D0953363

THE
PLAYER

ALSO BY BRAD PARKS

The Good Cop

The Girl Next Door

Eyes of the Innocent

Faces of the Gone

THE
PLAYER

Brad Parks

MINOTAUR BOOKS
NEW YORK

THE PLAYER. Copyright © 2014 by Brad Parks. All rights reserved. Printed in the United States of America. For information, address St. Martin's Press, 175 Fifth Avenue, New York, N.Y. 10010.

www.minotaurbooks.com

Library of Congress Cataloging-in-Publication Data

Parks, Brad, 1974–
    The player : a mystery / Brad Parks. — First edition.
        pages cm
    ISBN 978-1-250-04408-2 (hardcover)
    ISBN 978-1-4668-4269-4 (e-book)
    1. Ross, Carter (Fictitious character)—Fiction.   2. Investigative reporting—Fiction.   3. Environmental protection—Fiction.   4. Organized crime—Fiction.   I. Title.
    PS3616.A7553P59 2014
    813'.6—dc23

                                                                    2013045900

First Edition: March 2014

10   9   8   7   6   5   4   3   2   1

To Ga, ninety-five and still the classiest grandmother ever

THE
PLAYER

During seventy-seven years of scrupulous living, Edna Foster had survived whooping cough, encephalitis, breast cancer, one breach pregnancy, and two husbands. She figured she could handle the flu, no problem.

It struck on a Wednesday, the first day of spring's warmth had made it to New Jersey and visited her neighborhood in Newark. She had opened up the windows in the morning, tolerating the noise from a nearby construction site because she was ready for some fresh air after a long winter. By afternoon, she had caught a chill and shut the window. By nightfall, the chills had developed into a full-blown fever, with muscle aches and diarrhea to go with it. She called off the Bible study scheduled at her house that evening and consigned herself to bed. Too much fresh air, she supposed. By the next morning, she felt better.

The flu came back a week later. She hadn't opened the windows that day, but she had been digging in her garden. She chastised herself for not dressing more warmly as she suffered through another miserable night. But, again, the sickness took only a day to run its course.

Perhaps a month after that, she broke her tibia. She hadn't been doing anything more strenuous than walk through her living room when it happened. She had to drag herself to the phone to get an ambulance.

The doctor in the emergency room set the fracture, put it in a cast, then sent her home with crutches and enough Vicodin to get her through the discomfort. Edna used the painkiller sparingly for a few days, then flushed it down the toilet. She never drank or smoked—she was a good Christian woman, after all—and she didn't like how the drugs made her head feel fuzzy. Plus, there were too many junkies in her neighborhood. If word got out Mrs. Foster had pills, one of them would get it in his fool head to break into her house for them.

Without the painkiller, her mobility was even more limited. Her legs and ankles swelled, which she attributed to inactivity. She tried gritting her teeth and forcing herself to move about, if only to get her blood moving.

That's when she broke her arm. She had been crutching around her kitchen when her ulna just snapped. She crumpled into a heap on the floor and, unable to reach the phone this time, had to wait six hours until a neighbor came by to check on her.

The broken arm led to another hospital visit, another splint, and more Vicodin, which she promptly flushed.

Now fully laid up, the swelling got worse. She also kept coming down with the flu—at least once a week—which only added to her suffering.

But that wasn't all. Her skin felt itchy, no matter how much she moisturized it. She had a bad taste in her mouth almost constantly, even when she had just brushed her teeth. She developed back pain that ached nearly as much as the arm and leg fractures. Her lungs sometimes felt like they were on fire.

Her granddaughter, Jackie, the pride of the family—she was a college girl! she was going to be a doctor someday!—tried to force her to go to a physician. But Edna wouldn't have it. She was through with doctors. They would just give her more painkillers, and she didn't want any of that garbage. She would get by with her Bible, prayer, and some old-fashioned mental toughness.

Then her mind started to go. Edna had always taken her sharpness for granted—she was only seventy-seven, after all—and usually completed the Newark Eagle-Examiner crossword by seven thirty each morning. Yet, suddenly, she found she couldn't concentrate long enough to do even the simplest word games, the ones meant for children. She started blanking on simple things, like what she had eaten for breakfast or what day of the week it was. She had dizzy spells even when sitting down.

It was forgetting to flush the toilet that really got her in trouble. She barely urinated anymore, and what came out was often dark with blood and protein. She hadn't told anyone—her pee was no one else's business—but then Jackie walked by the unflushed toilet, saw the brownish water, and threw a fit, ordering her grandmother to go to the hospital immediately.

Once admitted, they quickly diagnosed Edna Foster with advanced-staged renal failure.

They put her on dialysis immediately but, again, Edna wasn't having it. She was in so much pain—her leg, her arm, her back—that sitting next to that machine for hours on end was unbearable. Her mental acuity was coming and going, but in her more lucid moments she managed to convince two doctors, a hospital administrator, a social worker, her pastor, and, most important, her granddaughter, that she didn't want dialysis anymore—and that she understood the consequences of that decision. She had been preparing to meet Jesus her whole life, she told them. If He was ready for her, she was ready for Him.

Finally convinced, they sent her home and, with help from Jackie, she got her affairs in order. During what turned out to be the final week of her life, she kept her Bible with her at all times. She slept most of the time, but when she was awake she asked Jackie to read some of her favorite passages. Often they were from the Book of Luke. He was a physician, after all. Just like Jackie would be someday.

The end, when it came, was merciful. She lapsed into a coma one night and slipped away two mornings later, around breakfast time. The ladies from her Bible study group speculated that Edna Foster was walking with the Lord by lunch.

CHAPTER 1

Even in an era when American print media has plunged into inexorable and perhaps terminal decline, even at a time when tech moguls are buying up venerated news-gathering organizations with their equivalent of couch change, even with the likelihood of career advancement dimmed by the industry's collective implosion, there are benefits to working for a newspaper that cannot be quantified by simple measurements like salary, benefits, or future prospects.

Kook calls are definitely one of them.

We get them all the time—from the drunken, the deranged, the demented—and they come in enough different flavors to keep us constantly entertained.

Some are just mild, low-grade kooks, like the ones who have newspapers confused with talk radio. They'll call up and start ranting about whatever subject is bothering them—the governor's latest cabinet appointment, the confusing signage that led them down the wrong exit ramp of the Garden State Parkway, the deplorable slowness of third-class mail—perhaps believing that if they just convince the reporter they're right, the newspaper will immediately launch a four-part series on the subject, written from the caller's particular point of view.

Then there are the conspiracy theorists, the ones who want us to "do some digging" into whatever fantasies they're harboring at the moment, whether it's that the local Walmart is importing illegal immigrants from Bangladesh in a garbage truck or that their town's animal-control officer is more of a dog person than a cat person.

There are also the old people who just want to talk. To someone. About anything. They'll call up with a "news tip," and of course it turns out they are the news, and the tip is that long ago—during, say, the Korean War—they nearly lost three toes to frostbite. And now, particularly on the mornings when they still feel that little tingle in their big toes, they feel the world at large needs to know about it.

Then there are the other standbys: the prisoners who use their phone time to call us, usually collect, and convince us of the gross miscarriage of justice that led to their incarceration; the paranoid schizophrenics who believe their delusions are worthy of front-page headlines; or the poor confused souls who, thinking newspaper reporters must be omniscient, will call and ask the name of the program they were watching on television last night.

As a group, they land somewhere between pitiable—particularly when they're obviously suffering from mental illness—and laughable. Except for the racists. We get a lot of those, too. They're just despicable.

Sure, Internet chat rooms and social networking have siphoned off some of our kooks over the years—there are more outlets for people to express their crazy now than ever before—but we at the *Newark Eagle-Examiner,* New Jersey's most widely circulated periodical, still get our share. Because the fact is, even with the increasing fragmentation of media, most people, even the nuts, realize a major daily newspaper like ours is still the best way to get serious attention for whatever cause or issue matters most to them.

Plus, we print our phone number in the paper.

Some reporters treat kook calls as nuisances. But most of us learn over the years to look forward to them. There's just nothing like going through an otherwise ordinary day, pecking away at some humdrum story, when suddenly you become aware one of your colleagues is talking to someone who lives off the grid and has found one of the three remaining working pay phones in the state of New Jersey to call and explicate his worldview.

If the reporter who takes the call is in a certain mood, she'll stand up in the middle of the newsroom and, for the benefit of those listening, start repeating key lines and questions in a loud voice, such as: "I realize you think Greta Van Susteren is trying to control your mind, but that doesn't necessarily mean Wolf Blitzer is going to try as well."

Or: "So you want to know if we're going to be writing about the rash of robberies in your neighborhood because someone keeps breaking into your house and moving your broom."

Or: "To make sure I understand this right, you're saying the Battle of Gettysburg didn't happen the way the history books said it did—and you know, because you were there in a previous life?"

The fun just never ends. So I have to admit I was mostly just looking for a good kook call on Monday afternoon when one of our news clerks wandered over to my desk and said, "Hey, I got a woman who says she has a big story for our investigative reporter. You want me to get rid of her?"

"Nah, I'll take it," I said.

I had just been killing time anyway, waiting for edits on my latest piece, a story about cash-strapped municipalities that were considering halting their recycling programs (corrugated waste products have seldom warranted so much attention). So when the forwarded call came through on my desk phone, I rubbed my hands together in anticipation, then answered with my most polite and officious, "*Eagle-Examiner*, this is Carter Ross."

"Hi, Mr. Ross, my name is Jackie Orr," came the voice on the other end. It was the voice of someone young, black, and determined.

"Hi, Jackie, what can I do for you?"

"Do you ever do stories about people getting sick?"

"That depends," I said. "Who's getting sick?"

"Everyone."

"What do you mean 'everyone'?" I asked. So far, so good: kooks often insisted that whatever troubled them also afflicted others.

"Well, first it was just my grandmother. Or we thought it was just my grandmother. But then it turned out to be the whole neighborhood."

"Sounds like you need a lawyer more than you need a newspaper reporter," I said.

"I tried that. I tell them people are sick and they're interested. But once they hear it's not some open-and-shut mesothelioma case, they don't want anything to do with it. I talked to one lawyer who sounded a little interested, but then he wanted a fifty-thousand-dollar retainer. If we had fifty thousand dollars, we wouldn't be bothering with lawsuits. We'd just move. Our case is a little more complicated than anyone seems to want to take on."

I felt myself sitting up in my chair and paying closer attention. There are certain words kooks tend not to use. "Mesothelioma" is one of them. So while that was a little disappointing—no kook call for me today—it was also more promising from a journalistic standpoint. As a newspaper reporter, I have a certain bias toward the disenfranchised, disadvantaged masses that others, not even sleazy lawyers, want to listen to. Maybe it's because, deep down, I fancy myself a good-hearted human being who wants to help the less fortunate. Or maybe it's because the Pulitzer committee shares the same bias.

"You said it's complicated. How so?"

"Well, we don't know what's making anyone sick."

"Okay, so you don't need a lawyer. You need a doctor."

"Everyone is seeing doctors. Or at least the ones who have health insurance are. The doctors just treat the symptoms and send them home. They don't have any answers."

I didn't either. But I was intrigued enough to have Jackie assemble herself and some of her ill neighbors to chat with me that afternoon. The headline MYSTERY ILLNESS STRIKES NEWARK NEIGHBORHOOD had a lot more promise for interesting journalism than MORRISTOWN WEIGHS COSTS AND BENEFITS OF RECYCLING NO. 6 PLASTIC.

Besides, as a reporter, I had learned to trust that little assignment editor in my head to tell me when I might be onto a good story. And my assignment editor was telling me, at the very least, that Jackie Orr was no kook.

Having gained a modest amount of seniority at the *Eagle-Examiner*—eight years counted as senior at a newspaper where most of the older reporters had been forced to take buyouts—I had wrangled myself a prime desk location in the corner of the newsroom.

It was strategic, inasmuch as it meant editors couldn't sneak up on me. But more than that, it was panoramic, inasmuch as it afforded me a sweeping view of the magnificent and picturesque vista that was a daily newspaper in action. In a single glance, I could see the anguish of the photo editors who had eleven assignments to shoot and only four photographers to do the shooting; the boredom of the Web site writers who were still repurposing yesterday's news until today gave them something interesting to do; the torment of the education reporter trying to make a story about teacher-pension reform sound interesting. And, okay, maybe it didn't fit conventional standards for beauty—unless you found splendor in forty-year-old office furniture and fifteen-year-old computer terminals—but it was my view and I loved it all the same.

Along the walls were the glass offices, home to the higher editors who sometimes conspired to limit my fun but were otherwise a decent group, albeit sometimes in a cheerless, party-pooping, adjective-hating kind of way.

In the middle were the desks filled with reporters. There were a few duds among them, too, but by and large they were a magnificently contemptuous set of brilliant, irreverent, fascinating folks, the kind of people who almost always had interesting things to say and entertaining ways of saying it. And in a strange way I could never quite explain to outsiders—who didn't necessarily understand how the cruciblelike forge of putting out a daily newspaper could bond people—I considered them my extended, mildly dysfunctional family.

Just beyond them was an area of the room known as the intern pod. If kook calls were one of the immeasurable benefits of life at a newspaper, the joy of working with interns was more quantifiable. Through the years, the newspaper industry had come to rely on an ever-growing collection of young, idealistic, energetic, just-out-of-college flunkies to do much of the news gathering that used to be done by more-hardened souls. And while you had to be careful not to let some of their naïveté get in the paper, they were fun all the same. At the age of thirty-two, I wasn't exactly Father Time. But I had been in the game just long enough that I knew there was a value to seeing the world through the nonjaded eyes of an intern. It helped keep me young.

Some of our interns, like Tommy Hernandez, now our city hall reporter and one of my best friends at the paper, started in this lowly post and quickly graduated to more important beats at the paper. Others had come and gone, leaving only their colorful nicknames—Sweet Thang, Lunky, Ruthie—and a smattering of stories in the archives by which we could remember them.

They were, most of all, cheap labor and eager helpmates. So it was that my eyes wandered toward the intern pod, looking for an enthusiastic aide-de-camp. Jackie Orr had promised me a room full of sick people. Interviewing them one by one, which is what I'd need to do, would take time. Having the assistance of an intern, presuming it was one who had been properly potty trained, would double my efficiency and halve my time. Plus, much like with kook calls, there was always the entertainment factor to consider. Interns were nothing if not amusing.

This being the middle of the afternoon, the pod was only partially populated. Half of them were out being good little interns, chasing stories. As I sized up the half that remained, my gaze immediately fell on Neesha Krishnamurthy, a smart—if a little too smart—young woman who had come to us from somewhere in the Ivy League. Columbia School of Journalism, if memory served. Poor thing.

Neesha's internship had thus far been distinguished only by an incident during the early days of her employment, when she stumbled across one of those only-in-Newark stories: a one-legged homeless man who had taken on a one-legged pigeon as a pet, training the bird to perch on his finger, arm, and shoulder.

Neesha somehow persuaded her editor to let her write a

human-interest story about the guy—some kind of misguided effort to tug on the readership's heartstrings with a tale of man and bird, bonded by their shared disability. Unfortunately for her, our Web editors thought it had what they liked to call "viral potential," so they sent along a videographer. And he had the camera rolling during that priceless moment when Neesha got the bird on her shoulder and it confused her for its favorite statue, depositing a salvo of white glop on her arm.

One point three million YouTube hits had guaranteed that, for the rest of her days at the *Eagle-Examiner,* Neesha would be known as Pigeon.

Hence, I strolled over to the intern pod, sat down across from her, and said, "Hey, Pigeon, what's up?"

She looked stricken. "How long are people going to keep calling me that?"

"Well, that all depends on one thing," I said, faux philosophically.

"What?"

"How long you plan on being alive."

She groaned. "What if I become executive editor someday? That would mean people would have to stop calling me Pigeon, right?"

"No, that would mean we'd have to stop calling you Pigeon to your face."

"It's so unfair!" she whined.

"No, unfair is being a pigeon in Newark, New Jersey with only one leg. What happened to you is just funny."

She pouted. Pigeon could be considered attractive—lots of long, dark hair and long, dark eyelashes surrounded by rather flawless skin—but after a dalliance with the aforementioned Sweet Thang, I had promised myself to swear off interns. Plus, I had enough complications in my romantic life at the moment.

"Anyhow, I was wondering if you wanted to help me report a story," I said.

"It doesn't involve pigeons, does it? Because Buster Hays tried to trick me into a story about a—"

I interrupted her by laughing. Buster Hays was the oldest reporter left, the only septuagenarian in a newsroom whose median age was roughly twenty-four. He hung around mostly because he was far too cantankerous to give us the pleasure of seeing him quit.

"No, no. I'm serious," I assured her. "No pigeons. No birds of any sort. I got a tip about a neighborhood in Newark where apparently a bunch of people are getting sick and no one knows why."

"Oh, cool," she said.

Yes, this was one who belonged in the Fourth Estate: only someone with a reporter's sensibilities would describe mysteriously ill people as "cool."

"Anyhow, there's going to be a group of them gathered at a house this afternoon, and I was hoping you could help me interview them. You busy?"

"Well, sort of. But it can wait. Let me just go tell Matt where I'm going."

Matt was her editor. And he was a decent enough guy, for an editor, but I didn't need Matt knowing about this. There was too great a risk he would tell my editor, Tina Thompson, with whom I had a somewhat complex relationship. The less Tina knew about my activities at the moment, the better.

"Don't do that," I said. She looked confused, so I continued: "Intern lesson number one: when it comes to editors, it's always better to beg forgiveness than ask permission."

"Are you sure?" she asked.

"Well, that depends. Do you want to be known around here for something other than bird poop?"

She followed me out of the newsroom without another word.

The address furnished to me by Jackie Orr was on Ridgewood Avenue, and as we made the short drive out there from downtown, I gave Pigeon a quick history lesson. Ridgewood Avenue used to be one of the South Ward's great streets, located in the Weequahic section of the city, one of Newark's great neighborhoods. Then someone got the fine idea to construct Interstate 78 through it in the late 1950s. It tore Ridgewood Avenue roughly in half, destroying the neighborhood and leaving behind a piece of the city that never quite recovered.

The house was located on the section of Ridgewood Avenue that survived just to the north of the highway, an odd wedge of real estate that had long been yearning for revitalization. It was a strange hodgepodge of residential and industrial, with everything from manufacturing and transportation companies to new public housing and old private housing, with some newly paved streets next to ones in such serious need of repaving you could see cobblestones under the asphalt.

Symbolically, nothing captured the area better than the South Ward Industrial Park. Originally conceived in the seventies as a $100 million economic engine that would employ more than a thousand residents, it was finally built in the late nineties as a $9 million facility that maybe—maybe—employed a hundred people and never did become the catalyst that anyone thought it would be.

Still, this being Newark, where urban renewal has been just around the corner for fifty years, there was a new project being touted as a neighborhood savior. Using eminent domain as something of a cudgel, the city had managed to scrape together a sizable piece of property across several city blocks, in the process leveling some abandoned factories and some houses that should have been abandoned but still had people living in them.

Then, with a variety of tax abatements and promises about streamlining approval processes, it had sold the parcel to McAlister Properties, a father-son development team who fancied themselves the Trumps of Newark. I was always a little unclear where the father, Barry McAlister, had gotten his seed money from—family? investments? bank theft?—but he and his son, Vaughn, had slapped their name on a couple of buildings in the city and, allegedly, they were going to toss up something sizable and shiny on this plot as well.

The last proposal I had heard about was for one of those mixed-use, mixed-income developments that have become all the rage among the urban-planning set. The numbers being touted by city hall always seemed to vary—anywhere from two hundred to three hundred affordable and market-rate residential units and 60,000 to 90,000 square feet of retail space—but it was, without question, going to be large. The total price tag was put somewhere around $120 million.

There were even rumors about a big-box store anchoring the retail space. A Kohl's? A Target? It was, so far, a well-guarded secret. But Newarkers got giddy when they spoke of it. That was one of the real ironies of life in a depressed city: all the people wanted was the same kind of national franchises—with their homogeneous, cookie-cutter architecture—that people in the well-to-do suburbs desperately tried to keep out.

The development was currently being called McAlister Arms—not to be confused with McAlister Center or McAlister Place, which were office buildings located downtown—and it was located just off an exit ramp to I-78. The thinking was that shoppers might be enticed into the stores by the lower sales tax of an urban enterprise zone and that commuters might be enticed to move there by the easy access to the highway.

That was another irony: the very roadway that had first rent the neighborhood asunder was now being seen as a hope for helping to bring it back. Some of the locals thought it would really turn into a boon for the area. Others thought it would be another South Ward Industrial Park, a project that promised salvation and delivered something well short of it.

Either way, it had to be better than what was there now: a big, empty lot.

It turned out the neatly trimmed single-family house where Jackie Orr had her group congregating was within shouting distance of the McAlister Arms site—or at least it was shouting distance if you could make yourself heard over the rumble of trucks and other heavy equipment that were readying the site for construction. As I pulled into a parking spot, I saw an earthmover pushing dirt into a pile that a backhoe was then scooping into a dump truck. Elsewhere, a crane was stacking steel girders. It was like watching very large Tonka trucks in action.

"So what's our plan?" Pigeon asked.

"Basically, you want to make like a doctor: ask them questions about what ouches, when it started ouching, and how it ouches. Then write down the answers. We'll sort everything else out later."

"Okay. Who's keeping the spreadsheet?"

"Who said anything about a spreadsheet?"

She looked at me like I had caught the stupid virus. "Investigative reporters keep spreadsheets," she said, as if quoting from a textbook. "It allows them to systematically track large volumes of data, identify emerging patterns, and draw conclusions based on their findings. It's how modern investigative reporting is done."

I made a show of stifling a fake yawn. "Really? Is that so? Says who?"

"Didn't you go to journalism school?"

"Thankfully, no," I said. Which is true. I had no formal training in journalism. And, frankly, I had never missed it. My undergraduate degree was from Amherst, a small liberal-arts college in Massachusetts where they had no journalism major and, in general, had tried not to teach us anything too useful. I grew more appreciative of how nonspecific my education had been with each passing year, as it became clear that in this breakneck world of ours, anything allegedly practical they might have crammed into me would have become quickly outdated anyway.

"Oh, well, I took several classes in investigative reporting and computer-assisted reporting," she said. "I'd be happy to help you set up a spreadsheet."

"Oh, no, thank you. Some of us reporters like to do their investigating a little more haphazardly."

"Why?"

"Because studies have shown reporters who use spreadsheets are seventy-two percent more likely to clog their stories with meaningless statistics," I said. "In fact, did you know that spreadsheets account for more than ninety-one percent of the deathly dull stories that get into the newspaper?"

She paused to consider these purely fabricated pieces of information as I turned off the engine. "You're making fun of me right now, aren't you?" she asked.

"Pigeon, you're about to meet real people, not data points," I said. "In my experience, human beings are too messy for spreadsheets. Stick around long enough and you'll learn to love them for it."

•   •   •

The woman who answered my knock on the door could not have been more than twenty-one. And if you told me she was fourteen, I would have believed that, too. She sort of resembled a mop held upside down: thin as the handle until her head, which exploded in a profusion of thick, black braids, loosely organized by a rubber band.

I smiled as she pulled open the wooden front door, noting she had not yet touched the clear Plexiglas storm door. She was going to size me up first, and that was fine by me. Newspaper reporters grow accustomed to being the Fuller Brush salesmen of the modern day: if we don't make a good impression on the front porch, we'll never get inside the house. For that reason, I'm always conscious of making my appearance as professional and noncontroversial as possible.

Hence, what the woman saw on the other side of her storm door was a smiling, six-foot-one, 185-pound WASP with the world's most boring haircut, pleated khaki pants, a freshly ironed white shirt, and a necktie that looked like it had been picked out by the Republican National Committee.

If she had looked really carefully, she would have noticed I double-knotted my shoes.

"Hi. I'm Carter Ross. Are you Jackie?"

She adjusted a pair of bug-eyed glasses that were too big for her small face. They were at least twenty years out of style and might have been charity giveaways. Or maybe that's just what The Kids were wearing these days. Either way, they gave Jackie an owlish look. I immediately pegged her as the girl in her high school class who spent lunchtime by herself in the corner of the cafeteria, reading fiction for pleasure.

"Yes, hi, Mr. Ross, thank you for coming," Jackie said, opening the storm door.

"First of all, please call me Carter. Otherwise you'll make me feel old. Second, this is my colleague Neesha Krishnamurthy. I hope you don't mind I brought her along to help me do some interviewing."

"That's fine. Please come in."

She showed me into a small entryway, with stairs immediately in front of me, a small living room to the right, and a kitchen in back. Nothing in the house looked to have been added within the last thirty years or so.

"Nice place," I said, because politeness is sometimes more important than honesty.

"This is my grandma's house," Jackie said, then corrected herself: "Was my grandma's house."

Right. Was. In case I hadn't already figured it out, Jackie added, "She just died."

"Sorry for your loss. How old was she?"

"Seventy-seven. It was actually at her funeral that we started realizing how many people in the neighborhood had been getting sick. We had been so busy caring for Grandma we hadn't noticed before that."

I considered asking for more details about Grandma, but I was aware there was a room full of people just to my right. They were all from the neighborhood, which meant they were all African American, and I got the sense they were sizing up the white guy who had just walked in. I figured it made more sense to talk to the living now and get details about the dead later.

"There are more of us than what you see here," she said, pointing me to the living room. "There are about twenty of us altogether. This is just who I could get on short notice."

I turned into the room and took stock. There were eight people: six women and two guys, roughly thirty to seventy years of age. They tended to be more toward the pleasantly plump side, but otherwise they looked . . . healthy, I guess. Or at least healthy for Newark, which is not an especially well city to begin with. In modern-day America, taking care of one's self requires money, good insurance, and ready access to primary care, none of which are things that people in a place like Newark tend to have.

"Hi, folks," I said. "How is everyone today?"

The replies were mostly mumbled, the faces downcast. I think people sometimes have newspapers confused with television, or at least they were acting like they were on camera. This little cadre of convalescents was ill, and they were going to play that part as long as they were in my presence. Then again, since Jackie's grandma had just died—perhaps of the same cause that was diseasing them—I suppose I shouldn't have expected a pep rally to break out just because I had asked them how they were doing.

After the introductions and a few necessary niceties, Pigeon and I divided the afflicted, went into separate quarters—me to the kitchen, her to the small dining room that was connected to the living room—and began interviewing them.

What I heard four times over the next hour or so was more or less the same story, told in slightly different ways. People kept getting what they thought was the flu, except it was happening too often to really be the flu. There was no discernible pattern to how or when it happened. There was no reliable predictor of when it would flare up again.

The symptoms beyond that were a little more scattershot, everything from puffy eyes to aching feet to a persistent cough and respiratory distress. And that could mean anything from diabetes to allergies. Being that my medical training didn't go beyond watching *Scrubs* reruns, it's not like I could place them as all being related to, say, a failure in the endocrine system. Mostly because I couldn't remember what the endocrine system actually did. I was proud of myself for even knowing we had one.

But there was one thing that caught my attention: broken bones. Three of the four people I talked to had fractured something recently, and they said others in their group had reported the same thing. That could just be coincidence, but I doubted it. Adults just weren't that clumsy.

What I liked about broken bones, from a journalistic standpoint, was that it wasn't the flu. A bunch of people who complained they were getting flulike symptoms too often felt like it could be an imagined thing, some kind of mass hypochondria. You couldn't imagine breaking a bone. It could be confirmed with X-rays. It was incontrovertible.

Plus, it suggested something truly strange was going on.

They all had theories as to what that was. One woman swore it was the water: she noticed it was suspiciously cloudy just before the onset of her most recent outbreak. Another woman thought perhaps the local grocery store where they all shopped had applied some kind of chemical to its produce. The guy I interviewed thought it had something to do with the neighborhood's proximity to I-78, which was more or less on top of them.

It was all possible, I guess. I just knew whatever it was had to be fairly local. The people I talked to didn't really have a lot in common. They ate different diets, worked different kinds of jobs (or not at all), lived in different houses. But the one thing they all shared was the neighborhood. It didn't take an epidemiologist to speculate that something very nearby—in the air, in the soil, in the water—was the culprit.

But I understood why the lawyers Jackie had talked to wanted nothing to do with her and her motley little group. Unless you had some kind of inkling to what this peculiar pathogen might be, it would take a lot of time—and money—to figure it out. That was assuming you ever could.

•   •   •

After finishing with our interview subjects, Pigeon and I dismissed them one by one, making sure to get their phone numbers and addresses in case we needed to ask them more questions. Jackie promised us more people if we could come back in the morning, after she had a chance to round them up. I told her Pigeon and I would be back, with bells on.

Once the last of the visitors departed, it was just Jackie, Pigeon, and I, standing in the living room.

"So I probably should have asked you this on the phone, but: how are you feeling?" I asked Jackie. "Have you been experiencing any of these symptoms?"

"Yeah, but only once. I don't live here."

"Where do you live?"

"Well, I grew up around here. I went to Shabazz," she said, pointing vaguely in the direction of Malcolm X. Shabazz High School, a few blocks to the north. "But I live in New Brunswick now. I go to Rutgers."

I was impressed. For kids from the expensive private school where I received my secondary education, Rutgers was a respectable safety school. For a kid from Shabazz High School, making it into Rutgers was like one of my classmates making it into Harvard.

"What are you studying?" I asked.

"Pre-med."

"Better you than me. What year are you?"

"I guess you could say I'm a junior and a half," she said. "I'll probably graduate a semester early."

"How'd you swing that?"

"Summer school. I love Newark and I want to come back here someday and be a doctor—a pediatrician, actually. But for right now? I just need to be out of here during the summer. I don't want to be hanging around on the bleachers when some whacked-out banger comes after me with a machete."

I got the reference. A few years earlier, four college students, back in Newark for summer vacation, had been sitting on the bleachers at a nearby elementary school, eating McDonald's and whiling away a summer evening, when they were attacked by a group of young men who may or may not have been going through initiation to the MS-13 gang. Only one of the four kids survived, and she still bears machete scars. One of the kids who was killed had been the drum major for the Shabazz High School marching band. He would have been a little older than Jackie. They might have known each other.

Jackie continued: "The only reason I was here so much this summer was because of my grandmother."

"Right, of course. I meant to ask you a little more about her. What was her name?"

"Edna Foster." She gave a thoughtful pause, then added, "She was the best."

"She sounds like it," I said, even though I didn't know a thing about the woman. "Do you have a picture of her by any chance?"

"Uh, yeah, sure, hang on," Jackie said. "There's one upstairs. Let me go get it."

Jackie departed the living room and disappeared upstairs for a moment, leaving me with a slightly bewildered-looking Pigeon.

"Why do you need to see what she looks like?" she asked, quietly.

"I don't," I said.

"Then why did you ask for a picture?"

"Because every good story needs a victim, and Edna Foster strikes me as a pretty good victim. So I need Jackie talking about her grandmother in a kind, loving way. If Jackie is looking at a picture of her grandmother while she talks, we'll get better stuff. Photos can be very evocative that way. Now do me a favor and get your notebook back out and write down whatever this young woman says next, because I guarantee we'll end up using it."

Pigeon still looked to be a little circumspect—this was yet another thing that wouldn't fit on her spreadsheet—but further conversation ended when Jackie came back down the stairs and into the living room.

"This is her and my grandfather," Jackie said, handing me a framed snapshot of a man and a woman who looked to be around thirty, standing on a sidewalk. The man had his arm around the woman, who was tall and thin, like her granddaughter. If I had to put a date on the picture, I'd say 1965.

Jackie went on: "That's a picture of them the day they bought this house. My grandmother was so proud of it. She was the first person in her family to own property."

I knew enough Newark history to be able to imagine the backstory. The mid-1960s was prime time for white flight and blockbusting. Whole neighborhoods changed complexion virtually overnight, thanks in part to less-than-scrupulous Realtors who roamed through neighborhoods, knocked on the doors of the white families who lived there, and said things like, "Just wanted to let you know you have new neighbors . . . Yes, it's a lovely family from South Carolina with eight kids . . . I hear they're going to plant watermelons out back."

Mr. and Mrs. Foster had probably bought this place from a nice Jewish family that couldn't wait to hightail it to Livingston.

"My grandfather got killed during a holdup a few years later. My grandmother remarried but he died of a heart attack. I still don't know how she managed to hang on to this place and raise three children by herself. She was tough."

"What kind of work did she do?" I asked.

"She worked for the city, in the engineering department. She was a secretary. She talked all the time about how she was the first black woman they ever hired, right after Gibson got elected"—Ken Gibson was the city's first black mayor—"and how it was hard sometimes, but she felt like she was going to make things better for her children and her grandchildren."

"You sort of look like her," I said, handing the picture back to her.

"Everyone says I act like her, too. She was the first in the family to buy a house. I'm the first to go to college. She just had . . . a lot of spirit."

It was the word "spirit" that got her. Jackie half blurted, half sobbed it, then immediately tried to compose herself.

"I'm sorry," she said.

"No, no, it's fine," I said.

"I just don't know what's going to happen now. My family is . . . I mean, we're no prize. I got a cousin in jail. I got another cousin who's bangin' so hard he'll probably end up there soon. But it's still my family, you know? When we get together, none of that stuff matters. It's just the family and my grandma and this house. This house is like our center. This is where we always gather, for holidays and birthdays. And now without Grandma, I just don't know . . ."

Jackie's voice trailed off again. I saw out of the corner of my eye that Pigeon was getting down every word. It's not that I wasn't absorbed in Jackie's story—I was—but I also remembered I had a story of my own to write. And it was in the best interests of Jackie and her sick neighbors that I write it well.

"So had she been in good health until recently?"

"Grandma? Oh yeah. She was like a dynamo. She finally retired maybe seven, eight years ago, but she hadn't slowed down at all. She still gardened and walked and was really active with her church. And then suddenly, it was like everything went wrong."

Jackie went through the symptoms her grandmother had experienced, and it was similar to what I had heard from the other victims. The flu. The swelling. Broken leg. Broken arm. Then it progressed to kidney failure, which might have been survivable except Edna Foster was too weak to put up with dialysis. Whatever this malady was had taken all the fight out of her.

"It just didn't make any sense," Jackie concluded. "And then at her funeral, people started talking, and it was like, 'Oh, she had that? That's strange, so do I.' Or, 'Oh, she had this? That's weird, so does so-and-so.' And maybe it's because of all these pre-med classes I'm taking, but it just didn't sound right."

"So what made you want to take this on as your cause?" I asked.

"I don't know. I guess I kind of thought it was what my grandmother would have done. But she wasn't around anymore, so now it was up to me. As I told you, I called a few lawyers, but I couldn't get anywhere with them. But I couldn't just give up. So I guess I was hoping that if we got in the newspaper and got some publicity, maybe someone would take pity on us and want to help us. A big law firm that might be willing to take us pro bono. Or a doctor. Or the state, maybe. I don't know. Do you think that might happen?"

"It might," I said. "Or it might not. Obviously, I can't make any promises about what happens after a story goes in the newspaper."

"I know. I know. Look, Mr. Ross . . . Carter . . . Thanks for coming. Just to listen to those people makes them feel, I don't know, like someone actually cares. I was beginning to feel like no one did."

I looked at Edna Foster's granddaughter, with her bug glasses, mop hair, and fierce pride. She was young enough and idealistic enough that when she saw something she didn't think was right, she believed something could be done—and had to be done. And she had found a newspaper reporter who felt the same way.

"There's a notion in journalism that one of the reasons we exist is to give a voice to the voiceless," I said. "People in my business tend to forget that sometimes. But I guess I try to re- member it's part of the reason we're here. It's really one of our highest callings."

Pigeon and I said our goodbyes and went back outside. The sun was getting low and I could hear the rush-hour traffic on I-78 zooming along behind me. But there was enough light that the guys at the construction site remained hard at it, their big ma- chines making their usual racket and kicking dust into the air. I figured if they were still working, I should be, too.

"What are you doing?" Pigeon asked as I passed my car and walked in the direction of Hawthorne Avenue.

"I'm taking a walk," I said.

"Where?"

"Just getting to know the neighborhood a little better."

"But . . . why?"

I gave her a palms-up gesture. "Don't know. It's called 'shoe leather journalism,' Pigeon. Hopefully they taught you about that at Columbia."

They must have, because Pigeon dutifully joined my tour. We walked along the sidewalks, some of them new, some of them old, all of them littered with occasional minefields of broken glass. I had spent enough years in Newark that I had long ago stopped trying to avoid them. My shoes had thick soles. Besides, if you closed your eyes and pretended you were down at the shore, the crunchy feeling under your feet was sort of like walk- ing on seashells.

As we explored the neighborhood, Pigeon gave me the brief version of her life story. She grew up in Edison, New Jersey, in the burgeoning Indian community there. She was valedictorian at J. P. Stevens High, where she hung out with other smart Indian kids. Then she went to Yale, where she hung out with more smart Indian kids. Her parents had made it clear they hoped she would marry a future doctor named Ranjit. You couldn't quite call it an arranged marriage; but he was Brahman and so was she, so it would sort of make everyone happy if she just went along with it. She said she probably would, even if she didn't really have feelings for the guy.

Yet, somewhere during this perfect, by-the-book, Phi Beta Kappa life of hers, she had been permitted one rebellion: she went to journalism school. And now it sounded like she was trying to make the most of it, in her own self-limited way.

As she wound through her little narrative, I kept my eyes peeled for . . . well, actually, I have no idea. But it is my general experience in matters such as these that you never know what you're looking for until you find it. Maybe there was some obvious source of local water contamination. Maybe one of the stoplights would be glowing radioactive orange. You never knew unless you kept your eyes open.

Except, in this case, all I really saw was a strange little Newark neighborhood that had been chopped off from the rest of the city. Interstate 78 formed a hard border to the south. The exit ramps filled the space to the east. To the west were some old brick warehouses that belonged to long-defunct companies, vestiges of Newark's manufacturing heyday. To the north was the McAlister Arms site and those clattering construction vehicles.

It created a little island on the south side of Hawthorne Avenue that was perhaps five blocks long and one block deep. And all nine of our sick people—ten, if you counted Edna Foster—lived on that island.

It brought to mind a tale I had read about in a geography class I had taken at Amherst. It was about a midnineteenth-century doctor in London who was studying a cholera outbreak. This was in the days before germ theory had been developed, so no one understood the mechanism by which cholera spread. But by putting a dot on a map for each house that had a case of cholera, the doctor was able to determine that the outbreak seemed to be centered around one public water pump that all the houses had been using to get their water. The pump's well turned out to have been dug a few feet from a sewage pit.

That doctor, John Snow, is considered the father of modern epidemiology. And, really, all I needed to do here is what he had done: find the equivalent of the water pump and then discover the sewage pit beside it.

By the time we completed our circumnavigation of the neighborhood, it was getting to be that time of night when the only white people meandering into that neighborhood were the ones there to buy drugs. I wasn't in the market for anything stronger than pale ale, so Pigeon and I returned to my car and I got us pointed back to the office. My ride is a used—and I mean well-used—Chevy Malibu with at least 111,431 miles on it, though that may be a conservative estimate. The odometer has been broken for a while. Suffice to say that if cars could win Purple Hearts, mine would have been awarded several by now. Still, it delivered us safely back to the newsroom.

If only it could have kept me safe once I got there. I had barely stepped off the elevator when my path was blocked by the curly-headed figure that was Tina Thompson. In addition to being the managing editor for local news and my immediate editor, Tina happened to be one of the two women with whom I had recently experienced the pleasures of the flesh.

This was merely the latest development in a relationship that had a way of making me feel like I was the last person to know what was going on. Tina had, once upon a time, looked at me as the ideal mate, in a strictly biological way. She was a single woman of a certain age—that age being the last number that still begins with the digit 3—and she had decided she was going to become a mother.

Not a girlfriend. Not a wife. Just a mother.

And I was to be her source of sperm. Not a husband. Not a lover. Just sperm.

I had always balked at that potential arrangement. I have these antiquated ideas about nuclear familyhood and, besides, I actually—this is *really* old-fashioned, I know—like her. She's smart and successful and passionate about life and a little nuts, all of which I found myself strangely attracted to. I tried to tell her this, though she seemed never to believe me. Instead, she tried to make herself seem tough and invulnerable, which only made me want to discover her vulnerable side that much more, which only infuriated her, which only charmed me further.

It never seemed to go anywhere beyond that. I had this long-harbored theory that we could make a great couple. She never let me test my hypothesis. And as a result we had reached this Balkan-style settlement where everyone left the table unhappy: I didn't get a relationship, she didn't get a baby daddy.

Then, without warning, she had decided motherhood, conventional or otherwise, was no longer in her future.

Then, with the possibility of procreation off the table, and with no apparent hope for any kind of relationship, we did the obvious thing couples who want neither children nor romance do: we had sex.

We hadn't really discussed the implications of this act. She insisted there weren't any and that I had been just a one-night booty call, a convenient way to fill a momentary craving. Ever since then, relations between us had chilled to temperatures not seen in Newark since the Pleistocene epoch. I can't say I fully understood the combination of idiosyncrasies and undiagnosed disorders that was Tina Thompson, but I at least understood she liked her distance. And after our clothes-free comingling, she had decided I had gotten a little too close. She had been making a determined effort to push me away ever since.

Hence, my greeting from her was not, "Hello, Carter," or, "Nice to see you, Carter," or, "Have you had a good day, Carter?"

It was: "Where the hell have you been?"

"Out for a walk," I said. Which was, technically, true.

"Oh, go ahead and play coy if you want. I saw Pigeon scurrying away just now. You know I'll be able to beat it out of her in seven seconds flat."

"Okay, so I was out working on a story. But it's not fit for your eyes and ears as of yet."

"Yeah, well the same could be said for that recycling story you wrote," she huffed. "The unfortunate thing is that you turned it in anyway."

"What's wrong with the recycling story?"

"It's a story about recycling but it's total garbage," she said. "In its current form, it's not deserving of the fifty percent postconsumer content it would be printed on. It's in your basket with comments marked on it. And it had better be returned to me—in a lot better shape—before you even think of working on anything else."

She gave me a look people usually save for backed-up toilets, then departed.

A responsible employee—thoroughly chastened and properly ashamed—probably should have gone straight to his desk and pounded on the keyboard until his fingers were bloody. Or at least chapped.

Me? I mostly just got thirsty for a frothy, 6-percent-alcohol-by-volume beverage, preferably one that was a nice, dark amber color—especially if I could share it with someone who might provide companionship and conversation while I drank it. And perhaps side benefits later.

The person most likely to supply all those things was Kira O'Brien, so I wandered over to her desk to see if I could talk her into an evening with me. Not that it would likely take much convincing. If Tina is the Pat Benatar of my life—because she makes love a battlefield—Kira is the Cyndi Lauper. She just wants to have fun. That she also sometimes dyes her hair purple is just a coincidence.

By day, Kira is one of the *Eagle-Examiner*'s librarians. She is twenty-eight years old and looks like a proper Irish girl, with brown hair, blue eyes, and a wardrobe that appears to have been coordinated by Ann Taylor. She is quiet, conscientious, and diligent in assisting reporters with their research needs. She sometimes puts her hair up with a pencil. And even if she does it just to be ironic, it still adds to the overall effect.

Then night falls, and she leaves work and morphs back into her true form, which is ten tons of uninhibited impulsiveness packed into a ninety-eight-pound body. Among her body piercings are parts I have never heard my mother say aloud (hint: one of them rhymes with "Dolores"). She enjoys it when certain private acts are performed in areas that might make them available for public viewing. And her closet includes numerous outfits that most people would refer to as costumes. She's the only woman I've ever met who, if you ask her to dress up as a vampiress, will ask you to narrow it down.

I'm adventurous enough that I can keep up with her. Sort of. One of these days, it's entirely possible she's going to get bored by me and my white and/or blue button-down shirts— even if I am seriously thinking about adding a third color to my repertoire one of these days—and leave me by the side of the road on her way to Comic-Con.

In the meantime, I just try to hang on and enjoy the ride. I hadn't really decided what I felt about her, other than that I enjoyed her company. She had indicated that she felt pretty much the same way about me. During one of our rare serious conversations, she said she viewed her twenties as a time to have fun and "experiment." She wouldn't even think about settling down until she was in her thirties, an age she spoke of like it was a strange land she could only barely imagine visiting.

Beyond that, we had yet to have any kind of talk about where our relationship was or wasn't headed—or whether we even *had* a relationship—and I sensed neither of us was particularly uncomfortable with that. If we had to name a magazine after our arrangement, we'd call it *Vague*.

"Hey, it's good you're here," she said as I entered the library. "My shift ends at seven and I'm sort of under a time crunch to get out of here. It would help if I could get changed now, but I'm the only one here. Could you cover the desk for a second?"

"What if someone asks a question I can't answer?"—which, in matters of library science, included just about everything.

"Just do what I do when I get stumped: pretend like the database is down and tell them you'll e-mail them when it comes back up."

"And you get paid for this?"

"Not well, believe me," she said. Then she grabbed a bag from under her desk and hustled down the hall to the bathroom.

I sat at her desk, mercifully alone. It was getting to be the time of night when reporters either had what they needed or had resigned themselves to faking it.

Perhaps five minutes later, Kira emerged from the bathroom wearing a helmet and a full-body leotard that was the color of bubble gum and festooned with various insignia and patches.

She looked like a storm trooper who had fallen into a giant cotton-candy machine.

"Okay, I give up, what are you supposed to be?" I asked.

"I'm Rose, the Pink Power Ranger," she said, like it should have been obvious.

"Uh, okay?"

"I'm going to a Power Rangers revival," she said. "I really prefer to be Lily, the Yellow Ranger. But last time there were like five Lilys and no Roses, and we couldn't form into a Megazord. The forces of Dai Shi nearly defeated us. The only reason they didn't is because there's never been a *Power Rangers* episode where that actually happened. So we sort of won on a technicality. But it was a hollow victory."

"Right," I said.

"You have no idea what I'm talking about, do you?"

"Not in the slightest."

"Didn't you play with Power Rangers as a kid?"

"Guess not," I said. I have dim memories of Power Rangers coming along, but I think by that point in my development, I had already moved on from things like LEGOs to larger, more challenging toys. Like redheads. If only I had been able to master them as thoroughly as I had the LEGOs.

"Oh, then you'll totally have to come along and check it out. It starts at seven thirty but it's in Jersey City, so we have to hurry. If I'm late, they'll morph without me."

"Well, we wouldn't want that," I said. "Let's get out of here."

Kira got a few curious looks as she threaded through the newsroom in full Power Rangers regalia. Chances were most of them didn't know it was our otherwise mild-mannered librarian underneath the helmet.

Except for Tina. She knew. Which was fine with me. I had expressed my interest in a relationship with her in every way I knew how and she had rebuffed me every time. If seeing me walk out the door with another woman made her jealous? Well, this may sound small of me, but: good.

I allowed myself a quick peek at her as I rounded the corner. All I saw was Tina shaking her head.

We took my car and within half an hour I was in the somewhat uncomfortable position of being in a room full of people in leotards, not all of whom had bodies intended for spandex. Apparently, there was an overlap between people who liked Power Rangers and people who liked cupcakes.

I had thought being the only person at the party not in costume would shield me from inquiry, but it turns out they just assumed I hadn't gotten into costume yet. As a result, I was pelted with questions about whether I was going to be one of the Jungle Fury Power Rangers or one of the Samurai Power Rangers—and what color I was going to be when that happened. My answer seemed to disappoint them. Apparently there's no such thing as the Khaki Power Ranger.

By the time it was over, I had consumed enough of this concoction they called "Power Juice" that I tossed my keys in Kira's direction and asked her to drive my zord—that's what Power Rangers call their vehicles—to my dojo. Or whatever.

I had hoped that shortly after arriving at my house in Bloomfield, I would start to be able to answer that age-old question: what *does* the Pink Power Ranger wear under her costume?

Except by the time we got there, I was just drunk and sleepy and, more than any of those things, exhausted. The day had taken more out of me than I had thought. It was all I could do to make my legs move once the car came to a halt in my driveway.

Somehow, I trudged up to the house and into my bed. I'm not sure I remember much beyond that, other than being confused.

What was my problem? Had I really had *that* much to drink? Had I just not eaten enough munchies at the party to sop up the booze I had poured into my stomach?

Whatever the answer, the night was pure misery. I couldn't get comfortable. If I lay on my side, it hurt. If I lay on my back, that hurt, too. My stomach was no great shakes. The rest of me was all shakes.

I just couldn't get my temperature right. At first I was freezing. Then I was too hot. I would wake up drenched in sweat, only to fall back asleep and wake up shivering.

I also kept having these strange, awful dreams. In one of them, I kept trying to file a story, only I couldn't get my laptop to work. In another, I had been granted this exclusive interview, except I couldn't find my notebook. Then I couldn't find my pen. At a certain point, I couldn't even tell whether I was awake or dreaming. I felt disoriented, whatever state I was in.

I'm not sure I got any real sleep. But when I woke up the next morning, Kira was still there. She was dressed in librarian clothes again and was lying next to me, a damp washcloth next to her.

"Good morning," she said, when she saw my eyes were open.

"Uhhhh," I groaned.

"You had a rough night," she said, as if I weren't already aware of it.

"I can't believe I drank so much."

"Oh, baby, this isn't a hangover," she said. "You're sick. I took your temperature in the middle of the night and it was like 103.5. You have the flu or something. Do you have any Tylenol? I couldn't find any in the medicine cabinet. It would probably make you feel better."

I directed her to the assortment of pharmaceuticals I kept stashed under my sink. She returned with two pills and a glass of water. I accepted both gratefully.

"You're a total sweetheart," I said.

"I just wish you had let me know you were going to get sick. I could have brought my nurse's outfit."

"Rain check? Pretty please?"

She just laughed. As I chased the Tylenol with the water and lay back down, she began running her hand through my hair, which felt delightful. The drugs kicked in a little and I thought I might finally get some good sleep. I was just on the edge of it when a thought wriggled its way into my consciousness:

"Oh, crap," I said.

"What?" she murmured.

"I totally forgot, Pigeon and I are supposed to do an interview this morning."

I started to hoist myself out of bed, but Kira pinned me back down. For ninety-eight pounds, she was pretty strong. Either that, or I still belonged flat on my back.

"You're not going anywhere," she said. "Nurse's orders. Pigeon can handle the interview by herself. She's a big girl."

I considered this and, more to the point, tried to talk myself into exerting the effort that would be required to rise, shower, drive to Newark, and be coherent. I failed to find the will to do any one of them, much less all four.

"Okay," I said. "But let me call Pigeon and let her know I won't be able to make it."

Kira handed me the phone, and I hauled up her number in my contacts—and, yes, it was stored as "Pigeon."

The phone rang once, twice, three times. Then finally I heard a thin, strangled, "Hi, this is Neesha."

"Pigeon, it's Carter. You sound worse than I feel."

"I feel awful, too," she said. "I was up all night. I think I've got the flu or something."

I felt a small prickle at the base of my spine. And it wasn't just from the chills. What were the chances that two able-bodied, healthy young people would simultaneously come down with the influenza virus during a time of year when it was not normally known to be circulating?

Very slim. I called in my regrets to Jackie Orr, telling her I had taken ill and asking her to reschedule until the next morning. And by the time I hung up, I was thinking, *What if this isn't the flu?*

What if it was the same thing that killed Jackie's grandmother?

Mitch DeNunzio always thought the mob got a bad rap.

Yeah, they ignored some laws. But only laws that were dumb in the first place. And, yeah, they killed people. But only people who deserved to die. And, yeah, they made money. But what's the point of being in the United States of Freakin' America if you can't make a little money?

In a strange way, he always thought some of his crime-family associates were the most principled people anywhere. They had rules and expectations—a code, as Hollywood liked to call it. They followed the code. And as long as you did, too, there was no problem.

Take, say, your friendly neighborhood bookie. Talk about a law that deserved to be broken: the ridiculous prohibition against gambling on sports, something that existed in forty-nine states (bravo, Nevada) for no other reason than that this country was founded by a bunch of Puritans. Now, sure, the local bookie was, technically, operating outside the law by taking bets on sports. But he was also providing a service that people clearly desired.

And he did it in an honorable way. He took all kinds of bets, whether he wanted to or not. If you won, he paid promptly. If you lost, all he expected was the same courtesy.

Now, if you couldn't pay? Well. In the short term, if you were a good customer, he might be understanding about a momentary shortfall. But if you still didn't pay? Well. Didn't he have the right to get upset?

He did. And there was no problem with that, where Mitch was concerned. Because the rules and expectations were clear all along. All the bookie was doing was following them.

Face it, from a moral standpoint, other industries—the supposedly legal ones—weren't nearly as clean. Take those scumbag bankers who threw the economy in the crapper with all the subprime-mortgage stuff, or the Wall Street types who gambled with people's retirement money, or CEOs who bolstered their bonuses by slashing the salaries and benefits of their workers. You want to say they're better than mobsters?

Truth was, Mitch slept fine at night. He was proud of the business he did. His old man had been what some would call a loan shark. Mitch never called it that—"shark" was such a loaded word. Plus, it had this small-time connotation.

Mitch wasn't small-time. And he thought of himself more as a venture capitalist than as a lender. He did his research. And when he put his money in a project, it was because he knew it was going to provide the kind of return that assured the borrower would be able to return Mitch's principal to him, with a reasonable rate of interest to compensate Mitch for his trouble and risk.

McAlister Arms had attracted his eye for a while. It was just the kind of project he liked—big, complicated, and lacking in oversight. There would be money flowing into it (and out of it) for years. And jobs. And contracts. These were the kind of things that were the grease for his wheels.

He just had to make sure his piece of it was protected. Like a good venture capitalist, he wasn't going to just throw his money at it and walk away. He kept tabs on his projects, made sure they stayed on track. And if he had to do a little something here or there to nudge it toward success?

Well.

Sometimes, that's just what a good venture capitalist did.

CHAPTER 2

Upon making the startling deduction that I had contracted the Ridgewood Avenue Mystery Disease—courtesy of some as-yet-undetermined toxin that had now invaded my body—I responded in the only way I could, given the circumstances: I took a nap.

I was prepared to remain prone for the rest of the day, but several hours later I began to feel marginally better. I woke to the sound of moaning, then realized it was my own: Kira was giving me a nice back rub. That gave me enough strength to get on my feet and into the shower. When I got out, I found a note from Kira, saying she was due at work.

It was disappointing, but she had been thoughtful enough to anchor the note with a Coke Zero. Like most journalists, I am a hopeless caffeine junkie. Unlike most journalists, I hate coffee. Hence, my caffeine-delivery mechanism of choice is whatever diet beverage the Coca-Cola Company has whipped up lately. Kira and I had not known each other very long, but she already understood and appreciated how a cold Coke Zero could make everything right in my world.

Thus fortified, I was again feeling human enough to face Tuesday and the same quandary that had occupied my mind on Monday: what, exactly, was making people sick?

This time, however, I had new information, namely my own experience. And that ruled out a lot. After all, I hadn't drunk the water, eaten the food, licked the walls, or done any number of things that might have exposed me to a variety of pathogens.

All I had done was sit on the couch and breathe the air. And since I had never heard of couch-sitting leading to a pandemic—well, unless you considered watching Jerry Springer a form of disease—that left me with the air as the most likely culprit. What was fouling the skies in that tiny little piece of the South Ward?

The highway seemed like a tempting possibility, but I had to rule it out. The way Jersey people drive could make anyone sick, sure. But if there was truly something noxious being ported along Interstate 78, there would be more than just a few folks who happened to live just off exit 56 getting sick.

It had to be something industrial. And there, New Jersey in general—and Newark in particular—had a long and tainted history. Over the past three centuries or so, the city had been a world leader at making everything from leather to plastics. It was good business back in the day, but a lot of the chemicals used in those processes were still just sitting there hundreds of years later—and would be for all eternity unless someone cleaned them up. New Jersey's reputation as a toxic-waste dump is both unfortunate and, largely, unfair. But it's not entirely unwarranted.

Fact is, there was all kinds of unimaginable goo lurking under our state's surface. Was something from long ago finally working its way to the surface? Had it been on top all along and was just now being stirred up? Whatever it was, some trace amount of it must have wormed its way into people's lungs. Including mine.

By the time I arrived at work, I thought that was the worst of my problems. Then I was confronted by a more immediate one: Tina Thompson was standing in front of the elevator, waiting for it to go in the same direction as I was.

Avoiding Tina had been high on my list of things to do, for reasons more professional than personal. But it was going to be difficult to accomplish that while riding up in the same elevator car. And even though she looked terrific—from floor up: calf-length black boots, gray tights, black skirt, form-fitting white blouse, curly dark hair swept up in a clasp—I tried not to look at her too much. There was no sense in antagonizing her.

"Good morning or, wait," she said, briefly glancing at her watch, "make that good afternoon."

"Hi," I said, keeping my eyes on the numbers as they ticked upward.

"Hey, I still need you to look at that recycling story in your basket," she said, without any hint of rancor.

"Okay," I said. I was waiting for a riposte of some sort, but none was forthcoming. Instead, we reached the floor for the newsroom and she gave me a cheery "See ya!" as we departed.

Suspicious, I logged in to my computer as soon as I got to my desk and hauled up my ode to reuse. Given Tina's previous comments about the story being unfit for the paper it would be printed on, I expected to see a file awash in red, which was the color editors' notes appeared in. But there just a small parcel of red text at the top:

"Carter: This is an outstanding piece of journalism, a pleasure to read and edit. There are a few minor questions below. Please address them and ship the story back to me so we can put it on A1, where it deserves to be!—TT."

Below, there were three questions so insignificant I was able to make the fixes on the spot. I saved the story, shipped it back to Tina, then walked to her open office door. She was seated with her long, lean body in a twisted position, like a minor maharani on her throne—yoga being one of Tina's pastimes.

"Was this a trick?" I asked.

"Huh?" she said, looking up from whatever had been transfixing her on the computer monitor.

"You said yesterday the recycling story was, quote, 'garbage.' Now suddenly you're thrilled about it. What gives?"

"Oh, yeah, I . . . Look, why don't you sit down?"

I sat.

She said, "Can I be honest with you?"

"Always."

"Okay," she said, uncurling herself and placing her hands on her desk and her feet on the floor. "Last night I saw you heading out the door with your girlfriend, the human lollipop, and at first it made me feel, I don't know, angry or jealous or something."

I was going to interject that Kira wasn't my girlfriend, but I didn't want to interrupt a verbal journey that sounded like it was heading toward Apologyland.

She continued: "But then I caught myself. You've given me ample opportunity to have a real relationship, and I've turned down every one of them. Because I don't really want one—with you or anyone, for that matter. So I can hardly blame you for pursuing one with someone else. Even if the person you chose treats every day like it's Halloween, that's hardly reason to despise her. She's got herself a great guy. I shouldn't hate her for that. Or you."

"Oh," I said. "Thanks."

"You're welcome. Anyhow, I'm sorry for being in such a snit with you lately. I really would like to go back to being friends. And colleagues. I hate that I've let our personal relationship cloud my judgment as your editor.

"Which," she said, making a big show of inhaling, "brings us to your recycling story. I went back and reread it last night and it struck me I had been guilty of malicious editing. I realized if anyone else had handed me that story, I would have been thrilled with it. The only reason I ripped it apart is because it said 'By Carter Ross' at the top. So I went back through and re-edited it more evenhandedly, and I was really quite pleased with what I found."

"Th-thank you," I stammered. I was always a bit uncomfortable when Tina was being contrite. As an editor, Tina was something of a fire-breathing dragon. As a reporter, I always fancied myself the brave and valiant knight, ready to do battle with her. But now suddenly my dragon wanted to stop and cuddle. It was enough to make me wish the fearsome lizard would just keep spitting fire. At least that way I knew to keep my shield up the whole time.

"I mean, let's be serious, I'm about to have to spend the afternoon rewriting Buster Hays. There's not enough Novocain in the world to numb that much pain. Next to him, editing you is a dream. And I ought to give you credit for that."

"Thanks," I said again.

"So what's this other story you're uncorking?" she asked. "Come on, don't make me sweat Pigeon for it."

Ordinarily, I never would have told an editor about a piece that was still such unmolded clay. There would be too much of a temptation for the editor to stick her hands in it and leave messy thumbprints all over. But given Tina's sudden softening, I made an exception to my usual policy and told her what I knew so far.

She agreed with my conclusion that Ridgewood Avenue deserved the *Eagle-Examiner*'s full attention. She gave me the official blessing to continue making use of Pigeon and to continue my search for the truth.

It would have been even better if she could have told me where to find it.

·　　　·　　　·

Emerging from Tina's office, I considered my options and quickly decided I needed to enlist the aid of some of my compatriots. Stick around a newspaper for any length of time and you'll realize that some of your best sources of information are the other reporters in the newsroom with you.

I immediately set my sights on Tommy Hernandez, happily clacking away on his computer. Tommy is about five foot seven, maybe 145 pounds, and gay as a box of Shrinky Dinks. He had his hair perfectly mussed and thoroughly moussed and was wearing a tailored shirt with more darts than a dive bar. He also had earbuds in. Tommy sometimes celebrates his Cuban heritage by listening to salsa music; other times, he celebrates certain stereotypes regarding his sexual orientation by listening to vapid pop music.

I couldn't say which he was indulging at the moment. He didn't appear to notice me as I approached him, but I was still a few paces off when he said, "Whatever the question you and your hideous pleated pants are coming to ask, the answer is, 'forget it.'"

Tommy is seldom shy about expressing his distaste for my fashion sensibilities. "How could you even hear me coming? You have music playing."

He looked up at me blank-faced. I pulled one of the buds from his ears. There was no sound coming out.

"You're doing the pretend-to-listen-to-music-so-people-won't-bother-you thing," I said. "You know that just makes me want to bother you more, right? Don't you at least want to know why I'm coming over?"

"No. And do you know why? One, because I'm very busy doing my own work. And, two, because you're coming out of Tina's office, which probably means she's told you not to do something that you are now going to ask me to help you do. I'm not going to be your stooge this time."

"When have I ever recruited you into an act of insubordination?"

"You mean this week? Not yet. But it's only Tuesday, so you're just about on time."

"Actually, I'll have you know, Tina is well aware of what I'm working on and I'm doing so with her full permission."

"Really?" he said, removing the other earbud. "That's sort of weird. What's her angle?"

"It's part of the new détente between us, apparently," I said. "Anyhow, if you're busy, I'll leave you alo—"

"No, I was just saying that so you wouldn't try to talk me into doing something I shouldn't have been doing. I'm really pretty free. What's up?"

I leaned against the desk across the aisle from Tommy. "I was wondering how much you knew about McAlister Arms, that new development that's being proposed in the South Ward."

As city hall reporter, I was betting Tommy would have heard any scuttlebutt surrounding such a large new project.

"Ah, Vaughn McAlister. He seems to be everyone's favorite subject lately."

"How so?"

"He's throwing money around like crazy," Tommy said.

"All aboveboard, I'm sure."

"Above the table, below the table . . . with New Jersey's campaign-finance laws, who can tell the difference most of the time?"

"What does he want?"

Tommy shook his hair-product-filled head. "I don't know, specifically. I think he just wants to make sure things keep moving smoothly. You know how it is with developers. Between the banks and their subcontractors and whatever options they might have on the land that are running out, they're always up against one time constraint or another. They're almost as bad as we are when it comes to deadlines. Plus, I'm hearing he has his sights set on bigger things."

"Such as?"

"I don't know. World domination."

"Seriously . . ."

"Well, the rumor is McAlister Properties is laying groundwork for something called McAlister Tower—some big skyscraper filled with Class A office space and a hotel on the top floors and all that. They'd build it right near Penn Station so they could get the PATH crowd and the New Jersey Transit crowd. It sounds like it could be really cool."

I just laughed.

"What?" Tommy said, frowning slightly.

"It's just funny that you haven't been doing this job long enough to get completely jaded yet. Ever hear of Harry Grant?"

"No."

"He was before my time, of course, but ask around. There are people around here who will remember him," I said. "He swept into town in the eighties with this plan to build the world's tallest building right here in Newark—one hundred and twenty-one stories. Everyone thought he had real money because he paid to have the dome atop city hall gilded with gold. But it turned out that was basically the only money he had."

"So what happened?"

"He built the facade for what he called the Renaissance Mall—this was the first stage of the tower—and then he went bankrupt and fled town. The facade stayed there for like two decades before someone finally knocked it down."

"So, what, you think the McAlisters are another Harry Grant?"

I didn't necessarily. Newark had come a long way from those days in the eighties, when it was so desperate for something—anything—to be developed that it was ripe to be plucked by whatever con man stopped off the turnpike. But I just said, "I don't know. You tell me."

Tommy leaned back and pondered it for a moment. "I don't think so. I mean, the McAlisters seem to be legit. This McAlister Arms thing is their first residential project, but they already have a couple of office buildings downtown."

"Yeah, except they didn't build those places. They just took existing buildings and slapped 'McAlister' on them when they bought them."

"True, but they do own and manage them now. That has to count for something."

"Do you know them at all?" I asked.

"I've never met the old man. From what I'm told, he's sort of the backroom guy. Vaughn McAlister is the front man. He's usually around if you want to talk to him."

Tommy pulled his phone out of his pocket and read off a number with a 973 area code.

"You've got his phone number programmed in your phone?"

"The McAlister name comes up often enough. I've probably quoted Vaughn a half-dozen times in the last six months."

"Is he a good guy to deal with?" I asked. And here, of course, I meant it in the way reporters define a good guy. It has little to do with, say, charitable works or a magnanimous personality and everything to do with whether they are quotable and return phone calls promptly on deadline.

"Yeah, good enough. He's a slut for good press. He'll pretend to be busy, but then he'll always magically be able to find time for you."

"Thanks," I said.

Tommy responded with a burst of Spanish, which he often does when he's insulting me.

"Okay, what did you just say?" I asked.

"It translates roughly as: 'Don't thank me. Just buy better pants.'"

As Tommy had predicted, Vaughn McAlister's schedule was absolutely slammed—completely and totally booked solid between now and next Labor Day, with not even a glimmer of hope that he would have time to wave hello if we passed in the hallway—except for the one small opening that happened to have popped up that afternoon. But only because the prime minister of England had canceled at the last second.

I had been somewhat vague as to why I was calling, saying only that I was writing about a neighborhood in the South Ward that was near McAlister Arms. I couldn't very well come out and say that I was worried his construction site was harboring toxic waste. Yet, it struck me during our brief phone chat—as he impressed upon me the monumental inflexibility of his colossally imposing schedule—that he didn't really care what I was calling about.

And, coincidentally, his magical opening was in twenty minutes. Which is about how long it would take me to collect myself, drive to his office downtown, park, and walk to his building.

Arriving at McAlister Place, I breezed through the downstairs security—I could have told them I was Jack the Ripper and they still would have waved me through—then faced a far stiffer inspection upon reaching the second-floor offices of McAlister Properties. A round-faced fortyish woman with shellacked brown hair and a gray skirt suit looked up at me as I entered.

"Hello, may I help you?"

"Hi. My name is Carter Ross. I'm a reporter with the *Eagle-Examiner*. I'm here to see Vaughn McAlister."

Her brow made a V shape in response to this assertion and she glanced at her computer screen. Her desk was as neat as any I'd ever seen. There was exactly one personal effect, a photo of a gawky-looking preteenage boy. Otherwise, the most prominent feature was a brass nameplate: "M. Fenstermacher." I was glad someone put in the "M." part. Otherwise it would be easy to confuse her with all the other Fenstermachers around.

I knew, from my days of high school language class, that "fenstermacher" meant "window-maker" in German. "Fenster" comes from the Latin "fenestra," which is also the root for one of the world's greatest words, "defenestration," which *Webster's* defines as "a throwing of a person or thing out of a window." It's also what M. Fenstermacher looked like she wanted to do to me at the moment.

"I'm sorry, I don't show you as having an appointment," she said. "Is Mr. McAlister expecting you?"

"He is," I said.

This brought another consternated look and another glance at the computer screen from M. Fenstermacher. Maybe the "M." stood for "Miss," because she didn't have a wedding ring on her finger. She struck me as a woman who did not like surprises. Her immobile hairstyle, impeccable manicure, precisely applied makeup, and utterly clean desk suggested that I was standing in front of a bit of a control freak.

"Wait here, please," she said, rising from her desk.

She rose and I got a whiff of Miss Fenstermacher's perfume. I don't know Chanel from chenille, but it smelled expensive. As she walked toward a set of double doors to her right, I saw her face was not the only part of her that was rounded. She rather amply filled out her gray skirt suit. She wasn't really my type—I like them a little more natural than the painstakingly produced Miss Fenstermacher—and it's not like she was going to win any beauty pageants. But in a (thankfully) bygone era, I'm sure there were bosses who would have chased her around the desk more than a few times.

Just then Vaughn McAlister emerged from the double doors. Miss Fenstermacher brightened considerably upon seeing him. This nightmare that was an unscheduled appointment was about to be over.

"It's okay, Marcia," he announced. "There was a last-second change to the docket and I was able to squeeze Mr. Ross in."

"Thanks for seeing me on such short notice," I said, playing along.

"Thanks for coming," he said.

I smiled at him. He smiled back. I extended a hand. He grabbed it. Vaughn McAlister was a real charmer—blow-dried blond hair, perfect teeth, firm handshake. I immediately recognized the type: he charmed people simply for the sake of charming them. Even if he couldn't immediately predict the benefits, he figured there would be some eventually. It was what he did.

He fancied himself not just as a player but as *the* player—the guy who could make things happen by sheer will and personal magnetism.

What he perhaps didn't understand is that part of being a mature newspaper reporter is being immune to such things. Most of us allowed ourselves to get charmed by a player once, in our early twenties, then learned our lesson.

The only thing about him I found truly impressive was his clothing. He was wearing a sharply tailored blue pinstripe suit that had probably cost more than every pair of khaki pants I had ever bought and Italian loafers that had easily set him back five hundred bucks. Now I knew why Tommy had such a soft spot for him: shoe envy is one of Tommy's tragic flaws.

Vaughn and I tested each other a little bit, swapping a few quick ha-ha lines—about traffic, about weather—then dropping enough names so that each of us knew the other was sufficiently connected. Then we gave up trying to impress each other.

"Hold my calls, Marcia," he said as he invited me into his office.

Miss Fenstermacher would, I was sure, eagerly comply.

There were no more attempts at small talk as I followed him into his nicely appointed office and settled into a chair on the other side of his sleek desk and Cross pen set.

"That's quite a large project you have going down in the South Ward," I said, hauling out my notepad so he knew we were on the record.

"Yes, we're very excited about McAlister Arms," he said with appropriate earnestness. "It's a mixed-use development, as you may know, so people will be able to live there, work there, and shop there. We've got the commercial space pretty well sold and we're going to start opening up the residential units for sale soon as well. We've already had people inquiring about it. This is going to be a real crown jewel for Newark."

Of course it would be. You have to love developer hyperbole: what is actually a very common construction project, built to the same code standards and with the same base materials as everything else, is always a "crown jewel."

"Care to say who the anchoring commercial tenant will be?" I asked.

"Not until the ink is dry on the contracts," he said, giving me his best Vaughn McAlister smile. "But it's a major national retailer. This is going to bring jobs to the people of Newark. We've written a first-source agreement into the lease, which means they have to use Newark employment agencies for at least fifty percent of their hires. We've also made our own promise to use eighty percent local labor during construction. This is going to bring jobs to this city. Make sure you put that in whatever you write."

It was a common gripe about development in Newark that it never ended up benefiting the people who lived there. I gave McAlister Properties credit for anticipating that criticism and doing something about it. I was about to ask another question, but I was interrupted by a knock on the door.

"Sorry," he said, then raised his voice slightly: "Come in."

It was Miss Fenstermacher. "I'm very sorry, Mr. McAlister," she said. "But this needs your signature ASAP."

Vaughn acted like he was annoyed by the intrusion, but I suspected he had told Miss Fenstermacher to interrupt, just so I wouldn't forget how Very Important he was.

He took a cursory glance at the document, then signed it with a big, bold "Vaughn McAlister." The "V" looked like a checkmark. The "M" looked like a bird about to take flight. The rest of it was just squiggles.

"Thank you, Marcia," he said. She smiled gratefully, then departed.

We were interrupted long enough that Vaughn was able to resume the conversation at a spot of his choosing, which, as it turned out, was in a soliloquy. "You may not know this, but my great-grandparents actually lived here in Newark. They came on the boat from Ireland and lived in the North Ward. So this city is really in the McAlister bloodlines and we want to see it thrive again. McAlister Arms is going to be a model for what we can do all over Newark. And the best thing is, it's really going to benefit everyone. We've got subsidized housing for low- and middle-income families mixed in with market-rate units. People from all walks of life will be able to live there."

Ah. So the crown jewel was also going to be capable of social transformation. It was nice to know his hyperbole had lofty goals as well. Now it was time to set the bait a little.

"Wow," I said, trying to sound gee-whizzish. "I was going to speculate whether McAlister Arms would be another South Ward Industrial Park—you know, something that doesn't live up to its hype. But it sounds like you guys have thought of everything."

"McAlister Arms is going to completely revitalize this part of Newark," he said. "And it's going to be good for the city's coffers, too. The city was willing to give us a ten-year tax abatement, but we insisted on only making it five. This is going to be a real ratables boon, and that's only going to help the city in the long run—more taxes means better schools, better police coverage, a better city."

"And this thing is really going to happen?" I asked. "You've got all the approvals and financing you need?"

He assured me he did, telling me in detail about how they were just finishing grading the property and were already moving materials on-site, and no one would be doing that if they didn't have the project green-lighted. I had already known that—after all, I had seen all the construction trucks the day before—but I wanted to make him feel like the interview was going well, like I was the skeptic who had now been won over.

I was really just setting him up for this question, which was meant to sound like a throwaway: "I don't even want to know what you must be doing to get that site ready for construction. I know there used to be a bunch of factories down there. They must have left all kinds of awful stuff behind, huh?"

I was hoping he would give me some kind of lead for what might be making these people sick. Something like, *Oh, yeah, we found a big pool of hexavalent chromium just yesterday.* Or, *Yes, they used to make lead paint on that site.*

Instead, he just said, "Oh, well, that's all been cleaned up already."

"It has? Because I heard there were some people getting sick down there. A whole group of folks from the neighborhood, actually," I said, again as an aside.

He absorbed this information, which didn't seem to cause a single hair on his perfect head to move askance.

"Well, they're not getting sick due to anything coming from us. Our remediation process was overseen by a Licensed Site Remediation Professional in strict accordance with state Department of Environmental Protection standards. It didn't even cost us or the city anything. The DEP has grants for brownfields redevelopment. For a private developer, the money can be a bit hard to get. But we had the city working with us. The DEP just loves public-private partnerships. They gave us six million dollars to clean up the site. That was done a while ago. We got it certified and everything."

I kept smiling like this was just more good news. But I was really a bit disappointed. If the remediation had been done a while ago, it meant McAlister Arms wasn't the culprit. After all, I had gotten sick the night before. It had to be a pollutant that was still active in some way.

I asked a few more questions about the development, mainly to keep my cover, then made a hasty departure. Vaughn was as charming upon exit as he was upon entrance. And he said that if I ever wanted to talk again, he would be happy to do so—assuming, of course, he could ever find the time.

It was just my luck that when I left the offices of McAlister Properties, it was three forty-five—which is known for, among other things, being close to four o'clock. And four o'clock, in Newark, meant Professor Rice's teatime.

Dr. Charles Rice was a history professor at Rutgers-Newark and was a much-loved institution in the city. Through some forty years at the university, he had perfected the art of pedantry—right down to the thick glasses and tweed jackets—and he delighted in the traditions and conventions of academia. He treated intellectual squabbles as if they just might lead to the Third World War if the wrong ideas prevailed, and he was known to weigh tenure proceedings with roughly the same seriousness as juries are instructed to consider death-penalty trials.

But he remained on enough of a corresponding basis with the outside world that those of us who lived there could still talk to him. He was eminently quotable, a man who spoke not in clipped phrases or short sentences but in full, eloquent paragraphs. And he was an absolute font of information on Newark. For time-strapped reporters who lacked the patience or expertise for serious scholarly research—self, meet self—Professor Rice was a one-stop shop for all things Newark history. If anyone would know what factory had once been down in that part of Newark, and how it might still be poisoning people now, it would be Professor Rice.

And, at four o'clock every day, he opened his humble office on the third floor of a growing-shabby university building to anyone who felt like visiting and served tea. It was his ode to eighteenth-century French salons, and he viewed it as a time for the intelligentsia of Newark to gather and discuss the important matters of the day.

Sadly, since the intelligentsia of Newark number about twelve—and most of them are busy at four o'clock—this often translated into Professor Rice sitting alone in his office, guzzling a pot of tea by himself. So he appeared to be delighted when I knocked lightly on his open door and said, "Anyone home?"

"Carter, my friend, how are you?" he said warmly.

"I'm doing fine, Professor, it's good to see you again."

We hugged—Professor Rice is a sixty-something-year-old African American man and an unrepentant hugger—and he pointed to one of the chairs in his office. It was a subtle thing, but his desk was shoved up against the wall, meaning you were never on the other side of a slab of wood from Dr. Rice. The chairs and sofas in his office, including his own, were roughly in a circle around the edges of the room. It was one small way he made his space more inviting for conversation.

"I'm so glad you came by," he said. "There's a book I've been wanting to give you."

Professor Rice was always giving me things to read. They were usually pretty good—if you didn't mind half-page footnotes—and they always had titles with colons in them. True to form, he handed me a book that would have made a fine doorstop, entitled *Marginal Color: Deconstructing Ethnicity, Race, and Class among Creoles and Non-Creoles in a Post-Revolutionary Pre-Antebellum Southeastern Louisiana Parish.*

"It kept me up all night," he said earnestly.

"Thanks," I said. "I'll try not to read it when I have any early-morning meetings."

"So what can I do for the *Eagle-Examiner* this afternoon?"

"Well, as usual, Professor, I'm hoping you can give me a quick history lesson," I said, taking out my phone and hauling up Edna Foster's address on Google Maps. "Can you tell me what kind of manufacturing used to happen in this neighborhood?"

I handed the professor my phone. He moved it around until he found the sweet spot in his bifocals, then considered it for a moment or two. He went to a larger map of Newark mounted on his wall and traced his fingers to the address I had given him. It was a modern map, complete with highways and the airport, but Professor Rice had a way of seeing through decades into what the city used to look like. It was actually somewhat uncanny.

From his wall map he went to one of his bookshelves and knelt down to the bottom level. He pulled out a platter-size, four-inch-thick book and hefted it onto a small coffee table with considerable effort.

"What's that?" I asked.

"The 1925 tax assessment of Newark," he said. "They had an extra copy at the Register of Deeds and Mortgages and they were going to throw it out. Can you imagine? Thank goodness someone had the foresight to ask me if I wanted it. Let me tell you, fella, I jumped on it. If you want a snapshot of Newark at its heyday, 1925 is about as good a year as any. The globalization that took the city's factory jobs away hadn't commenced, so all of the industry is still there. A few of the more prominent citizens had started moving out to the suburbs, but the outflow was really just a trickle. It was a good time for Newark."

Without so much as glancing at the index, he opened the enormous book to somewhere in the middle. He flipped two pages and studied it for another moment or two.

"Ah, yes," he said. "I thought so."

"What?" I asked.

"Dentures."

"Dentures?"

"Yes, come here," he said, patting a spot next to him on the couch. I joined him and he pointed to a piece of the map that was now within the McAlister Arms site.

"This was home to a company called K and J Manufacturing," he said. "This would have been a brick building several stories high which employed several hundred people. It was one of the nation's leading manufacturers of dentures."

"Huh," was all I could say.

"My friend, if I may ask, why are you curious about this?"

With any other source, I might or might not have said anything. But while Dr. Rice might be given to the usual academic gossip—like which assistant professors were sleeping and/or trying to sleep with which postdoctoral fellows—he knew when to be discreet with information. So I told him about the illness I was hunting and my suspicion that some long-ago industrial pollutant was the cause.

"Well, in that case, dentures are a good choice," Professor Rice said.

"Yeah, I guess they must have been made of, what, plastic or something?"

"Not in the nineteenth and early twentieth centuries, my friend. No, no. Back then, they were made of vulcanized rubber."

"You mean, like, tires?"

"Well, yes and no. The vulcanization process is part of making tires. But it also had many other industrial applications, including dentures."

"Think there's some byproduct of the vulcanization process that might be capable of making people sick a century later?" I asked.

Professor Rice struck an appropriately contemplative pose. "Well, chemistry isn't my area. But if I've learned nothing else about the kind of manufacturing that used to take place in Newark, it's that it's almost always unhealthy to someone somehow. You know what resource I refer to in matters such as these?"

Professor Rice was a scholar's scholar, so I was thinking it had to be some weighty academic publication. Something like, say, the *International Journal of Super-Smart Stuff Quarterly Review.*

"I couldn't even guess," I said.

"Wikipedia," he said, turning to his computer. "Let's see . . ."

He typed for a moment, then started muttering to himself, "Sulfur . . . that would smell awful, but I'm not sure it has any health effects like the ones you describe. Zinc oxide . . . I think that's part of most suntan lotions, so I doubt that's the culprit. Stearic acid? That sounds bad."

"Yeah, except I think it's found in just about every shampoo ever made, so that's not it."

"Then how about this: thiocarbanilide," he said, chewing over each syllable.

"What's *that*?"

"Well, I guess it was used starting in the early twentieth century as an accelerant in the vulcanization process."

"Is it harmful? Anything with that many syllables has to be bad for you, right?"

"I don't know," he said. "Let's see . . . Wikipedia mentions something about a lethal dose . . . huh . . . oh my."

He cleared his throat and started reading from another document: "'May cause ataxia, analgesia, convulsions, and respiratory distress, including cyanosis.'"

I had pulled out my notebook and was writing it down. "Ataxia, analgesia . . . None of this sounds very healthy, but do you know what they are?"

"Not at all, my friend," he admitted. "Oh, wait, look at this: 'Severe overexposure may result in death.'"

"Oh, I think I know what that is," I said. "I'm no doctor, so this is an unschooled opinion. But death . . . that's not a good thing, is it?"

"Definitely not," he confirmed. "Not good at all."

My parting gift from the good professor's office was a book called *New Jersey Makes: A Non-Marxian Sociohistory of Neo-Industrial Pre-Postmodern Manufacturing in the Garden State.* It made the doorstop of a book he had given me earlier look like a mere pamphlet. From a quick glance at the introduction, which was filled with prose as dense as it was impenetrable, it struck me as something that should have been regulated by the Food and Drug Administration as a sleeping aid.

But it did contain a chapter about K&J Manufacturing, which told the story of a son of Norwegian immigrants who rose from humble origins to become one of the most prominent men in New Jersey.

Klaus Josef Jorgensen had been the founder of K&J Manufacturing in the 1880s and perfected the process by which vulcanized dentures were manufactured. He eventually passed the business onto Klaus Josef Jorgensen, Jr., who turned K&J into a national denture powerhouse that supplied a significant portion of early-twentieth-century America's fake teeth—and compiled a significant fortune in the process.

Klaus Josef Jorgensen III took that fortune and diversified it, getting out of business—by then, dentures were starting to be made of different materials—and investing heavily in railroads, textiles, and other businesses that may have seemed like good bets in the midtwentieth century but were actually soon to go into significant decline. In the book, this was treated as more or less the end of the K&J Manufacturing story, except for one footnote.

It pertained to Klaus Josef Jorgensen IV, who recognized his father's blunder of being too backward-thinking. So, when he took over the family business in the mid-1960s, he again repositioned K&J to harness a technology that he was convinced was going to revolutionize the way data was collected and stored, leading to a flowering of information-sharing the likes of which the world had never seen. Yes, his vision was for K&J to be a global leader in the manufacture and supply of microfilm.

"By the year 2000, every American family will have a microfilm reader in its living room," Klaus IV confidently predicted in one document cited. "And microfilm will have replaced letter-writing as the preferred method of private communication among the middle and upper classes. The market for microfilm will be limited only by our capacity to produce it."

There was no mention in the book about how this bold prophecy had turned out. All there was, at the end of the chapter, was a picture of the Jorgensen family's Madison, New Jersey estate, shot from Route 124.

I recognized the part of Route 124 where the picture had been taken—it was a bend in the road just as you got out of Madison proper, on your way to Morristown. I didn't recognize the house itself. For as many times as I had driven that road— Route 124 used to be part of my beat when I worked in one of the *Eagle-Examiner*'s suburban bureaus—I was quite sure I had never seen anything like the stately mansion portrayed in the photograph. It looked like something that had been built by one of the Vanderbilts, all limestone and marble and Gilded Era opulence.

I was sitting in my car as I finished up my assigned reading and I made the snap decision to visit the mansion. Perhaps some member of the Jorgensen clan was living there and could tell me whether K&J Manufacturing was still alive in some form—and whether it might be willing to take responsibility for the medical costs and cleanup of the poisonous legacy it had left in Newark.

If not, then K&J Manufacturing and its heirs would still fill an important role in my article. Just as every good story needs a victim, which Edna Foster had so unfortunately become, it also needs a villain. And I didn't mind admitting that it would serve my purposes quite well if the villain happened to be some spoiled, wealthy, aloof lockjaw who couldn't bother to spit the silver spoon out of his mouth long enough to give me more than a hasty "no comment" when I knocked on his door.

I was still daydreaming about that scenario when I cleared the last of the lights in Madison and reached the spot on Route 124 where the picture had been taken. I understood immediately why I had never seen any palatial homes there: the property was overgrown with a dense forest of trees and shrubs, all of which were badly in need of trimming.

I turned into the front entrance, past a magnificent stone entryway and a wrought-iron gate that appeared to have been secured into the open position by a thicket of vines and brambles. I slowed so I could make out the tarnished brass nameplate on the gate. The place was named "Masticatoria."

Mastica . . . as in "masticate"? Someone in the Jorgensen family had apparently taken the dentures thing a little too seriously.

The driveway spiraled up and to the right. It had once been paved but was now just a crumbling patchwork of moss and broken chunks of asphalt. The landscaping continued to look as if it was being tended to by a manservant who was allergic to clippers. And trimming. And mowing. And weeding. And . . . work in general.

At the top of the drive was Masticatoria itself. It had clearly seen better days. There were places where the roof had lost its terra-cotta shingles. One of the stone chimneys was falling down. Another appeared to have become a well-populated squirrel nest. Ivy covered many of the windows. Things that should have been straight hung at odd angles.

The joint had an uninhabited feel to it. There was just no way some blueblood would allow the family manse to fall into such disrepair. Either it was abandoned or it was now the happy abode of the Munster family.

Still, I had come all this way. It would cost me nothing to knock on the door. I pulled my car to the top of the driveway, which ended in a massive half circle—for turning around four-horse carriages, no doubt—parked, and walked up a set of marble steps to a front door that was at least twelve feet tall. I grasped an enormous brass knocker, which let out a spine-tingling creak as I brought it toward me, then let it drop.

A heavy thudding sound echoed through the inside of the house. I thought that would be the only sound coming from this enormous and empty mansion before I turned around and called it a night.

Then, surprisingly, I heard footsteps.

The man who answered the door appeared to be about my age, about my height, and about my skin color. But that is where our similarities ended.

His hair looked like it hadn't seen a pair of scissors in a decade or a comb in twice that long. His beard could have been used to hide a week's worth of foodstuffs—and, for all I knew, it was. He was wearing a threadbare T-shirt over a torso that was more bone than muscle and a pair of jeans that were torn from long wear, not in any kind of fashionable way. He was barefoot. His body odor preceded him by several arm's lengths. But other than that, he seemed harmless enough.

"Hi, can I help you?" he asked in a friendly way.

Yeah, I wanted to say, *could you please, for the love of my olfactory nerves, take a shower?* Instead I went with: "Hi, my name is Carter Ross. I'm a reporter with the *Eagle-Examiner*. This is going to seem like an odd question, but is your last name Jorgensen by any chance?"

"Yeah," he said.

"Are you . . . Klaus Josef Jorgensen by any chance?"

"People call me Quint," he said.

Quint, as in Klaus Josef Jorgensen V. He was not exactly the lockjaw I was hoping for. He looked more like a body double for Tom Hanks's character in *Castaway*—after he's been on the desert island eating nothing but coconut for a couple of years.

"Nice to meet you," I said. "This is some place you got here."

"Used to be. Now it's a real dump, huh?" he said, still grinning.

"No, no, that's not what I meant."

"Yes it is," he insisted, and his smile went even wider, as if he was proud of it. "I wish I could sell it, but my trust explicitly states I can't. Seems like a waste to let it sit empty, so, well, this is where I live. Think it could use a touch-up or two?"

He was obviously joking, so I went along with it. "Well, maybe the trees could stand a bit of trimming."

Suddenly the smile went away. "Trim? Never! We need those trees to sequester as much carbon as possible! Come on, dude, get with the program!"

I looked at him closely to see if he was kidding. He wasn't. Not even slightly. Was it possible the heir to whatever remained of the K&J Manufacturing fortune was . . . a rabid environmentalist?

"Right," I said. "Right, of course."

I was trying to come up with something intelligent to say about global warming when he said, "Want to come in, dude?"

No, I want you to learn how to groom yourself, I almost said, but opted for: "Sure." Then, before it sounded too self-conscious, I added, "Dude."

Then I walked over the threshold of Masticatoria. As a reporter, I've been in all kinds of houses: the homes of hoarders, where there are nothing but thin trails of open floor between piles of stuff; the homes of OCD sufferers that smell like the inside of a Lysol can; the homes of collectors, who decorate their entire abodes with stamps/butterflies/purple unicorns or whatever their fetish happens to be.

But I had never been in a place quite like this. Every room was huge, beautiful, ornate, opulent—and empty.

So my brief tour of Masticatoria included a trip through

the (empty) foyer, down an (empty) hallway, past an (empty) library, and into a sitting room where there was nowhere to sit except for a few bamboo mats that had been arranged in a circle.

"Take a load off," he said, pointing to one of the mats. He caught my incredulous look, which I wasn't quite quick enough to hide, and added, "I'm not really big into furniture. It's a waste of resources."

"Yeah, I think I saw something like this on the Home and Garden Channel once," I said. "They called it 'barren chic.'"

I chose a spot that I deemed to be upwind from his aroma.

"So what can I do for you?" he asked.

"Well, I'm doing some reporting about a neighborhood in Newark that's near where one of your family's factories used to be," I said. "I was hoping you could tell me: what has become of K and J Manufacturing?"

"Oh, wow," he said, then launched into a version of the company history that was a bit more detailed—and a bit more sarcastic—than what I had read in the history book. But it ended in the same spot: Klaus Josef IV had mismanaged K&J into the ground and then died a brokenhearted early death. All that was left of the family fortune, Quint said, was the house—minus the furniture, which he gave to a museum—and something he called the 2077 Trust.

"The 2077 Trust?" I asked.

"It continues paying me a set amount a year until 2077, at which point I will turn a hundred and, the trustees assumed, either be too old or too dead to care."

He cast a sly glance to the left and right. "I tell the trustees all I do is sit around and smoke pot all day. And I always send them e-mails at four A.M. so they think I'm partying all the time. But the truth is, I've made all sorts of money that I've hidden from them. I'm currently invested in several very promising green-energy technologies. But you can't print that, because it'll ruin my fun."

"Okay," I said. "We'll make that last part off the record."

"Whatever, dude. Anyhow, I don't mean to be rambling. Why do you even want to know about this stuff?"

I was so thrown by what I was witnessing—the scion of industrialists living as a barefoot hippie in a decomposing mansion—that I couldn't even come up with a subtle way to phrase what came out next:

"Well, to be honest, I think something left behind by your family's denture-making operation is somehow surfacing and making people in the neighborhood sick."

"Really?" he said, like this intrigued him. "What are you thinking is the culprit? Do you know?"

"Thiocarbanilide."

Thinking back to the professor's rather grim warning—"severe overexposure may result in death"—I imagined that merely uttering the word would elicit a shudder from him, as if saying, "You've got thiocarbanilide poisoning" was the chemical equivalent of saying, "You married a Kardashian."

Instead, the face Quint made under his beard was more curious than menacing. "What kind of symptoms are these people reporting?" he asked.

I ran down the litany of problems, from the flu to broken bones. He was already shaking his head.

"That's not thio," he said, as if it were his friend and he was defending its reputation.

"How do you know?"

"Because I'm a Jorgensen. When I was a kid, we used to sit around at the dinner table talking about chemistry the way other families talked about the weather. Thiocarbanilide decomposes when left open to the elements, so it's hard to imagine any of it still being around after all this time. Besides, it's organic.

I'm sure it would kick your ass if you tried to eat it for break-fast, but there's no way it could cause the kind of stuff you're talking about."

I had taken chemistry in my sophomore year of high school. I remembered very clearly that Myra Merkle sat in the front row of that class. I remembered very little else about it.

"If you don't believe me, you can look it up," Quint continued. "Look, I'm not saying K and J didn't leave *something* down there that's making people sick. I'm just saying it's not thio."

"So what would it be?"

"Who knows? Could be anything. If you want, I could think about it, call some of my environmental people."

"You have environmental people?" I asked. Too bad he didn't have deodorant people.

"Well, yeah. My trust requires that I donate a certain amount of money each year, but it doesn't say where. That money was made by some industries that made the Earth a pretty dirty place. It seems only right to give it away to people who are trying to clean it up. So I give it all to a variety of small environmental groups."

"Oh, that's nice."

"To be honest, I'm mostly just in it for the protests. I do love a good protest," he said, allowing his mind to drift off for a mo-ment, doubtlessly to some picket-toting sit-in of yore. Then he snapped back to and concluded, "Anyway, when you donate fifty, a hundred grand a year to these small groups, they tend to pick up the phone when you call. Let me kick it around with them."

As tempted as I was to sit around and swap decorating tips, I didn't want to overstay my welcome. And, besides, Quint's stench was starting to make my eyes water. So we exchanged contact info and I made my way out of the odd netherworld that was

Masticatoria and back into the real one of Madison, New Jersey, where people viewed their trees more as landscaping than as carbon-sequestration devices.

It was after six o'clock, a perfectly acceptable hour for a reporter not on deadline to end his working day. It was also a time when, having now fully shaken off the effects of the dread mystery flu, I was getting a little hungry. So, knowing that my hometown of Millburn was just a few minutes away, I called a very familiar phone number and said five words I knew I would probably come to regret: "Hey, Mom, what's for dinner?"

My mom is a retired schoolteacher who still cooks like she has a family of five to feed. My dad is a retired pharmaceutical executive who tells her to cut it out. She seldom listens, and I occasionally avail myself of this fact to get a home-cooked meal in my stomach.

Of the three Ross children, I am the only one to have stayed in the great Garden State, though none of us went terribly far. My brother, Tyler, is a lawyer for a big firm in Washington, D.C. My sister, Amanda, is a social worker in Philadelphia.

None of us has produced offspring yet, but my parents remain forever hopeful. Tyler was married but childless. Whenever my parents asked him when he and my sister-in-law planned to have children, Tyler would tell them, "We're thinking about it." To which my father always replied, "Well, son, you know you have to do more than think about it, right?"

Then there was me. Girls had been telling me I was "marriage material" since I was sixteen. Yet, here I was, at thirty-two, still stuck in bachelorhood. Not even dating exclusively. When my parents asked if I ever thought about having children, I made vague noises without words attached to them. The fact was, future generations of Carter Rosses were not in my immediate or even intermediate plans. They were like the promise of more-energy-efficient cars: forever five to ten years off.

Given the disappointment that was their sons, my parents' great hope for grandchild production had become Amanda. After a series of boyfriends who seemed never to last very long, she had finally gotten serious with this guy named Gary. He was a New Jersey state trooper, and while this gave me endless amounts of material for ribbing—about their uniforms being inspired by Nazis, about the whole racial-profiling thing, about that racing club some of their troopers escorted down the parkway a few years back, and so on—the truth was I had always been impressed in my dealings with New Jersey's cops. There were a few rogue idiots who occasionally gave reporters like me a lot to write about. But generally they were top-notch professionals. And Gary was, all teasing aside, a heck of a good guy.

So when Amanda announced she and Gary were getting hitched, it was a cause for great celebration—and then, at least on my mother's part, obsession. Ever since the engagement, Mom had been treating mother-of-the-bride duties like it was North Africa and she was General Patton. In a tank. And now that the wedding was this coming weekend? She was no longer recognizing the Geneva convention.

Hence, I was barely inside the door before my mother started with:

"I've been thinking about the rehearsal dinner. Cocktails start at five, which I think is too early, but this is Gary's parents doing the planning for this part, so I didn't get a say. But it would be nice if we all went over together. If we leave here at four forty-five we should get there in plenty of time. So why don't you plan on being here by four thirty on Friday?"

"Hi, Mom," I said. "How are you?"

"And you're sure you're not bringing anyone to the wedding? It's not too late you know. There's an empty seat at your table."

From somewhere inside the house, my dad hollered, "Trish, would you leave him alone?"

"Bill, he's the only one without a plus-one. It's making the seating unbalanced," she yelled back, as if I weren't there. She turned her attention to me and said, "What about your friend Tina?"

Mom always referred to Tina as "your friend Tina." She always said the "your friend" part with this hint of collusion, like Tina and I were really deeply in love and not telling anyone, and Mom was steadfastly keeping our secret. It was clearly wishful thinking on Mom's part. She and Tina had met several times and they always hit it off fabulously.

"Sorry, Mom. That's not happening."

"She's such a nice woman and it would be so lovely to have her at such an important family gathering," she continued, as if I hadn't just spoken. "You just have to let me know by Thursday. That's when I have to give the caterer a final count."

"Mom!" I said sharply enough to get her attention. "Tina barely even talks to me anymore. We're"—I waved my arms in a frustrated gesture—"not going to any weddings, okay? Not someone else's and certainly not our own. So get Tina out of your head. She's out of mine."

Mom acted like she still didn't believe me, but nevertheless she said, "Well, maybe you'll meet a nice girl at the rehearsal dinner on Friday night. Maybe Gary has a cousin or something."

I hadn't told my parents about Kira yet. When I was a teenager, I learned not to give my parents too much information about my romantic life. I think there was a time in early adulthood when I started telling them more—after all, they couldn't ground me or take away my car anymore—then, after a little more time, I realized I had actually had the right idea when I was a teenager.

My parents tended to act as if our time together were a White House press briefing and I was the president. They would keep peppering me with inquiries until I finally stepped away from the podium and told them I wasn't taking any more questions. So I had learned that the less they knew when it came to relationships—call that area of my life domestic policy—the more time they would spend asking me about work, friends, or other subjects that might be called foreign policy. And, ask any president except perhaps the second George Bush: foreign policy is always easier to talk about.

Every once in a while my dad would try to pull me aside and, man-to-man, ask me if I was getting any "mud for my turtle"—or any number of other colorful euphemisms for The Act. But I wasn't fooled: he was going to report back to Mom a sanitized version of anything I said.

So I just deflected any more talk about my romantic life all the way through dinner, a delicious and suitably WASPy meal of tuna casserole, baby spinach salad, and couscous. We were just finishing up when my phone rang. Before I could think about the ears around me, I answered it with, "Hi, Tina."

Mom just beamed.

Then came five more words I knew I would come to regret, this time not from my mouth, but from Tina's: "Hey, wanna grab a beer?"

I somehow escaped the Ross ancestral home with only minor prodding about the nature of Tina's call or the implications of her invitation. It probably helped that this was one time I wasn't being intentionally obscure: I really didn't know what Tina's agenda was.

As I drove, I found myself daydreaming that she was finally going to drop all her walls and say she was ready to give our relationship the shot it deserved. Right. And then we would fly with a flock of unicorns to a magic palace in the sky where the friendly king would insist we spend the rest of our days having sex and eating bacon.

No, there were four real possibilities. One, she really was trying to reestablish platonic, friendly relations (surely a doomed effort, given our history and chemistry). Two, she was merely pretending to be friends, and was in fact sneakily renewing efforts to entice me into being her sperm donor (which I wasn't game for). Three, she was horny and looking for another booty call (which I promised myself I would resist, with the caveat that I was incapable of doing so). Or, four, Tina being Tina, I never really would figure it out; and we would continuing drifting on a round-the-world ocean current that kept us moving in the same waters a few feet apart (which seemed the most likely scenario).

And maybe, eventually, I would figure things out well enough with Kira that I could decide, once and for all, to launch myself into a different stream. At this point, Kira was still too new to make such bold decisions. To change metaphors, it would be like deciding to transfer to the college of a girl you'd just met.

Per Tina's instructions, I went to 27 Mix, a favorite Newark watering hole of ours. She was already there when I arrived, seated at a table against the wall. She waved when I entered, not that it was hard to pick her out. It was a Tuesday night at a time when the after-work crowd had thinned and the college crowd hadn't arrived yet. Plus, she was still in the same outfit from earlier in the day, the one with the long boots and the short skirt. The only difference was she had let her hair down. A man tends to notice the hottest woman in any room, and on this night—as with many others—that woman was Tina.

I went to the bar, grabbed myself a tasty, microbrewed IPA, then joined her at the table. In hindsight, the first thing that should have set off alarms in my head was that she wasn't drinking. But I didn't notice that. Not yet, anyway. We small-talked for about twenty minutes or so, until I drained my first beer. I stood and said, "I'm getting another. You want anything?"

"I'm not thirsty," she said.

And that's when I noticed she wasn't drinking.

"What do you mean you're not thirsty?" I asked. "Last I talked to you, you were about to edit Buster Hays. That usually makes you parched."

She forced out a laugh, tucked her hair behind her ear in a way she knew I loved, patted me playfully on the arm, and said, "Just go get your beer, silly."

I sat back down. "Okay, now you're trying to distract me by flirting with me. And usually that would work fine, because I'm a guy and I fall for that kind of stuff. But as you may or may not be aware, I'm also a newspaper reporter, which means I'm a trained observer of the human condition and have an inquisitive nature. So, with that in mind: what's up, Tina?"

She looked down at the table, grabbed the salt shaker, poured out a small pile, and began making patterns with the grains. I just sat there, waiting for an answer. Tina knew I wasn't going to let her dodge the question.

"So remember that night a little while ago when you came over to my house for dinner and you started rubbing me and one thing led to another?" she asked.

I was relieved: we were finally going to talk about It. The It that had been blocking any meaningful communication in our relationship like a series of strategically placed Jersey barriers. This was good. Great, actually. Maybe not as great as sex and bacon for eternity. But it was a good start.

"Yeah, I remember," I said. "I believe you said later it was a booty call."

"Right," she said. "And it was. Believe me, it was."

The unicorns and I were now hoping she was going to say that *at the time* it was a booty call, but she was realizing it was—and could be—so much more. Instead, she just played with salt a little more, mounding it into something resembling a circle and then spreading it out again.

"Tina?" I prompted.

"Yeah, right," she said, still not looking at me. "So, remember when I said I was on the pill?"

I felt the bottom of my stomach drop somewhere well below sea level. "Yes?"

"Well, they give you these little warnings about how you're supposed to take them at the same time every day, but I thought that was some kind of urban legend. I mean, how can that possibly matter as long as you remember to take it at some point, right?"

I was too stunned to say anything. She continued: "I started off saying I'd take them first thing in the morning, but it always seemed to slip my mind. So I thought I'd just take them when I leave work every night. The only problem is, sometimes I leave work at seven or eight. And sometimes, when I'm the one who's putting the paper to bed, I don't leave until one in the morning. And, well, apparently, that thing about taking it at the same time? That's not an urban legend after all."

"So you're . . ." I couldn't quite make myself say the word.

"Yeah," she said.

"How long?"

"I was supposed to get my period on Friday. By Sunday, I started getting suspicious. I've never been more than one or two days late my entire life."

"Oh," was all I could say, even if I wished I could be more articulate.

She finally looked up at me with those big, brown eyes that had a surprising amount of fear in them. Tina had been planning to have a baby for years—she was the only childless woman I knew who owned nipple shields. Even if she had recently changed her mind, I didn't figure it would take too much mental gymnastics for her to flip back to mommy mode. Yet, she looked somewhere between lost and terrified.

"I'm sorry," she said, tears welling in her eyes.

"For what?"

"I don't want you to think I . . . I don't know, tricked you or trapped you or something. I mean, there was a long time when I wanted you to, you know, get me knocked up. But I was never going to do it without your consent."

"Oh, I never thought—"

"And you should know I won't expect anything in the way of child support or anything," she said, straightening herself. "This was my fault. It's my baby. As far as I'm concerned, no one even has to know you're the father."

"Tina," I said. "I want to be the father. I want to be more than just the father. You know that."

She looked gorgeous and frightened and I just wanted to be with her. I went over to her side of the table to kiss her, hug her, do something to physically reassure her. But she jutted a flattened palm into my midsection.

"No," she said. "You are *not* taking advantage of my vulnerability that way. Forget it. I shouldn't have told you anything."

"Tina, I—"

"Look, I know what you're thinking," she said, and began mocking my voice. "'Oh, poor Tina. Oh, poor single mom. Whatever will she do without a big strong man like me to provide for her?'"

"That's not what—"

"You *love* to be Carter Ross on your big white horse, riding in to save the damsel. Well, guess what? This damsel doesn't need saving, okay? So you can just pack up your horse and go home."

She stood so violently she nearly knocked the chair over, grabbed her clutch off the table, and began walking with great determination to the front door.

"Tina," I said again, but she wasn't stopping. She slammed through the door and out onto the street. I gave chase until she whirled and faced me.

"Leave me alone," she yelled.

"Tina, can we—"

"I've got pepper spray in my purse," she said, reaching into her bag. "Am I going to have to use it on you?"

I stopped five feet short of her. I didn't really want to spend the next half hour of my life in agony, gasping for breath, wiping snot and tears off my face. More to the point, I recognized that, just perhaps, Tina was not yet in a place where she could have meaningful discourse on this subject.

Without another word, she turned from me, walked another twenty feet to her car, started the engine, and tore off.

For at least five minutes, I stood there on Halsey Street, contemplating what had just transpired. In one short snippet of conversation—most of which I spent watching a woman make patterns with salt—I had the profound sense that everything about my life had changed, even if I didn't fully understand how.

I had observed it in other parents, though. There was a kind of wisdom that having children seemed to bestow on them. Something about replicating life put their own existences in a drastically different perspective. I had seen it in my friends who had kids, who tried to explain to me what it was like—and how it had changed them—and after tossing out a few well-worn clichés, they just gave me that look that said, *Yeah, you won't get it until you've been here.* I had also seen it in the young—often too young—parents I had written about in Newark. For as much as I exceeded them in terms of education, life experience, and worldliness, they had a certain knowledge about humanity that I plainly lacked. It felt like they knew what It—the big It—was all about. And I couldn't even guess.

Yet, here I was, suddenly thrust onto that path. For whatever Tina had to say about it, I knew absentee fatherhood wasn't an option for me. It never had been, which is why I had never taken Tina up on the offer to be her sperm donor in the first place. Once Tina cooled down, she and I could sort out what this meant for us. But I was going to have a relationship with my child. That I knew.

I also knew that meant there was a time in my suddenly immediate future when I was no longer going to be happy-go-lucky bachelor Carter. And I wasn't just going to be a newspaper reporter, either. I was going to be someone's dad. If there was a more important-sounding job title, I hadn't heard it yet.

Okay. So. Fatherhood. I had thought it was like the promise of more-energy-efficient cars, ignoring that most major automakers already offer hybrids.

I couldn't really wrap my head around it. Right now, inside my colleague, editor, and sometimes-friend Tina Thompson, there was a small seed of a human being that was one-half me. In six weeks, as I'd learned from friends who had gone through this whole thing, that cluster of cells would have its own heartbeat. Sometime a little later—in time to be able to pick colors for a nursery, anyway—we'd know the gender. And then, if all went well, roughly nine months after an evening that started with an innocent booty call, an actual human being would come bursting out, howling and bloody and primed for a lifetime in which the world would change more than any of us could possibly imagine.

And I was going to be one of the two people explicitly charged with preparing the little bugger for it. I imagined it would start with the relatively simple stuff, like eating and pooping. Those are about the only tricks babies come out with, right? But I was reasonably sure more-complex operations would soon have to follow. Like walking. And riding bikes. And throwing balls. And being turned down for the prom. And writing college essays. And . . .

They were thoughts that, quite frankly, terrified me. I was barely a responsible cat owner, for goodness sake. Merely having to take Deadline to the vet once a year felt like an awesome burden. Was I ready for an undertaking roughly a million and fifty times more challenging? Could I honestly say, standing there on Halsey Street in Newark, New Jersey, that I possessed even one-tenth of the wisdom, patience, and stamina to deal with that?

Hell no.

The only thing that allowed me to so much as put one foot in front of another was the sneaking suspicion there were several billion other parents in the planet's relatively recent history who weren't ready for it either. Yet, it happened to them all the same. So I might as well get used to the idea that it was about to happen to me.

As best as I could see it, I had two short-term options. One, I could go back into the bar and get so mind-blowingly drunk I didn't have to remember the shame of being shoveled into a cab several hours later. Or, two, I could settle my tab and head to Tina's place in Hoboken—and make it clear to her I had arrived not on a white horse but in a used Chevy Malibu.

I have to admit, I was undecided as I stumbled, feeling a bit light-headed, back into 27 Mix and got the bartender's attention.

"Want another?" he asked.

And then it struck me: this was what fatherhood was about. It wasn't about having to figure out, right at this very instant, whether eleven was an appropriate age to get your ears pierced or whether it was okay to sleep over at Jackson's house. It was about trying your best, which you did by attempting to make one good decision at a time.

"Actually, I'll just take the check," I said.

I was feeling like a father already. That was good decision number one. Number two was going to Tina's house right now and insisting we talk about this. Yes, it was her fetus—possession being nine-tenths of the law and all that. But it was going to be my baby, too. And it wasn't fair of her to think she had the monopoly on all the worry, work, and anticipation that came with that.

Having made that decision, paid my check, and gotten back into my car, I pointed myself toward I-78 and Tina's place. There was a Devils game getting out of the Prudential Center, so I eschewed Broad Street and instead went through the neighborhoods to reach the highway.

And that was the only reason I happened to bump into the large collection of police vehicles congregated near one of the entrance ramps. I slowed when I saw that all the activity seem to be concentrated on the corner of the McAlister Arms construction site.

I glanced at the clock. I was perhaps ten minutes behind Tina—less, if she had gotten caught in hockey traffic. Deciding she could use a little more time to cool off, and perhaps a little too lost in deep and ponderous thoughts to make the more rational decision—like that this was a story I should have just sat out—I grabbed a fresh notepad and hopped out of my car.

More than likely, it would be another senseless, heartbreaking, run-of-the-mill ghetto shooting—some 'banger killing another 'banger for reasons that couldn't possibly matter as much as the value of the human life being lost. It was tragedy that was both unremarkable and unfathomable. If a newspaper actually tried to make some shred of sense out of it for its readership, we would exhaust every column inch of our news hole every single day and still barely scrape the surface. So instead we brushed it off with three quick paragraphs and a weary shrug. It would take me no more than ten minutes to gather those paragraphs and send them in.

There were floodlights up, but the police hadn't had time to set up crime scene tape. So I wandered as close as I thought I could get away with. I spied a uniformed cop who was just standing around, only slightly less guilty of loitering than me, and approached him. He was black and young, a rookie for sure. That was perfect, because it meant he wouldn't recognize me.

"Hey," I said. "What's going on?"

"Homicide," he said. "It's actually one of yours."

"What do you mean, 'one of mine'?"

"It's a white guy," he said.

"No kidding," I said. It wasn't unheard of for white people to be killed in Newark. Every once in a while, a suburbanite in town to buy drugs would be shot during a deal gone bad. Or it could be a bum who got rolled by a car whose driver hadn't bothered to stick around. But it was just unusual enough that my curiosity was piqued.

"Young guy? Old guy?" I asked.

"Somewhere in the middle," the cop said. "My partner is the one who found him. We were just driving along and we saw the body."

I was going to ask more questions, but a sergeant started steam-walking in our direction. "Hey, no reporters! This is private property," he barked.

I took three steps backward onto the sidewalk and grinned at him. "And now it's public property," I said. "Good evening, Officer."

He glared at me, but I walked away before he could invent some new reason why I was breaking the law. I continued on my way, rounding the corner, seeing if I could position myself for a better look at things.

Shortly thereafter, I got it. And it caused me to utter a phrase that would not be printed in a family newspaper. The blow-dried blond hair was the first thing I saw, followed by the sharply tailored blue pinstripe suit and the expensive Italian loafers.

The corpse was facedown and the back of its head was conspicuously concave—an arrangement that was likely made sometime around the time of death—but there was no question in my mind:

It was Vaughn McAlister.

They set him up, then they put him down.

Vaughn McAlister had been working late, poring over some contracts, when his office phone rang. It was an internal extension, from downstairs. The front security desk at McAlister Place.

"Yes, what is it?" he said, annoyed.

"There's a courier delivery here for you, Mr. McAlister," a man said. The voice wasn't familiar to McAlister, but he didn't give it much thought. The security company he used was constantly shuffling in new people.

"Okay, just tell him to leave it with you. I'll be down later."

"He says he can't," the man told him. "It's urgent and he needs to get the signature of the addressee. That's you."

"Oh, for the love of . . . Fine, I'll be right down," McAlister said. He wasn't expecting any urgent courier deliveries and the ones that came unexpectedly were seldom good news. Especially at this time of night.

McAlister took the elevator one story down to the lobby. The moment he emerged, the back of his head became impressed with the blunt end of an old-school Louisville Slugger, the heavy kind preferred by the home-run hitters of yesteryear and the thugs of

85

today. McAlister immediately crumpled, falling forward. Two more swings finished him off.

From there, the cleanup job started. A towel was wrapped around McAlister's head to soak up the blood. Another towel wiped down the few stray blood spatters. Then McAlister's body was tossed into a janitor's trolley and covered with trash bags—lest anyone come walking by.

Not that anyone did. It was late enough that the only people who hadn't already gone home were the workaholics who wouldn't leave their offices for a while yet. The security guard who worked in the lobby had been instructed to take a walk for a while, and he certainly wouldn't say anything. After all, he didn't see anything.

The body was loaded into a car, which soon left the parking garage. This led to the last dangerous part of the job. Ordinarily it was in the best interest of a killer to want a body never to be found. The Atlantic Ocean was invented for such things.

This killer was different. This killer wanted the body to be found—needed the body to be found. The world had to know Vaughn McAlister was no longer among the living. And quickly.

And there seemed no better way to make sure that would happen than by depositing the corpse on the work site that bore his family name.

CHAPTER 3

I never did make it to Tina's house that night, which was probably just as well. While we had much to discuss, I hear getting pepper spray out of khaki pants can be a real bitch.

Despite my certainty that the body I had seen was Vaughn McAlister, the Newark Police took their sweet time confirming it for us. It was sometime after midnight when they finally told me the victim was McAlister and that he had suffered a blunt force trauma to the head. I got the news into a few late editions and didn't get home until 2 A.M. I can't say the extra hours spent down at the scene helped me better understand why someone would want to bash Vaughn's blow-dried head in, but they sure did make me happy to crawl under the covers when it was all over.

I live in a two-bedroom house in Bloomfield, one of those Jersey suburbs developed at a time when they still made houses small. Up until this point in my life—which had not been marked by dependency in the form of a tiny person—it had fit me just fine. My only roommate is a somnolent domestic short-haired cat named Deadline, and his square-footage needs are not substantial. Food bowls and litter boxes take up only so much space.

As I drifted off to sleep, I wondered if, nine months from now, I would begin to understand why child-infected families moved to farther-flung parts of the world where the acreage is plentiful and the housing stock comes only in sizes XL and beyond. And when my phone rang at nine o'clock the next morning—and the caller ID told me it was Tina—I thought perhaps I wasn't the only one who had dozed off while doing the same kind of pondering.

"Hi," I said, sounding barely alive.

"Good morning," she said crisply. I thought her next words would pertain to having scouted out local Montessori schools—Tina is very proactive when it comes to things like that—but instead I heard: "Nice job on McAlister last night. None of the New York papers had a whiff of it. Their Web sites are all linking to ours. TV and radio have been giving us credit all morning and—"

"Tina did you seriously call to talk about work? Aren't we going to talk about last night?"

There was a long pause, during which time I imagined molars were being forcibly driven against other molars. It ended with: "No."

"Come on."

"I wasn't finished. I meant to say: no, not if you value your testicles. Because I swear I'm going to have them stuffed and mounted if you bring up that topic again."

"Tina, that's not fair. I have—"

"Drop it. Just drop it," she said, and I immediately knew she really meant it. She was using her quiet voice—the scary one, the one that always made me wish she were screaming instead.

I briefly considered pushing further, but resisted. As a member of the bigger-but-dumber half of the species, I am not necessarily endowed with the greatest instincts when it comes to dealing with the smaller-but-smarter half. But I at least try to learn from past mistakes. And those many errors had taught me that when Tina used the quiet voice, it was best to table further discussion until a later time. I couldn't imagine raging pregnancy hormones made this any less true.

"Okay. For now. But I reserve the right to talk about this at some later date. I'm not just going away, Tina. Whether you want to deny it or not, the fact remains that I am this child's father. And there's not going to be anything you can do to stop me from playing that role, so you might as well accept that I'm here to stay. I am fully committed to this baby."

I could barely believe the words that had tumbled from my mouth. They sounded so . . . *responsible*. What's more, Tina, in her silence, seemed to respect them. Not wanting to break this fragile win streak, I hopped off the field, concluding with: "But I understand that now might not be the right time. So let's start over with: good morning, Tina, what can I do for you?"

There was another beat of silence. Then she said, "Good morning, Carter. As I was saying, terrific work on McAlister."

"Thanks."

"The only problem is, you might have done a little too good. Brodie was so delighted he called me at seven o'clock this morning to talk about it. And he was fully engorged."

Brodie was Harold Brodie, our legendary executive editor. It had become part of *Eagle-Examiner* culture that his interest in a story was often described in terms of the intensity of the erection it gave him. This, of course, was all in very metaphoric terms.

Had it been actual, it would have made Brodie the most virile seventy-year-old on the planet.

"Okay, so what does he want?" I asked.

"He wants assurances that if anyone figures how and why Vaughn McAlister died, those details will appear in our newspaper, not someone else's," Tina said. "And therefore he wants his best reporter to dedicate all his time and talents to that task."

"What does that mean for the Ridgewood Avenue story?"

"Those people will still be sick next week. This week, we're full speed ahead on Vaughn McAlister."

This, of course, was the way the news business often worked. It wasn't necessarily the most important story that got covered. It was the most pressing.

"Okay," I said. "Can I please have Tommy and Pigeon to help me?"

"Sure. But only because you said 'please.'"

"Spoken like a true mother," I said.

"Shut up, Carter," she said, and ended the call.

As I shaved, showered, and generally made myself beautiful—and what was more pleasing to the eye than a solid white shirt, a muted-red tie, and charcoal pants made of some synthetic material that never wrinkled and may well have been bullet-proof?—I kept thinking baby thoughts, until I realized that Harold Brodie probably wasn't looking for a consumer-reports piece on the hottest new convertible strollers on the market.

So I engaged my brain's moving company, put the baby thoughts in a box that I marked "OPEN LATER," and made room for the story Brodie did want. Why would someone want to give Vaughn McAlister a premature trip to the Essex County Medical Examiner's office? I went through our conversation from the preceding day and ransacked it for any hint of that kind of trouble.

By the end of a bowl of Lucky Charms—still magically delicious after all these years—I hadn't come up with any more answers. McAlister had been full of well-groomed good cheer, well-mannered optimism, and well-intentioned exaggeration.

Which is not to say he was without problems. I just hadn't found them yet. Toward that end, I placed my first phone call to Tommy Hernandez. He answered by saying, "I'm not sure I want to talk to you."

"Why not?"

"Because yesterday you asked me about Vaughn McAlister and then last night he got all dead. That's pretty creepy. What happened? He took one look at your shoes and got so mortified for you that he died of embarrassment?"

Tommy is constantly telling me that my shoes are out of style. This is one of the many ways in which I know I'm not gay: my workaday footwear consists of two pairs of dress shoes, black and brown, and for the life of me I have no clue what's wrong with them.

"Too bad I wasn't smart enough to sell short on McAlister Properties stock," I said.

"Yeah, but you were smart enough to do something else."

"What's that?"

"Give me the name Harry Grant."

"Oh?"

"Yesterday after we talked, I ended up chatting with one of my favorite city hall moles and the subject of the McAlisters came up. I guess all is not well with McAlister Arms. I said something offhanded like, 'Well, it's not like the McAlisters are going to be another Harry Grant.' And the guy said, 'I'm not so sure about that.' I pursued it a little bit but he didn't want to say any more. Maybe he'll be more talkative today."

"That sounds interesting," I said.

"Almost as interesting as if you stopped shopping for your shoes at Thom McAn," Tommy said. "I'll talk to you later."

"What's wrong with Thom McAn?" I asked, but I was already talking to a dead phone line.

On my way out the door, I gave Deadline a quick pet. I did this not because I am the world's most loving cat owner but because he hadn't moved off my bed all morning and I wanted to make sure he was still alive. Sure enough, after about three strokes, he started purring like a small outboard motor.

"See you, pal," I said. "Don't exhaust yourself, okay?"

I left him, still rattling, and began the drive to Newark. As I slalomed between some of Bloomfield's most imposing potholes, I placed the call I didn't feel like making: I had to cancel on Jackie Orr. Again.

"Hello?" she answered.

"Hey, Jackie, it's Carter Ross."

"Oh, hi," she said. "I'm glad you're calling. I just heard from Mr. Robertson and he's not going to be able to make it this morning. He's come down with the flu again. But we still have Mrs. Tilley, DeAndre Mickens, Mrs. Torain, plus I was able to track down Mrs. James and convince her that talking to you was worth skipping a trip to the playground with her grandchildren. So that gets you up to twelve. Do you think that would be enough to get you started on your story?"

"Actually, Jackie, I'm really sorry about this," I said, "but I'm not going to be able to make it this morning."

"Oh. Are you still sick?"

"No. Unfortunately, there was a man killed in Newark last night and I'm probably going to be working on that story for at least the rest of the week."

"The developer?" she asked. Obviously, she had either seen that day's paper or read the Web site.

"That's right," I said.

There was a silence at the other end of the line. Jackie Orr was a thoughtful young woman, not a screamer. But I knew I had disappointed her.

"So all that 'voice to the voiceless' stuff," she said. "That was just talk, huh? A rich white man gets killed and that matters more than poor black folk getting sick."

"No, Jackie, it's not like that," I insisted. "It's just . . . from a news standpoint, the story about McAlister is a little more urgent. It doesn't make the story about your neighbors any less important. I'll be able to get back to it in a week or two."

"I understand," she said. She added a hasty: "Thank you for your time, Mr. Ross," then she hung up.

And I just found out I'm going to be a dad, and I had to work until really late, and I haven't had enough bonding time with my cat, I wanted to add, just to garner what I felt was a little well-deserved sympathy. But, of course, she was already gone. And she wasn't my therapist.

I tossed my phone onto the seat next to me and pouted, feeling guilty about having to jilt her but, at the same time, powerless to do much about it. I was still pouting—and still making my way through traffic toward Newark—when my phone rang. It was Pigeon.

"Hey, how are you feeling?" I asked.

"Better today. Yesterday was awful. I don't know how you made it out of bed."

"With my legs."

"Huh?"

"Never mind. I assume you've heard about Vaughn McAlister."

"Yeah, Tina Thompson just called and told me all about it. Then she told me she wanted me to work with you on the story. Did you . . . did you really ask for me?"

"Yeah. Is there a problem with that?" I asked as I veered around a particularly aggressive-looking pothole. It was the kind the municipality was either going to have to patch or turn into a community swimming pool.

"No, I just . . . I mean, thank you," she said. "That's, like, the nicest thing anyone has done for me since I got here."

Yet another sign Pigeon was for real: she defined being included on a story about a grisly homicide as "nice."

"Yeah, I'm a regular prince," I said.

"So, what do you want me to do? Can I make an FOIA request?"

FOIA stands for Freedom of Information Act. It was a wonderful piece of legislation that gave citizens access to the documents being generated by their government. For voters, it was a means of keeping tabs on their elected officials. For reporters, it was sort of like unlimited access to a never-ending beer tap, because it kept the good times flowing. Still, I didn't know what Pigeon was talking about.

"Uh, what exactly do you want to FOIA?" I asked.

"I don't know. But I learned in J-school that if I did an assignment that involved FOIA-ing something, I always got an A. There's got to be *something* we can FOIA."

That was when I made a hasty decision about what to do to keep Pigeon busy. "That's all well and good. But if you want to get an A in real life, you've got to get real people to talk to you. And the person I want you to talk to is Barry McAlister."

I heard her gulping over the phone. "You mean, the dead guy's dad?"

"Yep, the dead guy's dad," I said. This was a calculated gamble on my part. I had no inkling of who had killed Vaughn McAlister or why. But if it wasn't something in his personal life—a jealous wife, an angry mistress, a boyfriend who went all Andrew Cunanan on him—it was something in his business life. Barry McAlister was the only person who was positioned to be aware of both.

And all I really knew about Barry McAlister was that he must have been a pretty private guy. Why else would he have had his son act as the front man for the family business? So, chances were, if a seasoned reporter like me came at him, he would make like a shellfish and clam up. But maybe if a somewhat-naïve young intern approached him . . .

It was worth whatever slim chance of success it had. Sometimes reporting is about instinct. And sometimes it's about getting lucky when you throw something sloppy against a wall and it sticks.

Pigeon did her share of whining and protesting, but I pep-talked her into it. What I didn't tell her was that I was fully expecting whomever we sent to talk to Barry McAlister to strike out. And I'd rather waste her time than mine.

With Pigeon thus busied, I made a quick call to my best police source. Rodney Pritchard had floated around through various parts of the Newark Police Department during his years there, and I had written a few stories about him that had inclined him to be friendly to me. Currently he was in the Gang Unit, though he had been in Homicide recently enough that I knew he'd be up on their gossip. And a little gossip could go a long way just then.

"Hey, Pritch, what's going on?"

"Uh-oh, here's trouble," he said. I heard street noise in the background, which meant he was not in the office. Sometimes, if he was at Newark Police headquarters—known informally as "Green Street," because that was their location—he'd tell me I had the wrong number. Strictly speaking, Pritch wasn't supposed to talk to me without several layers of authorization. It was understood our conversations were just between us girls.

"What makes you say that?" I asked.

"I don't know. But when you're calling, it's always trouble somewhere."

"Well, I'm sure you can guess what that is today."

I heard a horn honking through his phone. "No, actually, I can't."

"The McAlister homicide?" I prompted.

"Yeah, what about it?"

"A major developer gets killed and dumped in a vacant lot within the boundaries of your fair city. I thought that would have all of Green Street jumping."

"I'm sure the case has been assigned to someone," Pritch said. "But I was in there this morning and it was pretty business-as-usual. I don't think this one is getting any extra attention."

"That's weird."

"Why?"

"I don't know. Usually when we go big with a story, you guys follow suit."

"Yeah, but a lot of times the only reason we do that is because when you guys get excited the mayor's office gets excited. And then you-know-what flows downhill. I don't think that happened this time."

"Why not?"

"Don't ask me. Ask the mayor. Better yet, don't ask the mayor. It's sort of nice not having him up in our business."

"Noted. If you hear anything, let me know, okay?"

"Sure thing," he said. "Anyhow, I'm just a guy out on a corner, looking at fresh graffiti, worrying we're about to have another war on our hands. So I gotta go."

"All right," I said. "Good luck with that."

Upon arriving at the office, I had not even set down my briefcase when I realized there was someone sitting in the intern pod who shouldn't have been there.

It was Pigeon. She was facing away from me, slightly stooped in her chair, in a failing attempt to make herself less noticeable. I walked toward her, thinking she would turn around when she heard me. Then I cleared my throat to get her attention. But, like a puppy who had just missed the paper, she couldn't look at me. She seemed incredibly interested in a small piece of the carpet opposite me and couldn't tear her eyes away.

I walked around to the other side and stood on the spot that had transfixed her.

"Hey, Pigeon, what's up?" I asked.

She lifted her gaze about halfway up but still couldn't make eye contact. "Oh, hi," she said.

"How did things go with Barry McAlister?" I asked.

"Imuddababa."

"Excuse me?"

"Addinnaddda."

"Pigeon, I'm getting to be an old man, so you're going to have to speak up."

Finally she said, "I couldn't do it."

"Pigeon!" I said, reproachfully, drawing out the second syllable.

"I just couldn't!"

"Pigeon!" I said, this time emphasizing the first syllable. I'd never known how wonderfully adaptable the word "pigeon" was.

"I got his address and I was going to go over to his house and everything. But then, I don't know, what was I going to say? 'Hi, Mr. McAlister, I heard your son died last night. Care to tell me about it?'"

"Well, yeah, that's about the size of it. What, you think you're going over there to swap brioche recipes?"

She lowered her gaze again and said, "I feel so ashamed."

This was one of the things I loved about interns. I have dim memories of a time in my career when talking to the relatives of dead people probably made me uncomfortable, too. It felt like a long time ago, but I forced myself back into the mind-set of what it was like to be a young reporter, filled with apprehension, scared to knock on a door.

"Oh, Pigeon," I said, hefting a grandfatherly sigh and giving her a pat on the shoulder. "Sometimes as a reporter, you have to pretend that every morning you put on a suit of armor. And then you make believe that armor makes you impervious to social awkwardness. I mean, it's like doing a man-on-the-street story. Would a normal human being charge up to a perfect stranger and say, 'Gee it's cold today. What do you think about it?' No, of course not. But as reporters working on stupid weather stories assigned to us by our unimaginative editors, we do it all the time."

"Yeah, but—"

"No buts!" I snapped. "I know asking a man about his dead son is a little harder than asking someone about the weather. And it's something that as normal human beings, we could never do. But when we have our armor on, it's something we can do. It's something we have to do, because it's our job. Look at it this way: we're going to be writing about Vaughn McAlister whether his dad talks to us or not. But if you were his dad, wouldn't you want the newspaper to talk to you, just so nothing inaccurate was written about your son?"

"Well, I gue—"

"Of course you would!" I interrupted, not because it's how Socrates would have done it but because I felt like I was on a roll. "You would want nothing more than for the final words written about your boy to be a hundred-percent, spot-on perfect.

"Besides," I added somewhat philosophically, "if we don't talk to him, *The New York Times* might. And Brodie would blow a gasket if the *Times* had something on a Newark-related story that we didn't. And when Brodie blows a gasket, the rest of the newsroom leaks oil. So let's go."

"Where?"

"To Barry McAlister's house."

"You'll come with me?" she said, actually sitting up for the first time.

"Sure," I said. "What are mentors for?"

"Wow, thank you," she said, a little too gratefully. But maybe, given the emotional wattage that was charging other parts of my life, I didn't mind a little uncomplicated professional admiration coming my way.

As we made for the parking garage, Pigeon gave me the address for the McAlister household: 7 McAlister Court in West Orange. What did these guys have about naming things after themselves, anyhow? It had to be some kind of egomaniacal disorder. Trump Complex.

I unhitched the Malibu and programmed Barry McAlister's address into the GPS, which recognized McAlister Court. We got rolling and I started giving Pigeon a brief geography lesson. Even New Jersey natives get the Oranges a little confused, because they come in three different cultivations: East, South, and West. It's really quite easy to keep them straight. The farther away from Newark, the higher the real estate values.

As such, I guessed that the McAlister home in West Orange would be a decent little shack. And it was. Though it wasn't anything ostentatious. It was an older, two-story, Tudor-style home with mature landscaping, nestled at the end of a private drive. It turned out the "7" on McAlister Court was quite superfluous. There were no numbers 1 through 6.

"I guess this is it," Pigeon said as I stopped the engine.

"Okay," I said, but didn't immediately get out of the car. Pigeon and I had been yammering so much on our way out—the geography lecture had given way to a lesson about *Eagle-Examiner* history—that I hadn't given much thought to the task at hand. I usually wanted at least to try to anticipate how an interview like this might go. Would Barry McAlister be angry? Welcome us with open arms? Give us a stiff upper lip and a few bland comments?

I wasn't necessarily afraid to knock on the door of a murder victim's family like I might have been as a cub reporter, but I still wanted to feel mentally prepared for whatever I might find when I did.

"What are you waiting for?" Pigeon asked.

I grasped the handle to the car door and said, "Just taking a moment to put on my armor."

I'm not sure what I expected Barry McAlister to be, but the moment he answered the door, I understood why he had made his son the front man for McAlister Properties. Barry McAlister didn't exactly present well.

He was overweight and smelled like a Marlboro. He was dressed in a timeworn flannel shirt, shapeless jeans, and once-white sneakers that had gone yellow with age. He had a nose that filled a large portion of his face and a jawline that was almost entirely jowl. His skin was sallow and flaccid. I pegged his age as somewhere in his late sixties but his health as somewhere in his eighties.

At least by appearances, he was the opposite of his perfectly turned-out son in just about every way. The only thing he had passed onto Vaughn was his hair, which was rich and full. Barry's was gray, not blond, but it was still an impressive mane.

"Can I help you?" he asked in a gravelly, Jersey-tinged voice.

I made the rather quick determination that if Vaughn McAlister had been all about show, his dad was all about substance. So I went with the direct approach: "My name is Carter Ross. This is Neesha Krishnamurthy. We're reporters with the *Eagle-Examiner*. I know this is a difficult time for you, but we're writing a story about Vaughn and we were hoping you could talk about him a bit."

His face didn't really move. He just opened the door a little wider. "Come on in," he said.

He trudged into a darkened living room and sat heavily in a leather recliner that faced an old, round-screen television that was on but muted. There was a small folding tray next to him with a full ashtray and an empty highball glass. I could forgive him the early start.

Then I realized, to my surprise, I could do more than just forgive him. I actually understood it, in a totally new way. There I was, less than twenty-four hours into my life as a future father, and already I felt its tug. Multiply what I felt by forty-odd years' worth of memories and experiences, and then lose it all in one violent moment? Forget drinking. It would be all I could do to stop myself from wanting to play in traffic.

I shook the thought from my head and looked around. The room appeared to have been preserved in a state that might best be described as 1977. The carpet was shag. The colors were predominantly brown and orange. The couch that Pigeon and I sat on was upholstered in a paisley pattern that was outlawed the day Reagan took office. The drapes were banned shortly thereafter as well.

There were a few pictures but they were also dated. Barry was absent from them—I can't imagine the camera liked him much—so they all either featured a younger-looking Vaughn McAlister or an attractive blonde with high cheekbones and feathered hair that last looked good on Farah Fawcett.

I was looking for a gentle start to our conversation, so I pointed to a photo of the blond woman and said, "Is that Vaughn's mom?"

"Yep," Barry said. "That's her just before she ran off with another guy and left me with Vaughn. Then she died of cancer."

So much for a gentle start. He lit a cigarette and stared at the television. I sneaked a glance at Pigeon. She looked like she would have gnawed her arm off it would have gotten her out of that living room.

"Vaughn looked like her," Barry continued. "Took after her, too, even though he barely knew her. She had a real sense of style, that lady. I was the one who raised Vaughn, but he always had more of his mother in him."

"Yet he went into business with you," I said.

"Yeah, well . . ." he said, let his voice trail off.

The whole vibe was weird—weird how the guy just let us into his house, weird how everything in the place felt so stale, weird how he just started talking like we were in the middle of a conversation—but I did my best to roll with it.

"So how did you and Vaughn become partners?" I asked, pulling out my notepad.

Barry let out a wry laugh. "I guess he didn't really have a choice."

"What do you mean?"

"Long story."

"We've got time," I said.

He looked at me for a moment, then returned his gaze to the television as he started talking. "I started off with one apartment building on Avon Avenue in Newark. It was a seventy-unit building—a big place for a guy who didn't know what he was doing. I bought it for next to nothing and I still had to take out a loan to swing it. The place was a nightmare. The boiler was busted all the time. The pipes leaked sewage into the basement. There were holes in the walls, holes in the ceilings. No one paid their rent. This was in the late sixties, just after the riots, and the quality of the tenants was awful. They were all on public assistance."

He took a drag on his cigarette and continued: "I thought I was going to lose my shirt before I even had a shirt. For a year, I worked night and day on that place. I poured money I didn't even have into it, fixed everything myself, got rid of the bad tenants, got better ones. They might have feared me a little bit, because I made it clear I'd kick them out if they didn't toe the line. But I think they respected me, too. They knew I was going to give them a fair shake. And they knew I wasn't like those absentee slumlords, because I was in the building all the time, making sure everything worked okay."

Another drag. "After a year, I had the place turning a nice little profit, so I took on another building. Another nightmare. A little bigger than the last one, actually. Same thing happened. I slaved on that building until I turned it around. Then I bought another one. I was starting to make some decent money but, damn, it was hard work. People think property management is just about cashing rent checks but it's a helluva lot more than that. At least it is if you want to make money at it. By the time Vaughn was born, I was doing pretty well but my wife started complaining about the hours. Not the money, mind you. Just the hours."

He hacked into his hand, looked at his empty glass, then went on: "I had bought us this place and I thought that'd make her happy, you know. I mean, the perfect little house in the suburbs. It's what every woman wants, right? But she was . . . it seemed like she was never happy. She kept complaining about me working all the time, but I . . . I guess I never took it seriously until one day she showed up at the office with Vaughn. He was maybe two. She handed me a Dear John letter, handed me the kid, and that was it."

The last cigarette wasn't quite done, but Barry wasn't leaving anything to chance. He lit another one before the first one could burn down, sucked on it until it was lit, then put it down. "After that, I tried to get babysitters for Vaughn, but I could never predict when I'd be home. They kept quitting on me that same way Vaughn's mom did. Finally I just said to hell with it and started bringing Vaughn with me everywhere. After day care, after school, Saturday, Sunday. The kid learned the business from the ground up. When you're a landlord, you see people at their best and their worst. Mostly their worst. Maybe I should have shielded him from it, I don't know. But I thought it was good for him to, I don't know, see what life really was. So if I had to clear out an apartment that had been used as a crack den, he did it with me. If I had some woman calling me hysterical because her boyfriend was trying to break the door down and the police wouldn't come, Vaughn would see that, too. He got an education, let me tell you—everything from fixing toilets to sitting in landlord-tenant court."

Barry grabbed the new cigarette, flicked the accumulated ash off the end, sucked on it briefly, then concluded, "So you asked me when Vaughn and I became partners. But the fact is, it wasn't really a decision. It was something life kind of thrust on both of us, and we made the best of it."

"So that's the residential side," I said. "I thought all of Vaughn's business was commercial."

"It was," Barry said. "Vaughn was like his mom in that he had a certain style—the clothes, the hair. He wanted everything to be fancy. He was like that in business, too. We could have both kept making a decent living doing what we were doing, but that wasn't good enough for Vaughn. He didn't want to spend his life managing ghetto buildings, chasing after deadbeats for their rent. He always had his eyes on downtown. He wanted those big, shiny office buildings. He wanted to wear nice suits to work. So he convinced me that McAlister Properties should add a commercial division and that he should be the head of it."

"How long ago was this?"

"Oh, I don't know. Ten years ago, I guess. I started selling off the residential buildings and Vaughn used it as seed money to go into the commercial side."

I felt I had gotten Barry McAlister sufficiently warmed up that it was time to ask the important question: "So, I know this isn't easy to think about," I said. "But do you have any idea who killed him?"

The television did its silent blare. The most recent cigarette sat smoldering in the ashtray. He sat stonily in his recliner, to the point where I feared I had lost him in some kind of trance.

Finally he offered, "Yeah. His secretary."

In certain ham-handed television shows, the sound technician would have inserted the sound of a record scratching, while the actors would have been instructed to stare dumbly into the camera.

"His secretary?" I said. "Miss Fenstermacher?"

"Yeah, that's her," Barry said. "Look, I don't want you writing any of this, so put your pad away. I didn't even tell the cops this, because I don't know anything for sure, but I got some history with some people at your newspaper. Some good history. I always felt like you guys worked hard to get a story. Maybe if I put you on the right track you can get this one too, huh?"

"Okay," I said, putting down my pad and closing the cover. "So what makes you think she did it?"

McAlister looked longingly at his empty highball glass, then hoisted himself out of the recliner.

"Want something to drink?" he asked.

"Sure," I said quickly.

"What's your pleasure?"

"What are you having?"

"I'm a Cutty Sark man."

Scotch. I absolutely despise scotch. I'd had a bad scotch experience long ago, in college, and had avoided the stuff ever since. There mere smell of it made me a little queasy. So, naturally, I said, "Sounds great."

He turned to Pigeon and said, "And you?"

I could tell Pigeon was about to make the terrible mistake of saying no, so I quickly interjected, "It's her favorite."

He disappeared into the kitchen and Pigeon glared at me and softly said, "What are you doing?"

"Well, apparently, I'm about to be drinking scotch. And so are you."

"We can't do that! We're *working!*" she said, with utmost gravity.

"Yeah, I know. News flash: when you're in this business, sometimes drinking with a source *is* working."

"But . . . I've never had alcohol before," she whispered, pronouncing the word "alcohol" like she was an international spokeswoman for the temperance movement.

"Is it some kind of religious thing?"

"No, I—"

"A health thing?"

"No, it—"

"Then live a little, Pigeon," I said as Barry returned to the room carrying three glasses filled with ice and an amber-colored liquid that didn't appear to have been mixed with anything that might lessen its potency or improve its taste. Scotch on the rocks. A Man's Drink.

He handed Pigeon and me our glasses, settled into his chair, and choked out a quick, "Here's to Vaughn."

He tilted back the drink and swallowed half of it.

"To Vaughn," I agreed. I took a less aggressive swig, but it was still enough to make my stomach feel like it had a small forest fire inside. As I brought my glass back down, I saw Pigeon was still just staring at hers. I shot her an urgent look.

"To Vaughn," she said at last, brought the rim of the glass to her lips, then took a tentative sip.

I saw the look on her face—the words "shock and awe"

came to mind—but I was proud of her for resisting the urge to spit it back up all over McAlister's awful shag carpeting. It was, I could tell, a struggle.

I'm pretty sure Barry missed it. He had settled back into his chair and was fiddling with his drink, tilting it back and forth to bring more of the scotch into contact with the ice.

"This is absolutely off the record," he said. "But you know Vaughn and his secretary had an affair, right?"

"No. I can say that didn't exactly come up when he and I spoke."

"I shouldn't even call it an affair anymore. I mean, well, where do I start. . . . Vaughn was married to this girl—nice girl, good-looking girl. I really liked her. They didn't have kids yet, but I kept hoping. And Marcia had a husband and a kid, too. Anyhow, Vaughn worked some pretty long hours. Marcia was always with him. So I suppose it was kind of natural for some sparks to start flying. It's not like he's the first guy to get the hots for his secretary, but, jeez, with those two it was like a forest fire. I walked in on them one time. Doing it right on her desk."

That explained why she kept it so neat.

Barry shook his head, took another swallow of scotch, and continued: "I told him to enjoy it for a while and then go back to his wife and shut the hell up about it. But he started all this, 'But, Dad, I love her,' crap. Sometimes she'd attach a sticky note to a file he needed to look at, and it'd say something like, 'I love you with every ounce of my being.' Mushy stuff like that. I'd tell them to keep it out of the office. I mean, that's what hot-sheet hotels are for, you know? Finally one thing led to another. He left his wife. She left her husband. It was a big mess. But he kept saying it was okay. They were in love."

He said the word "love" like he didn't believe it. I didn't

know if he was incredulous about it for his son and the secretary or just in general.

"So if they were in love, why would she kill him?" I asked.

"Because fires that burn hot also go out faster," he said. "Vaughn had told her they were done. I think maybe he was planning on going back to his ex-wife. He had mentioned to me she was moving back to the area. Maybe he told Marcia the same thing and she went nuts. You know what they say about a woman scorned. I always thought she might come unglued a little but I never . . ."

He broke it off, overcome with emotion. He drained the rest of his scotch, actually resting his forehead on the glass for a moment.

I thought about Miss Fenstermacher, her helmetlike hair, her flawless manicure. I couldn't necessarily envision her swinging a two-by-four at someone's head. But, then again, I also knew that she wouldn't have been the first jilted lover in history to exact the ultimate revenge.

"I saw him two days ago," Barry whispered. "I was just looking at him, in the prime of his life, feeling . . . I don't know. He had everything ahead of him. I mean, we weren't . . . We didn't talk about, you know . . . I didn't say 'I love you' all the time. We were . . . too busy. We always had other stuff to talk about. But he knew how I felt about him. Maybe I wasn't always the warmest guy in the world, but Vaughn knew. . . ."

Maybe he did. Maybe he didn't. I put that away in a mental file I had already started. Things I Would Do with My Kid: make sure I said "I love you" at least once a day.

Barry gripped the glass extra hard, then gave the ice one last shake before he set it down. He looked toward the fireplace, started at it for a moment or two, then continued: "He was really excited about how his new project was shaping up. He told me he was about to land a couple of big fish."

"Yeah, who was his big mystery tenant?"

He shook his head. "I don't actually know the details. Vaughn and I let everyone think I was still doing stuff behind the scenes, because we thought that would give him some legitimacy. No one would try to take advantage of him if they knew a crusty old battle-ax like me was still on the job. But the fact is, McAlister Properties is all Vaughn. I've been out of the game for a while. Like I said, I sold my buildings. I was getting too old to be diving into the ghetto anyway. I don't really know the commercial side the way Vaughn did.

"Anyhow," he huffed, "you didn't get that stuff about the secretary from me. I'm just a tired old man who doesn't know nothing."

He grabbed the remote control off his tray table and turned up the volume. Then he lit another cigarette, never taking his gaze from the screen. I suppose I should have tried to pump a few usable quotes out of the guy, but the old joke about trying to teach a pig to dance came to mind, and I just didn't feel like annoying the pig. I nodded at Pigeon as I stood.

"Thanks for the drink," I said.

"Don't mention it," he said gruffly, eyes still on the television.

Pigeon, also now standing, said, "I'm sorry for your loss."

He looked up at her and replied, "Thanks, kid."

He returned his attention to the television and we departed without another word. Though I did notice, as I was leaving the room, that a tough old man's eyes had gone watery.

My first act, upon departing the ode to polyester that was Barry McAlister's living room and making it outside, was to take three grateful breaths of non-tobacco-saturated air. As we made it to the end of the driveway, I spied a small shrine, set off to the side and nicely landscaped.

The centerpiece was a delicate marble statue of an angel, no more than maybe ten inches tall, with an inscription on the base:

Elizabeth A. McAlister
Beloved Wife, Mother
1945–1981

"Wow," I said. "Look at this."

"Oh my . . ." Pigeon started, trailed off, then came back with: "You don't think she's . . . buried underneath there, do you?"

"Pretty small for a headstone. Besides, that's against the zoning statutes in a town like West Orange."

Pigeon just stared at it. I added, "Safe to say he still carries the torch for his wife, though, huh? The pictures inside. The shrine outside. You'd think he'd hate her for running off, but . . ."

But there was nothing more to add, other than that it was one more unusual thing about Barry McAlister. I continued to the Malibu, mostly so I could go into its glove compartment and produce something absorbent for Pigeon. She had kept her composure all through the interview but now had lost it. I was a little surprised—Pigeon didn't seem like the weepy type—but I found two unused Quiznos napkins and handed them to her.

"Here," I said.

"Thanks," she replied. Between her leaky eyes and runny nose, she made short work of it.

"You okay?" I asked when she seemed to be done. I had already gotten us moving back in the direction of Newark.

"Yeah, I'm fine. I don't normally have this problem, I just . . . That poor, poor man. First his wife leaves him. Then she dies. Then his son gets killed. It's just so sad."

"Yeah," I said, because that was about the sum total of the situation.

"And now he's just going to sit in that room and drink himself to death and . . ." Her tears started again. "Does that really not get to you at all?"

"Of course it does," I said. "I'd be less than human if it didn't. I guess I've just learned that you have to stay in touch with your feelings without letting them overwhelm you. It's a fine line. If you don't stay engaged emotionally, your stories fall totally flat and you forget the meaning of what you're writing about. Yet you have to stay detached enough that you don't fall apart and lose the ability to function. It's something you learn."

"Uh-huh," Pigeon said, tears streaking down her face, like maybe she was still a little on the far side of the line.

"So, for example, we can reflect on the unusual bond between a father and a son who are both incredibly close and yet somewhat distant. Or we can talk about what kind of mental illness would drive a woman to leave her husband and son. Or we can talk about the perils of extramarital affairs. Or we can gripe about secondhand smoke because, I don't know about you, but I feel like the bottom of an ashtray right now."

Pigeon laughed a little bit at that. I continued: "But, the fact is, while all of that is important, and while all of that has its place when it comes time to start typing, none of that is going to get our story written."

She blew her nose into the napkin.

"You know what will?" I asked; then, without waiting for a reply, I finished, "A little visit to see Marcia Fenstermacher."

Pigeon was naturally dark complexioned, so it was hard to know for sure, but I'm pretty sure she blanched a little. "But . . . I thought she's the one who did it."

"Well, now, we don't know that for sure," I said. "It's innocent until proven guilty, remember? I'm sure it's possible there's some other logical explanation for how Vaughn McAlister ended up with half a head in that vacant lot, and, at risk of making a really bad pun, we should keep an open mind about it."

"That's horrible—" Pigeon started, but I waved her off.

"Anyhow, yeah, Miss Fenstermacher is our next interview."

"But shouldn't we, I don't know, wait or something?"

"Wait for what? For the police to pick her up and then we can't interview her? No way. The police aren't treating this thing like a very high priority, so they might not know about the affair yet. They'll probably hear about it soon, and when they do, Miss Fenstermacher becomes a person of interest. But for right now she's fair game. Think about it: an interview with the prime suspect in a high-profile murder case? Doesn't get much better than that."

Pigeon was biting her lower lip.

"O-okay," she said, unconvinced.

"So here's what we're going to do. Because time is of the essence, we're splitting up. I'm hitting her office. You're hitting her home. With luck, she's going to be one place or the other."

Pigeon had now taken her entire lower lip into her mouth and was gnawing on it like it was made of bubble gum. "But if she's home, what do I ask her? I can't just come right out and say, 'Hey, did you kill Vaughn McAlister?'"

"No," I said. "You probably want to be a little more subtle than that."

For the next few minutes, as we completed our drive to the office, I gave Pigeon some perhaps-helpful pointers on how to act and what to say. In truth, I was winging it a little bit. It's not like I had long experience in this area. The cops usually got to the killer before we did—it was sort of their job. Sweating confessions out of people was not something a reporter often found himself in a position to do. But I understood the general principle: get 'em talking and keep 'em talking until they slip up. Since it was the same principle that applied to any number of malfeasants—be they elected officials, public employees, or swindling businessmen—it was something I felt I could handle. I just hoped Pigeon could, too.

When we got to the *Eagle-Examiner* parking garage, I looked up the home address of Marcia Fenstermacher, thankful for her unusual name. It's not like I had to worry about sending Pigeon to the home of the wrong Marcia Fenstermacher.

It turned out Fenstermacher, Marcia and McAlister, Vaughn shared the same address in Florham Park. The house was in Vaughn's name, and it was assessed at $1.2 million, which made it quite the little love shack.

I briefly gave thought to sending a photographer with Pigeon, then talked myself out of it. At least for the time being, we wanted Miss Fenstermacher as disarmed and unsuspecting as possible. Presuming she had done it—and it was as good a theory as any at this point—it was best for her to think she had gotten away with it. Having a photographer firing away might spook her.

We'd get the photographs we needed eventually. In the meantime, we just needed to tread carefully, get as much on the record as we could, and hope that the murderer fell into our laps.

With Pigeon dispatched to Florham Park, I started the short trip to McAlister Place. I wasn't going to tell Pigeon, but I was fairly certain I'd find Miss Fenstermacher there. This was based on a guess, but I was assuming a guilty person would try to appear as nonguilty as possible. And the nonguilty-appearing thing to do would be to go into work, as if all were normal.

Or at least that was my best guess as I parked and once again traipsed more or less unbothered past the inattentive security guard.

I reached the second floor, paused briefly outside the door to gather my thoughts, then opened it.

Sure enough, there was Marcia Fenstermacher, sitting at her desk.

And she was a mess.

The hair was still perfect—nothing could budge the ultra-hold on that coiffure—but her round face was a soupy mash-up of foundation, blush, and eyeliner. It all might once have been in the right place, but that was before her tear ducts had gone into overdrive. The result was a swirl of colors and textures splattered across a blotchy canvas—like Tammy Faye Bakker in a blender.

She was clutching a Kleenex, which was obviously her preferred method of ooze containment, because her once-clean desk had at least a dozen crumpled tissues, each of them a mix of dampened pulp and smudged makeup.

She did her best to look up and pull herself together as I entered. She failed at both.

"Hello," she said, sniffing. "May I help you?"

Those were the same words she had used to greet me the day before, but the pretense of cool and calm efficiency that she had exuded then was gone.

"Yeah, hi, I'm Carter Ross from the *Eagle-Examiner*. I was here yesterday."

"Oh. Right. Of course. Sorry, I'm not . . . functioning that well."

She returned her face to her latest tissue, which already appeared to be ready for retirement. I had to give her credit: she was either legitimately distraught or she had missed her calling as a soap opera actress.

"I'm writing a story about Vaughn for tomorrow's paper," I said. "Do you mind if I ask you some questions?"

"Uh-huh," she said.

I didn't know if she meant "uh-huh" like she minded or "uh-huh" like I could ask her questions. But I slid my notepad out of my pocket and started firing.

"So how long had you worked for him?" I asked, figuring I'd start slow.

"Three years," she said. "It's been three wonderful years. Vaughn was the kindest, smartest, most . . . most caring man I've ever met."

"He was a good boss, then?"

This gave her pause. Slowly, quietly, she said, "He wasn't just my boss."

So at least she was going to admit that. "What do you mean?" I asked, playing dumb.

"We had . . . We had . . . He was my boy- boy- . . . God, would you listen to me? Vaughn and I were together. We had been almost from the day I started working here. He was my . . . I don't know what you'd call it. It seems ridiculous to call him my boyfriend. I'm forty-two years old, not some teenager. We lived together. He was my life partner. He was the answer to my dreams. We were . . ."

From a set of double doors to Marcia's left—the opposite side from Vaughn's office—another McAlister Properties employee appeared.

"Is everything okay, Marcia?" she asked.

But Marcia waved her off. "Yes, I keep telling you, I'm fine."

The employee and I shared a look at the wasted tissues on her desk. Yep, fine and dandy.

"Okay, well, give me a shout if you need anything," the woman said, giving me a suspicious up-and-down before disappearing behind the door.

"Anyway, as I was saying, Vaughn and I were together," she continued. "We had talked about marriage but we had both been married before. After his experience with his first wife and my experience with my husband, neither of us wanted to go through that again. But my son—I have a twelve-year-old—had started taking to him as a father figure. We were going to have him adopt Trevor so he could have some . . . legal status, I guess. It's ridiculous when you're not married, some of the things you have to put up with. Did you know the police didn't even find me to tell me about Vaughn's murder? I'm basically his wife, but I'm still not considered next of kin. It's like I don't even count."

"So how did you learn about it?" I asked. *Other than, you know, when you heard his skull crack.*

"He was working late last night, but then he was going to come home and we were going to have a late dinner together. Trevor was with his father last night, so it was supposed to be a . . . you know, a kind of romantic thing. I was expecting him at ten and I was shocked when he wasn't home. He's never late. So I kept calling him and calling him. I swear, his phone must have like thirty missed calls on it. I never imagined . . ."

She shook her head. She was smooth enough in the delivery that I got the feeling she had rehearsed this story. Or maybe she had told it to enough co-workers that she already had it grooved in.

"Eventually, I went to bed. I thought maybe he had just fallen asleep at his desk. He did that once before, and he's been working so hard lately. I kept expecting he'd slide into bed next to me. But he . . . he never came home."

She barely squeaked out the word "home." She took a few moments to compose herself, then continued: "When he still wasn't back in the morning, I thought, okay, he slept at the office. So I came in here, ready to give him hell for not calling. But then he wasn't here, either, of course. Do you know how I learned about it?"

"How?" I asked.

She swiveled her still-perfect hair from side to side. "Google alerts. I had a Google alert that sent me any mention of Vaughn's name, so I could let him know about it. So I had this e-mail this morning with the story from your Web site."

She suffered another minor breakdown from reliving that experience, then offered a quick, "I'm sorry."

"It's understandable."

"I think I'm still mostly in shock. I mean, you see those murder victim's family members on TV who say, 'It hasn't hit me yet.' And I always used to think, 'How is that possible? What are you, some kind of idiot?' But I can tell you, absolutely, it hasn't hit me. Not really."

"Have you talked to the police yet?".

"Nope. Nothing," she said, like this still offended her. "I still haven't heard word one from them."

Just wait, I thought. *You will.*

"So the last time you saw Vaughn alive was . . . ?"

She puffed her cheeks and let out a gust of air. "I don't know. I probably left around seven last night. He said he just had a few more things to go over and he'd be home at ten."

Right, I thought, *keep repeating that story.*

"Do you have any idea who might want to kill him?" I asked, paying careful attention to her mottled face.

But she gave no reaction, at least none that I could read. She was just shaking her head. "No. I mean, I can't . . . Who would want to hurt Vaughn? He was doing such good things for the community. Everyone was so excited about that new project. It just doesn't make any sense. Are you sure it wasn't . . . I thought maybe it was a robbery or something. We've unfortunately had some problems with break-ins. Maybe he tried to stop it, or . . ."

Right. A robbery. Sure, lady. It was time to push Miss Fenstermacher a little and see what happened.

I cleared my throat and said, "Marcia, I know this probably isn't something you want to talk about. But were you and Vaughn having any trouble?"

"No. Never. Who told you that?"

I couldn't tell her it was Barry McAlister, because he had put it off the record. "I'm afraid I can't say. But I had heard he was going back to his ex-wife."

That had merely been supposition on Barry's part, of course. But it sure brought Marcia Fenstermacher's fangs out in a hurry.

"*Her?*" she spit. "That's completely untrue. Vaughn and I were totally happy together. He didn't . . . I mean, we fought from time to time. But every couple fights. It was never anything serious. Even if he did leave me, he never would have gone back to *her.*"

"What makes you say that?"

"Because he didn't have anything to do with her anymore. At first she'd call and ask for money and for a while he had been giving it to her. But even that had stopped. So to suggest they might be getting back to . . . I don't know why anyone would . . . Why would that even matter?"

"Well, think about it. If there was a change in Vaughn's situation," I started, then I saw her spine straighten.

"Wait," she said. "You don't . . . you don't think I did this, do you?"

"I never said that," I said. Though it sure was interesting her brain would be so quick to reach this conclusion.

"But when you ask me if we were having problems." She let out an indignant huff. "That is just the most offensive, most horrible thing . . . As if this wasn't already the worst day of my life. The nerve you have! I'm going to have to ask you to leave, Mr. Ross. Immediately."

She looked at me with hatred in her eyes. I wondered if Vaughn McAlister had seen that face at some point before his life ended.

I escorted myself from the office and, once outside, called Pigeon and filled her in on the world according to Marcia Fenstermacher. Pigeon was already out in Florham Park by the time I was done, so I instructed the intrepid intern to case the neighborhood to see what, if anything, she could learn about the happy/unhappy couple.

Then I turned to my next task. If Vaughn McAlister had been getting ready to leave his mistress—or his girlfriend, or his life partner, or whatever we ought to call such people—and possibly rekindle with his ex-wife, it made the ex-wife my next logical contact.

Alas, whereas Fenstermacher was an unusual name, McAlister was not, which I knew would complicate the task of finding her. I steered my car out of the parking garage to a spot where my smart phone would have decent reception and started asking my dear old friend, LexisNexis, for some help.

They say that an elephant never forgets. But, truly, pachyderms have nothing on a good digital database. If you know your way around inside them, it's amazing how much of a person's biography you can start to assemble.

Thus, I was able to find some old property records that linked McAlister, Vaughn to a McAlister, Lisa. Then McAlister, Lisa moved to Florida and reverted to her maiden name: Denbigh, Lisa.

She didn't stay long in Florida. From there, she'd gone to Arizona. Then California. Then Oregon. Without casting aspersions on Lisa Denbigh's reputation, it's fair to say she got around.

It's funny how you get a sense of a person just from the public records they leave behind. If you have someone who lives a stable life, doing dependably mature things—like buying a house, registering to vote, paying her taxes, and keeping up with her bills—she establishes a certain profile. It's neat. Tidy. Simple.

Lisa Denbigh, on the other hand, had created a swampy morass. In addition to the transient lifestyle that resulted in a dozen or so addresses across four states, she had an assortment of civil complaints against her for unpaid bills: $554 from her electricity provider in Florida; $897 from an electronics store in

California; $734 from a cell phone provider; $17,554 from a credit card company; and so on. Some of them had progressed rather quickly to summary judgment, which meant she hadn't bothered to answer them.

She also had an assortment of speeding tickets, including one that had resulted in a bench warrant in California; and unpaid parking tickets, for which the county of Broward, Florida felt it was owed $570.

It was all relatively small-time—there were no felonies or violent crimes, no DUIs or drug offenses, at least not that I could find—but it didn't exactly paint Lisa Denbigh as the most fiscally responsible person in the world.

It also wasn't going to make her very easy to track down. I was able to find telephone numbers associated with some of her addresses, but not all of them. And, of course, none of the numbers was any good. Three were disconnected. One was clearly a wrong number—it led to a sandwich shop. One was for a fax machine. One forwarded to another number that was also disconnected. Another led to an answering machine that told me, "This is Roy. You know what to do. So do it."

I left a message, telling Roy if he knew where Lisa Denbigh was to have her call me. But it didn't exactly instill in me a lot of confidence. She had likely left a long trail of bill collectors in her wake, all of whom were trying to call her on phone numbers that they, too, were finding on LexisNexis. That would only make her change numbers more often—because who the heck wants to be pestered by bill collectors all the time?

Instead of attempting the impossible task of guessing where she might be now—somehow, I was thinking it wasn't Oregon anymore if she and Vaughn were getting together again—I decided to go backward. Going through her history, I went past when she was Lisa McAlister to when she was Lisa Denbigh for the first time.

I tracked her through a variety of addresses in Manhattan, then to Gainesville, Florida at a time when Lisa would have been roughly college age. And that meant more than likely she had been a student at the University of Florida. Good to know.

Going back in time even further, the earliest address I could find was on Thagard Road in Empress, Georgia, an unincorporated piece of Brooks County. The address was, as far as I could tell, still the home of Robert and Martha Ann Denbigh—presumably, Lisa's parents. Their dates of birth were about right. Their public-records profile was more of the neat/tidy/simple version. There was only one phone number associated with them, so I called it.

"Hello?" a friendly sounding southern gentleman said.

"Hi, is this Robert Denbigh?"

"It is."

"My name is Carter Ross. I'm a reporter with a newspaper in New Jersey. I'm trying to track down your daughter, Lisa."

"Oh, well, it shouldn't be too hard for you. She just moved back up your way."

"She did? Do you know where?"

"Well, no, to be honest. We just got a note from her on that Facebook thing maybe two weeks ago saying she was moving back to New Jersey. She didn't say where. We figured we'd get a note from her once she was settled down."

"Do you have a number for her by any chance?"

"Well, now, I don't know if I feel comfortable sharing that with you," he said.

"I can understand that. Could you maybe give her my number and ask her to call me?"

"I don't think she's very good about checking her messages, to be honest. When we want to get ahold of her, we usually just send her a message on Facebook. I don't have much use for it, but my wife's got an account. Why don't you do that?"

I thanked him for the suggestion and ended the call, a little embarrassed I hadn't thought of it sooner. I know there are differing opinions about Mark Zuckerberg and the phenomenon he created and/or stole, but most reporters I knew were ready to make him one of our patron saints. When it came to snooping on unsuspecting citizens—"FaceStalking," as sometimes we called it—few things were better than Facebook. It was amazing how much of their lives people would put online. Yes, Facebook has privacy controls. But a lot of people don't even bother using them.

By that point, I had enough information about Lisa Denbigh that I knew I'd find her easily, presuming she was one of the 7.5 billion people on this planet of 7 billion who have Facebook accounts. Sure enough, I came up with a Lisa Denbigh who had studied at the University of Florida and Brooks County High School.

I clicked and started chuckling. Everything was falling into place. Lisa Denbigh was a statuesque bottle blonde with high cheekbones, fake boobs, a flat stomach, and very straight, very white teeth. She actually looked a bit like the picture I had seen of Vaughn's mother, suggesting that, at least when it came to some people, maybe Freud wasn't that far off after all.

I now had the missing piece that more or less allowed me to put together a good guess at her life story. She had been head cheerleader and homecoming queen at Brooks County High School. Or maybe Brooks County Junior Miss.

No matter. Point is, she was pretty and popular. Then she went to the University of Florida, where she was in the same sorority as all the other pretty, popular girls. She graduated, went to Manhattan, and got one of those jobs that beautiful young women can always find—hostess at a high-end restaurant, receptionist at an image-conscious business, pleasing face for hire at trade shows, whatever. There were always men around to buy her clothes, buy her drinks, buy her a boob job—anything she needed.

About the time when she started realizing her youthful good looks weren't going to last indefinitely—when younger, prettier girls started showing up to replace her—she met Vaughn. He was a developer on the come who wanted some arm candy. They were a perfect couple, except for the fact that they had nothing to talk about.

After a few years, the physical attraction stopped being enough. Vaughn made a real, deep connection with his secretary and ran off with her, leaving Lisa adrift. She started moving around the country, running away from her problems. Her half of the divorce settlement had run out—which might not have taken long, since Vaughn had probably been smart enough to get a prenup. And she had never really learned how to be accountable with money. She thought beautiful people didn't have to play by the same rules as everyone else. Hence all those collection accounts I saw.

Finally she made a desperate attempt to reconnect with Vaughn—maybe on Facebook, who knows? By that point, Vaughn had grown tired of Marcia Fenstermacher, who was, while reasonably attractive, no Lisa Denbigh. And so she moved back to New Jersey and they rekindled, much to Miss Fenstermacher's consternation. And two weeks after his ex-wife showed up back in down, Vaughn had ended up dead because of it.

Or at least that was the narrative I had assembled, based on stereotypes, guesses, and certain well-honed reporter's intuition. There was only one way to find out if my version was reasonably true: I clicked on the button to compose a message to Lisa, typed out a quick request for her to please call me, and hit Send.

I just hoped she checked Facebook more often than she paid her bills.

• • •

I had more or less completed inventing Lisa Denbigh's life story when Pigeon called me, sounding out of breath.

"Hey, it's Neesha," she said, panting.

"Hey," I said. "Why do you sound like you've just run the New York Marathon?"

"Because I hate dogs," she said quickly, in between two large gulps of air.

"Come again?"

"I"—inhale—"hate"—exhale—"stupid"—inhale—"dogs," she said, with one final huff. "Sorry. I just got chased through the neighborhood by one."

"What was it, like a pit bull or something?"

"No," she said, her breathing still fast but at least not desperate. "I think it was one of those . . . what was the kind of dog they had on *Full House*?"

"*Full House*?"

"Yeah, you know. That show where Mary-Kate and Ashley Olsen played the same girl, except you always knew whether it was Mary-Kate or Ashley because Ashley looks ever-so-slightly weirder than Mary-Kate?"

"Yeah, what about it?"

"They had a dog. What kind was it?"

"Pigeon . . . wasn't that a golden retriever?"

"Yeah, that's it. A golden retriever."

"So you were being chased through the streets by . . . a golden retriever. What, were you worried he would lick you to death?"

"Look, I told you, I *hate* dogs, okay?"

"Duly noted," I said. "So did you just want to tell me about your harrowing escape from this slobbering yellow menace or was there another reason for your call?"

"Oh, yeah, so I talked to one of the neighbors, and you know what she said? She said that she heard that Vaughn and Marcia had, quote, 'a big row' on Monday night."

"Really?"

"Yeah, she was kind of old—I guess that's why she used the word 'row'—and at first I was surprised that she could hear anything, because she asked me to repeat every question like five times. But she said she was walking her dog this morning—what is it with people in this neighborhood and dogs?—and she bumped into another neighbor who said she heard a lot of yelling coming from the house on Monday night."

"So this is a secondhand report of yelling," I said.

"Yeah, I guess."

"She give any details?"

"Not really. She just said everyone in the neighborhood was talking about it. The lady was a bit of a busybody, so really it might have just been her talking about it to everyone. But after what you said about Vaughn going back to his ex-wife, I thought maybe Monday night was when he told Marcia Fenstermacher and that's when she flipped out."

"Okay, good stuff," I said. "See if you can find the neighbor who actually heard this fight. And, in the meantime?"

"Yeah?"

"Watch out for wandering Pomeranians. We lost three interns just last year to those vicious brutes."

"Don't be mean," she said curtly. "That golden retriever was out to get me."

I was still laughing when she hung up on me.

Putting the Malibu in drive, I started weaving through some back streets toward the office, then decided on a quick detour to Green Street. At some point, I'd have to get a comment from the Newark Police Department about the McAlister investigation. Might as well cross it off the to-do list.

I parked at a meter and fed it—Green Street being the one place in Newark where Parking Enforcement consistently lived up to its name—then went inside the ancient and thoroughly outdated building that still housed Newark's Finest. I announced I was there to harass Hakeem Rogers, the NPD's public information officer and my occasional nemesis.

After a ten-minute wait, he came downstairs, greeting me with: "Why can't you just call me so I can have the pleasure of ignoring your message all day?"

Officer Rogers and I don't always get along very well. But at least we don't pretend otherwise. And, truth be told, I think we both enjoy the antagonism.

"Because," I told him, "I wanted to get your thoroughly unhelpful quote early on so I could have the pleasure of making fun of your bad grammar all day."

"Yeah, you're so smart. Anyway, what do you want?"

"I'm writing about Vaughn McAlister," I said.

"Yeah, I figured. What about him?"

"He was murdered in your fair city last night."

"Yeah, I heard. My comment is: Too bad it didn't happen to you instead."

"Is the Newark Police Department investigating this heinous act?"

"Of course we are," he said.

"Do you care to update the city's newspaper on the progress of your investigation?"

"Sure. You ready?"

I pulled out my pad and said, "Go."

"The Newark Police Department is actively investigating the murder of Vaughn McAlister. Anyone with information relevant to this or any other crime is urged to contact the Newark Police Department's twenty-four-hour Crime Stoppers anonymous tip line at—"

"Seriously? You're already going tips line on this one?"

Rogers usually gave us the tips-line quote when it was another thug-on-thug gang-related killing they knew they'd never be able to solve.

"That's all I got for you," Rogers said.

I debated tipping him off about Marcia Fenstermacher, if only because it would speed things up. If the Newark Police arrested her, I'd be back to Jackie Orr and Ridgewood Avenue by the end of the week. But, maybe because I was annoyed at Rogers, I decided against it. Let the cops do their job—or not, as the case may be.

I was about to announce my departure when Hakeem Rogers did something that, while not unprecedented, was at least unusual.

"Hey, Ross?" he said.

"Yeah?"

"Put your pad away for a second."

I obliged.

"Off the record?" he said.

"Sure."

"Don't hold your breath on this one," he said.

"What does that mean?"

But Hakeem Rogers was already walking up the stairs, his back turned to me, saying more with his silence than he had with words.

Under ordinary circumstances, Marcia Fenstermacher had no trouble keeping her wits about her. She was orderly, logical and relentlessly organized. It was why Vaughn had hired her in the first place, poaching her from another developer by offering her a five-thousand-dollar raise. It was why Vaughn had become so dependent on her, relying on her to know even the smallest detail of his business. Sometimes she swore he wouldn't know where the bathroom was without her.

But, these being anything but ordinary circumstances, it took her a while to finally reach a conclusion about what to do next. There was just so much to process. Plus, everyone kept coming up to her with these big, weepy eyes, wanting to console her, inquiring how she was doing, asking if there was anything they could do. It was all well-intentioned, of course, but it kept distracting her from what she knew she really should be doing.

Yes, there was a lot to be done. And everyone would expect Marcia Fenstermacher to be the one to do it, just like always.

She needed to contact a funeral home, arrange for a viewing, find a minister to officiate at the service. Vaughn was a seriously lapsed Episcopalian who probably hadn't darkened the doors of a church since his wedding day. But it would be nice to hear some comforting words from someone in a stiff white collar. It all had to look good.

Except, of course, there was something she knew that had to be done first.

Wanting to be alone, she waited until everyone was out of the office at lunch—or at least would not be coming to bother her about anything. She quietly rose from her desk, tossing her latest overloaded tissue into the wastebasket as she stood. She walked as quietly as she could across the hardwood floor to the door to Vaughn's office.

There, she paused. She hadn't been in there since the night before, since . . .

She took a deep breath, then pulled on the handle. Everything looked the same as it had the thousands of other times she had pushed through those doors. She reminded herself she was not a superstitious person. She didn't believe in ghosts. Vaughn's spirit was not in there.

Only his files were. She walked over to the filing cabinet in the corner—the one he kept locked—and produced her key. What she needed was in the second drawer from the top.

She pulled it open and found the folder, exactly where it was supposed to be. Inside was a sealed, plain brown envelope. There was no writing on it, but she knew it was the right one.

Not bothering with a letter opener, she slid her finger under the flap, creating a series of jagged edges in her haste to get to the contents. Then she pulled out the document inside.

Her eyes paused on the words atop the first page: "Last Will and Testament of Vaughn J. McAlister."

With one last deep breath, she started reading. She went slowly at first, then started skimming as she got closer to the end. It was all there, in black-and-white.

He had left her everything. The house. Every dime in his savings account. His cars. The 401(k)—or what was left of it after he had raided it three times. His 50 percent interest in McAlister Properties. Everything.

She slid the drawer closed, her hand shaking just slightly.

CHAPTER 4

The reluctance of the Newark Police to engage in solving Vaughn McAlister's murder was curious. It's not that they were terribly concerned about what it would do to their clearance rate. With eighty or a hundred killings a year, one sliding under the boards wouldn't budge the numbers that much. Only about half the murders in Newark got solved anyway. Still, the Vaughn McAlisters of the world usually belonged in the half of the murders the Newark Police did solve. He was a regular citizen, after all—a well-known member of the business community, at that.

And yet Pritch was telling me no special resources were being put toward it, because city hall didn't seem to be making a fuss about it. And Hakeem Rogers was telling me not to hold my breath waiting for it.

Did Marcia Fenstermacher somehow possess the connections or political wherewithal to get an investigation squashed? That seemed to strain credulity. She was secretary of McAlister Properties, not secretary of state.

So was there something else about Vaughn McAlister's life or death that someone high up in the police department or the city of Newark didn't want exposed? Or was there some other actor or element out there I had yet to even discover?

It begged an explanation that I could not, at the moment, produce. So, halfway back to the *Eagle-Examiner* offices, I broke off my usual route and turned toward the Clinton Hill section of the city. My Malibu, as sensitive to the unexpected course change as any Trigger or Silver, whinnied and neighed.

"That's right, boy," I told it. "We're not going to the newsroom. We're going to visit an old friend."

When official sources don't know much, or won't say much, unofficial sources often do. And one of my best unofficial sources for all things related to the streets of Newark was a T-shirt-shop owner who more or less grew up on them.

Tee Jamison is one of those people who proves that adage about the dangers of judging books by their covers—or, in his case, brothers by their tats. Because while he's got the tattoos—and the braids, and the muscles, and a certain look that tends to make old white women nervous—he's about as much of a thug as Betty Crocker. Put it this way: I once caught him in the back of the store with a box of tissues and a bootleg copy of *Love, Actually.*

His real name is Reginald. In return for my never telling any of his friends that, he has been known to help me with an occasional story or ten. He enjoys sharing his knowledge of urban culture with me, and I'm happy to oblige by playing the part of the clueless white guy. He keeps claiming he has a second white friend, but I'm skeptical.

The street outside his store was empty, as it tended to be in the morning. By afternoon, there would be an assortment of young men that Tee semi-lovingly referred to as "the knuckleheads." They were a mostly harmless group who acted like they were in a gang—they wore gang colors, flashed one another gang symbols, affected gang attitudes—but were really just faking it. I asked them about it once, and it turns out pretending to be in a gang is a great way to get left alone by people who really *are* in a gang.

I rang Tee's doorbell and got buzzed in. From his back room, I heard, "Hey, why don't black people take aspirin?"

"Oh, my," I said. "I don't know, Tee, why don't black people take aspirin?"

"Because they're too proud to pick the cotton out of the top of the bottle," Tee said, emerging into the front of the store with a grin on his face.

"That's beyond horrible."

"Yeah, and if you told me that joke, I'd have to organize an angry mob to stomp on your pasty white face. But since it's me telling it to you, it's just funny. That's what you white people like to call 'ironic.'"

"Well, maybe Alanis Morissette would, but I was never sure she quite got the definition of that word right."

"Who's Alanis Morissette?"

"She's Canadian. And angry."

"Man, I would be too if I had to live in Canada," he said. "Ain't nothing but snow and polar bears up there. Hey, what do you get if you cross a black man and an Eskimo?"

"No. I'm not playing along this time. I can't run the risk you're an informant for the NAACP."

"A'ight," he said. "Fine. Ruin my fun. Anyhow, what's up? You never come around no more."

"I was here last week."

"You was?"

"Yeah."

"Aw, man, I thought that was my *other* white friend. You guys all look alike, you know."

"So I've heard," I said. "Anyhow, I'm actually not just here to swap racially insensitive witticisms."

"Oh yeah, what's going on?"

"You've heard about McAlister Arms, right?"

"Yeah, gonna get us a Best Buy!" he crowed.

Like I said, Tee knows stuff about Newark. "The identity of the tenant is supposedly a big secret. How do you know it's a Best Buy?"

"Because one of the knuckleheads told me they saw some dudes in Best Buy shirts walking around the property a couple weeks ago," Tee said. "It's all over the city already. Every shoplifter I know is looking forward to it."

He was kidding. I think.

"Anyhow," I said, "the property's developer got killed last night. He has a jealous girlfriend, so it might be pretty straightforward. But the cops don't seem to be doing much with it. So I was hoping you could keep an ear out for any talk about it."

"What kind of talk?"

"The usual who-done-it and why."

"Oh, well it's probably one of his workers," Tee said definitively.

I felt my head recoil. "One of his workers? What makes you say that?"

"They all getting sick."

"Sick?" I asked, getting another small jolt. Just when I thought sick people were out of my purview for the time being, here they were again. I had dismissed the possibility of the McAlister Arms site as the source of the Ridgewood Avenue mystery disease because Vaughn McAlister told me it had been cleaned up. But if construction workers were having the same symptoms as Edna Foster and her neighbors, I'd have to start digging a lot harder into McAlister Arms. Perhaps literally.

"Yeah, sick. They been hiring a bunch of people from the neighborhood down there. And at first everyone was like, 'Wow, a construction project that's actually hiring black folks.' Because usually they just bring in people from out of town, you know what I'm saying?"

"Sure."

"So they start throwing around jobs, and then we figured out why they must have wanted black folks. It's because whatever they're doing down there is making them all sick. And, you know how it is, don't nobody give a damn about sick black folks."

"Yeah, so I've heard," I said. "What kind of sick are they?"

"I don't know. I just heard everyone working there is getting sick. But when they complain or don't show up for work, they get fired. There's enough people in this city who need jobs that there's always someone to take their place. Some of the workers figured out the score and just stopped complaining—it's good money, you know what I'm saying? But I know some other dudes who are really pissed off. One of them probably got pissed off enough that they, you know, handled it hood style."

An angry construction worker was certainly a lot more likely to be proficient with a blunt object than a secretary was. Then again, I'm not sure this simplified anything. I had seen dozens of workers down at that site. That would make for a rather sizable suspect pool.

"Do you know any of these guys who were working down there?" I asked.

"Yeah, I know all of them. But ain't none of them gonna snitch."

"No, no. I'm not looking for a snitch," I said, then told him all about the people I had met on Ridgewood Avenue and how the construction workers sounded like victims of the same malady.

"Well, I'll be damned," Tee said when I was done.

"What?"

He grinned and said, "Guess someone might care about sick black people after all."

. . .

Tee and I made arrangements wherein he'd contact some construction workers on my behalf and I'd be the beneficiary of his efforts when I got to interview them at some later date.

I was just out the door when my phone started ringing. The call was from the 973 area code, which meant it was local, but neither my phone nor I recognized the number.

"Carter Ross."

"Yo, Bird Man," I heard back. Bird Man is what people on the streets of Newark sometimes call reporters from my paper because of the more avian aspects of the *Newark Eagle-Examiner*'s banner. The person hailing me this way was young, African American, and vaguely familiar-sounding. But I couldn't quite place his voice.

"Hi, how can I help you?"

The man lowered the phone and, chuckling, announced, "He asking, 'Hi, how can I help you?' " This prompted laughter from his audience, which sounded like three or four other young men.

"Damn, Bird Man, you really do got a funny way of talking," he said.

That's when I knew who it was. "Bernie Kosar! Is that you?"

He laughed again and said to his friends, "He just asked if it's Bernie Kosar." The buddies seemed to enjoy this, too, and Bernie returned to the phone. "You too funny," he said.

"Thanks. Anyhow, to what do I owe the pleasure?"

I thought Bernie might feel compelled to repeat that line, too. But he answered, "You might want to come by Brown Town. Someone here wants to tell you something."

"Okay. I just happen to be in the neighborhood. I'll see you in five minutes."

Brown Town was the quasi-secret world headquarters of the Brick City Browns, one of Newark's more-venerated street gangs. In an increasingly partisan gang world of Bloods, Crips,

Latin Kings, and MS-13—to name just a few—the Browns had remained staunchly independent. They had their hustle and answered to no one.

Not long ago, while reporting a story, I had become an honorary member of the Brick City Browns. I had done this by earning their trust—this may have involved smoking a mildly psychoactive controlled dangerous substance—and then by giving them a fair shake in the newspaper. As a "member," I was allowed to visit whenever I pleased. Which, admittedly, was not too often.

Nevertheless, I remembered the way well enough. So it was actually four minutes later when I knocked on the door. Bernie Kosar—I had given him that name because he usually wore the retro uniform of former Cleveland Browns quarterback Bernie Kosar—answered. Except he wasn't wearing Kosar's number 19. He was dressed in droopy jeans and a brown camouflage hunting jacket.

"Hey, what happened to your uniform?"

"We ain't been wearing those lately," he informed me.

"Why not?"

" 'Cuz the Cleveland Browns football team been stinking it up so bad. It don't look good for our organization. I mean, if you're wearing Patriots jerseys, people say, 'There goes a winner.' But the Browns? Man, the Romeo Crennel era was a joke. And don't even make me start talking about that fool Eric Mangini."

"Fair enough," I said. "Anyhow, you said someone here wants to talk to me?"

"Yeah, come on in."

I entered Brown Town, which was basically unchanged from the last time I had been there. On the outside, it was a tired-looking, three-story, wooden single-family dwelling, a genus of house Newark had in plenty. On the inside, it was one seriously pimped-out pad, with leather sofas, big-screen televisions, and enough mirrors to make you think it was being used as a set for *Feng Shui Gone Wild*.

Bernie led me into the living room, where Kevin Mack—or the guy who used to wear Kevin Mack's retro uniform, before that became untenable—was playing a shoot-'em-up video game with some other guys. Bernie nodded at him and Kevin put down the controller and said, "No fair killing me while I'm gone."

I followed the two of them into the kitchen, which was in its original, non-pimped-out condition. That meant we were sitting at a table that might be characterized as pre-Internet, surrounded by a whole lot of linoleum flooring and particle-board cabinetry. Bernie shot another look at Kevin, who started talking.

"So I was down on Peshine Avenue last night when I saw something you might be interested in," he said. "But, you know, you can't tell no cops where you heard this."

"Okay," I said. The Browns were, perhaps understandably, not fond of law enforcement. "What were you doing down there?" I asked.

Kevin glanced at Bernie.

"We've got some, uh, commercial interests in the area," Bernie said.

Back when I had gained membership, the Browns funded their activities through the sale of bootleg movies. I wasn't sure if they were still in that business or if they had moved on, and I knew better than to ask. Sometimes, even a newspaper reporter doesn't want to know the full truth.

"Anyhow, I'm, you know, doing my thing, kind of waiting for . . . someone," Kevin continued. "And suddenly this black car comes cruising down the street. I'm thinking maybe it's the dude I'm waiting for, even though that ain't his usual ride. So I'm watching it. Next thing you know, it stops, and these two white dudes get out and, real fast, haul this other white dude out of the backseat and toss him in this construction site. And then they leave real fast, and I'm like, what the . . . ? Then I look at the dude they tossed out, and I was like, 'Whoah shee! That dude is dead!' And then I got out of there real fast, because I do *not* need to be the nigga they pin that on."

He didn't need to tell me that the construction site was McAlister Arms or that the dead dude was Vaughn McAlister.

Bernie Kosar cut in: "Then we saw in the newspaper this morning you was writing about that dude. We thought you'd want to hear how it went down."

"I appreciate that. A lot," I said. "Thanks."

"Hey, man, you a Brown, you a Brown for life," Bernie said, then made some kind of hand gesture that, for as many times as I had seen it, I lacked the manual dexterity to duplicate.

"So, these two white guys," I asked Kevin. "Did you get a look at them?"

"I mean, yeah and no," Kevin said. "They sorta looked alike. They was both big. And they had they hair all slicked back. And they was wearing black leather coats. That's probably all I saw. It all happened pretty fast."

And then Kevin added what I had already been thinking: "They looked like they was from *The Sopranos* or something."

It was possible. Mobsters in Newark, once a common sight, were now more of a rarity, having retreated from the neighborhoods along with the rest of the white population. But they still made the occasional foray.

So it could be the mob. Or it could be professional killers.

Which could still mean his secretary was behind it. It could also mean it was anyone with a few grand to spend and a grudge to settle.

•   •   •

We chatted for a little while, though Kevin Mack didn't know much more than what he had already shared. Before long, they were extending an offer to partake in some of the aforementioned CDS, and I thought I was going to have to come up with a creative excuse as to why I couldn't when my phone saved me by ringing.

"Sorry, guys," I said without looking at it. "I'm expecting a call from my editor. I gotta take this."

They bade me a fond adieu and as I darted out I promised to visit again soon. The phone was already on its fourth ring—dangerously close to going to voice mail—when I yanked it from my pocket and saw it wasn't my editor. It was Tee.

I answered the way he always does: "Yeah."

"Hey, that's my line," Tee said.

"I know, but haven't you learned yet? We let you blacks invent stuff and then if it's good, we whites steal it."

"That's true. But y'all stole the Neville Brothers, too. So you can't be *that* smart."

"Well, there's no accounting for taste," I confirmed.

"Anyhow, I was going to try to round up a few of the guys who had been working on that construction site. But then one of them just walked into my store. You wanna talk to him?"

"Yeah, I'm actually close-by. I'll be there soon."

"Okay. He in the back watching a Sister Souljah tribute. So he ain't going anywhere for a while."

"I'll be right there anyway," I said, hopping into my car.

There was still no sign of any knuckleheads when I arrived. Tee buzzed me in and hollered, "We back here."

I went to the back room, where Tee was sitting on the couch with a young black man, who looked up from Sister Souljah as I walked in. He was dark skinned and neatly kept, with close-shaved hair and a thin mustache. He had a small gold earring in his left ear only, but I didn't know if that meant anything anymore—other than that he didn't feel like buying two ear-rings.

The far more interesting accessory was the one he had on his right leg. It was a white splint, and it ran from his ankle to his thigh. There were crutches leaning against the far side of the couch.

"Hi. I'm Carter Ross," I said. Had he stood, I would have extended a hand to shake. But he was, for obvious reasons, stay-ing seated.

"'Sup," he said.

"As Tee probably told you, we're writing a story for the *Eagle-Examiner* about McAlister Arms and some of the things that are going on in that neighborhood. You worked down there?"

He nodded.

"What's your name?" I asked.

"Do I gotta give him that?" the young man asked Tee.

I had told Tee enough about how my business worked that he knew how to answer. "That's how they roll. But you ain't got nothing to hide and you ain't done nothing wrong, so it ain't no big thing. You can trust him."

"Yeah, yeah," he said, like he was convincing himself of this fact.

"So what's your name?" I said again.

"DaQuan Richardson," he said. I made him spell "DaQuan" for me—hey, you never know—and got some of his basic infor-mation. He was twenty-three. He had lived in Newark all his life. He had gone to West Side High School. He'd done a se-mester of community college but it hadn't stuck. Now he was bouncing from job to job. He was going to try to get hired by United—the airline was one of Newark's largest employers—but that was on hold, on account of his leg.

"Yeah, about that . . . what happened to it?" I asked.

"I was just ballin' with some of my boys and it snapped," he said. "I wasn't even doing nothing. Just dribbling the ball and *crack*. Hurt something bad."

"When did it happen?"

"About two months ago. I had a hard cast for the first six weeks. Now it's in this thing," he said, gesturing toward the splint. "It ain't much better, but at least when it itches I can scratch it."

"And you were working for McAlister when it happened?"

"Yeah." And then he offered an unprintable word about McAlister Properties, suggesting that its bosses had a rather unnatural affinity for their mothers.

"So you're not a big fan," I confirmed.

"When I broke my leg, they just fired me. No disability. No severance. Nothing. They said I didn't qualify for nothing. It was just 'see ya later.' At first, I was pissed. But then I was like, 'Thank goodness.'"

"Why is that?"

"Because, man, I kept getting sick the whole time I was working there."

"What kind of sick?"

"Oh, you know. It was like the flu or something. You'd feel it coming on and then it would just hit you. It got so you knew when it was going to happen. I worked there three months and I probably got sick ten times. Since I quit, I been fine. It's the same with a bunch of other dudes, too. We all been getting sick. Some of them complained and they got fired. Some just quit. Some of them kept their mouth shut. They still working there, still getting sick. I heard one dude had to go on dialysis."

Just like Jackie Orr's grandmother. "What about broken bones?" I asked. "Anyone else break a bone?"

"Yeah, a couple other dudes, actually. One of them broke his collarbone on-site."

"Ouch," Tee said.

"Yeah," DaQuan said. "But that's okay, the lawyer said we gonna get us some money for that."

"Lawyer?" I said. "What lawyer?

Fifteen minutes later, I left Tee's place armed with the name of Will Imperiale, Esquire, and some vague details about the lawsuit he was planning against McAlister Properties.

The name, I already knew. Anyone in New Jersey who had ever glanced in a telephone book, watched daytime television, or received junk mail knew the name Will Imperiale. Probably anyone who had slipped and fallen in the local grocery store knew of him, too. He was the heavily advertised king of the local personal injury lawyers.

And, according to DaQuan, he had somehow gotten word about sick construction workers and had been quietly signing them up—there were several dozen—with assurances of a quick and sizable settlement. Thousands of dollars for anyone who had been ill even once, he had said. Thousands more if someone had lost his job for any length of time. Hundreds of thousands for a broken bone. For anyone who had more serious complications? It could be even more. Plus, all their medical bills would be handled.

They were bold promises, and I was unconvinced how much he could back them up. Because, sure, in a grocery store slip-and-fall, things were relatively straightforward: there was no question how the plaintiff had gotten hurt, nor was there any doubt that the defendant had likely caused it. The lawyers would go into a conference room and come out an hour later with an agreement that a broken leg was worth, say, $200,000 in pain and suffering, $60,000 in medical bills, and $30,000 in lost wages. Not bad for an hour's work.

I couldn't imagine things were as easy in a case like this. The defendant's lawyers would know that proving the construction site was making people sick was no easy task, from a legal standpoint. Who's to say they hadn't just picked up some bug that they kept passing to one another?

You'd have to be able to find the chemical culprit, prove it was in the ground/air/water, prove it was capable of causing the maladies in question, and furthermore prove there wasn't some other toxin—from some other nearby source—at work. It would involve complicated science, painstaking documentation, a raft of expensive experts, and a whole lot of moving parts that might or might not come through for you.

Plus, you needed the rare jury that would be smart enough to understand all the science involved but still compassionate enough—or angry enough—to sock the responsible party with a large judgment. Then you needed to hope the dollar amount didn't get knocked too far down on appeal.

Oh, and the whole thing could take ten years.

I couldn't imagine Will Imperiale was mentioning any of that to his new clients. Right now, the game was just to get the maximum number of people to entrust their legal fate to him. The more clients he signed up, the more his reward grew—because he'd get a third of whatever he could ultimately collect for them.

With multiple defendants, the math got big in a hurry. Say he could sign up forty people and get them an average of $200,000 after medical bills, pain and suffering, and lost compensation were factored in. That was a tidy $8 million, of which he'd get a nice little $2.6 million slice. So it behooved him to talk big now, even if his chances of being able to deliver later were anything but assured.

If nothing else, it was, in the short term, a good follow for the next day's paper: the dead man's company was allegedly making construction workers sick and was about to be sued for it by a prominent and successful personal injury lawyer. At the very least, it was something to momentarily requite Harold Brodie's amour for the story.

I called Pigeon, told her about the lawsuit, and instructed her to stop bothering Vaughn's former neighbors—which she was more than happy to do. It didn't sound like she'd had luck finding any who were as chatty as the old lady from earlier in the day. Her new assignment, I informed her, was to start calling some of the other construction workers; Tee had given me a few names and numbers as a parting gift. I, meanwhile, was going to make an unannounced visit to the offices of Imperiale & Trautwig.

It would have made for better copy if those offices had been located in some seedy strip mall. And they may once have been. But business had obviously been good enough for Imperiale & Trautwig that they were in One Newark Center, alongside a variety of upstanding law firms, masquerading as one of them. Perhaps I shouldn't totally denigrate the practice of personal injury law. Certainly there were times when the negligence of others caused real harm to certain individuals, and they had every right to be compensated for their suffering. I just wished the whole racket weren't quite so opportunistic.

Imperiale & Trautwig took up half of the twelfth floor, and I told the receptionist just inside the main doors that I was there to see Mr. Imperiale and, no, I didn't have an appointment. This immediately became of less concern when I announced I was a reporter with the *Eagle-Examiner*, and two minutes later I was sitting inside Will Imperiale's office, across from the great man himself.

Will Imperiale was perhaps fifty, with dark hair whose color came from a bottle. The most prominent feature on him was his nose, which was large and hooked. All through our brief introductions, I couldn't help but stare at it. It was an impressive nose.

"So I met a new client of yours today," I said when it was time to stop with the preambles.

"And who is that?"

"DaQuan Richardson," I said.

With that, the nose had a smile appear underneath it. He was doing his best not to look like a man who had just hit the lottery. He rearranged some things on his desk and tried to make his eyes seem like they were full of concern—not just dollar signs.

"Ah, yes, Mr. Richardson," he said. "How was his leg looking?"

"Just fine," I assured him. "He said it's a lot more comfortable now that the cast is off."

"He still has a long road ahead of him," Imperiale said. "He's going to be out of work for some time yet. He's a laborer, you know. Can't labor with a broken leg. Medically, there's going to be more doctor's visits, rehab, a long recovery—and that's assuming it's healed properly."

Will Imperiale was obviously hoping it hadn't. If doctors had to break it again and reset it, that would be worth, what, another hundred grand?

"All things I'm sure you'll be pointing out to the defendant's lawyers," I said. "Speaking of which, who are the defendants?"

He once again was attempting to tamp down his smile. "May I ask your interest in the case?"

"Yeah, sure. You may have heard Vaughn McAlister is no longer with us."

"Yes, I read it in the paper today."

"And I wrote it in the paper today. The thing is, we also have a paper tomorrow. So I need to write something for that.

The fact that Mr. McAlister's company is being sued—and may have been making construction workers sick—smells like news to me."

That there were also residents in a nearby neighborhood getting sick made it even more newsworthy. But I wasn't going to tell him about that yet. Nor was I ready to put it in the newspaper.

"Well, it's premature to . . ." Imperiale started, then stopped himself.

He chuckled lightly. There were obviously things bouncing around in his head, and I could tell he was having a debate with himself about how much to tell the newspaper reporter. Lawyers, personal injury lawyers especially, often have this problem. Because, on the one hand, he didn't want anything printed that might damage his case or tip off the other side as to his strategy. It was not unusual for trials to have newspaper clippings among their exhibits as the result of lawyers or clients who had said too much. On the other hand, the threat of bad publicity could be a powerful weapon for the plaintiff in any legal proceeding. Civil suits were often settled just to keep things out of the newspaper. And in a case this complex, a quick settlement benefited the plaintiff's lawyer more than anyone.

I let Imperiale have a little debate with himself. Finally, he said, "Can we talk off the record?"

"As long as I can get something on the record by the time I leave here. I'm not here strictly for the charming conversation, you understand."

"Sure, I understand," he said. "Okay, off the record: the complaint hasn't been filed yet. So, technically, there is no lawsuit. Yet."

"When were you planning on filing?"

"Soon. We were still gathering plaintiffs. You can always

add more by amending the complaint after you file, of course. But I always like to feel like I've beaten the bushes pretty thoroughly before I file. I was probably going to give it another week or two. But the development with Vaughn McAlister and your interest could . . . change the timeline, I guess."

"Right, of course," I said. I understood what he was talking about: Will Imperiale didn't want to risk losing his case. If I brought attention to the fact that people were getting sick and there was no law firm of record, every ambulance chaser who had ever passed the New Jersey bar might start scouring Newark, looking for clients. But if Imperiale & Trautwig had already planted its flag in that legal ground and it was known it had already signed up a few dozen clients—perhaps all the clients there were to be had—it would become much less attractive to the competition.

"We've been writing the complaint as we went, so it's pretty much ready to go, but . . ." He stopped himself. The smile went blinding for a second, then he reined it in. "What would it be worth to you to be the first to get your hands on the complaint?" he asked.

Without hesitation, I shot back, "We're not a tabloid. We don't pay for stories."

"No, no, I'm not talking about that," he said. "No money."

"Then what?"

"I could get the thing filed by five this afternoon. No one else in the media would be able to see it until it was processed, which wouldn't happen until Thursday morning at the earliest. But I could e-mail you a copy when I filed. It would be a guaranteed scoop for you."

"And in exchange?"

"Whatever you wrote would need to say 'Imperiale and Trautwig' at least four times," he said smoothly.

Now it was my turn to smile. I got it. He didn't want money.

He wanted something more valuable: free advertising. He knew a front-page story that mentioned his law firm prominently was gold. It would scare off other firms and also possibly flush out additional plaintiffs.

From a strictly by-the-book standpoint, we didn't cut deals like this with sources. And perhaps if Pigeon had been around, I would have told the guy to screw off, simply to set a good example for her. But the sausage-making enterprise that was putting together a daily newspaper could sometimes get a little messy. And while I wouldn't go bragging about this at the next Society of Professional Journalists cocktail party, I was going to mention his law firm in what I wrote anyway. So there seemed little harm in engaging in a minor gentleman's agreement that didn't involve cash considerations or anything else that would be a serious ethical foul.

"Okay, but four times is a little much. It'll start to read like a billboard for Imperiale and Trautwig," I said. "Three times."

"Three times, plus you mention our Web site."

"No Web site. It'll make me feel like your whore, plus I guarantee you the copydesk would cut it out, and I have no control over that."

He eyed me. "Okay, three times," he said, reaching across the desk to shake my hand. "I'll send you the complaint by five. You can quote from it whatever you want."

"Deal," I said. "By the way, I assume the complaint will say what is making people sick?"

"No," he said.

"Isn't that something you kind of need to know?"

"Not really," he assured me. "Not yet, anyway. We can keep it vague for the time being. Eventually we'll get into chemical testing. For now, we just need plaintiffs with problems."

"Well, you certainly seem to have that."

"We do," he said.

As I excused myself from his office, his parting shot was: "Remember. Imperiale and Trautwig. Four times."

"Three times," I reminded him.

"Oh, right," he said. "Three."

Had to give him credit for trying.

I returned to the office, exacted a Coke Zero from the break room vending machine—Coke Zero being as necessary to my writing process as air—and hunkered down. My plan was to craft the shell of a story, then fill in the details when Will Imperiale sent me the complaint. I had barely settled into my chair when Tommy Hernandez ambled my way. Well, maybe it was more of a sashay than an amble. Tommy even walked gay.

"So I'm going to tell you some things about Vaughn McAlister, but first I have a question for you: What do your shoes have in common with Hurricane Katrina?"

I looked down at my feet, still unsure what he found so offensive about how they were shod, then decided to play along. "I don't know, Tommy, what do my shoes have in common with Hurricane Katrina?"

"They both qualify as federal disaster areas."

"Okay, seriously, what is the problem with these shoes? There's nothing—"

"Laces," he interrupted.

"Excuse me?"

"Laces are what's wrong with your shoes. Unless you're trying out for the lead role in *Death of a Salesman* and you need to look like you're from the fifties, there is no need to have laces in your dress shoes. Laces are for sneakers, hiking boots, and certain avant-garde peasant blouses. I mean, those things on your feet almost look like wingtips."

"What's wrong with wingtips?"

"Are you a hipster wearing them ironically or are you playing the part of the one percent in an Occupy Wall Street protest demonstration? Then fine. Otherwise: everything. Everything is what's wrong with wingtips."

"I just . . . I don't understand."

"I know you don't," he said gravely. "Believe me, I know."

He bowed his head, moment-of-silence style, as if mourning the death of fashion.

"Anyhow," I said, "if you'll excuse me, I have a story to write."

"Oh, yeah! I knew I came over here for a reason," he said, delighted with himself for remembering. "I learned some very interesting things about the dead guy formerly known as Vaughn McAlister."

"Oh?"

Tommy sat down at the desk across from me, which was empty, and crossed his legs. "Well, remember I told you about that city hall source that likened him to Harry Grant?"

"Yeah."

"Well, I got the guy talking a little more and it sounds like Vaughn McAlister was in trouble money-wise."

"How so?"

"Apparently, McAlister Properties hasn't actually paid the city for the land that McAlister Arms sits on. The city already deeded it over to him, but he'd yet to give them a dime."

"Oh, that's neat."

"Yeah, but there's more," Tommy said. "From what this guy says, the city sold Vaughn the land for $1.4 million, but it promised McAlister Properties $1.1 million to help clean it up."

"So he basically paid three hundred grand for a big chunk of prime real estate. But it goes in the books as $1.4 million so no one howls that the city is giving him too cozy a deal."

"Well, there's that, and also there's an accounting thing going on. I didn't exactly understand it, but I guess the money comes out of different pots, and for tax reasons, it made sense for the city to have a $1.4 million credit in one place and a $1.1 million debit in another. It's something to do with state aid."

"Okay," I said. You had to love the vagaries of municipal accounting, which were designed seemingly to keep lay people as confused as possible. The problem is, it often had the same effect on the professionals hired to understand them.

"Except here's where it gets really good," Tommy said, getting so excited he had uncrossed his legs and was now leaning forward on the desk. "The city gave Vaughn the cleanup money even though he still hasn't paid them for the land."

"So he's walking around with what is essentially a free $1.1 million loan, all while owing them $1.4 million."

"Yep. My source said no one in city hall wanted to make a big deal out of it, because they were afraid they'd end up looking as bad as McAlister. And the South Ward councilman hadn't made a fuss because he's afraid if he presses too hard, Mc-Alister Properties will pull the plug on the project—and I guess he was planning on making McAlister Arms a centerpiece of his reelection campaign. My source said he was starting to think that McAlister might be able to get away with never paying."

"Meaning the city would have paid him $1.1 million to take ownership of a property with a fair market value of at least twice that?" I said.

That, perhaps, started to explain why city hall wasn't putting any stress on the police department to solve Vaughn's murder. Men like Pritch and Hakeem Rogers were usually antennae for political pressure—due to the aforementioned axiom about what flows downhill. But neither of them had sensed that pressure this time, because, if anything, it was being applied in the opposite direction. No one in city government wanted this murder to get much attention, and therefore no one was calling the police department to demand justice.

In short, there was a bit of a stench around Vaughn McAlister, and the less it was fanned, the fewer people would have to smell it.

"You got it," Tommy said. "So I'm thinking maybe we do a follow that says something like, 'Slain developer was broke as a joke.' You think that would be good?"

"Well, I'm all for following the money. So yeah, let's try and do a piece about McAlister's finances," I said. "But let's not put him in the poorhouse just yet. Developers are always playing games with cash flow. He might have just known he could wait a little while before paying Newark, while some of his other creditors were a little more insistent."

"Or he could have used it for bribe money," Tommy said, giggling. Tommy giggled about such wanton breaches of trust from public officials mostly because Tommy giggled about everything.

"You might want to pull his campaign contributions to see if he tried to do some of it legally," I suggested. "As for the other stuff, how much of that can we get on the record?"

"All of it. It's just going to take a little while. Now that I know what to ask for, I've requested the necessary documents from the city clerk's office. It's a question of how long they sit on it."

"What's their average these days?"

"They've been pretty good, actually. I've got a girlfriend there who helps me out."

"A girlfriend with apparently no gaydar whatsoever," I pointed out.

"Well, she's a lot older than me. So who knows? Maybe she has a son that she's just waiting to set me up with. She's Puerto

Rican and she's pretty fine for an older woman. I bet if you put her mouth on a guy, it would—"

"Okay, okay. I don't want you to have to take a cold shower," I said.

"Yeah, speaking of which, *your* girlfriend is approaching," Tommy said.

It said a lot about the precarious state of my existence that I had to turn to discover whom he was talking about. But when I did, I saw Kira O'Brien slinking toward me, wearing one of her conservative work outfits—pink sweater set, gray slacks—with her hair up in a little bun. Seeing her made me feel vaguely guilty, simply because I had been thinking a lot about Tina—for understandable reasons—and quite a bit less about my favorite librarian.

"Hi, Tommy," she said.

"Hey, Keer," Tommy said.

Then she looked at me and announced, "Carter, I've given this a lot of thought and . . . I think I'm ready to take the next step in our relationship."

Sensitive interpreter of social situations that he is, Tommy took that as his cue to leave. Kira planted herself in the seat he had just vacated. I found myself wishing this conversation—wherever it was leading—didn't have to take place in the middle of the newsroom. Kira was unconcerned about public displays of, well, just about anything.

"Uh, okay, what next step?" I said, trying to keep my voice hushed.

"Well," she said, sitting up very properly, with a special twinkle in her blue eyes. "I know we haven't really talked about our relationship or put any labels on it. So I don't want this to be too sudden. And you can tell me if you think it is. You'll tell me, right?"

"Uh, yeah, sure, I guess," I said, but inside I was already flinching.

"Seriously, I want to be careful that we're not moving too fast for you," she continued. "I know how guys are with the C-word."

"The . . . C-word?" I asked. The only C-word I could think of that I had serious problems with was "celibacy."

She glanced left, then right, then whispered, "You know, the C-word: 'commitment.'"

Oh no. Not now. Not here. I suddenly felt my internal temperature rising. The last time a woman had started talking in these kinds of terms with me, it was a few years back. The girl I had been seeing at the time told me her lease was up, and she strongly suggested—to the point where one could say she informed me—that she was moving in with me. I'll spare the details and say it ended when she moved out, having strongly suggested and/or informed me that she was having an affair with a guy from her office.

And it's not that, under ordinary circumstances, I would mind having a girl as cute and spunky and smart as Kira want to progress our relationship. I mean, true, we had never really had a serious conversation about anything. But that wasn't the issue. It's just that, in matters such as these, my circumstances were T-minus nine months from changing dramatically.

"So," she continued. "I don't want you to freak out or anything but . . ."

I may have winced as I waited for her next words.

"I want to take you to the Zombie Ball," she said. Then added, "As my date."

I waited for there to be more. Like, *I want to take you to the*

Zombie Ball and I want you to propose to me there. But there was nothing more forthcoming. Then I remembered: this was Kira. Simple, fun, easygoing Kira. She called it the "C-word" because she was more afraid of it than I was.

"Oh," said, feeling my body instantly cool off. "Sure. No problem. When is it?"

"Friday night," she said.

I winced again, but for different reasons. "Ugh, I can't make it that night," I said. Kira immediately looked hurt, so I explained, "My sister is getting married this weekend. Friday night is her rehearsal dinner."

"You . . . you have a sister?" Kira asked.

Like I said, we had never had a serious conversation. "Yeah. She lives in New York and I don't see her a lot, so I guess you haven't had a chance to meet her yet."

"And she's getting married?"

"Yeah. On Saturday," I said.

"Around here?"

"In Millburn, yeah."

"Are you . . . going with anyone?"

"No," I said.

"Oh," she said, and suddenly she wasn't looking at me anymore.

And then, with roughly the same speed as continents divide and mountains grow, it occurred to me: Kira wanted to go to the wedding. With me.

I was so proud of myself for realizing this, I didn't think about the long-term implications of what I asked next. Let me be more clear about this: I really, truly wasn't thinking. Sometimes people—and by people, I mean women—don't get this about guys. They'll get all haughty and superior and snap, *What were you thinking?* And that fact is, we weren't thinking anything at all. We just weren't.

This was one of those times. I just cleared my throat and tried to make it sound like I was still in the flow of the conversation. "You want go to with me?"

"Of course!" she said immediately, her entire face lifting upward, the twinkle back in her eyes. "I mean, it's your sister's wedding. I love weddings. Why wouldn't I want to go?"

"I don't know. I just didn't think you'd be interested. I mean, you do know the only person at a wedding who's allowed to be in costume is the bride, right?"

"Wait, you mean I can't wear my pink Power Rangers outfit?" she said, deadpan, then gave me a wink.

"Well, as long as it's not white," I said.

She snickered and rewarded me with a genuinely happy smile. "Oh, this is going to be great. I'm so glad you asked me. I actually have the perfect dress for a wedding. I got it last year for my friend's wedding. There's just one problem with it."

"What's that?" I asked.

She rose from her chair, walked over to me, leaned in close, and whispered, "It's kind of tight. And the only way to avoid having panty lines is not to wear—"

"*Carter Ross!*" came a loud, female voice, jolting us both.

It was coming from the opposite side of the newsroom, from the mouth of Tina Thompson. I looked over and saw she was crooking one finger at me in a repeated motion, the internationally accepted sign for "get your ass in here."

"Excuse me," I said to Kira. "I like where this conversation is going, and I would like to continue it. But in the meantime, I do believe I'm being paged."

"Okay," Kira said. "I can't wait for this weekend. Rehearsal dinner Friday night, wedding Saturday night?"

"You got it," I said.

With her face still about two feet from mine, she gave me a devilish look that made my insides do a backflip. "We are going to have an awesome time," she said. "Weddings make me so—"

"*Carter!*" Tina hollered again.

"To be continued," I said, lifting myself from my chair and walking toward Tina's office.

On the way, I heard Buster Hays growl, "I miss the days when it was nothing but guys in here."

During the final twenty feet of my walk to Tina's office, I thought hard about what the source of her ire might be. Usually, I was pretty good at knowing my transgressions, a self-awareness I could use to assist in preparing a rigorous defense.

But, in this case, I was lost. I had put a good scoop in that day's paper. I was working on a story for the next day's paper that she—and, more important, Brodie—would like. I had not gone behind her back about anything I could remember. And, I mean, sure, Kira and I had just been talking in rather close quarters, but she kept insisting she didn't care about that.

Then I thought, well, maybe I hadn't done anything wrong. Maybe she was just feeling impatient because deadlines had been moved up for some reason. Maybe the pregnancy hormones were starting to make her a little nutty. Maybe this was no big deal.

"You wanted to see me?" I said with forced innocence.

"Close the door," she ordered.

Close the door. Never good. I complied.

"Take a seat," she said, taking one of the two chairs that faced her desk.

And that's when I felt what it was to be a turkey. In mid-November. With a farmer who was sharpening his ax. When Tina really wanted to take my head off, she always chose one of the chairs that faced her desk, because it pointed away from the newsroom. That way, none of the gossips in the room would be able to read her lips. Tina always liked her most serious scolding to be done without closed-captioning.

My butt had just barely met the chair when she clenched her teeth and bristled, "What the hell, Carter?"

"Uh, what hell are you referring to?"

"You didn't tell anyone my . . . condition . . . did you?" she said, fiercely.

"No. Why would I want to? I've barely even had the chance to—"

"No one?" she demanded again.

"No."

"Not even *your mother?*" she seethed.

"My mother? Why would I tell my mother? She's not exactly the first person I'd rush to with the news that I'm about to have a child out of wedlock."

"So you're sure she has no idea?"

"Not unless she's telepathic. I haven't even talked to her since I got the news myself. Why do you ask?"

"Because I just got off the phone with her," Tina said. "She just called and invited me to your sister's wedding. She wants me at the rehearsal dinner, the wedding, the Sunday brunch, the whole thing."

"And what did you say?"

"What else could I say? I said yes. I don't seem to be having any luck convincing you to pretend this baby isn't yours. So, unless you come to your senses, this woman is going to be my child's grandmother. Your sister is going to be the aunt. Plus, your mom has always been so sweet to me. I couldn't very well tell her to go pound sand."

"You could have said you already had plans."

"Yes, I suppose I could have. But I didn't think of that. In any event, it's too late now. It's settled."

"Yeah, I guess," I said.

I swallowed hard. The implications of my unthinking so-licitation of Kira as my wedding date just a few scant moments earlier were now clear to me. For the record: it is generally un-wise to ask one woman to a significant family function when another woman is carrying your seed.

"Sorry I accused you of having told your mom. The last thing I want is anyone's sympathy. But I'm still just, I don't know, a little freaked out about this whole thing. I feel like I can't get my head around it."

"Believe me, I know what you mean."

Tina's boil had already cooled to the point where it wasn't even a simmer. "Well, I guess there are worse things than going to a wedding as your date."

I gulped. "Yeah, about that . . ."

"What?"

I wanted to be honest with her and tell her I had just invited Kira so we could share a good laugh about this awkward little predicament. Except there were at least four factors to consider. One, she might not find it so laughable. Two, it wouldn't be good for the health of my unborn child to make Mommy's blood pres-sure spike dramatically. Three, there was an entire newsroom full of eardrums behind me, and I had to be considerate of their pain thresholds. And, four, I'm chicken.

So I just said, "Never mind."

"Okay," she said, giving me a nice pat on the knee as she got out of her chair and went around to her normal position behind her desk. "By the way, how's the McAlister follow coming?"

I enlightened her on the most recent developments, agreed to have something filed by seven, then exited her office. But in-stead of returning to my desk, I peeled off down the back stair-way and out the side entrance—an emergency exit whose alarm had long ago been disabled by the smokers who sneaked out that way to grab a cigarette. It seemed to be clear of loiterers for the moment, so I pulled out my phone and speed dialed the Ross family home in Millburn, with the intention of fixing this little dilemma.

"Hello," my mother answered.

"Hey, Mom, it's me."

"Hi, honey!" she said brightly; then—because I never call during the day—she quickly asked, "Is everything all right."

"Yeah, fine," I said tersely. "Except . . . Mom, why did you invite Tina to the wedding?"

"Well, she's your friend, dear, and there was an empty seat at your table and I just thought it would be perfect."

Oh, it was perfect all right. A perfect disaster. "Mom, did it ever occur to you that if I had wanted Tina at the wedding I already would have asked her?"

"Well, I thought maybe you were just being obstinate. You get that from your father's side, you know. What's the problem? Are you two having a spat?"

No, Mom, we're actually having a baby, I wanted to say. But instead I stuck with the more immediate issue: "The problem is I just invited someone else."

"Oh, did you ask Tommy?" Mom asked. Then, before I could mount an answer, she started gushing: "Because I thought you knew I already asked him. There was an opening at your cousin Glenn's table, and I've always wondered if he might, you know, lean that way. He's never been married and he's so good-looking. Everyone says he looks just like Dirk Pitt."

"Brad Pitt, Mom. Everyone says he looks like Brad Pitt. Dirk Pitt is the guy in the Clive Cussler novels."

"Right. *Brad* Pitt. The one with all those children. No danger of Glenn doing that." She chuckled at herself and continued: "But it really would be great if he and Tommy maybe took a shine to each other. Is that an okay word? A "shine"? Is that what you say with gays? I really have learned to be open-minded about this sort of thing. I even voted for gay marriage on the—"

"Mom! This isn't about Tommy. It's about me. I invited a girl."

This gave Mom a hitch in her conversational stride. "A . . . a girl?" she said, and I could picture the confused, hurt look on her face. "Do you have a girlfriend, honey? You never told us anything about a girlfriend."

I started sputtering and stammering. It was amazing how, even as a thirty-two-year-old man—fully grown and independent for many years—I could still be made to feel like a blushing teenager by my mother. Finally I spit out: "I have a girl who's a . . a . . . friend. We don't really know each other that well yet. Her name is Kira. She's a librarian here at the paper. And I just invited her to be my date for the weekend."

"Oh. That is a problem."

"It sure is."

"That will unbalance the seating," she said, heavily.

"Among other things it will unbalance."

"Well, we'll just have to make the best of it," she said, as if she had just been informed the daffodils in one of the flower arrangements were being replaced by tulips.

"No, Mom, you'll just have to call Tina and tell her there's been a terrible mistake and you have to trim the guest list."

I could hear Mom recoiling. "Oh, honey, no! Absolutely not. That would be tacky beyond tacky. I just couldn't . . ."—she was interrupted by the click of her call-waiting—"Oh, that's the caterer! I have to go."

Then she hung up. I stuffed my phone into my pocket, then buried my face in my hands, sure that things couldn't get much worse. Then I looked up and realized I wasn't alone.

Buster Hays was sucking down the remains of a cigarette, a malicious grin on his face.

"You heard all of that, didn't you," I said.

The grin spread a little wider. "Lucky for you, my silence can be bought."

"What's the price?" I said, trying to be cagey, but knowing I was basically at his mercy.

"I got an All-Slop shift tomorrow night that could have your name on it," Buster said.

All-Slop was our cute name for what was formally known as the NonStop News Desk—the division within the newsroom whose job it was to feed the Web site, twenty-four hours a day. We called it the All-Slop because that's roughly what we shoveled into it. There were a few reporters dedicated exclusively to the All-Slop, but the rest of us were forced to pick up the slack on a rotating basis. It amounted to about one shift a month. I am still waiting to hear where I can apply to get that time back at the end of my life.

"Fine," I said. "I'll take your All-Slop."

He grinned. I suspect if he had one, he would have lit a victory cigar.

Waiting for me upon arrival back at my desk was an e-mail from wimperiale@imperialeandtrautwig.com. The subject was "Civil suit." The message read:

MR. ROSS,

PER OUR DISCUSSION, THE ENCLOSED WAS BEEN FILED TO ESSEX COUNTY SUPERIOR COURT AT 4:56 P.M. TODAY.

SINCERELY,

WILLARD R. IMPERIALE, ESQ.
IMPERIALE & TRAUTWIG

ONE NEWARK CENTER

NEWARK, NJ 07102

I opened the document to find one of the most crowded captions I had ever seen. There were a total of twenty-eight plaintiffs, plus "John and Jane Does, 1-100." The defendants included McAlister Properties, the city of Newark, the state of New Jersey, the New Jersey State Department of Environmental Protection, the federal Environmental Protection Agency, a few corporations I had never heard of, and, strangely enough, K&J Manufacturing, good old Quint's family business. I had thought it was defunct. Maybe Will Imperiale had discovered it still had assets that could be attacked.

The document was 156 pages long, and there was no way I'd be able to read the entire thing and have my story filed by seven. So I skimmed to the end. It did not leave me terribly impressed with Imperiale's lawyerly skills. As a reporter, I had read a lot of civil complaints, enough that I had a decent sense of which ones were well-grounded in law and fact and which were long shots.

This one fell more to the Hail Mary side of things. Imperiale obviously still had a lot of work to do. Nevertheless, I grabbed some pull quotes about the gross negligence of the defendants that had led directly to the illnesses of the plaintiffs, and started cobbling together a story.

I was just getting into the flow of it when I heard a sound behind me that made my butt muscles clench. It was a pocket full of spare change being rattled around.

Which meant it could only be one person: Harold Brodie. The *Eagle-Examiner*'s executive editor almost never left his office, but when he did, he was a notorious change jangler. He always seemed to have a pocket full of the stuff—quarters and nickels to make the lower sounds, pennies and dimes for the higher registers—and it was a favorite strategy of his to walk up behind you and give it good shake so you knew he was there. Brodie had made many a tuchus tighten that way through the years.

"Hello, Carter, my boy," he said in a voice that was thin and high and belied the extent to which I feared the man behind it. I don't know why a stooped, slender seventy-year-old with over-grown eyebrows and a weak bladder intimidated me so much, but to me Brodie was the equivalent of a beefy, three-hundred-pound biker with a temper. I just didn't want to provoke him.

"Good afternoon," I said. I deliberately never address Brodie by name, because while I didn't want to call him "Mr. Brodie"—it seemed too obsequious—I also didn't have the testicular presence to call him "Harold" or "Hal."

"You did a fine job on the McAlister story," he said.

"Thanks."

"And I understand we have a follow cooking?"

"Yes, sir," I said and didn't elaborate. Long experience had taught me that the less I said around Brodie, the better.

"Have you spoken with Barry McAlister yet?"

"I did this morning, as a matter of fact."

"How was he?"

"Pretty broken up, as you might imagine. I didn't get much out of him. He was also a little drunk, to be honest."

"Ah, yes, Barry always did like the bottle," Brodie said.

"You know him?"

"He's an old friend. I was a young reporter assigned to Newark cops when I met him. Or maybe I should say he met me. I was working a story in the ghetto when a group of punks tried to mug me in front of one of his buildings," Brodie said; then, oddly, he started chuckling. "Barry McAlister came charging out of that building with a double-barrel shotgun, fired one shot in the air, and told them he'd put the other shot in one of their asses if they didn't clear off."

Brodie chuckled again and said, "He told them they could mug all the people they wanted, but they damn sure weren't going to do it in front of his building. I'll tell you, boy, he sure got me out of the soup."

"Sounds like it," I said, now understanding Brodie's interest in this story. McAlister had mentioned he had "some history" with people at the *Eagle-Examiner*. I hadn't realized the history was with our top guy.

"After that, I'd see him from time to time. He was one of those sources who you might not be able to quote, but who always knew the score. I'd buy him a drink or two, just to listen to him talk. A lot of the landlords remaining in the neighborhood were shysters, there to wring whatever money they could from their crumbling buildings without giving anything back. Barry McAlister wasn't like that. He cared for his buildings and the people inside them." Brodie shook his head. "It's a shame what happened with him and Elizabeth. He was never really the same after that. She took something from him and I'm not sure he ever got it back."

Brodie was on memory lane now, a side of him I had never really seen before. He had been the top editor at the *Eagle-Examiner* for a quarter century, and it was easy to think he had come out of the womb that way. But Brodie had a past like everyone else.

"I remember Vaughn when he was just a little boy," Brodie continued. "He was a smart little fella, just like his father. This whole thing is terrible. Terrible. Any ideas who would do such a thing?"

I paused, because I wasn't sure how much I wanted to say, under the theory of The Less Your Editor Knows, The Better. But he seemed to have a personal interest, so . . .

"Well, he seems to have a girlfriend who might not be terribly pleased with him," I said. "And I talked to a not-for-attribution source who said he saw two white guys get out of a dark sedan and dump Vaughn's body on the McAlister Arms construction site. They made it sound like a professional hit."

"Were you planning on putting that in the newspaper?"

"Not with the level of sourcing I have right now," I said. "But it's definitely something to keep in mind."

Brodie closed his eyes. It was something he always did when he was thinking deeply, never minding that it was, frankly, a bit unsettling. He stayed in this contemplative pose for a long moment, then opened his eyes.

"Well, keep on it, my boy," Brodie said, giving his change one last jingle before he departed.

Will Imperiale knew how other lawyers scoffed at him. He heard their catty little comments at bar association events—cheap shots about his ads in the Yellow Pages or his billboards. He knew the disdain they had for him.

He also knew most of them couldn't have hacked it in his line of work. Say what you will about personal injury lawyers, but they worked for a living. And hard. They didn't have regular clients with recurring legal work. They couldn't bill by the hour, knowing they'd get paid no matter what the result. They couldn't pad accounts to help make up for a lean month.

All a personal injury lawyer had was his current caseload. If it was heavy with winners, he was going to prosper. If it was light or had too many losers in it, his overhead—all those paralegals and assistants on the payroll, all the money for office space and advertising—would eat him alive.

As such, good new cases were like air for Will Imperiale. He needed them to survive.

Yeah, sometimes they came at him easy. Someone saw one of the ads and walked in with a good case. Former clients referred their cousins, girlfriends, or neighbors.

But he had learned there were other ways to get them, too.

He had emergency-room nurses on retainer at several of the local hospitals and offered them a bounty for each case they tipped him off about. He had a network of ambulance drivers with the same kind of arrangement. He was a major supporter of several of the largest police charities and he made it clear to them what would earn future donations.

Sleazy? Perhaps. Expensive? Sure. Worth it? Absolutely.

That's what made the McAlister case such a pleasure. It came at him unsolicited. One day, a man he didn't know simply made an appointment. And he refused to meet with one of the paralegals who normally did the intake work. Ordinarily, Will Imperiale wouldn't waste his time with those initial meetings. Too many of them were sob stories without a decent claim. But the guy insisted he meet with The Man himself, and Imperiale was intrigued enough to humor him.

He was glad he did. The case was an opportunistic lawyer's dream: lots of sick people with heavy medical bills; lots of significant injuries, with very legitimate pain and suffering attached to them; and a defendant with deep pockets. Plus, the victims were poor. That always helped if it went to a jury.

Plus, poor people asked fewer questions.

The man wanted a kickback, of course. They all wanted kickbacks. And this guy was looking for a big one, much larger than Imperiale would normally even consider.

But this man was promising to serve up McAlister Properties on a silver platter. It would be guaranteed money. Plus, the guy was going to provide Imperiale enough dirt on McAlister—quite literally—that Imperiale stood a good chance of being able to go after some of the other defendants.

After all, the city of Newark had its fingers in this thing. So did the state of New Jersey. The company that had once owned the land—K&J Manufacturing—was surely still good for something. Even the Environmental Protection Agency could be liable.

It was a can't-miss case. The kickback would be worth it. There would still be lots left over for Willard Imperiale, Esq.

CHAPTER 5

There is a certain joy to being a newspaper reporter on deadline that almost makes me sorry for other types of writers. I always chuckle when novelists say they're "on deadline" and you ask them what the deadline is and they say, "October." In my world, October is not a deadline. It's a month.

In the magazine business, it's no better. They'll say they're "on deadline" because they've been told they must deliver copy in "mid-October" or "ideally by October 15, if at all possible." And, again, that's not a deadline. That's a suggestion.

No, a real deadline is something that cannot be measured in months or days. It can be measured only in hours or, better yet, minutes.

And missing it comes with consequences. The word "deadline" originally came to us from the penal system. Once upon a time, a deadline referred to an actual line on prison grounds that an inmate could not cross, or else he'd be shot dead. The newspaper business long ago took this concept and ran with it, with only slightly less drastic penalties for offenders.

When you have a deadline like that—a real deadline, a deadline with fangs—it takes on its own necessary momentum. There's no time for writer's block, to grope around for that perfect phrase or to wait for some mythical muse to inspire you. You just have to write. What comes out isn't necessarily going to be poetry. It might be downright awful. But it comes out all the same—because the alternative is to get fired. As a writer, knowing that can be very freeing.

Hence, my Vaughn McAlister follow-up story was not something I had planned on submitting to the annual New Jersey Press Association Awards. But I filed it at 6:58—with a whole two minutes to spare—so I marked it in the win column and moved on.

I was just starting to think about Kira and Tina and the baby—and the mess my imprudence had created—when my phone rang.

The caller ID told me it was Pigeon, whom I had neither seen nor heard from in several hours. The last I knew, she had been hard at work with Tee's list of names and phone numbers of construction workers. But it suddenly occurred to me she hadn't reported back with anything. I answered with a casual, "Hey, where ya been?"

My phone's earpiece broadcast a cacophony of background noise. It sounded human, but it was all indistinct.

"Hello?" I said.

"Hey. You Carter?"

The person asking this question was not Pigeon. His voice was about two octaves too low. It also lacked the elocution and precise diction I had come to expect of the J. P. Stevens High valedictorian.

"Yes, this is Carter. Who's this?"

He didn't answer that question, just said, "You got to come get your girl."

"My girl?"

"Yeah, I told her she had a bit much and was there someone

I could call. She handed me her phone and said, 'Call Carter.'
She says her name is, I don't know, Mischa or something."

"Neesha?"

"Yeah, that's it."

"Uh, okay, where is she?"

"She at Pop's. You know where Pop's is at?"

I did know Pop's. It was on Springfield Avenue and it was
one of the seediest dive bars in Newark—a distinction that was
not easily earned in a city where many of the drinking establish-
ments had attained quite a low position. It was the kind of place
where the proprietor had long ago resorted to serving drinks in
plastic cups and beer in plastic bottles, because it made the bar
fights safer and easier to clean up after.

What I didn't know was how Pigeon had gotten there.

"Yeah, I know where Pop's is," I said, already standing up
and heading to the elevator.

"Good. You might want to come fast," he said.

"Why is that?" I asked.

There was no answer. Nor was there any more noise coming
from the phone. Mr. Deep Voice had ended the call. So I scram-
bled out to the parking garage, fired up the Malibu, and made
good time out to Pop's, which was only three turns and five
minutes from the office. I parked a block down—there were no
spots immediately outside the bar—and as I approached, I heard
a lot of loud, excited, male voices. There was obviously some
kind of disturbance going on inside.

Then I walked through the front door and saw why: Pigeon
was dancing on top of the bar.

Someone had found "Brick House" on Pop's ancient jukebox, and Pigeon was thrusting her body in near-rhythm to the
Commodores' classic. That Pigeon's booty was perhaps not as
generous as was often preferred in that ZIP code bothered none

of the patrons, because she had removed her bra and was waving it over her head like a lasso.

This, naturally, was very popular with the twenty-or-so men who had gathered around the bar to encourage her. They were all black, most of them on the beefy side, and their sturdy boots and dirty jeans told me they were all employed in one blue-collar industry or another. They had finished a hard day's work and now they were blowing off steam.

One of them yelled, "Show your tits!"—most likely not for the first time—and Pigeon started playing with the hem of her sweater, lifting it just enough to show a flash of bare midriff, then lowering it.

This brought a boisterous roar from her audience, which seemed only to embolden her. She pulled up the sweater a little farther, about halfway up her torso, then kept it there for a few beats of the music before letting it drop.

The one guy who had said, "Show your tits!" kept repeating it, until soon the whole pack of them was chanting that bawdy instruction. Pigeon seemed to be of the mind to oblige them, because she brought up the edge of the sweater until it was just under her breasts and started dancing with it in that position, gyrating her hips clumsily, like some kind of intoxicated belly dancer.

And that's when I decided everyone had enjoyed enough of the show. I started shoving my way through the throng until I reached the front row, then called "Pigeon!" in a voice filled with rebuke.

But she didn't hear me. She just kept right on dancing and I feared we were mere seconds away from an entire bar full of men seeing more of Pigeon than her future arranged-marriage husband might appreciate. So I reached up, delicately grabbed the hem of her sweater, and pulled it down.

This brought a chorus of angry boos from the mob. It momentarily occurred to me that interrupting the peep show, while good for Pigeon's reputation, might end up being bad for my face. I wasn't sure I could take on one of these guys, much less twenty of them, and they were making their unhappiness with me known.

Then Pigeon solved the problem for me. She been already been knocked slightly off-balance by my grabbing her sweater. And she was probably not very steady to begin with, given the amount of liquid courage it had likely taken to get her up on that bar in the first place. So she began teetering to the left, then tottering to the right; then, in a desperate attempt at overcorrection, she ended up falling, lying full out on the bar.

Her landing knocked over a small tidal wave of beer and malt liquor. The men had been so tightly bunched there was no avoiding the deluge, and enough of it splashed into them that it quite literally doused their anger. Several of the more-enthusiastic guys in the front row, including the one who had started the chant, got a rather thorough soaking. They just stood there, half stunned and dripping. Had I been the one spilling the drink, I'm quite sure I would have gotten a beating. But since it was Pigeon, they couldn't summon much anger.

The song had ended anyway and now that the entertainment had gone down, the crowd dispersed—some to the men's room, to get paper towels, and some to other parts of the bar. I helped Pigeon dismount from the bar, then handed her a few napkins so she could at least wipe her face. She was somewhere beyond blotto and had grabbed on to my shoulders to help keep herself up.

"Oh, Pigeon," was all I could say.

"You were the one who told me to live a little," she slurred.

"Yeah, this may have been a little too much living," I suggested.

"I know, I know. It's just the guys were all so nice and they've got these things call Yay ... Yay ... Yaygerbuhs ..."

"Jägerbombs?"

"Yeah! That's it! How did you know?"

I knew, because I do believe anyone of a certain drinking age—and I imagined that included anyone who had gone to a college party or a rowdy bar in the last ten years or so—had at least one run-in with a Jägerbomb. It was a combination of Jägermeister and Red Bull that, between the alcohol in the former and the caffeine in the latter, got the imbiber both buzzed and buzzing.

"Drunk on Jägerbombs," I said, shaking my head.

"Yeah! They're so much nicer than that awful drink Barry McAlister gave us earlier. It tastes kind of like cough medicine, but in a good way."

"Right," I said. "Just, in the future, try to remember they have a little more kick."

As I steadied Pigeon, a man approached us. He was dressed like everyone else in the bar—a working stiff—but he appeared substantially more sober.

"You gotta be Carter," he said. I recognized this as Mr. Deep Voice, the man who had summoned me to the rescue.

"Yeah, that's me."

"Looks like you got here just in time."

"Or maybe a little on the late side," I suggested.

"Yeah, sorry about that. Your girl and some of us was just talking a little bit at the bar, having a drink. Then one of my boys bought her a shot. She liked it, so we got her another. I didn't think nothing about it, but then . . ."

"She doesn't exactly have a lot of practice handling her liquor," I informed him.

"Yeah, I see that."

Pigeon was still trying to find her equilibrium, using me as her fulcrum. Her eyes appeared not to be focusing on anything, then suddenly they zoomed in on the guy in front of us.

"Oh heyyyy! This is one of my friends!" she said, so drunkenly happy to see him that she gave his chest a thump. He was solid enough that Pigeon's hand just bounced off him.

"Yeah," he confirmed. "That's me."

"Tell him about the dirt!" she blurted.

I looked at the guy and felt my head cocking. "The dirt?" I said.

"Wait," Pigeon interrupted. "I seriously think I need to sit down. The room is getting all . . . woooo . . ."

From long experience with drunks, I knew Pigeon was about ten to twenty minutes away from communing with the porcelain goddess. But she wasn't quite ready for that, so I guided her to the nearest open table. "Won't you join us?" I asked her friend.

He complied and we sat. Now that Pigeon was no longer relying on me as her sole means of support, it was a little easier to concentrate on the guy. He was roughly my age, though I always have a bit of a hard time telling with African Americans—darn them and their unwrinkled skin. He had a plump face atop a thick body, and short black hair.

"So you're friends with Tee?" I asked, just because I wanted to establish a little rapport with the guy.

"Yeah, we go back. You know him?"

"Good dude," I said.

"Yeah," he agreed.

I stole a quick peek at Pigeon, who had slumped in the chair and settled into a semicatatonic state. At least she wasn't feeling any pain. Yet.

"So, I'm sorry, I don't think I got your name," I said.

"Alan Sutherlin."

"And I'm Carter Ross."

"You with the newspaper, too?"

"Sure am."

"Nice to meet you," he said, and we shook hands properly.

"I assume you've worked down at McAlister Arms?" I said.

"Yeah."

"You still working there?"

"Nah, my part of the job is over."

"Are you with the lawsuit?" I asked.

"Not me. I never got sick. I know a bunch of guys who did. I just drove a truck, so I wasn't there most of the time."

"Oh," I said. "So what's this about dirt?"

Someone had put 50 Cent on the jukebox, and now we were all, officially, In Da Club. Alan was moving his head to the music a little. He seemed comfortable.

"Yeah, I was just telling your girl about it. How much you know about brownfield remediation?"

"I mean, a little. I guess. Why?"

"Well, here's how it's supposed to work, right? You take a truck full of dirt out. You dump it somewhere safe, like in a landfill or something. Then you bring fresh fill back in."

"Okay," I said. "I'm following you."

"Yeah, except with McAlister Arms, we weren't doing that."

"What do you mean?"

"First of all, we didn't have near enough trucks. Normal job, you get like ten, twenty trucks, so you can keep 'em going in and out all the time. You follow me?"

"Right."

"We had, like, two," he said, then leaned back in his seat.

"That seems . . . inefficient."

"Not for what we were doing."

"What do you mean?"

"This is what I was just telling your girl. We didn't take the dirt nowhere. We was told to just drive around with it, then bring it back and dump it like it was fresh. They told me I couldn't tell no one. Said I could get in trouble for participating in illegal dumping, or something like that. I didn't think nothing of it. I was like, 'Hey, man, you pay me union rate, I do whatever.' But then dudes started getting sick."

"But, wait, I'm confused. Why wouldn't they just have you do it the right way?"

"I don't know. Money, I guess."

"How so?"

"Because you got to pay a lot to get someone to take your dirty dirt off your hands. There are only certain facilities that can handle it, and most of them are in Pennsylvania, which is a long haul. That costs money. Plus, you got to pay for clean dirt. That costs more money. Plus, you got to get the right number of trucks going. That's like fifteen, twenty more trucks with fifteen, twenty more drivers. It all costs money. They wanted to make it look like we was cleaning up that site, but they didn't want to pay for it."

I thought back to Vaughn McAlister smugly telling me that the state's Department of Environmental Protection had given him $6 million for the cleanup and signed off on its completion. The city of Newark had given him another $1.1 million. He had obviously spent a small fraction of that money on the charade that was his cleanup process. I didn't know what he had done with the rest of it, but it was becoming apparent he hadn't actually remediated the site.

Which explained why people were becoming ill. Whatever chemical had been left in that dirt long ago was still there. And Vaughn McAlister had been doing the worst thing possible: stirring it up, getting it in the air so everyone—construction workers, the good people in the neighborhood, even the friendly local newspaper reporter—could suck it into their lungs.

"What a bunch of bastards," I said.

Alan nodded his head. "And then they act like the people

getting sick are just faking it. That's what really pissed me off. I wasn't gonna say nothing, because I didn't know who to say it to. But then Tee told me about you, said you would know how to handle it."

I was glad Tee had that kind of faith in me. I wasn't going to tell Alan, but I didn't even know where to start.

Alan's disclosure gave me new leads to pursue, but in the meantime, I had the more immediate problem of what to do about my alarmingly blitzed intern. I escorted her into the men's room—the guys wouldn't care—and assisted her through the aforementioned purge of at least some of the poison coursing through her body.

Once that grim task was accomplished, I considered my next steps. Since she seemed incapable of walking unassisted, I figured driving was out of the question. So I helped her out into the street to my car and, with misgivings—because she was still wet from the booze soup she had spilled all over—shoveled her into the passenger seat. I momentarily lamented what this would do to the Malibu's cloth seats, which would likely end up smelling like a brewery for a week or more. But I also didn't see much alternative.

I got into the driver's seat and studied her for a moment. Her neck seemed incapable of supporting the unbearable weight that was her head.

"Pigeon," I said loudly, as if that would penetrate the haze. Nothing.

"Neesha," I said.

She slowly swiveled her head toward me and let out a "Wa?"

"Where do you live?"

She groaned.

"Pigeon, come on, I have to take you home. Just tell me where you live."

She sank into the seat, her eyes half lidded. Realizing I wasn't going to get much of a response out of her, I started gently poking around on her person, trying to find a driver's license or something else that might have her address on it. The front pockets of her pants had been sewn shut—why twenty-first-century women put up with that kind of nonsense was beyond me—so I rolled her toward me and checked for back pockets.

She responded by flopping her arms around me, which was not exactly the response I was looking for. It got even more awkward when she buried her face in my neck and started nuzzling me. Not that I took it seriously as any kind of come-on. In her current state, she would have nuzzled Newt Gingrich.

"Easy there, Pigeon," I said, but that just made her squeeze tighter.

Still, it did make the job of checking her back pockets a little easier. Lightly, so she would not confuse it with groping, I ran my hand down her back until I found a rectangular lump that turned out to be a credit card and a driver's license. I pulled them out, untangled myself from her by gently shoving her back into the passenger seat, and found her address in Edison.

I read it out loud and said, "That's where I'm taking you, okay?"

"Noooooo," she said, moaning. "Tha's my parents' house."

I imagined her parents as a pair of strict, traditional Indian Americans. Mom in a sari. Dad with a mustache that looked like Gandhi's. The kind of mom and dad who had raised themselves an Ivy Leaguer and then pledged her in marriage to a doctor. Then I imagined myself, a white man they had never met, showing up with their daughter, drunk and braless.

Right. Edison was out.

"Okay, so where should I take you?"

No answer. She seemed to have slipped into some lower level of consciousness. I asked the same question two more times and got nothing more than a series of incomprehensible moans. Finally I just gave up and started driving to my Bloomfield abode. It looked like a night on the couch was forthcoming.

On the way to my house, I started pondering my next move. I now knew why the McAlister Arms site had been making people ill, even if I hadn't identified the chemical agent at work. I strongly suspected that Vaughn McAlister had pocketed the money earmarked for its cleanup. The question was how Vaughn McAlister had gotten the state DEP to sign off on a remediation that clearly hadn't been done. Was the DEP just duped by the parade of dump trucks that had come and gone from the site? Shouldn't there have been more oversight?

That was about as far as my thinking had advanced by the time I pulled into my driveway, with Pigeon now fast asleep beside me. I prodded her half awake, shucked her out of the passenger seat, and helped her stumble inside. Then I sat her down at my kitchen table and made her drink a full glass of water. I didn't know if she would remember it enough to thank me later, but operating under the golden rule of inebriation—do unto other drunks as you would have them do unto you—I thought it humane.

The water seemed to give her a little bit of life. It also seemed to make her aware of how sticky she was, because she asked if she could take a shower. I guided her into my bathroom, provided her a towel and a change of clothes. I didn't own pajamas for myself, much less for a woman, so a T-shirt and a pair of boxers—which is what I always slept in—would have to do. Then I cleared out, thankful she was functional enough to take care of things from there.

Eventually, I tucked her into my bed—in pain, but alive.

Deadline was already there, and he responded to the presence of a perfect stranger by immediately curling up next to her and purring. I know there are cat owners who imagine that their pets are bonded to them and them alone. I am under no such illusions. My cat is perfectly indiscriminate about human contact. He'll cuddle with anyone whose body heat is in the neighborhood of 98.6 degrees.

I was going to find myself a hunk of couch and call it a night, but I checked my phone one last time. During all my shuffling of poor, incapacitated Pigeon, I had missed a call and had a message.

It was brief: "Hey, it's Quint. Call me."

I guess when you go by "Quint," you can get away with being first-name only. I checked the time he had left the message and it was only a half hour earlier, so there was no danger I'd be waking him up by calling at a late hour. Besides, I had the feeling Quint was a bit of a night owl.

Sure enough, he answered on the first ring. "Quint here."

"Hey, Quint, Carter Ross."

"Hey, man, didn't want you to think I forgot about you. It just took a few days for some of my people to get back to me. But it should be worth the wait, because I think I figured out what you're looking for."

"Oh yeah? What's that?"

"Cadmium," he said.

"Cadmium?" I repeated.

"Yeah, know anything about it?"

"How to spell it. But that's about it."

"Well, I tossed those symptoms you gave me off of a bunch of my people. And then finally one of them said 'cadmium' and it was a major duh moment, because I should have thought of it sooner. It's a perfect fit. Every symptom you described is a potential side effect of cadmium poisoning."

"Huh," I said. "Did K and J use cadmium?"

"Not that I know of."

"So who did down in that part of Newark?"

"Oh, I have no idea."

"But, I mean, was there a specific kind of industry that used cadmium?"

"A lot of them did," he said. "It was used in dyes, in plastic, in electroplating. Then people started figuring how bad it was for you, so it's been phased out of a lot of things. It's still used in some batteries—that's why you have to be careful about how you dispose of them. It doesn't surprise me that there's cadmium down there. What's weird is that it would now be surfacing."

"Oh, it's not so weird."

"What do you mean?" he asked.

I told Quint about Alan Sutherlin's admission to me—that all that dirt was not only still dirty, it was being freshly stirred up. "What I can't figure out is how the site managed to pass muster with the state DEP when it was only fake remediated," I finished.

Quint let out the kind of laugh that told me he didn't find anything funny. "Yeah, unfortunately, that doesn't surprise me."

"Why do you say that?"

"Because I hang around with all these environmentalists, and they complain more about the state DEP than they do about the people actually doing the polluting. All I hear about from them is how the DEP doesn't actually do its job anymore. It makes other people do it."

"Explain, please."

"This is New Jersey, right? We lead the nation in Superfund sites. And we've got a list of something like eighteen thousand other contaminated sites around the state. That's down from twenty thousand or so, but we're still finding new ones all the time. Some of them are pretty small potatoes—any place that used to be a gas station or a Laundromat is probably contaminated. It used to be, anyone who wanted to do something with one of those properties had to hire an environmental consultant who had to submit a series of documents to DEP and then wait for approval before they could go on with their project. And it could take forever, because you would, say, submit an assessment and then wait ten months for DEP to say it was okay. Then you'd submit a remediation plan and wait another ten months. You had stuff that was literally getting held up for years.

"So," he continued, "a few years back, everyone got so fed up that they changed the laws. They invented something called the Licensed Site Remediation Professional. LSRP for short. The environmental consultants had to apply to become LSRPs, but once they did, they were essentially allowed to do everything on their own. They still have to submit paperwork to DEP, but they don't have to wait for approval anymore. The LSRP's green light is enough to keep things moving forward. I guess the DEP still reads the paperwork. Eventually. Theoretically. So there's still some oversight. But, in some ways, my environmental buddies are right: the DEP is letting the LSRPs do its job for it."

"So, if I'm being generous toward DEP, I'd say they streamlined an onerous regulatory process by privatizing it," I said. "But if I'm being unkind, I say they're opening themselves up to the possibility that the foxes will be guarding the henhouse."

"More or less, yeah. The LSRP is supposed to act independently and is bound by a code of ethics that says they can't get too cozy with the developers. I'm not sure if it actually works out that way all the time. The DEP hopes it can keep the fear of God in these LSRPs because it's ultimately their ass on the line. If the LSRP certifies a site as being clean and it turns out later to be causing groundwater contamination because of shoddy work by the LSRP? The LSRP could get fined or lose his license. But otherwise? But there's nothing beyond the LSRP's say-so that a cleanup has actually been done."

I absorbed this for a moment. "But you said the LSRP does have to file a bunch of paperwork, yes?"

"Yeah, I guess. But I've seen it and I think even I could fake it. I'm sure someone who really knew what they were doing would have no problem filling in the forms in a way that passed muster. So why would that matter?"

"It matters because those are public documents, which means a nosy reporter can easily get his hands on them," I said.

"Don't get too excited. A lot of it is pretty technical. It wouldn't necessarily make a lot of sense to you."

"Doesn't matter. As long as it has someone's name at the bottom."

"I don't follow."

"Now, Quint, you know I'm a journalist and thus prone to cynicism," I said. "But you don't suppose, here in the very righteous state of New Jersey, that perhaps an unscrupulous LSRP might, say, take a little something under the table to sign off on a remediation that didn't actually occur?"

His laugh was genuine this time. "Yeah," he said. "I suppose I can imagine that happening easily enough. But it's not like someone is going to admit taking a bribe to a newspaper reporter."

"No, but I can make it obvious enough in what I write to make it clear that's what happened."

It was one of the things that a few years in the newspaper business had taught me: readers were smarter than we sometimes gave them credit for. You didn't always need to tell them the answer to the question was four. Sometimes you just had to tell them it was two plus two and have the confidence they'd figure it out.

It was a nice thought, as I drifted to sleep on my couch, that this would be one of the times I could make the math simple for them.

The next thing I knew, there was a ringing sound. It was coming from somewhere near my front door. I was unsure what that might mean, but then, slowly, as I emerged from the grogginess of sleep, it occurred to me: someone was on my front porch, ringing the doorbell.

I opened my eyes. Light was pouring in through the window of my living room. That meant—wait, don't tell me—it was now morning.

I wasn't hungover. Or at least I shouldn't have been hungover. I hadn't even been drinking the night before. I just felt like my brain had been dipped in peanut butter. Maybe some of the alcohol Pigeon had consumed had leaked into me by osmosis.

As I got to my feet, the doorbell rang again. "Coming," I said.

I looked around for big-boy pants, but they were upstairs. Oh well. Whoever was paying me a visit at 8:00 A.M. would just have to accept me in my sleeping attire. I went over to the front door and, through the side window, saw Tina Thompson.

And this is how sleepy I was: it didn't occur to me I was doomed.

"Good morning," I said, opening the door.

She was carrying a Dunkin' Donuts bag, which had to be for me, because she ate carbohydrates only on her birthday and select holidays. She was also carrying a Coke Zero. Again, clearly for me. She was dressed for work—brown slacks, tapered white blouse that flattered her narrow figure—and had probably already been jogging. I would have told her she was glowing if I'd thought it wouldn't get me slapped.

"Good morning!" she said, brightly. "Sorry, I knew I might

be waking you up. I just thought this would be a good time for us to talk about, you know, things."

Perhaps subconsciously, she looked down in the direction of her uterus.

"Great," I said, still not thinking for even half a second about my houseguest. "Yeah, definitely. Come on in."

Tina had just made it inside when, as if following instructions from the Awful Timing Handbook, Pigeon descended the staircase, rumpled and rubbing sleep from her eyes. She was wearing my T-shirt and boxers—and nothing else—and was clearly coming from the direction of my bedroom. She had gone to bed with wet hair, and it was now tousled in a way that made it appear she was coming off a very active evening.

Tina took one look at her and froze. Pigeon, likewise, stopped about halfway down the steps.

"This isn't what it looks like," I said quickly.

Tina's eyes were wide and I could practically see the synapses in her brain jumping to conclusions. What else could she think? Pigeon and I were both in our underwear—or, rather, *my* underwear—and she obviously hadn't just stopped by for breakfast.

Without a word, Tina turned and walked out the door. Heedless of my indisposed state, I went after her.

"Tina," I said, charging down the steps. She was already halfway to her car and walking with considerable determination.

"Tina, wait!" I said, having now made it to the driveway. "Let me just explain . . ."

As she reached her car, she whirled and threw the Dunkin' Donuts bag at me, hitting me square in the chest. The Coke Zero followed but, luckily, it sailed just to the right of my head.

"Explain what?" she spit. "How many different positions you used? Save it for *Penthouse Letters,* big guy."

"Tina, this isn't—"

"What? Are you about to tell me what happened in there depends on what your definition of 'is' is? Because that didn't work for Bill Clinton and it's sure as hell not going to work for you."

"She got very drunk," I said. "She couldn't . . ."

"Oh, terrific. Congratulations. So you only take advantage of twenty-two-year-old interns when they're drunk? That makes it all better, then."

"No, no. Would you please listen to me? She was drunk. I didn't know where she lived so I just let her sleep here. Nothing happened."

If Tina was listening, I couldn't tell. She was fumbling with her car keys, trying to find the little "unlock" button on the keypad—more than likely, so she could get into the car and try to run me over.

"You know, I can't believe it, but I actually feel bad for Kira," Tina said. "Because at least I know what an ass you are, and she's still going to have to find out someday."

"Would you please just come back inside? I didn't lay a finger on that girl. You can ask her, if you want. She'll tell you everything."

"Believe me, I don't want to hear it," Tina said, having gotten her car door open and taken a seat.

"Nothing happened," I insisted.

"I don't really care, Carter," she said. "Coming here was a huge mistake. Thinking that you were really serious about being a father was a huge mistake. Everything about you is a huge mistake."

She slammed the door. I had half a thought about standing behind her car to block her exit. But then I had another thought, one that involved Tina having to explain to her child someday that he didn't have a father because she had rolled over him with her Volvo.

So I let her go. She backed down the driveway, splattering the Dunkin' Donuts bag in the process, then pulled out into the street without looking back at me once.

I walked over to the bag. It appeared there had been two pastries in there, one filled with crème, the other with jelly. The insides were now oozing out of the bag, which had been thoroughly flattened.

At the moment, I knew exactly how it felt.

Over the next hour, as I readied myself for another hard day of finding news, I accepted at least seven apologies from Pigeon, both for her behavior the night before and for fouling things up with Tina. Eventually, I returned her to her car so she could go home, stop babbling at me, and change into something that wasn't imbued with ossified Colt 45.

The irony was that once I got rid of her, I immediately had to do what would have been her kind of thing: FOIA some LSRP reports from the New Jersey Department of Environmental Protection.

Technically, the New Jersey version of FOIA was known as OPRA, the Open Public Records Act. But that made it no less magnificent, in my view. I made a hasty return to the office, ready to paper the state capitol in Trenton with requests.

In my experience, there are two ways to go about this kind of thing. One, which is favored by some of my compatriots in the news media, is the Bull in the China Shop Approach. They assume that government doesn't want to give up its precious documents unless the issue is forced. They assume state employees are foot-dragging malingerers. They know the law—make that The Law—is on their side, so they storm in, making demands that they know must be met, no matter what. And they shake their angry fists until they get it.

The problem with this method is that, yes, your requests will be fulfilled. In approximately four years.

Hence, I go for a much gentler tack. Call it the Possum in the Auto Parts Store Approach. As a possum, I don't know which oil filter to use. I certainly don't have the opposable thumbs needed to install one. So I need help. And I assume the state employee actually wants to provide it—which, unfair stereotypes about government bureaucrats aside, most of them actually do. I approach with meekness, because possums are a very docile kind of animal, make it sound like I'm asking a favor (not making a demand), and thank them profusely for every small kindness they extend.

With this in mind, my call got forwarded around the DEP until I ended up talking with a nice-sounding woman named Gina, who, just my luck, happened to be the administrator of the Licensed Site Remediation Professional program. We established a quick rapport and I had already made two jokes and three self-deprecating comments about my cluelessness. Then I told her I was a reporter. She stiffened for a moment, informing me she wasn't supposed to talk with reporters. All reporter calls were supposed to go to the public affairs office. I promised her I wouldn't tell and pointed out I couldn't put her in the paper because I didn't know her last name. With that, she relented. She wasn't allowed to talk to reporters but, apparently, she could talk to possums.

She said if I had the LSRP's license number I could easily request whatever documents I needed. I told her that was the problem: I didn't know who the LSRP was. And there came my big break. Gina could do a search by property-owner name. And thus she could tell me that the McAlister Arms site had been overseen by an LSRP named Scott Colston, license number 510552. She even gave me his date of birth and business address.

Gina then directed me through the maze of the DEP's Web site to the form where I could make an OPRA request for all the documents filed by that license number. She even told me what to put in certain blanks so the request would be filled quickly—in a week or so. I thanked her profusely, stopped just short of promising to name any female children I had after her, then ended the call.

That it would take a week to get the documents was not a problem. I already knew they were going to tell me that Scott Colston had signed off on a cleanup that had never happened. Now I just had to do the fun part: find him and ask him why.

I certainly planned to stop by his place of business. But there was undoubtedly more in the public record about Scott Colston. So I wandered back to the Info Palace, as our newspaper's library scientists called their lair, where Kira was staring at her computer screen like it perplexed her. She had put her hair up with a pen—they must learn how to do that when they get their MLS degree—and was wearing another one of her prim and proper sweater sets, this time in lime green.

"Good morning," I said.

"Is it?" she asked, then looked down at her watch, which appeared to have mouse ears on it. "Oh, I guess it is."

"Do you really have a Mickey Mouse watch?"

"Yeah, isn't it cool?"

I just shook my head. It was getting hard to keep up with whether there were any cartoon characters/fantasy series/superheroes she didn't like.

"So I have two favors to ask," I said.

"Shoot."

"One, Pigeon got obnoxiously drunk last night and ended up sleeping at my house. But I swear to you, nothing happened."

She took in this news without reaction. "Uh, I'm sorry. What's the favor?"

"Just to believe me that I was pure and chaste and nothing untoward happened."

"Oh, okay. That's easy enough. What's number two?"

I slid her a piece of paper with the date of birth and business address of Scott Colston, plus a bit of background as to why I was interested in him. "Give this guy the full workup. I want everything you can legally give me on him, plus any illegal stuff, too."

"Oh, you're giving me a DOB? Hot stuff!"

"Is that all it takes to get you excited? A date of birth?"

"Well, for right now, yeah. You'll have to do a little better later."

"You trying to make me blush?"

"Would you like me to?" she asked in her I-live-dangerously voice.

Giving Kira that kind of challenge in the newsroom would be engaging in a game of chicken I couldn't possibly win. "No," I said. "Definitely not."

"Too bad," she said. "So how high a priority should I make Mr. Colston?"

"If I bat my pretty blue eyes at you, will you make it your top one?" I said, blinking rapidly and trying to look endearing.

"Let me just finish this thing I'm working on right now, then I'll get to yours. You are lucky I find nerdiness charming."

"In so many more ways than one," I said.

"Okay, let me get to work," she said, making a little shooing gesture. "Now go."

One of the many advantages of being male—or at least of being the kind of guy I am—is the ability to compartmentalize. Yes, I seemed to have more than one woman in my life. Yes, one of them was furious with me, while simultaneously being pregnant with—still trying to get my inner air-traffic controller to land this fact—my child. And, yes, they were both my date to my sister's wedding.

But as I went out to the parking garage to get my Malibu, I put those issues in separate rooms, to be dealt with at some later time. All that mattered now was Scott Colston and his business address, which was on Route 46 in Fairfield.

I enjoyed my ride out on I-280, passing a spot I had once written about. It was a patch beside the highway where authorities had found a sizable field of marijuana plants, being grown and cultivated by a group of miscreants who were, if nothing else, bold. To me, it spoke of the obliviousness of the road's travelers. According to highway-usage stats, roughly 150,000 vehicles had passed that spot every day for two years without one driver or passenger noticing anything. It was amazing what you could keep hidden in plain sight.

Leaving the highway, I merged onto Route 46, a four-lane divided road designed with collision-repair-shop owners in mind. They were the only ones who could enjoy a road so heavily trafficked with so many merges, bends, dips, and blind spots—and, hence, so many car wrecks.

My GPS eventually led me to Colston's address, which turned out to be in a strip mall on the westbound side. But I immediately became concerned that I had the wrong place. The strip mall was small, and its tenants included a cell phone peddler, a tax preparer, a dry cleaner, a tanning salon, and a pizzeria.

There was nothing that looked like the office of an environmental consultant.

I pulled into a parking spot and let the car idle while I double-checked my reckoning. Yes, I was in the right town. Yes, I had the right road. Yes, I had the right number.

It was just that the number corresponded to the pizzeria, a place called Tomaselli's, that occupied the unit on the left corner. Curious, I got out of my car to check it out. As I approached, it looked like any other server of tomato pie in a state that very well may lead the nation in pizza parlors per capita. It had a variety of come-ons in the window: Tuesday, for example, was family night, with two one-topping mediums and a two-liter bottle of soda for $13.99. It had plastic booths for seating. It had pictures of Venezia, Firenza, and Roma on the walls.

The only thing unusual about it was that when I pulled on the door, it didn't open. Tomaselli's was, apparently, closed. I checked the time on my phone. It was after eleven, a time when your typical pizzeria is gearing up for the lunch rush. There appeared to be enough of a workday crowd around here, and certainly enough traffic on the road, to justify being open.

Especially in a town like Fairfield, which a half century ago had become a repository for all the Italians fleeing Newark. Even now, it had to be close to 50 percent Italian. People in this part of New Jersey took their pizza very seriously. You could start a heated discussion by asking which establishment in town had the best crust or the best sauce. Places that couldn't compete went out of business rather quickly, and I couldn't imagine being closed for lunch was helping Tomaselli's stay afloat.

With my curiosity thus addled, I went next door to the tanning salon. Tanning is an Olympic sport in New Jersey, and the woman at the front desk looked like a serious medal contender. I couldn't say what race she was because, to paraphrase the immortal Snooki, she was neither black nor white. She was tan.

A few years back, a woman from Nutley, New Jersey gained brief notoriety when she was accused of taking her six-year-old into a tanning bed with her. Part of what made the story go national—all the way to *Saturday Night Live*—was that the woman's skin had approximately the color and consistency of a saddlebag. The six-year-old, who was very fair skinned, also ended up getting some face time on TV. For most of the nation, the tanning mom's alleged transgression was exposing this pasty little girl to potentially harmful UV rays. For a small subset of people in New Jersey, the only sin was that Mommy had not used enough bronzer.

The woman in front of me appeared to be in that subset. She was that kind of midforties where no one had the heart to tell her she couldn't pass for midtwenties anymore. Her name tag identified her as Vicki. She was about five foot four—five nine, if you counted her gelled-up bangs. She had hoop earrings that could have doubled as stirrups and her well-developed jaw was getting a workout on a piece of chewing gum. A Jersey Girl if ever there were one.

"Hi, welcome to EverTan. How are ya?" she said, with a thick-enough Jersey accent that "are" came out more like "awe."

"Hey, I'm good," I said; then, before I could form my next sentence, she jumped in:

"Lemme guess, you're going on a cruise with your girlfriend, and you want to get a good base before you go south. I have just the right package for you. I get guys like you all the time," she said, pronouncing "all" like it was a piece of equipment that should have been found in a woodworker's shop.

"No, actually, I'm not going on a cruise, I—"

"Why not, don't you have a girlfriend?" she asked not so innocently.

"Uh," I said, because that was a deeply complicated question.

"A cutie like you doesn't have a girlfriend? What's the matter? Too many to chose from?" she asked, and I may have been imagining it, but she thrust her left hand—with its bare ring finger—a little closer to me.

"No, not . . . not exactly."

"Well, if you get one, you should take her on a cruise. Have you ever been on a cruise? I love cruises. All I do is pack a dress and two bikinis and I just tan on the deck all day. It's awesome."

Vicki was leaning halfway across the counter at me in a way that made me think that if I felt inclined to ask her to go on a cruise—or to tan with her in one of her two bikinis—she would be inclined to say yes.

"I'm sure it is. I'm actually not here to tan, sadly enough. My name is Carter Ross. I'm a reporter with the *Eagle-Examiner*. I was curious, what's with that pizzeria next door?"

"What, you doing, like, an investigation or something?" she asked, like she found it amusing.

"Something like that."

"Oh, well, what do you want to know?"

"Why isn't it open?"

"Tomaselli's? Oh it's, like, never open."

"Never?"

"Well on Friday and Saturday nights it's open, yeah," she said. "But even then, no one goes."

"So the advertisement in the window about Tuesday being family night . . ."

"Yeah. I know. Funny, right?"

"Yeah, funny. You know who owns the place, by any chance?"

This stopped her. Up until this point, Vicki had had a rather pleasant smile stretched across her bronzed face. The moment I inquired about ownership, it disappeared.

"What does that matter?" she asked.

"Do you know who it is?"

"Maybe. Why do you want to know?"

"I told you: idle curiosity," I said, trying to keep it low-key, but she wasn't buying it.

"Are you a cop or something?"

"No, as I said, I'm a newspaper reporter." I dug out a press pass and a business card and handed them to her.

"Yeah, okay, so you're a newspaper reporter," she said, taking a cursory glance at the two items. "But how do I know you're not wearing a wire for the cops or something?"

"Uh . . . I don't know. Because I have an honest face?"

I thought she was going to suggest that she frisk me, but suddenly her smile was back.

"No," she said. "I have an idea."

Her idea started with my buying the BeachComber InTANsive package, which would entitle me to six twenty-minute sessions in the SuperBronzing SunBlaster 2400. It was the least expensive package they had—cheaper than the SunWorshipper FanTANstic package, for sure—and I was amenable to it, if a little curious as to how it would look on my expense report.

It was the second part of her idea that gave me pause.

"You want me to do what?" I asked, because I wasn't sure I had heard it right the first time.

"Tan in the nude," she said, matter-of-factly.

That, unfortunately, was what I thought she had said. "And what will that accomplish?"

"It'll prove you're not wearing a wire. That way I can talk to you. And I can tell you stuff about what goes on over there. But I don't want to end up being like Adriana on *The Sopranos*. You know, like, you're just going for a ride with your boyfriend, not thinking about anything, and then he pulls you off into the woods and, blam, that's it. And why? Because you talked too much."

The word "talk" came out as "tawk." The rest of it just came out as paranoid blabber. But there was no talking—or tawking—her out of it.

"So I just, uh, take off my clothes and *that* will prove to you I'm not wearing a wire for the cops?"

"Exactly," she said, like it needed no more explanation.

"Uh, okay. I guess."

"Don't worry, I won't peek," she said, then threw in a quick wink.

"Right. So where do I—"

"Come on," she said, grabbing me by the arm and escorting me through a set of curtains and into a room that had four doors on either side. She went to a door on the left side that had "3" on it, pulled a set of keys off her wrist, and unlocked the door.

"Here you go," she said, holding it open. "Just holler when you're ready."

I walked inside. Vicki closed the door. As I hurriedly stripped down, I eyed the SuperBronzing SunBlaster 2400. It looked like a coffin lined with fluorescent bulbs. I suddenly got what the 2400 signified—it was the number of places you'd get skin cancer if you spent too long in the thing.

I removed most of my clothes, then paused when I reached my boxers.

"You sure I can't keep my underwear on?"

"No," she yelled from the other side of the door. "You could have a wire hidden in there. Besides, you'll get awful tan lines."

I shook my head and went Full Monty. Then I climbed inside the tanning bed, turned it on, and closed the top.

"Okay, I'm ready," I shouted inside my crypt.

I heard the door open and close. Then, for some reason, I thought I heard what sounded like my car keys jingling.

"No offense, but I'm putting your clothes outside," Vicki informed me. "Can't be too careful."

She reentered the room. The next thing I knew, she was lifting the SuperBronzing SunBlaster's lid.

"Hey!" I said. "I thought you said no peeking!"

"Just had to make sure you didn't still have the wire on," she said. "You've got nice abs, by the way."

I groaned. She continued: "Besides, it's a good thing I checked on you. You forgot to put your glasses on."

She handed me a pair of green goggles with a black circle in the middle of each lens—like some kind of angry, black-eyed frog. I placed them on my face, feeling ridiculously exposed the whole time.

"Okay. Good," I said. "Now could you please lower the . . ."

"You know, you're pretty pale. Sure you don't want some tan accelerator? I've got this stuff called Black Storm that could really brown you up fast. I could help you put it on if you—"

"Just lower the lid, please."

She complied. As I was enveloped in simulated sunshine, I heard her pulling a chair next to the tanning bed.

"Okay, so," she started. "My girlfriend Trina has a cousin named Eddie whose best friend is this guy Tony. Now I don't really know Tony all that well, but I see him around, you know? He doesn't work but he always seems to have money. And he always pays for things in cash, if you know what I mean. And he's a little gross because whenever I see him he's like, 'Oh, baby, I could treat you so good, baby. I could buy this for you. I could buy that for you.' He makes me feel like a whore."

The word "whore" came out with an extra syllable: "whoor." She continued: "So Trina was talking to Eddie one day and she was saying, 'Oh, yeah, my friend Vicki just got a job as a manager at EverTan, and I guess Tony was around and he just started laughing. And Trina was like 'what' and Tony was like 'nothing' and Trina was like 'no really' and finally Tony told her."

I was so blinded by the lights of the tanning bed I was finding it a little hard to concentrate. But I sensed that Vicki wanted me to contribute to the conversation, so I said, "Told her what?"

"That this whole building . . . is owned . . . by . . . the mob," she said, inserting pauses between the words to make her delivery more dramatic. "I'm not sure if the other businesses even know it. I mean, the dry cleaners are Korean, so they're, like, too busy eating rice or whatever. And the guy who does taxes is, like, I don't know, Armenian or something. The guy who owns Ever-Tan is from Iowa and people from Iowa are, like, too straight for the mob, you know? But you were asking about Tomaselli's, and . . ."

"And?" I prodded.

"Well. After Tony told Trina and Eddie and me about this building being owned by the mob, I started paying attention to Tomaselli's a little more. Because they're never open—which is weird—but every once in a while you'd see these guys just showing up there and going inside. They'd stay in there for a little while and then they'd leave. It was like they were having a meeting or something. And then this one day, I'm sitting here and I see this really nice SUV roll up. It was a Cadillac Escalade. It was silver. Really nice—though I would *not* want to parallel park it. And you know who stepped out of the back?"

"Who?"

"I swear, it was Mitch DeNunzio. The boss himself. It was like something out of *The Godfather*."

I nearly sat up so I could look at her. Then I remembered I was in a tanning bed. And naked.

So I just asked, "How did you know it was him?"

"Well, I don't know, I've seen him on the news and stuff. I told Eddie about it and he was like, 'Yeah, that's him. He rides around in a silver Cadillac Escalade.' I guess Eddie had started doing some little things for Tony—which is *so* not a good idea— and he had seen the Escalade a couple of times. It's just wild, you know? You always hear about this kind of stuff and then, wow, there it is next door. I wonder if they kill people over there at night or something."

I was quite sure they didn't, which wasn't to say there weren't other nefarious things going on there—like Licensed Site Remediation Professionals using it as a mail dump.

"Have you ever heard the name Scott Colston?" I asked.

Vicki thought for a second, then said. "No. Doesn't sound familiar. Are you sure you're not with the FBI?"

"No, no," I said. "Just the newspaper."

"Yeah, I guess I believe you," she said. Then she lifted the tanning bed one more time and added, "You pretty clearly have nothing to hide."

I eventually was permitted to get dressed and leave EverTan, albeit with one more not-so-vague intimation from Vicki that we should go on a cruise together and a rather stern reminder that I should come back in a few days if I wanted my new tan to last. Also, she impressed upon me the importance of moisturizing.

As I aimed the Malibu back in the direction of Newark, my mind began churning. According to Vicki, whom I had no reason to doubt—and who had no reason to lie to me—Tomaselli's was a mob front in a mob-controlled building. It was like the former marijuana patch I was once again passing: illegal, but hiding in plain sight.

And Scott Colston, whoever he was, was having his mail delivered there, which meant Scott Colston was likely mob controlled, too.

Which raised more than a few questions about Vaughn McAlister. Had he merely paid the mob for a fake remediation? Or did his ties to organized crime run deeper? Was his entire business mob owned, with Vaughn merely serving as the legitimate face of it? Had he run afoul of the bosses in some way?

I thought about who the more likely killer was: a jilted lover like Marcia Fenstermacher or a jilted mobster like Mitch DeNunzio. It wasn't much of a contest. DeNunzio beat her on body count alone. He also was more likely to have a pair of black-sedan-driving hit men on his speed dial.

I suppose I shouldn't have been exactly flabbergasted that McAlister would have ended up involved with the mob. This was New Jersey, after all. But, in truth, I was a little surprised. For whatever New Jersey's reputation for organized crime may have been—and for whatever HBO Productions might lead you to believe—there weren't mobsters under every rock in the Garden State.

Yeah, there was probably a rumor floating around every town in the state that this pizzeria or that gas station was a front for organized crime. But the reality was that outside of a few industries—hello, waste management—the mob's influence had waned greatly, to the point where the rumors were likely all that was left.

Personally, I had never dealt with the mob. The mob to me was like an exotic elemental particle was to a physicist: I knew it was there, somewhere; and I had a variety of ways, both theoretical and experimental, to prove its existence; but I had never actually seen it.

Luckily for me, there was a staff member at our paper who had long experience with it. Buster Hays was our resident mob-beat writer. Within his several Rolodexes—Buster refused to digitize his contacts list—were a variety of old men with crooked noses and last names ending in vowels. And they were all legitimate businessmen. They just tended to have jobs that didn't involve showing up.

Buster had been writing about organized crime for us long enough that I think he knew every mobster in the state—just as they knew him. He treated them with no special deference. He was fair and forthright with them, yes. But he was fair and forthright with all his sources. The mob was just another institution he covered. It was no different than, say, the Episcopal Diocese was to the religion reporter. It was just that the Episcopal Diocese marked the bodies it buried with headstones, whereas the mob tended not to stand on such ceremony.

I tried to call Buster's office phone and cell and got no answer at either. I thought about texting him, then laughed at the absurdity: I'd have better luck texting the plant near his desk. Buster had only very recently acquiesced to e-mail as a valid form of correspondence. And even then, he still printed out all the messages he wanted to read.

Resigning myself to a far more ancient form of human interaction, I went into the newsroom and found him sitting at his desk.

"Hey," I said. "I was just trying to call you."

"I know you were," he replied in an accent that, much like Buster, came from the Bronx.

"And you didn't answer because . . . ?"

"Because I looked on the calendar and it's not Do Favors for Ivy Boy Day," he said. Buster refuses to accept that Amherst is a proud member of the New England Small College Athletic Conference, not the Ivy League. Hence, I am either "Ivy" or "Ivy Boy," depending on how patronizing he feels like being.

"What makes you think I need a favor?"

"You got that desperate look about you."

"Then I suppose it will please you to learn that you're right, as usual," I said.

Up to that point, Buster had not been looking at me—one of his favorite ways of making it clear to me I'm not worth his time. He finally turned, looked at me over the top of some drugstore granny glasses, and said, "Whataya want?"

"I want to know why the mob killed Vaughn McAlister."

He snorted. "What makes you think the mob did it?"

Without compromising Kevin's Mack's anonymity, I related to him what my reliable eyewitness had seen. Then I told him about Tomaselli's Pizza and Mitch DeNunzio.

"Great," he said. "Let's just drop by Kenilworth Heating and Air Conditioning and ask Sam the Plumber why he had the guy iced."

"Uh, okay. Where—"

"Never mind. It was before you were born," Buster said, removing the granny glasses and tossing them onto his desk. "Look, this may surprise you, Ivy, but even though I've written about them from time to time, the local crime families are not in the habit of sharing the more intimate details of their operation with me."

"Yeah, but maybe you talk to someone who talks to someone who might be willing to gossip a little," I said. "I mean, how did McAlister Properties even get involved in the mob in the first place? And which mob family?"

"Well, I do have a guy who might hear some of the stuff coming out of the DeNunzio family, and . . ." Buster stopped himself. "No. Forget it, Ivy. I'm not getting involved. The mob isn't like the Department of Community Affairs. They don't have public information officers whose job it is to take our calls."

Even as he was making a fuss, I could tell his brain was already churning. He just needed a little encouragement.

"I know," I said. "That's why I need you. Come on, Buster, you're the only guy left at the paper who even has a shot at getting something like this."

It was a naked appeal to his ego. But I knew it would also be an effective one. Buster took great pride in being the last of the old guard, a staunch preserver of The Way Things Were (And Still Ought To Be).

He let out a gusty sigh and shook his head. "Okay, fine. I'll make a few calls. But the last time I looked, I'm not running a free lunch program. What are you going to do for me?"

With Buster Hays, there's always a price.

In the end, it was just too much for Vicki to keep to herself. The visit from that cute Eagle-Examiner reporter had been the most gossip-worthy thing to happen at EverTan in months. And Vicki, who felt rather gossip starved ever since leaving her job at the health club, had to share. Just once.

Thus began the conversation chain. The first was between Vicki and Trina. It was one of those swear-to-God-you-can't-tell-anyone type conversations.

So, naturally, Trina called her cousin Eddie and told him all about it. She felt she was acting in Vicki's best interests—she wanted to know if Vicki could get herself in some kind of trouble for having blabbed about Tomaselli's to a reporter—and she swore Eddie to total secrecy.

Eddie hung up the phone and immediately dialed Tony. Eddie's primary concern was that Mitch DeNunzio knew where the information had come from, knew that Eddie was being loyal, and that therefore Eddie was worthy of more of the work DeNunzio had been tossing him. Tony thanked him for the information and assured him it would improve his standing with DeNunzio.

Tony had, in fact, never mentioned Eddie to DeNunzio. Not once. He was subcontracting those small little tasks he had given

Eddie—paying Eddie half of what DeNunzio had paid for the jobs, telling Eddie they were being ordered by DeNunzio himself.

Thus, Tony immediately began angling for ways this information could improve his standing with DeNunzio. Stuff like this was gold. It would make Tony seem like he was connected. Important. Worthy of promotion, even. He relished telling DeNunzio all about it.

DeNunzio thanked him for the tip, but wasn't terribly concerned. He could avoid Tomaselli's for a while, no big deal. Scott Colston had obviously been compromised. But that was almost inevitable. He had perhaps hoped to use Colston for some other projects, perhaps turn it into another nice little sideline. No matter. Now that he had the idea, it would be easy enough to create a new Scott Colston. He dismissed Tony and didn't give it much more thought.

It was when DeNunzio heard Buster Hays was snooping around, asking questions about Vaughn McAlister, that be became concerned. He couldn't, under any circumstances, allow himself to be publicly linked to McAlister's death. No venture capitalist wants to be known for knocking off the principals of the firms he invests in. It's bad for business.

Plus, the FBI reads the paper, too. And there's nothing more the Fibbies like than a high-profile case. Mitch had associates who liked messing with the feds, but Mitch never got the wisdom of that. He prided himself on keeping himself off the FBI's list, not closer to the top of it.

Yes, he had to do something about this. Buster Hays, he didn't worry about. He had dealt with Buster before and could call him anytime and trust him to be reasonable.

But Carter Ross? He was more of a variable. He might not be as reasonable.

So Mitch made a quick phone call.

"I need you to track someone down," he said.

"Who?"

"He's a reporter for the Eagle-Examiner. His name is Carter Ross."

"No problem. What do you want me to do with him?"

"For now, just find him," came Mitch's reply. "We'll deal with the rest later."

CHAPTER 6

I left my negotiation/blackmail session laden with two more of Buster's All-Slop shifts—a triumph, since he was trying to pin me with four of them—then took a trip back to the Info Palace to see how Kira was doing in her search for Scott Colston.

She was sitting in almost the exact same pose as the last time I'd seen her, except she had taken the pen out of her hair, which I found mildly disappointing in a way I couldn't quite place.

"Hey, how's it going?" I asked.

She looked up at me and frowned. "Did you get so drunk with Pigeon last night that you forgot how to spell?"

"No. Sadly, I was sober last night. That's not to say my spelling is completely beyond reproach. Why do you ask?"

"Because I think you spelled Scott Colston incorrectly. Is it C-O-L-S-T-O-N?"

"Yeah, I think so. I haven't actually seen it in print yet, because I got it over the phone. But I can't imagine there are many alternate spellings. Why?"

"Because he doesn't exist," she said. "I checked every database I know how to check. The nearest Scott Colston I found lives in Virginia. His DOB doesn't match the one you gave me. I

FaceStalked him just to make sure and he's just this guy who sometimes does karaoke under the name DJ Scooter. He doesn't have a criminal record, in case you were wondering."

"I'm sure his mother is very proud of him," I said. "I hate to ask, but would you mind looking at other spellings?"

"Already did it. I looked up Collston with two 'L's, Scot with one 'T,' Colstun with a 'U,' Colsten with an 'E.' I ran as many permutations as I could think of. Nothing came up with that DOB."

"Huh," I said again.

"You want me to tell you which databases I checked?"

"No, no. I'm sure you were thorough. Thanks for making it a priority."

"My pleasure," she said.

I took a quick glance around the Info Palace, which was momentarily empty. "So," I said. "You want to tell me more about that dress you're wearing to the wedding?"

"You mean the one that doesn't have room for—"

Her next word was interrupted by my phone ringing. It was Quint Jorgensen. "Ugh, I'm sorry," I said. "Believe me, I want to hear all about it. But I do need to take this call."

She exhaled noisily. "It's probably just as well. There's no point in getting all worked up when I'm just going to have Buster Hays walk by any minute and try to hit on me again."

"Ew," was all I could say. "Sorry to have to leave this conversation on that note, but . . ."

"Yeah, go," she said. I hit the button to answer the call.

"Carter Ross."

He didn't bother with introductions. "Dude, I just read the newspaper"—having just woken up, no doubt—"and I saw your article about the lawsuit. Why didn't you tell me about it last night?"

This was as agitated as I had heard gentle Quint since I'd

suggested he trim his trees. "Well, to be honest, I didn't even think about it," I said. "But I suppose I should have. I assume you figured out K and J Manufacturing is one of the defendants?"

"No, that's not . . . It is?"

"You mean you didn't know?"

"No."

"Then why do you sound so upset?"

"Because!" he burst, like it should have been obvious. "This is a lawsuit against a major polluter? This is the perfect thing for my environmental people to protest! I'm going to call up that lawyer. I'm sure I can get him interested in a protest. I'm going to get some of those construction workers to show up. We'll get the news media. This is going to be big. Huge!"

"But . . . you sure you aren't worried about K and J being sued?"

"Oh, no," he said, dismissively.

"Why not?"

"There's really nothing left of K and J."

"So you're not—"

"You're missing the point. This isn't about K and J. It's about the protest."

"But what are you hoping to accomplish, exactly?"

"Accomplish?" he asked, like it was some kind of distraction.

"Yeah. You've got to have goals. Demands. Something like that."

"I don't know. It doesn't really matter. What matters is that we're right and they're wrong and we can use the protest to bring awareness of it. It's so perfect. Everyone is going to have such a great time."

Quint had mentioned his love of protests once before. I hadn't quite understood it back then. Now I was beginning to think maybe it was just because he was lonely.

"Right, sure. Like a party," I said. "And when are you going to have this protest?"

"Tomorrow. Ten in the morning. I've got my car charged up and I'm taking a trip into Newark to file the permits right now. This is going to be great. Can you put something in the paper about it?"

"Maybe. I don't know. I can definitely get something on the Web site. They're more desperate for content. The paper might be a little more discerning, but I might be able to slip it into whatever follow we do on the Vaughn McAlister killing for tomorrow."

"Okay. Great. You don't mind that I tell everyone the *Eagle-Examiner* is going to cover the protest, do you?"

"Quint, I'm not sure I—"

"Aw, come on, pleeeease?" he begged. "Trust me. I throw a *great* protest. We'll have two hundred people. Minimum. We'll come up with really creative placards for your photographers. I promise!"

He seemed so excited—and I felt like I owed him, for putting me onto the LSRP thing—that I didn't have the heart to turn him down. Besides, if he really could get some of those construction workers and a decent crowd around them—and if Will Imperiale grandstanded a little bit—it might smell just enough like news that it would keep Brodie distracted.

"Sure," I said. "Count me in."

Quint's call reminded me that I had yet to follow up on his tip about cadmium. I wandered back to my desk and tried to get the computer sitting there to come to life. The computers in the newsroom are old enough that their processors are really a series of winches and pulleys, powered by running water—or at least that's about how fast they work—but eventually I got Google up on my screen.

Sure enough, a search on cadmium poisoning brought up a list of symptoms that matched what the people on Ridgewood Avenue had experienced. It often started with achiness, fever, and chills that resembled the flu, which I had experienced. It included respiratory problems, like the cough that some of my interviewees had reported. It could lead to kidney failure, like what had taken Edna Foster's life.

And it even could lead to broken bones. People who had repeated exposure to cadmium developed something called "osteomalacia"—which was a hard-to-pronounce way of saying their bones got soft. Soft enough that sometimes they just snapped.

I read about the first documented cases of cadmium poisoning, which were identified in Japan during the 1950s. A mining company had been releasing cadmium into the Jinzu River, which local farmers used to irrigate their rice fields. People who ate the rice were ingesting low levels of cadmium. But apparently it doesn't take much cadmium to have deleterious effects. So many people were suffering broken bones, the locals started calling it "Itai Itai Disease"—*itai* being Japanese for "ouch."

That soon led me to another unfortunate aspect of cadmium poisoning: there was no treatment for it. All you could do was treat the symptoms and try to stop inhaling the stuff.

Speaking of which, I realized I owed Jackie Orr a visit. She and her neighbors deserved to know what I had discovered, even if there wasn't much they could do about it. I pulled out my notepad, found her phone number, and dialed it. There was no answer, and I was in the middle of leaving a message when I got a phone call from her.

"Hi, Jackie, it's Carter Ross," I said.

"Hi," she said, her tone noncommittal. I could guess she was still feeling a little betrayed by the reporter who had so quickly dropped her story for another one.

"So I think I've got a line on what's making your neighbors sick," I said. "Ever heard of cadmium poisoning?"

"No," she said. "What is it?"

I gave her my full book report on cadmium and delivered it in an authoritative voice, based on the twenty minutes of googling I had just done. At the end, she said, "So how do you cure it?"

"Unfortunately, you don't," I said. "According to what I read, there are things you can do if you swallow cadmium, but if you've inhaled it, you just have to wait until it works its way out of your system."

"That's okay. Mr. Imperiale says he's going to take care of us."

"Mr. Imperiale?"

"Yeah, that lawyer you wrote about," Jackie said. "I saw your story about those construction workers and I thought that if he was representing all of them he could represent us, too. I called him up this morning and told him about all of us. He was really nice."

I bet he was. The twenty-odd residents of Jackie's neighborhood had probably just added to his potential score by a couple of million bucks, presuming he was ever able to get a score.

"He wants to meet with all of us tonight," she said. "He said everyone just had to sign a sheet of paper saying he was their lawyer and then he'd be able to add us to the lawsuit. He said everyone could get their medical bills paid for, plus damages."

"If you win."

"What do you mean? Why wouldn't we win?"

"These kind of lawsuits can be very complex. It's one thing to think you know what's caused everyone to get sick, it's another thing to actually prove it. Take your grandmother. You said she broke her leg. Weakened bones is a classic symptom of cadmium poisoning, but it's also a symptom of aging. Who's to say it wasn't just an old lady breaking her leg? Who's to say there's even cadmium? And, if there is, who's to say where the cadmium came from? The defense is going to come in and argue that there's no cadmium anywhere on that site. Then it's going to say that even if there is cadmium, the defendant had nothing to do with it getting there. Then it will say even if the defendant was responsible, the cadmium wasn't to blame for her broken leg or her kidney failure or anything else. There are a lot of steps to proving this thing, and Will Imperiale has to nail every one of them if he wants to win. You see what I mean? So you might want to tell your neighbors not to go on any spending sprees. Even if they do eventually get something, it could be years before they see the money."

Jackie met that news with her usual considered silence. I felt like the guy who had just delivered the news that the leprechaun didn't really have a pot of gold.

"Oh," she said. "Well, I'd just as soon put my faith in Mr. Imperiale. He seems to be a lot more positive about being able to help us than anyone else. At least I know he won't run off and write about a rich developer instead."

It was a well-delivered punch to the gut. And I probably deserved it.

"Well, just try to remember that a guy like Will Imperiale is ultimately serving his own interests," I said. "That his interests and yours happen to align is merely a coincidence."

Having already delivered the body blow, Jackie went for the big uppercut:

"He's not really so different from you then, is he?"

Hopelessly behind on all judges' cards, I had my corner wave the white towel by ending the call. I knocked together a quick story for our Web site about Quint's big protest, then my stomach told me it was getting to be pizza o'clock.

Thinking I might as well make it a working lunch, I located Tommy, who was talking on the phone. I pointed at my mouth while rubbing my belly. He gave me the finger—the polite one that Jersey people reserve for when they're not driving—and then, after wrapping up his call, started appraising me with a scowl on his face.

"Why do you look like an Oompa-Loompa?" he asked.

"An Oompa-Loompa?"

"Yeah, haven't you ever seen *Charlie and the Chocolate Factory*?"

"Which one," I asked, "the creepy one with Gene Wilder or the even more creepy one with Johnny Depp?"

"Doesn't matter. You could be cast as an Oompa-Loompa extra in either one."

"I don't understand."

"Have you looked at yourself in a mirror lately?"

I felt an instant sense of dread, like a woman who had tucked her dress into her panties but didn't realize it until she had already walked across a crowded room three times.

"Not . . . I mean, not really," I said.

"Come on, then," he said, marching off to the men's room. I followed him, entering when he held the door for me.

"Look. See?" He pointed to my image in the mirror. "Oompa-Loompa."

I stared at myself, unsure of whom, exactly, I was looking at. The features were about where they should have been and resembled the ones I knew. It's just that they had all turned this deviant shade of orange, like something faintly reminiscent of a Creamsicle.

Or an Oompa-Loompa.

"Oh my," I said, gently poking my face. Every place I prodded, the skin momentarily reverted to its natural color, but then quickly went Oompa-Loompa again.

"Yet another tanning-bed tragedy," Tommy said, shaking his head.

"How did you know?"

"Spend as much time around gay men as I do and, trust me, you know. Tanning-related accidents are a serious problem in my community. By February it can be like an epidemic, all these orange men wandering around bars. The ones who are also on steroids have these big heads, too, so they start to look like pumpkins. It's sad." Tommy sighed wistfully. "Anyhow, what led you to the dark side?"

"Would you believe I was feeling a little low on vitamin D and I was out of milk?"

"No."

"Well, that's my story and I'm sticking to it," I said. If I told Tommy the truth—that I had stripped to get a story—it would just become another thing I could never live down. I wasn't ashamed of having done it. But only because I was the only one who knew about it besides Vicki. And Vicki wasn't telling. She was too busy helping her face make the final ascent from caramel to chestnut.

"Anyhow," I said, before Tommy could continue his line of inquiry, "let's go grab some pizza. Having radioactive skin really stokes your appetite."

He followed me out of the building and down to our favorite pizzeria. On the way, I updated him on my various findings. Once we were settled in front of a proper meal—two steaming slices and a twenty-ounce bottle of Coke Zero—I asked him what he had been up to.

"I've been trying to follow Vaughn McAlister's money," he said. "Though, to be honest, it's a little hard, because he didn't seem to have any."

"Do tell."

"Well, start with his major existing properties—McAlister

Center and McAlister Place. I talked to a commercial real-estate guy who kind of walked me through some stuff. McAlister Properties is a private company, of course. So some of this is guesswork. But the guy said that Vaughn was having major problems keeping the buildings full. He had lost a couple of big tenants in the last year or two."

"Why?"

"Bad management. Bad luck. Some combination of both. My guy said there have been some security problems at both places—some break-ins, things like that. Computers stolen. Televisions stolen. The kind of heavy stuff that thieves shouldn't be able to take if the security force you've hired is even half awake. But Vaughn's wasn't. Same with cleaning. I guess his buildings had started to slip there, too. You can't go charging someone thirty-five bucks a square foot for Class A office space and then not keep it up. People have other options. And apparently all the commercial brokers in the area had started telling clients to avoid McAlister Properties buildings."

"That sounds like a problem," I said.

"Yeah. My guy did some rough math for me that said, based on the square footage of his two biggest buildings, based on when he bought them—and based on the debt service he likely had on them—that unless Vaughn had a roughly eighty-five-percent occupancy rate, he was going to start getting in trouble. Now, ordinarily, that shouldn't be a problem, because the vacancy rate for Class A office space in Newark generally isn't much more than ten percent. But I did a little undercover work. Now this, mind you, is another rough estimate. But I walked the stairways and hallways of both buildings and as best I can tell they're about sixty percent occupied. That means he's taking a bath on them."

I took another bite of pizza. "What did he pay for them?"

"McAlister Center went for forty-four million. McAlister Place was seventy-one million."

"A total of one hundred and fifteen million."

"Very good, Einstein. Now, again, this is a little bit of guesswork. But, basically, my guy said Vaughn had to come up with about six hundred grand every month just to meet his debt service. And that doesn't count staff salaries, security, cleaning, things like that. Plus, Vaughn had people working the McAlister Arms site. Even if they were just moving around dirt, that still costs money. My guy made a pretty convincing case that at sixty-percent-occupancy level, Vaughn McAlister was probably losing at least three hundred grand a month, maybe more."

I whistled, pulled out my phone, and punched up the calculator app. "So we're potentially talking about four million bucks a year," I said.

"Yeah," Tommy said, munching on pizza. "Tells you pretty fast where that cleanup money really went, doesn't it?"

"Or at least a good portion of it," I said.

"But that's not even the worst of his problems," Tommy said.

"Oh?"

"My guy said that, particularly after the financial crisis, banks are very vigilant these days about something called DSCR—debt service coverage ratio," Tommy said. "Basically, they want to know that you have enough money coming in from your existing properties before they loan you money for any new ones. And, in this case, he said Vaughn McAlister's DSCR was probably a disaster. There's no way any bank would have loaned him money for that project down in the South Ward with those other two buildings hemorrhaging so much money."

"Unless he had a couple of blue-chip tenants who might have turned his cash flow problem around," I said, then told

Tommy what Vaughn had said about his supposed "big fish" and the rumors about Best Buy.

"But if he didn't have Best Buy, he was pretty much dead in the water," Tommy said.

"Yep," I confirmed. "And sinking fast."

Tommy and I batted various theories around for a while, eventually deciding that he would stay on Vaughn McAlister's finances while I would pursue other angles.

We soon settled into small talk—Tommy was urging me to continue tanning, saying it was the only way to make the orange go away—and we were just about done with our pizza repast when my phone rang.

The number came up "Restricted." Ordinary people often choose not to answer such calls. Reporters typically answer them on the first ring. An overdeveloped sense of curiosity can be annoying that way.

"Carter Ross."

"Hi, this is Lisa Denbigh. You were looking to speak with me?" she said in a southern accent that was thick as a Georgia pine forest.

"Yes, hello, Ms. Denbigh. Thanks for getting back to me."

Tommy tilted his head as soon as I said, "Denbigh." I had told him all about the former Mrs. McAlister.

"I got your Facebook message yesterday," she said. "Then I heard from my parents you had called them, too. So I thought you were probably pretty eager to talk."

"I am. Did you . . . I assume you heard about Vaughn, yes?"

A brief silence was followed by, "Yes."

"Sorry for your loss," I said.

Another silence. Then: "To tell you the truth, I'm not sure

how to feel about it. There were times a few years ago when I probably would have killed the cheatin' son of a bitch myself."

Now the silence was on my end, mostly because I didn't know what to say. She quickly filled it with: "I'm sorry. That was . . . I didn't mean it like that, I just . . . We've been through a lot, Vaughn and I. And when I saw the article about him being killed, it brought back a lot of memories, some of them good, some of them bad."

"Tell me about the good first," I said, just to get her talking.

"Are you doing some kind of obituary or something?" she asked.

"Something like that, yes."

"Well, Vaughn was . . . He was like a big, bright comet flashing through the sky. We both ran in a pretty fast crowd but he was still hard to keep up with. Everything was big, bigger, biggest when it came to Vaughn. My friends thought I fell in love with him because of his money, but I really fell in love with him not for what he was but for what he was going to be."

"What do you mean?"

"Vaughn was a dreamer. But he wasn't one of those pathetic dreamers whose dreams were never going to come true. You felt like he was the kind of dreamer who was going to work so hard he was going to force things to turn out just the way he said they would. He could . . . see things in ways that ordinary people couldn't, but he could also make them happen. He was so focused. He always said he was going to be like Donald Trump, but with good hair."

"So the money was just a side benefit?" I asked.

"Oh, honey, he never really had money. He just acted like he did, because he knew the only way people would give him money is if they thought he already had lots of it. We had a prenup that protected his share of the company but said I got half of everything else. Well, let me tell you, five years later, half of nothing was still nothing."

That certainly helped explain the variety of debts she had rung up.

"Had you been in touch with him recently?" I asked.

"Yeah, we probably talked about a week ago, actually."

"Did you talk to him frequently?"

"I guess we talked from time to time, yeah. Vaughn was the kind of guy who wanted to be friends with everyone, even his ex-wife. I think he kept in touch with everyone he ever met. It used to drive me nuts when I was married to him, because he would talk to old girlfriends. Then I just sort of realized that's who he was. He couldn't stand the thought of anyone not liking him. It was sort of sad, I guess. But sort of sweet, too."

"So you were still fond of him?" I asked, trying to circle around to the question I really wanted to ask.

"Oh, I suppose. Vaughn McAlister was hard not to like. Even when he cheated on me I couldn't hate him too much. He had a big heart, and if he was guilty of anything, it was following it everywhere it told him to go."

"Where had it been telling him to go lately?" I asked.

"What do you mean?"

Time to spit it out: "Were you two talking about getting back together?"

She didn't immediately answer my question. She just laughed. It was a real laugh: high and clear and strangely sunny, given the topic of conversation.

"Oh, shoot, honey, where would you get a crazy idea like that?" she asked.

"Someone told me you guys might be rekindling."

"Who?"

"Can't say."

"Let me guess. It was his dad, right? You don't even have to tell me. I know it was his dad."

"What makes you say that?"

"Vaughn's daddy was always sweet on me, bless his heart. He always had this joke that he was going to run off with me. I think he always hoped Vaughn and I would get back together and have a bunch of babies. But, oh goodness, no. That ship has sailed. It sailed three years and three therapists ago. I'm not saying I've got much in my life figured out. I'm probably a bit of a mess, actually. But I can say this: no way were Vaughn and I getting back together. I wouldn't if he begged me, and I don't think he was going to be begging me anytime soon."

"Why not?"

"He and Fenstermonster . . . sorry, that was my little name for her. He and Marcia were really quite happy together."

"They weren't having any trouble?" I asked.

"No, they seemed pretty blissful. In a way, it made me feel a little better about how things ended between Vaughn and I. We weren't that happy anyway. He probably did me a favor by cheating on me. And at least he cheated on me with a woman he really ended up loving, not some bimbo. I think if anything he was fixing to marry her. Or at least that was how he was talking."

"So let's just say, hypothetically speaking, that Barry McAlister said Vaughn and Marcia were having trouble. What would you make out of that?"

"Probably just wishful thinking on Barry's part," she said. "He never really liked Fenstermonster that much. Sorry, he never liked Marcia that much. He was just talking out of his ass, if you'll excuse the expression."

"No, no, it's fine," I said.

"Anyhow, I'm here at the hairdresser and she's ready for me. Anything else you want to know about Vaughn?"

"That depends. Anything else you want to tell me?"

"Not really," she said.

I thought the call was going to end there, but then she added, "Except I really do hope he rests in peace."

We ended the call and I drummed my fingers on the table for a moment. It was becoming apparent that Vaughn McAlister's problems had gone well beyond a jealous girlfriend—and that the girlfriend in question probably wasn't even jealous. Weighing my sources objectively, the sober ex-wife with no real skin in the game had more credibility than the drunk father who was too distraught to think straight. I had to face that I had been a little quick to judge Marcia Fenstermacher.

"Well?" Tommy said.

"Well, I think I know what I have to do next."

"What's that?"

"Apologize to Marcia Fenstermacher for accusing her of murder."

"Why?"

"Because, one, I don't think she did it," I said. "And, two, she might help us figure out who did."

It seemed only right that I make my apology in person, so I packed myself off for another visit to McAlister Place. The security guard appeared to have been recently anesthetized, so I walked right past him and took the stairs to the second floor, where I pulled on the door.

Except the door didn't yield. I yanked again. Locked. I knocked. Nothing.

Obviously, whoever was currently in charge at McAlister Properties had declared a day of mourning for the boss. Either that, or they all realized there was no point in coming to work at a place that was on the verge of bankruptcy.

That made Florham Park my next obvious place to look for Marcia Fenstermacher. I had the address from when I had dispatched Pigeon there the day before, and I was soon headed in that direction. I was about halfway there, having just merged onto Route 24—not terribly far from the Millburn exit—when my mother, as if imbued with a sixth sense that her son was passing nearby, decided to call me.

And, because I knew she wouldn't call me during work unless she had a very good reason, I decided to answer.

"Hi, Mom."

"Hi, honey," she said. "Do you have a minute?"

It was never just a minute with my mother. But I said, "Yeah, sure."

"Oh, good. I have *great news.*"

"What's that?"

"Uncle Louie's gout has flared up."

"Why is that great news?"

"Because Aunt Linda says he's not going to the wedding."

"And . . . ?"

"He was sitting at your table!" she said, triumphantly.

"Yeah, still not getting why that's something to celebrate."

"Sorry, honey. I forget that you haven't spent as much time with the seating chart as I have. If Uncle Louie doesn't go, that means there's room at your table. You, Tina, *and* your new girlfriend can sit together!"

"Oh that's . . . that's just . . . super," I said. Then, to dull the pain of that news, I head-butted the steering wheel. Twice. The second one was hard enough to make the horn blow. It made me feel a little better. But only just.

"What's that?" my mother asked. "Was someone honking at you? Are you driving?"

"Yes, Mom."

"You're using a hands-free device, right?"

"Yes, Mom," I lied. My Bluetooth had been broken for three months.

"I don't want you getting a ticket. Plus, it's not safe. You know your cousin Jennifer got a ticket for that not long ago."

"I know, Mom. I was there when she told you about it, remember?"

"I just want you to be safe. Anyhow, one more thing. Do you have another minute?"

"Yes, Mom." I said, knowing her sense of time probably hadn't improved.

"Your father wants you to say a few words at the rehearsal dinner on Friday night."

"Why?"

"Well, you know the father of the groom is going to say something on behalf of his family and you know how your father feels about public speaking. So he was hoping you could say something on behalf of our family. You're really very good at that sort of thing. I'd ask your brother but he treats everything like it's a courtroom and it starts sounding like an argument. Do you think you could come up with something?"

"Okay, sure."

"It has to be something nice,"

"Yes, Mom."

"And thoughtful."

"Yes, Mom."

"Maybe you could quote Auden or something?"

W. H. Auden was Mom's favorite poet. I'm not sure he ever wrote a word about love that didn't make it sound like one of life's most tortured exercises. Also, in Auden's world, it usually involved two dudes. But I said, "Okay. Auden. How about 'Funeral Blues'?"

"Carter Morgan Ross, don't you dare!"

Yes, my middle name is Morgan. It's a family name. And,

yes, I know I shouldn't have given my mother such a hard time. It was my small bit of revenge for her giving me three last names.

"I'm kidding, Mom," I said.

"Okay. Okay. And you're going to be here at four thirty on Friday, right?"

"Yes, Mom."

"So we can leave at four forty-five."

"Yes, Mom."

"And get to the rehearsal dinner at five, when it starts."

"Yes, Mom."

"And you won't be late."

"Mom, you're talking to your son who named his cat Deadline. When am I ever late?"

"I know. I know. I just want everything to go smoothly. You know how your father hates to be late for things."

"Yes, Mom."

"Okay. Remember: four thirty!" she said one more time. Then, feeling like I had sustained enough henpecking for one conversation, I hung up.

I completed my drive to Florham Park, to a neighborhood that was an even mix between modern McMansions and future teardowns. McAlister's was, naturally, one of the former—a boxy, beige thing that only went to prove that $1.2 million doesn't necessarily buy you good taste.

Before long, I was knocking on the door, ready to duck when Marcia Fenstermacher answered it and tried to kick my teeth in. Instead, the door was opened by an older woman who immediately answered the question as to where Marcia had gotten her round face.

"Hello," she said in a not-unfriendly way. "Can I help you?"

I introduced myself and told her I was hoping for an audience with Marcia. She told me her name was Sandy and that Marcia had just gone to the store for a second. But I could wait for her if I liked. I informed her I liked.

She invited me into a large kitchen and pointed me to a seat at the island in the middle. The kitchen opened into a great room, where the gawky preteenage boy I had seen in the picture frame on Marcia's desk was sitting in the corner, typing furiously on a desktop computer.

"That's Trevor," Sandy said. "He's our burgeoning computer genius. Trevor, this is Mr. Ross. Please say hello."

The kid mumbled something that may have sounded like "hello." He was freckled and flat-topped and I found myself wondering who my son—or daughter, or whatever the speck in Tina's womb would eventually turn into—would end up looking like. It stood to reason the kid would be tall and dark haired. I wondered if the hair would be curly like Tina's or—

"He's on that thing constantly," Sandy said, interrupting my inner monologue. "I really don't understand what he's doing."

"I'm just coding," Trevor said sullenly, like he was tired of explaining himself.

"As I said," Sandy said, "I really don't understand what he's doing."

"Yeah, can't say as I do, either."

Trevor tore himself away from the screen for a brief moment to size me up in a way that suggested he couldn't figure out why his grandmother let a six-foot-one moron into the house.

"Well, at least he'll never lack for employment," I said, then added, "I wish I could say the same for newspaper reporters."

"Well, I just hope he—" Sandy started. But she was interrupted by two things. First was Trevor saying, "Hi, Mom." Second was Trevor's mommy giving me a scalding glance and demanding, "What do *you* want?"

•　　•　　•

Sandy and Trevor froze. This man who had waltzed into the house had seemed friendly, but Mom was obviously pissed off at him. So they were no longer sure what to make of me. Marcia was still fixing me with a face that belonged in the Nasty Glare Hall of Fame

"I wanted to offer you an apology," I said.

"What for?"

I glanced at Trevor and asked, "Is there somewhere we can go and talk?"

This turned out to be a brilliant move, because it made Marcia realize that even though I was imprudent enough to have wrongly accused her of killing the man she loved, I was not so inconsiderate as to discuss it in front of her son and mother. Plus, by the time we moved into the study, which is where she shunted me, she had cooled off a little bit. She was wearing jeans and a sweatshirt and while her hair was still perfectly immobile, the rest of her was presented more casually than when she had to play the part of Vaughn McAlister's secretary.

"Look," I said as soon as the door behind us closed, "I asked you some pretty pointed questions yesterday, and I just wanted to say I was sorry. I had caught hold of a little bit of gossip about you and Vaughn being on the rocks and him jumping back to his ex-wife. I know now it wasn't true, but it made me jump to certain conclusions. Then we heard from one of your neighbors there was loud yelling coming from the house Monday night . . ."

"Uff, probably Mrs. Peters," Marcia said. "She's a busybody of the first order but she also can't hear that well. I just . . . Trevor and I got in a little fight about his homework."

"Yeah, anyway, I'm sorry. You were pretty clearly having the worst day of your life and I didn't make it any better. Sometimes the first quasi-plausible explanation is the one that a lazy mind seizes, but that doesn't make it right."

She had her arms crossed—I do believe they call it a defensive posture—but most reasonable people have a hard time staying too mad when someone is laying the mea culpa on three layers thick. If there's one good thing about screwing up as often as I do, it's that you become a virtuoso at apologies.

"Why are you telling me this?" she demanded.

"Well, to be honest, my executive editor knew Vaughn as a kid. So he's got a personal interest in this story, which gives me a personal interest, too. Plus, I'm more than a little curious myself at this point. So I'm hoping maybe you can help me figure out who did this."

"Why should I?"

"Well, let me ask you this: have you heard from the police yet?"

"No."

Her arms were still crossed. But at least now I had redirected some of her anger at a different target.

"Don't you think it's a little strange that they wouldn't have contacted you by this point? You're not only his significant other, you're his secretary. Wouldn't any diligent investigator want to talk to you? I mean, no one knew every facet of Vaughn's life better than you."

"Yes, I just thought . . . I thought maybe they just hadn't gotten to me yet."

"I'm sorry to tell you this, but they might not get to you ever," I said. "Our sources are telling us no one in city hall wants to bring much attention to Vaughn's life or death due to some of his property purchases. I had two officers in the Newark Police Department tell me in different ways that the case wasn't a priority. And lord knows they've got other murders to solve. At this point, it seems like the *Eagle-Examiner* is the only institution in Newark that wants to see Vaughn's killer brought to justice. So I'd really appreciate your help."

The arms finally dropped to her sides. She flopped into one

of two easy chairs in the corner of the study and pointed me to the other one.

"Have a seat," she said.

"Thanks."

She rubbed her temples and closed her eyes for a moment. Her brain had been experiencing a serious bear market, but it was doing its best to stage a rally. Finally, she said, "Okay, what do you want to know about?"

No point in sugarcoating things. "This is a hard question to ask. But please try to understand I'm trying to find the truth. And the truth isn't always pretty. Is it possible Vaughn had gotten involved with the mob?"

She looked legitimately dumbstruck. "The mob? Why would he do that?"

"Maybe he needed the money? Maybe he went to them for a loan for the company that he couldn't pay back?"

"But he . . . The company had plenty of money."

"It did?"

"Well, yeah. I saw everything that crossed Vaughn's desk. One of the things that he always had to sign off on were the quarterly profit-and-loss statements we submitted to the banks where we had loans. You always have to list assets and equities. I can't pretend like I knew how to read everything on those statements. But in the last one, I swore I saw the McAlister Properties reserve account had something like eight million dollars in it."

"Seriously? Do you have one of those statements for me to take a look at?"

"Not here. But I can show you if you come into the office tomorrow."

"Okay." I was still trying to process what I had just heard as I moved on to the next topic of interest. "Another question: do you know the name Scott Colston?"

She looked down and to the right as she groped through her memory. "Yes, but . . . why do I?"

"He's the Licensed Site Remediation Professional who signed off on the cleanup of the McAlister Arms site."

"Oh, right. Yes. I guess I've seen that name on some documents."

"Have you ever met him?"

She gave this ten seconds of thought before saying, "No. But that's not unusual. Someone like that would do his work on-site and I never . . . I never went to the site. Vaughn wanted me to stay in the office. So I wouldn't have had the chance to meet someone like that."

"Ever talked with him on the phone?"

Five seconds this time. Then: "No."

"This may seem like a strange question, but . . . are you sure he exists?"

"Well, I . . . Why do you ask?"

I told her about having traced him to a pizzeria that was seldom open and known to be frequented by mobsters, including one Mitch DeNunzio.

"Wait," she said. "Mitch DeNunzio is in the mob?"

"Mitch DeNunzio *is* the mob."

"But I thought he was—I mean, I never . . ."

"Did Vaughn have interactions with Mitch DeNunzio?"

"From time to time, yes," she said, quietly. She brought her hands to her face. They were starting to shake. "Oh my God. Oh, Vaughn, how could you?"

"Did Vaughn ever say what their meetings were about?"

"No. And it's not like I was sitting in on them. Mr. DeNunzio came to the office maybe one or two times. And there were probably another few times Vaughn went out to see him. I never really knew what it was about. I thought DeNunzio was . . . I don't know, an investor or something."

"I suppose in a manner of speaking he was," I said. "He's just not the kind you can afford to cross."

Another twenty minutes of conversation made it apparent Marcia Fenstermacher didn't know anything more about the woes that might have led to Vaughn's demise. She promised to keep pondering matters and said she'd call Vaughn's dad to see if he knew anything about Vaughn's interactions with Mitch DeNunzio. I promised to keep her in the loop about anything new I discovered. I departed with a friendly nod to Sandy and Trevor, who was still buried in his computer screen and oblivious to the world.

As I drove back to Newark, I rang up Kira, telling her about the four-thirty-or-else deadline being imposed by my mother and giving her my parents' address. I wasn't worried about her getting to the place. Kira was a librarian. She had been trained to find a children's fiction book that had been filed in the 700s, next to the books about how to draw bugs. Finding my parents' house would be no problem.

With the call completed, I settled in for a good drive-time think, trying to iron out this newest wrinkle. In some ways, it made sense that Vaughn might have had some cash in reserve. After all, he had gotten a big pile of money—$6 million from the DEP and $1.1 million from Newark—for a cleanup he'd only pretended to do. That didn't quite add up to $8 million, but maybe the business had stashed away some profits back before it started losing tenants and going into the red.

Still, that did nothing to address the main question: if Vaughn had eight million bucks in the bank, why would he feel the need to go to the mob for money? I can't say I was an expert in business financing, but in general I knew that La Cosa Nostra should be treated as a lender of last resort.

It perhaps spoke to my level of desperation and ignorance that I was starting to think my best hope for further understanding of this issue was Buster Hays. I found the newsroom's resident grouch at his desk, reading his e-mail—which he had, naturally, printed out. I wondered if he'd send his reply via the town crier.

I took measure of the newsroom clock, which read 5:48, then made my move.

"Okay, Buster," I said. "It is exactly twelve minutes until your All-Slop shift. If you expect me to be sitting in that chair in your stead when it begins, I'm going to need a little information from the organized-crime-beat writer. You got anything yet?"

"Just hold your horses, Ivy, I—" He stopped when he looked up at me. "What happened to you?"

"What do you mean?"

"You look like you took a bath in Cheetos."

"My unnatural coloring should not be an issue here," I snapped. "Don't be racist."

"Fine. Have it your way. Anyhow, I did talk to one person who might be in a place to know a thing or two about your fair-haired boy. He said Vaughn McAlister had needed a favor from Mitch DeNunzio, and that he might have been willing to provide a favor in return."

"What does that mean?"

"Ivy, I keep telling you, this isn't exactly an organization that prides itself on transparency."

"Yeah, but . . . a favor. So does that mean money or what?"

"No. No money. My source made it sound like a service of some kind had been performed. I don't know exactly what."

"And in return?"

"Oh, I don't know. Maybe they just wanted free office space? I kind of had to get this on the sly. The guy thought I was calling about something else and I dropped this into the conversation. If I asked too many questions, he would have stopped talking."

"So that's all I get? I'm going to spend all night chained to the All-Slop and all you give me is that Mitch DeNunzio and Vaughn McAlister exchanged unspecified favors?"

He leaned back, grinning in self-satisfied fashion. "Correct me if I'm wrong, Ivy, but that's a lot more than you could have gotten on your own. I got a few other lines in the water. I'll let you know if one of them jiggles."

"Fine," I said, feeling a little disappointed.

"Have fun shoveling," he said, then started waving me off. "Now go away, kid. You bother me."

"Trust me, it's mutual," I said, if only to offer a parting shot.

I returned to my desk. At least Buster had potentially solved one thing for me: a guy with eight million dollars did not need a loan from the mob. This, however, only renewed my curiosity as to why Vaughn McAlister was no longer breathing. Had he somehow reneged on the favor he had promised? Was that worth killing him?

I must have been lost in thought, because the next thing I knew a hand was being passed in front of my face.

"Hello? Anyone home?" Tommy was asking.

"Oh. Sorry," I said, shaking my head a little bit.

"And stop that," Tommy said.

"Stop what?"

"Chewing on that pen," he said. I hadn't realized it, but in my distracted state, I had taken a pen off my desk and stuck it between my back molars and was apparently giving it a good chomping.

"What's it to you?" I asked.

"One, it's gross," he said. "Two, never let a gay man think you've got an oral fixation. It just leads us on."

"What do you . . . Oh, never mind," I said, suddenly getting it. I'd never look at a Bic in quite the same way. "Anyhow, what's new?"

"More bad news for Vaughn McAlister."

"Worse than being dead?"

"Well, maybe not that bad. But it was probably a serious bummer for him right before he got that way."

"And what's that?"

Tommy settled himself behind the empty desk across from me. That was one of the only good things about being in a business with ever-declining staffing levels: plenty of open seating.

"Well," he said. "I started looking into Best Buy. I called up their corporate offices in Minnesota and got the usual runaround from their spokesman about how they don't comment on their plans for expansion until the leases are signed and blah blah blah."

"Which means they hadn't signed a lease yet," I said. "That's something."

"Yeah, but that's not all. I started doing a clip search and found out the guy who brokered the deal for their store in Springfield is a guy I know."

"Better to be lucky than good sometimes."

"Yeah, so I called him and started chatting him up. And what he told me—not for attribution, of course—is that they had been in serious talks about moving into Newark. They had their advance people out on the site and everything. It looked like it was going to be green-lighted, but then it all fell apart about a week ago."

"Why?"

"He said there were serious concerns about the financing of the project," Tommy said. "Basically, Best Buy became convinced the thing was never going to get off the drawing board so they had told McAlister Properties they were pulling out."

"But that doesn't make sense," I said. "According to Vaughn's secretary, he had a reserve account with eight million bucks in it."

"Do you believe her?"

"She's offered to show me their most recent P-and-L statement when she's back in the office."

Tommy considered this for a moment. "Yeah, but that still doesn't take into account McAlister Properties' problem with its DSCR."

"Uh..."

"Debt service coverage ratio," Tommy reminded me. "Remember, in the postrecession world order, no bank is going to extend money to a developer unless it's convinced the business has significantly positive cash flow to be able to repay it. Vaughn wasn't even breaking even. Heck, he was *losing* money. So to a certain extent it didn't matter how much money he had in reserve. McAlister Arms was a hundred-and-twenty-million project. Eight million in the bank is vending-machine money compared to that."

"And unless he could get his existing buildings back into the black, he was never going to get another dime in financing," I said. "And he was losing roughly four million bucks a year, give or take, which means he was running out of time to turn things around."

"You got it," Tommy said. "And obviously Best Buy had decided that was never going to happen."

I wanted to keep kicking around ideas with Tommy, but I caught the newsroom clock out of the corner of my eye. It was straight-up 6:00, which meant my time was no longer my own. The next eight hours of my life were going to be spent in service to the All-Slop. I excused myself from Tommy's company and trudged over to that part of the newsroom, ready to do my part to feed the digital monster.

When I got over there, I was surprised to see Pigeon already seated at one of the other desks.

"Hey, what are you doing here?" I asked.

"The All-Slop intern called in sick," she said. "They asked me this morning if I wanted to fill in. Since it meant I could sleep all day, I said yes immediately."

I stifled whatever sly comment I was about to make about that because Tina was walking by and I didn't want it to appear Pigeon and I were being friendly, talking, or even acting as if we were members of the same broad taxonomic family. I had successfully avoided Tina all day, and I hoped that had afforded her ample time to cool down and realize there were many explanations as to why Pigeon had spent the night at my house, and some of them might have actually been innocent.

Alas, she was eyeing me like she wished she had another Dunkin' Donuts bag to throw at me.

"What are you doing here?" she asked.

"What does it look like? I'm creating original content so it can be stolen by aggregators who profit from my hard work without paying for it."

She ignored my commentary and said, "Why is Buster's name on the schedule?"

"I suppose 'extortion' would be one word for it. I needed his help with something, and Buster's help never comes free."

Tina shifted her glance to Pigeon, who was pretending to busy herself with a computer keyboard that had suddenly become terribly interesting.

"Cute," Tina said. "You two plan this?"

My lungs expanded with the air I would need to object, but she didn't give me the chance to let it escape. "Never mind," she said. "I don't even care. What I do care about is why you don't have a follow on Vaughn McAlister."

"I filed the thing about the protest . . ."

"I meant a real follow. With actual news in it. Something that signals to our readers we care about this story and they should, too. More importantly, something that signals to Brodie he shouldn't replace you with a twenty-three-year-old that he'll pay half as much to work twice as hard."

"Brodie would never do that."

"Spoken like a reporter who hasn't seen the latest newsroom budget," she said.

Tina wasn't serious. I knew that. And if there was any further consolation, it's what I had learned through hard-won experience with Tina: when she was out for blood like this, she didn't really mean what she said. She just wanted to make sure she cut me somehow. I decided my best tack was to appear mortally wounded and hope she felt she had gotten her pound of flesh.

"Stop trying to look pathetic. It won't work," she said. "Does Tommy have anything?"

I thought about Tommy's contributions: one not-for-attribution source saying Best Buy had pulled out of McAlister Arms; another background source, with no direct knowledge of McAlister Properties' balance sheet, doing back-of-napkin math that said it was losing money; an anonymous tipster in city hall who said McAlister was sitting on more than a million dollars of Newark's money. They were valuable additions to my understanding of Vaughn McAlister's precarious financial situation, but it wasn't really stuff I could put in the newspaper—at least not responsibly.

"We're getting there," I said. "You're just going to have to be patient."

"Oh, I'm plenty patient," she said, then jerked her thumb in the direction of Brodie's office. "It's Mr. Hot Pants who's pitching a tent."

With that rather graphic image, she left me to the All-Slop and the relative peace that was, journalistically speaking, a fairly mundane task. By that time of night, it was mostly routine stories about car wrecks, homicides, the weather, and whatever other disasters, natural or unnatural, were unfolding across the Garden State. We reacted to the stuff that seemed interesting and ignored the rest of it.

When you're on the All-Slop, you're basically hoping the news comes in at what might be called Goldilocks speed. If you get too much, it starts to feel hectic. Too little and you get bored. You're looking for juuuuuust right.

This one was a little on the fast side, so I hadn't really noticed the passage of time until around midnight, when things started to slow down. I was in the middle of some idle chitchat with Katie Mossman, one of the All-Slop's regular editors, when she took a glance at the Web feed from the fire/police incident-pager network.

"Uh-oh," she said.

"What?"

"I've been keeping an eye on this house fire in West Orange. Sounds like a big one and now, apparently, it's a fatal. Incident pager said they just found a body."

"A fatal in *West* Orange?" I said, because if there was going to be a deadly fire in the Oranges, East Orange was the most likely culprit. It had far more aging tenements, the type that tended to burn easily and catch inhabitants unaware—because the tenants stole the batteries from the smoke detectors in the hallways.

"Yeah. I'm afraid you're going to have to write it up."

"I got two hours left in this shift anyway," I said. "Might as well fill it with something. What's the address?"

She looked at the screen again and said, "It's in the one hundred block of McAlister Court."

I swore loudly. There was only one house in the 100 block of McAlister Court—only one house on McAlister Court, period. And there was only one body likely to be found in that house.

Barry McAlister.

They rode past the house twice. Any more than that and someone might notice.

There were three of them—two thick guys and a thin guy, the same crew that had been hired to do the first McAlister job.

Two passes turned out to be enough. The place was exactly as their employer said it would be: a two-story Tudor on a private lane, reasonably secluded, with enough trees that it couldn't really be seen by its neighbors. At least not until the leaves fell.

Still, they didn't want to take any chances. So they stole a car, taking it from the parking lot of the West Orange train station. It was a Buick, at least fifteen years old—the kind that are easier to steal, because the antitheft safeguards hadn't gotten too sophisticated yet. They aimed to have it back before the owner would even be aware of what had happened.

They just wanted to make sure that if anyone saw a car turning onto Barry McAlister's private lane, it wasn't theirs.

In truth, arson wasn't really their specialty. They knew guys who were real artists at it, guys who could make it seem like a wire had shorted or an oven had been left on. Neither the two thick guys nor the thin guy knew any of those tricks.

But that didn't seem to matter to their employer, who said it didn't matter if the authorities knew it was arson. The only instructions they had been given was that Barry McAlister's house—and, in particular, his living room—needed to burn, and it needed to be a fire that would cover up as much of the evidence as possible.

Cook everything. And leave the body behind.

The body had to be found. Once again, that was key. The world had to know that Barry McAlister was dead. Same as it had been with Vaughn.

So they pulled up in the driveway in their stolen Buick and went to work. They had enough lighter fluid for a decade's worth of wiener roasts, and they used it to soak the living room. They thought about pulling some of the recycled newspapers out of the garage, so the fire would have enough fuel to get good and hot. Then they looked at Barry McAlister's shag carpet, paisley couch, and ancient drapes and decided there was enough polyester to keep things raging for a while.

The thin guy was the one who actually struck the match. The flame instantly leaped across the carpet, up the drapes and onto the easy chair where the corpse was resting.

The fire alarm started ringing shortly thereafter and that spooked them a little bit. Even though they knew none of the neighbors would be able to hear it, it made them feel like they were attracting too much attention to themselves.

So they took off, leaving a funeral pyre behind them.

CHAPTER 7

Before Katie Mossman could have much say in the matter, I told her I was heading out to West Orange. I'm not sure there was precedent for an All-Slop reporter being allowed to leave the desk. I'm also not sure there was anything Katie could have done to stop me.

It was always possible the fire had been an accident. Barry McAlister was a chain-smoker who obviously enjoyed a drink or two. He wouldn't be the first alcoholic to combine his two vices in a tragic way, dropping a lit cigarette on the couch as he passed out—to name just one way it might have happened.

Then again, it was also possible someone, perhaps some minion of the DeNunzio crime family, had killed Barry and given his house the ol' gas 'n' go, knowing that if the place was torched properly, it would incinerate enough evidence to assure the assailant of getting away with it.

I had been operating under the assumption Mitch DeNunzio had developed a serious grudge against Vaughn McAlister—for reasons I had yet to fully uncover—and had decided to take him out. Perhaps that grudge extended to Vaughn's old man. Had he seen something he shouldn't have seen? Had he known something he shouldn't have known?

Whatever it was, I wondered if Barry had even been aware of it. He was so lost he'd thought Marcia Fenstermacher had something to do with this. You would think that if Barry was aware Vaughn had been having dalliances with the mafia, that would have been the first thing he told me—not some revenge fantasy involving a jilted secretary.

When I got to West Orange, the short private drive that was McAlister Court looked like a staging ground for a disaster-training session, with an impressive assortment of firefighting equipment on hand. The municipalities in this part of the state are tiny—many just a few miles square—and yet they all have full fire departments that, on a given night, don't have anything better to do than respond to fires in other towns. I counted at least six fire departments represented.

There were also two ambulances; five marked police cars; six unmarked ones; a crime-scene-unit truck; and a K9 car, whose purpose I couldn't begin to fathom, unless they feared one of the fire departments forgot to bring its Dalmatian and would need a spare dog. There were people in uniform everywhere, most of whom were present probably only because this was the most exciting thing that was going to happen to West Orange all year and they didn't want to miss it.

There was also, front and center, a car from the Essex County Arson Squad, which perhaps began to answer my question about whether the fire had been set accidentally.

Then there was the house itself. Or, rather, what was left of it. I had covered a lot of fires in my time as a reporter, including some fatals. There weren't many as thoroughly torched as this one. What had once been a nice Tudor house was missing most of its roof. It was hard to find a place on the shingled siding untouched by flame once you got much beyond the first floor.

You generally didn't get a fire like that unless it had a

little bit of help from several dozen gallons of Shell's finest 93 octane.

I got out of my car and started skulking around. The blaze had been extinguished, though the air still had that sickly, unnatural stench that house fires get from the burning of things that were never meant to be burned, like plastic and insulation. There was enough darkness and confusion that no one really paid attention to me, the first reporter at the scene. So I had free rein to cast about until I found someone who might tell me what was going on.

It didn't take long until I found him. Michael "Sully" Sullivan was the mayor of West Orange. He was a good guy—as Sullys everywhere tend to be—and I had dealt with him a couple of times before. He was a local Realtor, a better-than-average quote, and had been mayor for at least a decade, mostly because no one else really wanted the job. In a town like West Orange, being mayor was a part-time gig that paid precious little—maybe ten thousand a year—and came with more headaches than that stipend could possibly be worth.

I was glad he was there, if for one reason only: when it comes to fire and/or crime scenes, mayors are great. They have absolutely no official purpose and are as essential to any investigation as nearby manhole covers. Yet, they often get briefed and will use the information to make themselves seem important to their constituents. You can usually get them to tell you stuff the fire and/or police department never will.

"Hey, Mr. Mayor," I said as I sidled up to him. He was looking at me blankly, so I said, "Carter Ross from the *Eagle-Examiner*. Isn't this past your bedtime?"

He took a moment to recognize me, registered mild surprise when he did, then recovered with: "Hey, Carter, nice to see you again. Isn't it past yours too?"

"Ordinarily, yeah. I happened to be pulling a night shift when this went out on the incident pager. I recognized the address as being Barry McAlister's place. You may have heard about what happened to his son, Vaughn?"

"Yeah, I read about it," Sully said.

"So you understand my curiosity. What's the deal? Did whoever went after the son decide to go after the father and turn this into barbecue season?"

He shook his head and said, "More like hunting season."

Even in the dim, whirling light cast by the various fire trucks and emergency vehicles, I could still make out the pained expression on Mayor Sullivan's face.

"What do you mean?" I asked.

He pulled his hands out of his pockets, blew on them, then shoved them back in. "Can I just talk on background and then we'll put something on the record later?" he said.

"Sure."

"Chief Delaney thinks Barry was dead before the fire started," Sully said. "We found Barry's car in the garage. The inside of it had blood all over it."

"Blood?"

"Yeah. A lot of it. Chief's theory was that someone waited for Barry in the backseat and, when he got in, reached around and slit his throat. The chief was saying the only way there could have been that much blood in the car is if someone severed Barry's carotid artery."

"Ugh," I said, flinching.

"Yeah, so basically the chief was saying it looked like Barry was killed in his car and then dragged into his living room—there were blood smears on the stairs, too. The perp then lit the body on fire, perhaps to cover evidence of the throat slashing.

One of the firemen said he had never seen a body burned so badly."

"Oh, man," I said, feeling that bit of news in my stomach.

"Yeah, but the perp didn't do as good a job in the garage. I think maybe he hoped if he set a fire in the living room, the garage would catch fire, too. But there's not much about a concrete-slab floor that will burn, so most of the garage survived intact."

"So, what, he was hoping the whole house would burn to the point where no one would be able to investigate and they would just chalk it up as an accident?"

"Maybe. Who knows? Whatever his hope was, he wasn't very good at it. One of the Arson Squad detectives said the living room still smelled like lighter fluid."

We stood there for a minute or so, both of us with our hands in our pockets, looking at this singed house. There was enough here to keep some determined investigators busy for a while. The crime scene guys would work on what was left after the fire. The Arson Squad guys would determine what kind of accelerant had been used to light the blaze. The medical examiner would get what he could from the charcoaled body.

There would be more information. But none of it, I suspected, would actually help to solve anything. The answers weren't in whatever forensics were left behind in that house. They were somewhere outside. I wondered if I'd ever be able to figure it out definitely myself.

"Did you know him?" I said at last.

"A little bit. I think everyone in town knew about what happened with him and his wife—it was a bit of a scandal at the time, her just leaving like that. After that, you'd see him around, at the grocery store and that sort of thing, but he was always sort of a tragic figure. I've probably sold ten houses in this neighborhood over the years and never once seen him outside or interacting with his neighbors."

My cell phone buzzed in my pocket—most likely Katie, asking if I had anything to report. I wasn't going to answer it, but it did prod me enough to ask, "So you mind giving me that on-the-record quote you promised?"

"Yeah, sorry to ramble so much," he said. "Just put me down as something like, 'This is a profoundly sad day for West Orange and the McAlister family. Our hearts go out to them. Yet even as we mourn this terrible loss, I am confident that Chief Delaney and his detectives will bring this killer to justice.'"

I jotted the canned quote in my notebook. Just as I was finishing, Sully said, "Now, if you want to do me a favor, please make it clear in whatever you write that this poor guy was targeted for some reason and that the police believe this was an isolated crime. I don't need everyone in town thinking there's some kind of homicidal maniac going around West Orange slitting throats and torching homes."

"Bad for property values?"

"No kidding," he said. "Just when they were finally starting to get better."

I peppered Sully with a few more questions; then, when it was clear he had told me all he knew, I called the mayor's quotes in to Pigeon, whose job it would be to immediately disseminate them to the insomnia-suffering masses surfing the Web at this hour. Before long, I started to feel like I was about as useful as all the unneeded cops hanging about. Chief Delaney, whom I was meeting for the first time, brushed me off with a "no comment." I couldn't find any investigators from the Essex County Prosecutor's Office. And I didn't know what the Arson Squad guys looked like, or if they'd even talk to me.

Around the time the last of the out-of-town fire trucks pulled away, I decided to call it a night, too. It was 2:00 A.M. My time on the All-Slop was, technically, at an end. Anything else the authorities might have to say could wait until the light of day.

The last thing I noticed before getting into my car was that the little angel statue, the one that commemorated the life of Elizabeth McAlister, beloved wife and mother, had disappeared. Maybe it had been knocked down by one of the fire trucks or shattered by an ambulance that went on the lawn or who knows. But it had somehow gone missing.

She was the last of the McAlisters. And now she was gone, too.

It took forever to get to sleep—lingering adrenaline being what it is—and morning came too fast. I had set the alarm for 9:00 A.M., knowing I had promised Quint I would cover his piddling protest. I swore that only a half hour had passed when it rang.

I dragged myself out of bed, ran the shower extra-hot, then finished it off extra-cold. It did some good, but not much. Sometimes, a shower just feels like polish on a garbage truck. I dressed in my best pleated khakis and finest white shirt and took the unusual step of packing a blazer, knowing I would likely have to go straight to the rehearsal dinner from work without time to stop at home to change.

Before heading out, I sent quick e-mails to Tommy and Pigeon. I asked Tommy to keep working on Vaughn's finances. I figured Pigeon could handle the follow on the fire/murder of Barry McAlister.

That left the protest for me. And not even my morning Coke Zero could generate much enthusiasm for that. I had covered enough protests to know how they normally worked: the organizers promised a big crowd of outraged citizens, only to get a dozen people, half of whom were actually there representing their own pet cause only tangentially involved with the issue in question. I could only imagine what kind of unemployed and underemployed environmentalists would crawl out from under the rocks at ten o'clock on a Friday morning for Quint's little gathering. The Society for the Preservation of the Yellow-bellied Atlantic Squid. Left-handed Ukrainians for Environmental Fairness. Friends of the Roadside Puddle by Mrs. Jones's House. I was convinced it would be a sorry assortment of souls.

Instead, as I turned down Irvine Turner Boulevard and neared the McAlister Arms site, I had to come to a halt. A long line of traffic had formed. And it wasn't moving. I saw some kind of commotion a few blocks up ahead. There were police vehicles already on the scene, parked at odd angles on the sidewalks. Some drivers were honking their horns. Others were trying to turn around and get out of the mess. A few had given up and were just standing by their cars.

I did my own U-turn, then pulled onto a side street so I could park and walk closer. As I neared the area, I saw a large collection of humanity that, if it decided to, could have turned into a very respectable mob. I'm not exactly the National Park Service when it comes to estimating crowd size, but there were at least five hundred people. And that *didn't* include the Shabazz High School marching band—in full uniform—assembled off to the side.

I heard their chanting from several blocks away. It was the old standby: "What do we want? Justice. When do we want it? Now." I found that pretty funny, since Quint had told me the day before he didn't really have a goal for his protest—meaning the people didn't even know what justice they were seeking.

It was only when I got close that I saw what was happening to snarl traffic. Roughly fifty of the protesters had linked arms and sat down in the middle of Irvine Turner Boulevard, blocking anyone trying to get to I-78.

The police on the scene were just watching them, clearly unsure of what to do. Quint had mentioned he was going to Newark to get the permits, so I was sure the protest was legal.

Blocking the street wasn't, but the cops were probably edgy about cracking down too hard. They didn't want to incite a crowd this large. Newark and riots don't have a good history together.

Out of curiosity, I sidled up to the first protester I saw. She was a young woman with long brown hair that actually had flowers in it, like she was trying to follow some sixties protest manual passed down from her grandparents.

"Excuse me," I said. "I'm a reporter with the *Eagle-Examiner*. I'm wondering: what are you here protesting?"

"I think there's some pollution or something?" she said, absent anything resembling guile. "But don't ask me. I don't actually know."

"If you don't know, why are you here?"

"I'm a friend of Quint Jorgensen's," she said, then corrected herself: "Actually, I'm more a friend of a friend. I don't really know him. I more know *of* him."

"And so you came to his protest because . . . ?"

"Are you kidding? Quint organizes the *best* protests. I never miss them. The food alone is worth coming for."

"The food?" I asked.

"Oh yeah, didn't you see? There are vegetarian sandwiches over there," she said, pointing to a long table with what appeared to be two five-foot-long sub sandwiches and a pair of volunteers behind them, cutting off pieces and passing them out. She pointed to a guy with a large foam Snickers for a hat: "That's the candy man. He passes out candy bars and that sort of thing. That tub over there has chips—don't worry, they're made from organic, locally grown potatoes. Somewhere around here, there's another lady passing out home-baked cookies. Protesting can work up an appetite, you know. Quint tries to think of everything."

As she was speaking, I had caught a whiff of marijuana smoke. I wondered if Quint had thought of that, too. I guess when you have millions of dollars and nothing better to do with it, you need not spare the extra trimmings.

I was about to ask the young woman more questions—to see just how facile her understanding of the issue at hand was—when the Shabazz High School marching band decided to add to the bedlam. With three sharp whistle blasts, the drum section began a thunderous salute. Soon every kid in the band was doing some kind of fancy dance step in perfect unison with the others. They circled around the street blockers, to the encouragement and delight of the other protesters. Then they climbed a temporary stage that had been erected and began belting out the Shabazz High fight song.

It was total chaos.

And in the middle of it was Quint, holding a bullhorn, grinning at it all.

Picking my way gingerly through the crowd—a good portion of whom turned out to be smoking a substance that was not tobacco—I eventually made it to Quint, who was waving his arms in the air, acting like he was conducting the band. The kids were blaring away, not paying him any mind. He pretty clearly didn't care. The homemade cookies weren't the only things that were baked.

"Hey, you made it!" he said, clearly pleased to see me, yelling so he could be heard over the music.

"Yeah, this is . . . this is something," I yelled back.

"I told you: I throw a good protest."

"I see that."

"Please tell me you've managed to come up with some demands," I said.

"My hands?" he said. "What about my hands?"

"No," I yelled, then got closer to him so he could hear better, to the point where I was practically yelling in his ear. "*De-mands*. Do you have any *demands*?"

"Oh, no. Not yet."

"So what are you going to do with these people?"

"I don't know, actually," he said, still seeming unconcerned. "The lawyer was supposed to handle the entertainment."

"The lawyer? Who, Imperiale?"

"Yeah. I called the dude yesterday, told him about the protest and he was all excited about it. He said he'd get some of his clients here to talk about the injuries they suffered. But now here it is game time and I don't even think he's here. You haven't seen him, have you?"

I glanced around the crowd, trying to locate a man with a big nose and fake black hair who looked like he'd be comfortable on the back of a Yellow Pages. I didn't see him anywhere.

"Nope," I said.

"Stood up by a freakin' lawyer," Quint said, shaking his head, but seeming in good humor about it. Cannabis tended to have that effect.

"Maybe he got called into court on some other matter?" I suggested.

Finally, the band stopped playing. Everyone gave them an enthusiastic round of applause.

"How the hell did you get a marching band to come?" I asked when the noise finally died down.

"Will introduced me to one of his clients. A girl named Jackie? She lives somewhere around here. She pulled some strings."

"Jackie Orr?"

"Yeah, that's her. She's right over there—the black girl with the bushy hair," he said, directing my gaze with a point until it fell on Jackie. "Anyhow, if you'll excuse me for a second, I got some work to do."

Quint walked over to the temporary stage and climbed its stairs and was soon acting as emcee, thanking the Shabazz marching band, getting another roar out of the well-fed, mildly buzzed crowd. I slid over to Jackie.

"So I understand you and Quint have joined forces," I said.

She hitched her antiquated bug glasses up her nose, readjusted the bag she had slung over her shoulder, and gave me her usual critical stare-down. "Yes," she said, and was not going to offer anything else.

"Look, I know you're upset with me, because you feel like I abandoned you. But if you had given me a little more time, I would have come back to you."

She shoved her hands into the pockets of the Aéropostale hoodie she was wearing. But something in her posture told me she was coming around, so I pressed on:

"And, besides, in some ways, things have worked out pretty well. You wanted a lawyer. You got one. You wanted attention for your neighbors' problems"—I gestured to the throngs of people around me—"and you pretty clearly have that, too. So what do you say we call a truce? I'm still going to write some kind of story about this. Even if I don't know what it's going to say or how this is going to play out, I'd like you to be a part of it."

I held out my right hand. She let it dangle there for a minute, then grabbed it and gave it a good, firm pump.

"My grandmother always told me to judge people on their intentions as well as their actions," she said. "I guess your intentions are good."

"They are," I confirmed. "They are."

Up on the stage, Quint was still revving up the crowd. He was asking if any of the plaintiffs in the McAlister Properties lawsuit were present, inviting them to give their "testimony." Obviously, Quint wanted to provide the entertainment, colorful lawyer or no.

"So what about Will Imperiale," I said. "How are his intentions?"

"Good. Really good."

"You sure? He was apparently supposed to be here this morning but he didn't show."

"Well, he showed up at my grandmother's place yesterday afternoon when he said he would," she said. "He talked us through what was going to happen, what we'd have to sign and what it said and all that. It all sounded pretty good. Everyone ended up signing with him."

That was unsurprising. Knowing how to work a living room full of potential clients was something of a necessary survival skill in the field of personal injury law.

"Please tell me you asked him some hard questions," I said. "About the timing of everything. About the difficulties of the case. About how long it might take before you got paid—if you got paid at all."

"I did. He said it was no problem. He said we'd all get paid. He promised."

Well, at least the man didn't lack for confidence. I wondered if he had somehow learned about Scott Colston, the fake Licensed Site Remediation Professional. Maybe Quint had tipped him off. Something like that would go a long way toward proving negligence. Still, nothing was ever assured in a court of law.

"You know he can't really do that," I said. "No lawyer, no matter how sure he is about his case, can guarantee a victory. Juries are fickle. Even if he got a bench trial, where it's going to be decided by judges, he might get tripped up on some minor statutory point. The defense is going to have smart lawyers, too, you know."

"No, no, that's the thing: he said the defense has already agreed to settle."

"It has?"

"Yeah. He said the details were still being worked out. And we might not get all the money owed to us, but that if we signed with him, we'd at least get something."

"Really? How much?"

"He said even someone like me, who only got sick once, would probably get like ten thousand. He said some people would get a lot more. Maybe fifty or a hundred thousand."

"Wow, really?" I said, mostly because I was too astonished to say much more.

She nodded.

I looked up at Quint, who was railing about the wanton negligence of McAlister Properties, the greedy corporation that cared only about its profits. Now it was starting to sound more like a stump speech for a midterm election campaign. No matter. The crowd was loving it.

"So, wait," I said, still trying to make sure I understood what was happening, "which defendant settled? There were at least fifteen of them in the complaint I saw. I mean, even Quint's family's old company was a defendant."

"This one, I think," she said, pointing to the ground. "McAlister Properties."

That was curious, to say the least. Between the construction workers and Jackie's neighbors, Imperiale had something like fifty clients, some of them with broken bones and kidney failure. One of them had even died. It was a multimillion-dollar claim if ever I'd heard one. And it's not like McAlister Properties' insurance would cover it, because the insurance company could rightly point out that its policy didn't cover negligence on the part of the insured. So the settlement would be coming out of McAlister Properties' piggy bank. Why would the McAlisters fork over millions without a fight?

Even though I knew the company had money—that eight-million-dollar reserve—I couldn't imagine Vaughn would so willingly give up his nest egg. His only chance of surviving was to get his two main buildings profitable again, a turnaround that could take months or years, if it happened at all. He needed all the padding he could get. Why would McAlister Properties—which sounded like it was creeping toward the cliff of insolvency as it was—agree to pay a settlement that would push it over the edge? And would the settlement, which presumably was negotiated when both McAlisters were alive, hold now that both McAlisters were dead?

"Well, I still wouldn't go on any spending sprees," I said.

"He said it was as good as done."

"Did he put it in writing?" I asked.

"I don't think so."

"What do you mean, you don't think so?"

"I . . . I mean, I didn't actually read it," she said, and at least had the good sense to be embarrassed about it.

"Do you have the agreement you signed with you?"

She fished around in her shoulder bag, produced an envelope that had Imperiale & Trautwig's logo printed on it, and handed it to me.

"Thanks," I said.

I opened it and pulled out a four-page document. It all looked pretty standard. And, sure enough, there was no mention of any kind of settlement or of any kind of guaranteed payments. Imperiale was too cagey to put any of that on paper.

Really, the only unusual thing about the agreement was the part about compensation. This was usually where there was language to indicate the undersigned attorney was entitled to one-third of any reward recovered by the plaintiff. But apparently that wasn't good enough for Willard R. Imperiale, Esq.

The bastard had conned these poor people—who probably didn't know any better—into giving him 50 percent.

"Thanks," I said. "Interesting reading."

•   •   •

Quint had finished up his speech and had finally been joined on stage by DaQuan Richardson, the first plaintiff to testify before this mock court of revelers. But first, the Shabazz band was going to strike up another song.

This rendered further attempts at conversation somewhat pointless, so I bade Jackie farewell and wandered around the crowd for a while. One speaker after another kept coming up to the podium to complain about the malady McAlister Properties had visited upon them, each of them encouraged by Quint. It made for some odd pairings—the superrich heir from Madison and the downtrodden people of Newark—but, then again, this was an odd gathering.

Eventually, I felt like my time at the show was drawing to a close. I had enough in my notebook to file something. The crowd was growing bored and starting to dissipate. The people sitting in the street had been persuaded to let traffic go. The marching band had high-stepped its way back to Shabazz High, a few blocks away.

Not wanting to be the last princess at the ball, I meandered back to my car, only to find it double-parked by an extra-long, silver Cadillac Escalade. I stared at the car peevishly for a moment, not understanding what was happening and certainly not noticing that a rather large man had approached behind me— until I heard his voice.

"Carter Ross," he said.

I turned to see a gentleman who had about four inches and a hundred pounds on me. He was wearing a black peacoat, even though it wasn't that cold. And I don't think it was because he had a circulatory problem.

"There's someone who wants to talk to you," he said. "Get in the truck."

I looked at the vehicle and that's when it hit me: a silver Cadillac Escalade. Mitch DeNunzio's vehicle. I tried to appear unworried, even nonchalant, which is hard to do when you're worried about soiling yourself.

I cast a few furtive glances to my left and right to see if there was room for me to make a getaway. Although I couldn't have beaten this goon in a wrestling contest, I was pretty sure I could outrun him. The problem was that I couldn't outrun the bullets in his gun.

"I don't suppose I could politely decline your offer," I said, bending my knees slightly so my legs would be ready to propel me somewhere else. And fast.

Then another voice behind me said, "Not really."

It was another gentleman, a little shorter, but thicker. He was wearing a windbreaker, which meant either circulatory problems were contagious, or he was also packing. My odds of escape, which were already small, had become infinitesimal. I thought about making a break for it anyway. But then I started to think more rationally: if my choices were, basically, get shot now or get shot later, didn't it make sense to delay the pain?

"Well," I said. "Can I ask where we're going?"

"Just get in the car," Goon One said, closing in and grabbing my arm.

I couldn't believe, given that I had so recently been surrounded by hundreds of people—not to mention a full marching band—that I was now alone, with no one to witness that I was being abducted in broad daylight. But the little side street where I had parked was deserted.

Goon Two opened the door for me as Goon One shunted me inside with something less than the courtesy he might have shown his grandmother. The seats had been arranged limousine-style, with one of the benches turned backward so it could face the other one. Goon One got in behind me and planted me in the middle of that backward-facing bench. Goon Two went around and sat on the other side of me.

Facing me was a sixty-something-year-old Italian man, dressed in a silver suit that was nearly as shiny as the Escalade. His shirt collar was open and unbuttoned more than, in my opinion, a man's shirt ought to be. Not that I was going to share that reflection at the moment.

"My name is Mitch DeNunzio," he said as the SUV got moving. "That name mean anything to you?"

"I know you're, uh, probably not a big fan of the RICO statutes," I said.

He chortled. "Ha. You're funny. This kid is funny, huh?"

Having been given tacit permission to express their pleasure, Goon One and Goon Two chuckled.

I wasn't laughing. I was still looking for some kind of escape. We were trolling through Newark at a very reasonable speed, stopping at lights, obeying traffic laws. Could I overcome the six hundred pounds of meat bracketing me and hop out at an inter-section? I wondered if Vaughn McAlister had been making the same calculations shortly before his head met the thick end of a baseball bat.

"So," he continued, "I understand you've been asking around about me. Having Buster Hays make some inquiries about me and Vaughn McAlister? Is that right?"

"Yeah," I said, cautiously. No sense in denying what the man already knew. Obviously, whomever Buster had spoken with had reported back to the boss. I wasn't sure how they had found me. But since I had written about the protest in the paper today, it wasn't hard to guess that I'd be covering it.

"Well, in that case, I'm glad we're talking," he said. "I know that sometimes certain . . . rumors . . . can tend to take on a life of their own with me. And I don't need bad publicity of that sort at this moment. So I want you to know: I had nothing to do with Vaughn McAlister."

Half of me wanted to say, *Great to hear. Now how about you let me out of this car and I'll go write that up?*

"You, you didn't?" I said, sounding more incredulous than was perhaps polite.

"No. Never. I actually wanted to be one of his investors. I thought McAlister Arms had a lot of promise and I know he might have needed some financing help. But we hadn't solidified anything. So why would I want to kill him when I stood to make a lot of money off him?"

"I don't know, actually," I said. "I'm told you two had some . . . meetings? And that maybe you did some favors for each other?"

"We did."

"So maybe that arrangement stopped working out as well as had perhaps been promised. And maybe you decided he didn't need to be around any longer because of it."

He was shaking his head. "Not true."

"Are you sure?" I said.

He chortled again. "You got a lot of balls. This kid has got a lot of balls, huh?"

Goon One and Goon Two followed suit and laughed. So did I. Though maybe mine was a little more nervous than theirs.

"Look, kid, I tell you I didn't kill the guy, I didn't kill the guy," he said. "We had a business relationship, yeah. That's it."

"Did this business relationship involve Scott Colston?"

This time the chortle was more of a chuckle. "Ah, Scott Colston."

"Does he . . . does he even exist?"

"Well, I'm sure I don't know," DeNunzio said, fairly winking at me with a tone that had gone appropriately sarcastic. "Because, of course, I have no association with Mr. Colston and know nothing about him. But let's just say it's possible that

Mr. Colston is not very good at his job. And therefore he may have signed off on Vaughn's remediation job a little prematurely. And if that's the case, well, the state of New Jersey ought to take away Mr. Colston's license."

"Yeah, if it can find him."

"I wish them all the luck in the world," he said.

"Okay, so you may have introduced Vaughn to Scott Colston's services. What did Vaughn do for you?"

"Nothing. He was one of my customers, actually."

"Your customers?"

"Yeah. I own a security company. We have contracts all over New Jersey. One of them is with McAlister Properties. We offered Vaughn some highly competitive rates and he took advantage of them."

My mind flashed to the last guy I had seen sitting at the front desk at McAlister Place—a guy who offered about as much security as a guard dog. A dead one.

Then I got it: Tommy had mentioned there had been a rash of break-ins at McAlister Properties buildings. Of course there had been. DeNunzio had probably been giving his goons free rein to steal anything they wanted in those buildings—which Vaughn allowed, as a way of payment for those so-called competitive rates, and as compensation for the so-called services of Scott Colston.

Mitch DeNunzio wasn't going to confirm any of this for me. But he didn't have to. I already knew. I also knew it meant it really was unlikely DeNunzio had ordered Vaughn or Barry killed. Why slaughter a golden goose like that?

"Okay, okay, I get it," I said. "So if you didn't kill Vaughn, who did?"

"I don't know. I really don't. I give you my word on that. All I can tell you is it wasn't me."

"Okay. Well. Thanks for . . . setting me straight, I guess."

We had circled back around so that we were nearing my Malibu again. The Escalade was slowing down. My ride with the boss was coming to a far more gentle end than I had ever thought it would.

"No problem, kid," he said. "And, hey, just so you know, I think that girl Vicki likes you. Cute girl. She kept talking about how maybe you'd go on a cruise with her. You want, maybe I could send you two on a cruise. Would you like that?"

"With all due respect, Mr. DeNunzio, no, thank you," I said, then added, "Trust me when I say I have enough girl trouble right now."

They had two more jobs to do. This was the second-to-last. And, in truth, they were a little disappointed. This employer had been awfully good to them, paying promptly, generously, and, of course, in cash. The employer seemed to be rolling in it.

The only real difficulty in the job is that they'd probably have to do it during the daytime, because it had to happen when the homeowner wasn't there. And time was getting tight. That's what their employer had told them.

So the three of them—two thick guys and a thin guy—rented a silver Honda Odyssey. "The silver bullet," one of them called it, jokingly. A soccer-mom car. Suburban camouflage. Perfect for a place like Florham Park. Perfect for this job, in particular.

They stole plates off a car at a local Kings supermarket and swapped them out, just in case, then parked outside the target home shortly after sunrise.

Then they waited.

All around them, the neighborhood came to life. The commuters left first. The high school kids went next. The men kept their eyes on the target house. Their employer told them there would be a woman and a kid inside—and maybe an old lady. Or maybe not.

264

They watched. They saw the woman. They saw the kid. There was no old lady. That was good. One less person to worry about.

A little before eight o'clock, the kid walked down the driveway and to the end of the block, where he caught a bus to school. He never once glanced at the Honda.

The three men kept waiting. An hour passed. Two. Their employer had said the lady probably wouldn't go to work, but she would definitely leave at some point.

Finally, after a few more hours, the automatic garage door opened and a minivan—noncoincidentally, a Honda Odyssey with tinted windows—backed out. It turned around at the top of the driveway and went out front-first. The woman was driving. She didn't look at them.

They waited until the minivan disappeared around the corner, then made their move. There was no time to waste. They pulled into the driveway and the thin guy hopped out. He went around to a back door and quickly jimmied the lock.

There was a security system—they had been warned about that—but it was an inexpensive model that was easily defeated. The door had two pressure-activated sensors, one on top and one on bottom. The thin guy carefully stuck Silly Putty over them so they remained depressed the entire time. He slipped inside the house and disabled it, using a device designed to trick the central monitoring computer into thinking the system was still on.

Then he hustled down to the garage and pressed the opener. The Odyssey slid inside. The thin guy closed the door behind it. From the perspective of anyone passing outside, there was absolutely nothing unusual going on at Marcia Fenstermacher's house that morning.

Once inside, they worked quickly. They were there to steal only one thing, but, of course, they knew they were going to have to turn the place inside out to find it. So they had to make it look like they were there to steal everything.

They took the kind of things a gang of home invaders—or a couple of fiending hopheads who needed money for drugs—might take, quickly throwing it all into the Honda Odyssey. All the way, they kept an eye out for the one thing they had come for.

After about five minutes, one of the thick guys found it. It was in a drawer in the office.

"Got it," he announced, loudly enough his partners could hear it.

"Great," said the thin guy. "Let's spend three more minutes trashing the place, then get the hell out of here."

CHAPTER 8

During my new-employee orientation many years earlier, I had been taken on a tour of the plant where the *Newark Eagle-Examiner* was printed. For a young reporter who had just come from a much smaller daily in Pennsylvania, the *Eagle-Examiner*'s operation was awe-inspiring, from the soaring towers used to print the color sections, to the rolls of newsprint so massive they required a forklift to move them, to the stacks of ink barrels, each one a latent source of literally millions of printed words. Newspaper economics were better back then, and the plant was cranking out something like 450,000 copies a day, employing hundreds of pressmen and a fleet trucks to carry it all.

Seeing all the work it took to put my stories into print was both powerful and sobering, and I have long endeavored to compose articles equal to that effort. I'll never forget the chill I felt as I was ceremoniously handed a fresh, slightly damp copy of that day's edition.

Then, at the end of the tour, I was taken back outside through the employee break room, where I met Inky the Parrot, the pressmen's mascot. And when I looked down, I got a different kind of reminder of the newspaper's place in many people's lives:

there, lining Inky's cage, catching his compositions, was the preceding day's edition.

It was more with Inky in mind that I wrote my story on the protest. I finished by two o'clock, at which point my lousy night's sleep was beginning to wear on me. After finessing a fresh Coke Zero from the vending machine, I returned to my desk, feeling like a new man. I was still curious about this alleged settlement that Vaughn had agreed to before his untimely demise. And, of course, I couldn't exactly ask him about it.

But I could ask his lawyer. I just had to cajole my computer's winches and pulleys into letting me search the paper's archives and figure out who that attorney was. After tripping through a few stories that led nowhere, I found a caption that went with a photo we had run of a ribbon-cutting at McAlister Place a few years earlier. I couldn't see the photo in our archives—just the text—but it told me all I needed to know. Pictured next to Vaughn McAlister was Kevin Ryan of McWhorter & French.

And that was a break for me. McWhorter & French was Newark's biggest—and probably best—law firm. And Kevin Ryan, the partner who headed its real estate division, was a guy I knew. Newark was a big city, but like a lot of big cities, its tall buildings were just a mask for the small town that lurked underneath. And in small-town Newark, Kevin Ryan was someone I bumped into all the time, at cocktail parties, at lectures, at charity functions.

As such, when I called his office, his secretary put me through.

"Hey, Carter, how're you doing, buddy?"

Kevin Ryan was an affable sort of guy who might have overused the word "buddy." We were more acquaintances than buddies. But I suppose there are worse words to overuse.

"Hey, I'm good," I said. "How are you?"

"I've been better, to be honest. I'm still pretty shaken up

about this whole Vaughn thing. Then Barry, too. And to hear the fire was arson. It's . . . it's unbelievable. I just don't know what's going on."

"Me neither," I said.

"Vaughn was . . . He was a gem of a guy. He was one of my best friends. This has been . . . This has been hard."

"I didn't realize you guys were that close."

"We really started out together," he said. "I was a young associate at McWhorter when Vaughn was getting out from under his old man's wing and starting to do his own thing. I did all his early deals for him. And it was sort of like as he grew, I grew with him. And you know what it's like when you're young. You work together a lot—long hours, that sort of thing. Then you start socializing together. I was there when he met his first wife. I was an usher at his wedding. It was . . . I mean, we started as a business relationship. But then it became more than that. I'm not sure I realized it until he died, but Vaughn was really one of my best . . . I'm sorry, I'm rambling. Is this what you're calling for? You working on some kind of appreciation piece or something?"

"Not . . . exactly. I am definitely working on a story about Vaughn. But it's less an appreciation and more an investigation at this point."

"Okay, right. Sure. Sorry. How can I help?"

"Well, I'm curious about this lawsuit against him. The one I wrote about."

"The one filed by that sleazebag Imperiale? I haven't seen it yet. But I'm sure it's crap. A guy like that would sue his own grandmother for giving him lukewarm chicken soup."

"Yeah, so why would Vaughn agree to settle it?"

There was no delay in Ryan's answer: "What? Vaughn wouldn't have done anything like that."

"Then why is Will Imperiale is going around signing up

plaintiffs by telling them he's already gotten McAlister Properties to settle? He's been promising some of them they'll get fifty, a hundred grand a pop."

"I don't know. I mean, with a guy like that, who the hell knows what he says and why? I wouldn't put it past him to lie, knowing that the bigger his class, the more he can get for their pain and suffering. But I can tell you, unequivocally, there is absolutely no way Vaughn agreed to any settlements."

"Are you sure? Could Vaughn have settled the thing without telling you? I mean, you do real estate law. Maybe he consulted an attorney who defends personal injury stuff who told him that it was in his best interests to make the thing go away?"

"No," Ryan said quickly. "I just—I mean, that would be . . . I wasn't kidding when I said Vaughn and I were best friends. We talked almost every day. You want to tell me he wouldn't have at least mentioned that he had been sued? And that he was thinking about negotiating a settlement? Even if he didn't want me to do the negotiation, which is reasonable given my lack of expertise in that area, I'm sure he would have asked me to recommend an attorney. Or at least he would have told me who he picked—whether it was someone here or at another firm. I just can't tell you enough: there is no settlement."

"Okay, I get it," I said, more confused than ever, particularly when it came to the motives and actions of one Willard R. Imperiale, Esq.

Was it possible he'd had something to do with the early demise of the McAlister boys? Had he forced them into a settlement and killed them before they could change their minds? That hardly made sense. Anyone who felt like challenging that deal later would easily win.

And yet, who else would profit from their death? Especially given that he had weaseled his way into getting 50 percent of the payout. Speaking of which:

"Got another question for you," I said. "I saw the agreement Imperiale had his clients sign. He's got them giving up fifty percent of whatever he's able to recoup. I had never heard of that before. Is that legal?"

"Good grief. That guy is unbelievable," Ryan said, and I heard what sounded like a hand slamming on a desk. "Okay. Sorry. You asked whether it was legal. The answer is: yes. Obviously, the standard is one-third. And I think it's pretty unethical to go for half under the circumstances. But the law says attorneys are entitled to 'reasonable' fees and the courts have determined that up to fifty percent is reasonable in certain circumstances."

"So there's no recourse for his clients when they realize they've been screwed?"

"Not really," Ryan said. "If he went for more than half, you could get him disbarred. But as long as he doesn't go for more than that, he can make an argument that he was taking a significant risk with a case this complex and that the higher percentage was merited. And unfortunately he could find case law to back him up."

"Okay, just wondering," I said. "Thanks."

"Don't thank me," he said. "Just nail the guy who did this to Vaughn, huh, buddy?"

There wasn't much more Kevin Ryan was willing to tell me—he couldn't exactly discuss McAlister Properties' financial difficulties when he was still the company's lawyer—so we ended the call.

As I stood up and stretched my legs, I saw Tommy and Pigeon sitting at their desks, looking suspiciously unproductive. It's never good to give interns idle time, so I decided to huddle them and see what they had been able to learn. I went and collected Pigeon, then presented myself at Tommy's desk.

"Hey, we're having a team meeting," I said.

Tommy looked up at me. "My god, what's the team name? The Newark Raccoons? Didn't you sleep last night?"

"Not enough," I confirmed.

"That will take its toll on your skin, you know. That's something you need to consider. Especially at your age."

"At my *age*? I'm thirty-two."

"Brittany Murphy died when she was thirty-two," Tommy informed me. "Something you should think about."

"I feel pretty good about my chances of outliving Brittany Murphy."

He just shook his head. "I'm sure she thought the same thing before, you know . . ." He made a strangling sound.

"No, I'm pretty confident Brittany Murphy didn't think she could outlive Brittany Murphy."

Tommy got a far-off look, then said, "Wow. I never thought of it that way. That's deep."

Missing Tommy's mordant wit, Pigeon was looking at us like she couldn't believe she was wasting a Yale education hanging out with people like us.

"Anyhow, back to business," I said. "Either of you learn anything of note or interest yet today?"

"I just got off the phone with Kathy Carter," Pigeon said. Kathy was the spokeswoman for the Essex County Prosecutor's Office and a friend. Pigeon continued: "She said the medical examiner's office determined that Barry McAlister not only had his throat slashed, he had also been shot in the head. It has officially declared the manner of death a homicide."

"Shot *and* slashed *and* burned. Jeez. Someone wasn't taking any chances. Did the medical examiner's office also officially declare who did it?"

"No such luck," she said. "She said the Crime Scene Unit bumped up the case in the queue, so they've gotten some stuff back. The blood in the car is definitely Barry's. I think maybe they were hoping Barry had put up a fight and that maybe some of the blood belonged to the perpetrator. But it was all Barry."

"My, the prosecutor's office was awfully forthcoming today, wasn't it?" I said. "We usually never get results like that this early."

"I think the Crime Scene Unit's funding is on the chopping block," Tommy interjected. "So they're taking every opportunity they can get to show everyone what a good job they're doing."

"I'll take it," I said. "What else?"

"The Arson Squad is referring all calls to the prosecutor's office. They haven't formally called it arson yet."

"Yeah, but those guys like to take their time," I said. "And we pretty much already know it's arson. So I'm not too worried about that. What else?"

"That's it," she said.

I pondered this all for a few seconds, then said, "Okay, type up what you got and send it to Tommy and me. And when you're done, why don't you go out to West Orange and work the neighborhood a little bit. See if anyone knows anything about the life and times of the former Barry McAlister that we don't. Or, better yet, ask if anyone saw anything shortly before he became the former Barry McAlister. I'm sure the police have already done that, but it'd be cool if we got it, too. And . . ."

I was trying to think of what else I could have Pigeon work on when Tommy raised his hand, as if waiting to be called on.

"Yes, Tommy?"

"She also might want to ask if there were any signs he was having money troubles," he said.

"Oh? Him too?"

"Yeah. I had sort of reached the end of my snooping on Vaughn, so I started looking into Barry," Tommy said.

"Which is exactly what I would have told you to do if you had asked. My little intern has grown up so fast."

"Yeah, whatever," he said. "Anyhow, it turns out Barry started selling off his apartment buildings about ten years ago."

"About the time Vaughn was starting the commercial side of McAlister Properties," I interjected.

"Exactly," Tommy said. "It looks like he was sort of selling them off one at a time. In dribs and drabs over the course of the last decade, he sold seven buildings for a total of $10.2 million."

"I'm sure he had loans left on some of those. But even assuming that wasn't all profit, that's not a bad little retirement account."

"Yeah, but I don't think any of it is left," Tommy said. "About a year ago he applied for a reverse mortgage on his house. And he just took out a home equity loan, too. So it seems like he was scraping around for cash."

"Jeez, what's with these McAlister boys and money?" I said. "They kept acting like they didn't have any cash, yet all the while they had lots of it."

"Yeah, are you *sure* about that?" Tommy asked.

"It's what Marcia Fenstermacher told me. And I don't think she was lying to me. She even promised to let me have a look at their P-and-L statement."

"Did you take her up on the offer?"

"Not yet. We talked at her house and she said it was at the office."

"You think she'd mind if I looked, too?" Tommy asked. "I might see something in there that lets us make sense of everything. I've done so much work on McAlister Properties' finances at this point I feel like I could apply for a job as their accountant."

"She probably won't want you to print things that are proprietary," I said. "But I think she knows the cops aren't showing much interest in Vaughn's murder, so we're kind of her only hope. But there's one way to find out."

Interns are sometimes wont to make things harder than they really need to be, so with Tommy and Pigeon looking at me curiously, I completed the thought for them:

"Call her and ask her."

Breaking our huddle, I returned to my desk. There was no answer at the offices of McAlister Properties, so I tried Marcia's home number. It rang four times and I was thinking I'd have to leave her a message when she answered.

"Hello?" she said, breathing heavily.

"Hey, Marcia, it's Carter Ross," I said. "You okay?"

"Yeah, sorry, I was outside and I thought you were going to be the insurance company calling back and I didn't want to miss the call so I sprinted to the phone."

"The insurance company?"

"Yeah. My house was broken into this morning. The police have already been out here. The insurance company is supposed to be sending an adjuster out. It's just, ugh, like I didn't have enough going on with Vaughn's funeral and now Barry and—"

"Wait, wait, slow down, your house was broken into?" I said.

It could have been a coincidence, sure. But this was another one of those things—like the fire at Barry McAlister's place— that felt decidedly un-random. There was some kind of unknown, unseen actor, constantly setting things into motion, but I still didn't know who it was or what was motivating it all.

"Yeah," she said. "Can you believe it?"

"What did they take?"

"Oh, I can barely even tell yet, they made such a mess of the place. All of my jewelry is gone, for sure. So are some of the electronics. And Trevor's computer. And the silver. They didn't take the crystal, but they grabbed pretty much anything else they thought would have quick resale value."

"And it happened this morning?"

"Yep. While I was out running some errands. The police think that maybe they were watching the place and waited until I left. It's so creepy. People always talk about how violated they feel when something like this happens, and it's true. Some of what was stolen was Vaughn's and it's like, I don't know, losing another part of him. I know it's just stuff and I should be happy no one was hurt. But I don't know how much more I can take right now."

Her voice was faltering. The woman whose life had been all about control was doing her damnedest to hold it together in the face of a series of events that could have unhinged anyone. Resilience in the face of tragedy is a fascinating area of study, and psychologists are only beginning to understand why some people are more resilient than others. But, whatever the secret ingredient was, Marcia Fenstermacher seemed to have it.

"Marcia I'm . . . I don't even know what to say. I'm so sorry. That's . . . awful."

I heard her sniffle twice and breath heavily before she said, "Anyhow. Sorry to dump that on you. Were you calling about something?"

There comes a point when even the most dogged reporter has to put his humanity first. And there was no way in good conscience I could dump more on this woman. So I just said, "Yeah, but forget it. You've got enough to worry about."

"No, what is it?" she said.

"Marcia, seriously, it's just something for the story about Vaughn. It can wait."

"Please. I want to help. I . . . I . . . really could use any distraction at this point. I promise I'll have a good, long nervous breakdown when this is all over—I've got it scheduled for two weeks from now. But in the meantime, you're the only person who is trying to make any sense of what's going on. So, please, distract me."

I allowed a small pause into our conversation before saying, "Seriously?"

"Seriously," she confirmed.

"Okay. Well, you said I could look at that P-and-L statement you had at the office. I was hoping maybe a colleague and I could do that this afternoon."

"How long do you think it would take?"

"I don't know. Fifteen minutes?"

"What time is it?"

"Five minutes to three."

"All right. Why don't you meet me in the office at three forty-five."

"Are you sure it's not too much trouble?"

"Absolutely. We had all decided to close the offices for the rest of the week—it's not like anyone was getting anything done anyway—but I actually have to be in the office at four anyway. Will Imperiale's secretary called to set up an emergency meeting."

Will Imperiale. There he was again. "And what did he want?"

"I don't know exactly. She said he was going to make some kind of take-it-or-leave-it settlement offer that's going to be so good I won't be able to refuse it. But it's only on the table through the end of today."

"That's sort of curious. You know he's been telling his clients that the thing is settled already," I said, then filled Marcia in on the conflicting conversations on this subject I'd had with Jackie Orr and Kevin Ryan.

"Well, as far as I know, Kevin is right," Marcia said when I was done. "Vaughn never mentioned anything about a settlement to me, either. And it's hard to believe he would have kept something like that from me *and* Kevin."

"Yeah, I guess so," I said. "But, wait. Imperiale wants a meeting with you? Why you? No offense, but what authority do you even have to make a settlement on behalf of McAlister Properties?"

"Oh, didn't I tell you? I'm now part owner of McAlister Properties. Vaughn left his share of the company to me in his will."

"I see. So if you own half, who owns the other half?"

"Actually, that might be me, too. Barry McAlister had owned the other half. I haven't seen his will yet, but I'm guessing he left his half to Vaughn. It's not like he has any other close relatives. And if that's the case, then it's mine, too."

So the woman who had started as a clerical employee was now, perhaps, the sole proprietor of McAlister Properties. That was an interesting twist.

"You like being the boss?" I asked.

"Believe me, I was a lot more happy being the secretary. I don't really even know what to do. Vaughn used to talk to me about all this stuff, so I basically understand it. But when it comes to the banks and the tenants and all the vendors and everything . . . I don't mean to sound like an idiot, but he was always the one who made the decisions. I'm not sure . . . Well, anyway, I guess it's just one more thing I'll have to deal with before I have that nervous breakdown."

"Right," I said. "So I'll see you at three forty-five?"

"Yep. See you then."

As I hung up the phone, I was feeling pretty good about things, with the afternoon all mapped out:

I needed to be at my parents' house at four thirty, or else my mother would send out the National Guard to hunt me down. But it was only a twenty-minute ride from Newark to Millburn, twenty-five with traffic. As long as I left Newark at four, I would make it to Millburn in plenty of time.

My good mood lasted for another twenty-eight seconds, which is the amount of time that I was able to sit in my chair unharassed before I heard a loud noise coming from Tina's office.

Worse, it sounded like my name.

"Carter Ross!" she repeated.

I looked over and once again saw her standing near the entrance to her office, doing that finger-crooking thing. I complied and was barely inside when she said, "It's about the wedding. Close the door."

I shut the door behind me, then sat down. I immediately feared the worst: she had heard that Kira was coming as my date. And now I was going to get in trouble not only for that but also for not having told her. She would, of course, insist it was the second part that bothered her—she would lay it on thick about trust and communication and all that. We would never acknowledge that the first part was really the sticker, because then she'd have to actually admit she cared for me.

She was drumming her fingers and shaking her head.

"It's just a shame," she said.

"What?"

"That your baby is going to be born fatherless."

"Why?"

"Because, I swear, I'm going to kill you. Your mother called last night and asked if I could come to her house at four thirty today so we could all go over to the rehearsal dinner together."

She said "together" with special disdain. Like she was saying "anthrax" or "cholera outbreak" or *The Bachelor*: season 18." But I was actually feeling strangely buoyed. I still had, what, ninety minutes or so to figure out how I was going to finesse the situation in a way that didn't involve Tina severing my head from my shoulders.

"And why is that my fault?" I asked. "I can't exactly control my mom. You're the one who is such good friends with her. *She* invited you to the wedding, not me, remember?"

"Yeah, but you're supposed to serve as a buffer between me and that which might be upsetting to me. I'm pregnant! I'm . . . in a delicate condition!"

"With all due respect to the future mother of my child, I'm not sure you and 'delicate' belong in the same sentence."

"Whatever. I shouldn't have to survive one-on-one time with your family without you there to run interference for me. Your mother stays on good behavior when you're around. But if you're not there, she starts asking all these questions. It might get ugly. Just tell me you *will* be there on time."

"Yeah, I'll be there. I've got a meeting with Marcia Fenstermacher at three forty-five but it's in downtown Newark at McAlister Place and it'll only take fifteen minutes. I'll be prompt. I promise."

"Marcia Fenstermacher," she said, giving her head a tilt that indicated her confusion. "I thought we were thinking she was the one who killed Vaughn."

"Yeah, that theory is now out of fashion. It's so . . . so yesterday afternoon. We've got a much more nuanced understanding of the situation now."

"And what is that?"

"Actually, I have no idea. But it doesn't look like Marcia Fenstermacher is our culprit."

"Why not?"

"Because the theory was that Vaughn was going back to his ex-wife, Lisa Denbigh, and Marcia killed him out of jealousy. But I talked to Lisa and it really sounded like nothing of the sort was happening. And, I don't know, I think Marcia and Vaughn were really in love. Besides, if this was a lovers' quarrel, Barry McAlister would still be alive, not sitting in a pile of ashes at the Essex County Medical Examiner's Office."

"So you're sure she has no motive? Nothing to gain financially by Vaughn being dead?"

"Um," is all I could say. Otherwise, I would have had to make a baaing sound, because I was feeling a little sheepish. As usual, Tina had a point.

"What?"

"Well, I was starting to think that maybe this sleazy lawyer, Will Imperiale, had something to do with this, because it seems like everywhere I turn, he's there. But now that you mention it, Vaughn *did* leave Marcia his interest in McAlister Properties in his will. And . . . uh . . . ."

"Yes?"

"Well, we don't know what Barry's will says. But if Vaughn is his sole heir, that means Marcia would get that, too. So McAlister Properties would effectively become hers alone."

Tina was shaking her head at me. "Did you know that 'gullible' is not in the dictionary?"

"Aw, come on," I started, but she cut me off.

"Actually, I don't care. We're not playing Columbo here. We don't need to crack the case. What we need is something to put in Sunday's newspaper. Brodie still has major wood for this thing. He's like a teenage boy who has found his father's stash of porno magazines."

"I think most teenage boys know how to get porn off the Internet these days."

"Don't quibble with my metaphor. Just tell me you can cobble together something for Sunday."

I sat with my chin in my hand for a moment, because I figured that would make what came next seem more thoughtful.

"Let's go big picture," I said. "Make it one of those 'The Rise and Fall of McAlister Properties,' the homegrown company that once had so much promise but now appears to be in tatters."

"That sounds kind of soft. What would it conclude?"

"It wouldn't. It would just sort of lay out what we know."

"Talk it out for me," she said.

"Okay, you go with the big doomsday opening, about how death, destruction, and apocalypse has rained down on this once-prospering, Newark-based company. Then you go to the narrative. Start with Barry's slow rise as a landlord in rough-and-tumble postriot Newark, then with him selling his buildings so Vaughn can go into commercial real estate. Vaughn acquires some nice-sized buildings downtown and slaps his name on them, but he wants the brass ring—McAlister Arms, the shiny project he develops himself and really puts him in the big time. And then things start going awry. Thanks to a rash of break-ins, his buildings start losing tenants and bleeding cash, so in desperation he pockets the money that's supposed to be earmarked for cleaning up this new property, getting a fake LSRP to sign off on it. Then people start getting sick. Then McAlister Arms loses its blue-chip tenant. Now McAlister Properties is getting sued by the sleazy lawyer and the McAlister boys are getting dead for reasons the authorities are still investigating."

"Sounds good. But can you deliver all that?"

"As long as you don't get too picky with me on the sourcing? Yeah."

"And you have time to write it?"

"I'll let Tommy and Pigeon come up with a rough draft tonight, then I'll have time to make it pretty—and you'll have time to edit it—tomorrow before the wedding."

"Okay. But why do I feel a little sick?"

"It's probably the baby."

"No," she said. "It's because, as usual, you have no real idea what's going on and I'm afraid it's going to get you in trouble."

"My soon-to-be brother-in-law Gary is a state trooper. If you're worried, just call him. I'm part of the family now. Besides, I thought you were the one who's 'in trouble.'"

"What do you . . ." she started, then the double entendre caught up with her. She just shook her head and said, "You're awful."

"Sorry," I said, grinning.

"Just be careful with Miss Fenstermacher," she said as I rose from the chair. "I know you think she's just the harmless secretary, but it's just a little too convenient how this has lined up for her."

"I promise," I said. "I won't turn my back on her."

Departing Tina's office, I gathered Tommy and Pigeon one last time to talk them through the story we were going to craft for Sunday's edition. I told Pigeon to head back out to Barry McAlister's neighborhood and see if she could gather any more string there. Then Tommy and I made our departure for McAlister Place, taking separate cars so I could make my Millburn getaway at the appointed time.

As I drove, I thought through that basic story sketch I had laid out for Tina. I kept trying to pinpoint what might have been the catalyst for the murder and mayhem that had visited the McAlisters. Some of it seemed a long time coming—the business hadn't started struggling with vacancy overnight—while other factors, like losing Best Buy and getting sued, were more immediate. Those things seemed more likely triggers. But, again, until I developed a better theory on who was doing this, I was likely to be a little lost on the why.

Finally, I gave up. Thinking too hard was a dangerous thing

in my line of work. I flipped on one of the local all-news radio stations, which had a mention about Barry McAlister's homicide at the top of the hour. It referred to Barry as "Newark real estate mogul Barry McAlister." I thought about the wrinkled, chain-smoking, broken old man I had visited in his unfashionably decorated West Orange home and shook my head. Some mogul.

Traffic came next, and I heard about the tractor trailer that had jackknifed and then spilled its contents all across I-280, creating an eastbound delay of eight miles—and growing—and rubbernecking delays westbound. There's a kind of schadenfreude you get from listening to New York-area traffic. You know there's going to be traffic somewhere on a Friday afternoon, and you get this perverse joy knowing it's hitting someone else. I was heading to Millburn on I-78, meaning the tractor trailer wasn't my problem.

I pulled into the parking garage with Tommy just behind me. Together, we walked past the lobby security guard, who was actually asleep.

"Do you think we should we wake him up?" Tommy asked.

"No, he looks peaceful."

"Hard to believe Vaughn was having a problem with break-ins with this kind of crackerjack security staff."

"Yeah," I confirmed. "DeNunzio Protective Services—on the job!"

We were still snickering as we reached the second floor, but the mood changed the instant I opened the office door. Marcia Fenstermacher was already inside. She was wearing business-casual clothing and a dour countenance that could have been due to at least a dozen different factors. But it seemed to be mostly the result of whatever she was looking at on her computer screen.

I introduced Tommy, then asked, "You look troubled. What's the matter?"

"It's this," she said, pointing to the screen. "It's . . . Something's very wrong."

"What?"

"Well, this P-and-L statement is more than a month old, because we only have to file them quarterly," she said, picking up a spreadsheet printout that was on her desk. "So I wanted to get you the most up-to-date number on what's in the reserve account."

"Yeah, and?"

"Look at the number on the bottom right of the last page," she said, handing me the printout.

I flipped to the end of the document and looked at the all-important bottom line. It listed the total reserves as $8,054,772.19—otherwise known as eight million bucks.

"Okay. What's the problem?" I said.

"Now look at this," she said.

She turned the screen toward me and I peered at it. It was the summary page for McAlister Properties, and there were several accounts listed. The largest was $35,483.22—which, while I'm not a Fields medalist, is substantially short of eight million bucks.

"Are you sure this is the same account as the one listed on the P-and-L statement?"

"Absolutely. Look at the account numbers."

I looked from page to screen, then from screen to page. "Yeah," I confirmed. "There's definitely a problem."

"I think I'm going to have that nervous breakdown right now," she said, and I didn't doubt it. Even her immutable hair had been slightly mussed by her pulling at it.

"It couldn't have just disappeared," Tommy said. "Have you looked at the recent transactions?"

"Right, of course. I'm sorry, I'm just . . . I can't think straight."

She clicked on the appropriate button and, sure enough, there was an eight-million-dollar wire transfer that had been completed at 4:38 P.M. on Thursday.

Marcia was starting to hyperventilate and was stammering out her questions. "But this isn't . . . Who could have . . . Where . . ."

"Why don't you call the bank and ask them what's up?" Tommy said gently, casting a wary glance in my direction that I'm sure Marcia didn't catch.

"Right, of course," she said. "I'm sorry. Come on, Marcia, pull it together."

She hit the speakerphone button on her desk and dialed the bank's 800 number. She went through the prompts until she got a real human being, who identified himself as, "This is Robert in customer relations." He went through the steps of verifying Marcia's identity.

"I see you're listed on the account as having administrative privileges," Robert said. "What can I do for you today Ms. Fenstermacher?"

"There was a large amount of money transferred out of the account yesterday afternoon," she said, obviously making an effort at keeping her voice controlled. "Can you tell me who authorized it?"

"Yes, ma'am, let me check that," Robert said, and we heard him typing on his computer. "That transfer was made in person at our branch office on Broad Street in Newark. It was authorized by a Mr. McAlister."

"That's impossible," Marcia burst. "Vaughn McAlister wasn't even alive yesterday afternoon."

"Not Vaughn McAlister," Robert informed her. "This order was put in by a Barry McAlister."

Barry McAlister. So one of the last things he did before being shot, stabbed, and burned was to give away the family fortune.

"Can you tell me where the money was wired to?" Marcia asked.

"Yes, ma'am. It was sent into the escrow account of Willard R. Imperiale, Esquire."

"Him?" Marcia said.

"Yes, ma'am."

"But that was never . . . Is there any way you can, I don't know, cancel the order?"

"No, ma'am," Robert said, and had nothing more to add.

There wasn't, of course. Banks didn't give you backsies. The money was gone. Maybe she could recover it eventually, but that would require time, lawyers, and figuring out why Barry had given it away in the first place. I watched as this reality landed on Marcia Fenstermacher's face.

Finally, Robert asked, "Is there anything else I can help you with today?"

"No . . . no, thank you."

Marcia ended the call and for a moment there was more silence. Marcia was seated at her desk. Tommy and I were standing on the other side of it.

"Why would Barry fork over eight million dollars to that scumbag Will Imperiale?" she asked.

"I don't know," I said. "But I'm betting the authorities in West Orange will be very interested in asking him that question."

"Oh, believe me, I'm going to ask him first," Marcia said. She looked at her watch, then said, "He's due here in less than five minutes."

As if on cue, I heard the door open behind me. I turned to see two people, neither of whom I was exactly expecting under the circumstances.

One was a woman whose cheekbones I recognized instantly, from having gazed at her Facebook photos. She was brunette now, not a blonde, but there was no question in my mind she was Lisa Denbigh.

The other was a man I couldn't quite place, but mostly because he was wearing a hat and dark glasses. Then he removed them and I realized he was someone I had seen before as well. His hair was different, too—he had dyed all the gray out of it. But there was no doubt about his identity, either.

It was Barry McAlister.

In retrospect, I should have given him the bum's rush: just lowered my shoulder, wrapped my arms around him, and kept him down there for as long as it took. I'm not the brawniest guy alive—or the bravest—but I'm pretty sure I could take out a chain-smoking septuagenarian.

Except, as he closed the door behind him and pressed the lock button, I was still trying to process it. Barry McAlister was alive? As in, not dead? Not shot, stabbed, and burned?

By the time I had put this together, Barry had already reached into the black duffel bag he was carrying and pulled out a gun—also black—and, in doing so, had taken control of the situation.

"Barry!?" Marcia said. "Where's Mr. Imperiale?"

"Mr. Imperiale is no longer with us," he informed her. "Would you like to meet the 'secretary' who set up this little meeting?"

Lisa just gave Marcia a sarcastic little wave.

Marcia was still trying to catch up to what was going on, stammering, "But what are you—"

"Shut up," Barry cut her off, pointing the gun at her. "I didn't expect you'd have so much company. You were supposed to be alone. Is anyone else here?"

Marcia didn't answer. Without taking his eyes off any of the three of us—or his aim off Marcia—he slipped the bag off his shoulder and set it down. His left hand disappeared inside for a moment and produced yet another gun.

"Here," he said, extending the second gun to Lisa. "Take this. Check the rest of the office and make sure there's no one else here."

Lisa accepted the gun. Other than her obviously augmented breasts, she was a small, slender woman—having been underfed since puberty—and the gun looked too big for her hand. Alas, it wasn't so large that her fingers couldn't make it to the trigger.

She entered the door to my left, the side that wasn't Vaughn's old office. Barry kept his gun pointed in our direction.

"You look a lot less dead than you're supposed to be," I said.

"Shut up, wiseass," he said. "Or do you want some of this?"

He cocked the gun and trained it in the direction of my mouth, which I promptly closed. I thought back to what Brodie had told me about Barry chasing muggers away with a shotgun back in the seventies. I decided not to test if his proficiency with firearms had stayed with him in his old age.

"Yeah, that's what I thought," he said. "Okay, first things first, I want to see everyone's hands. Let's get 'em up."

Tommy, Marcia, and I complied.

"Good," Barry said. "Oh, and let's be clear, let's keep it nice and quiet, too. I don't want anyone doing any yelling or, trust me, I will make this hurt."

None of us responded. He collected our cell phones next, going one at a time, not giving us any opening to make a move.

"There's no one here," Lisa said, having returned from her office tour.

"Okay, very good," Barry said. "Great job, sweetheart."

She smiled at him in a sickly sweet way, and it struck me: oh, lord, they had been sleeping together. A little part of me felt like hurling, and not because their tryst strained the acceptable limits of a May-December fling. Lisa had once been Barry's daughter-in-law. Thirty-year age difference aside, that's just nasty.

Marcia was obviously on the same wavelength as I was, because she spit out, "*Sweetheart?* Don't tell me you two are . . ."

"Zip it, bitch," Lisa said with her Georgia twang. "After what you did to Vaughn and me, I've heard enough out of you for an entire lifetime."

"After what *I* did?" Marcia fired back. "Maybe if you had actually—"

"Enough!" Barry roared. "Marcia, I keep telling you, shut the hell up. I don't want to hear anything else out of you. Now, Lisa . . ."

"Sorry, baby . . ." she started.

"Forget it. Just stay focused, honey," he said. "Don't make it emotional. Let's take care of business first."

"Yeah, this is no time for a lover's quarrel," Tommy said.

"That's enough out of you," Barry said, pointing his gun at Tommy. "Unless you want the last thing you see in this world to be a bullet heading toward your face. And you"—he swiveled the gun at me—"let's keep those hands up."

I lifted my hands a little higher.

"Now, first things first," Barry continued. "Lisa, hand me your gun back, sweetheart."

Lisa presented her gun to Barry, handle first, barrel pointed away. He closed his hand around it, and was now pointing both of them at us.

"Great," he said. "Now I need you to go in the bag. I got a hammer and a cloth bag in there."

"Okay," she said, withdrawing the requested items. "Now what?"

"I want you to put the phones in that bag and start busting them up," Barry said. "Bust 'em up good."

"Oh . . . okay," she said, clearly a little confused.

"I've read stories about some of these things having tracking devices," he said, answering the question she hadn't even asked. "Nobody needs to know where these three are."

There was a crunching of plastic as Lisa started swinging the hammer at the bag. I glanced at Tommy and Marcia. She looked calm, more calm than I'd expected she would be; he looked stricken by what was happening to his phone. I might have felt the same way, but I sensed we had even bigger problems ahead.

I couldn't figure out why Barry had asked Lisa to put the phones in the bag before crushing them. The only thing that made sense was that he planned not only to make our cell phones disappear, he planned to make us disappear. And when he did that, he didn't want McAlister Properties' employees to find little smashed-up bits of our phones on the carpet.

It also told me something else: whatever he was planning on doing to us, he wasn't planning on doing it here. We were going to be taken somewhere else. My suspicion was confirmed when Lisa announced she was done with her demolition job.

"Excellent. Now let's tie them up," Barry said, pulling an industrial-size roll of duct tape from his duffel bag and handing Lisa both guns. "Let's do Mr. Ross here first." He herded me over to the corner of the room.

"Take a seat please," he said to me. "Lisa honey, stand right over there. If he tries anything funny, put a couple shots in his ear. We can clean up the mess later."

It was kind of surreal, watching Barry duct-tape various parts of my body together. Lisa kept a wary eye on Tommy and Marcia. As Barry went to work, unwinding a not-inconsiderable length of duct tape on my ankles and then my knees, I let my brain go to work on what, exactly, was going on.

The first, most obvious, thing was that Barry had faked his own death. He wanted to be able to disappear with no one looking for him. And, what's more, he had apparently succeeded.

"The blood," I said. "The crime scene guys said the blood was yours. They DNA tested it and everything."

He said nothing.

"The West Orange police chief said there was tons of it— enough to make it look like your throat had been slashed," I said. "How is that possible, unless . . ."

The answer hit me: "You were banking your own blood. You got yourself a big enough stockpile and then spread it around. You've been planning this for a while."

Barry allowed himself a chuckle. "Very good, smart guy," he said.

"You're sick," Marcia said.

"Can I shoot her?" Lisa asked.

"No, honey," Barry said, patiently. "Not now."

As he started in on my hands and wrists, I kept trying to put things together. Okay, so Barry had successfully played dead. And he must have found a way to take that eight million dollars with him. There seemed to be little point in disappearing broke.

So that's why he had killed Vaughn—or, rather, had Vaughn killed. The two white guys in the black leather coats that Kevin Mack had seen disposing of Vaughn's body, the two guys I had assumed were DeNunzio henchmen, were, in fact, hired by Barry.

But why had he also killed Will Imperiale? I could only presume that's what Barry meant when he'd said Mr. Imperiale was no longer with us. It stood to reason the burned body in Barry's house was Imperiale's.

For that matter, why involve Imperiale at all? If you needed a body to burn in a fire, you wouldn't grab someone like Imperiale. Sure, he was about the same height—that could help fool the medical examiner, who wouldn't test the DNA of a corpse that everyone assumed was Barry's. But Imperiale was a high-profile personal injury lawyer. Why not grab someone more anonymous who happened to share roughly the same bone structure?

It didn't make sense. Adding a lawyer into the mix would just seem to complicate things. If you're going to steal eight million dollars, filtering it through a lawyer's escrow account wouldn't seem to give you any advantage I could think of. There had to be easier ways.

Barry finished with me and turned to Tommy next, making him sit in the corner next to me. I surreptitiously tested my duct-tape bonds and couldn't make them budge. He had done a thorough job: my legs up to my thighs, my arms up to elbows, then my forearms to my thighs. It didn't exactly leave a lot of wiggle room. And you'd be surprised how strong multiple layers of duct tape can be.

I looked outside at the street traffic one story below me—people in their cars and on foot, hurrying home on a Friday afternoon. I could see them, but of course they couldn't see in through the tinted windows. A hostage scene was playing out just a few feet from them, but they were completely unaware of it.

"You know I'm due at my mother's house at four thirty," I said. "If I don't show up, she's going to start to worry. And she's a champion worrier. I once saw her worry a coat of paint off the walls."

Barry didn't pause in his task to comment on this—not even to tell me to shut up. He was too intent on getting Tommy trussed up in the same fashion as he had done me.

When he was through, he turned to Marcia and said, "All

right, before I take care of you, you've got a little paperwork to do for me, Miss Fenstermacher."

"What are you talking about?" she said, proudly. "I'm not doing anything for you."

Barry grabbed a gun from Lisa, walked deliberately up to Marcia, who was still seated at her desk, and roughly grabbed her hair. He pressed the gun to her lips, grinding the barrel into her teeth.

Marcia turned her head so that the gun was pressing into her cheek instead. "Oww, stop that!" she protested. "That really hurts."

"Let's be very clear about something here," Barry said in a low, deadly serious voice. "You're going to do what I tell you to do. You're going to sign what I tell you to sign. And you're going to do it without complaining."

He gave the gun one final jab into her face, then stood up and went to his black bag once more. He removed a legal-size manila folder that contained a thick stack of paper. As he opened it, I saw it contained five stapled documents of identical thickness. He placed the first one down in front of Marcia.

"Settlement agreement?" she said. "I'm not going to sign a settlement agreement! Barry, this is going to bankrupt the company!"

"Yeah, but not for at least a hundred and eighty days. It'll take at least that long for anyone to even figure out what's happened."

"But, Barry, you built this company," she said. "It's half yours."

"No, actually, it's all yours," Barry said. "I'm dead, remember? My will leaves everything to Vaughn. Which means, in essence, I've left everything to you. You are right now the sole owner of McAlister Properties, with total authority over the company's decisions. Let me spare you reading all that fine print: you are signing off on an eight-million-dollar settlement."

And that's when I finally got it. The settlement. The 180 days. Why Barry needed to involve Imperiale. Why Barry needed Marcia even more.

Or, more accurately, why he needed Marcia to disappear, and Imperiale to disappear along with her.

I got it then. It was twisted. But, then again, so was Barry McAlister.

As Marcia Fenstermacher signed away a fortune—all the while swearing to Barry that he wouldn't get away with it, that he was a fool, that he was going to hell, etc.—I worked it all out.

Start with the obvious: if Barry had tried to just transfer eight million dollars out of the company account and into his own, it would show up on the quarterly P&L statements that McAlister Properties submitted to its mortgage holders. Those lenders would take appropriate legal action to make sure they could still get their mitts on the money and Barry would have to fork it right back over.

But if that eight million was being paid to settle a lawsuit, the banks wouldn't be able to do anything about it. Barry would only have to pay the money back if McAlister Properties went bankrupt within 180 days. In bankruptcy court, any transaction a company makes in the final 180 days before it declares bankruptcy can be reviewed by the court and voided.

Yet, Barry was leaving McAlister Properties in such disarray, there was no way it would be filing for bankruptcy—or doing much of anything else—in the next 180 days. Of its two namesake architects, one was dead, the other one was presumed dead; and its new owner, Marcia, would be considered missing in action.

The company would limp along for a year or more before anything would be decided. The settlement would be untouchable.

Enter Imperiale. The money had been dumped into his escrow account, as any good settlement money should be. It would look to all the world like Will Imperiale, sleazebag personal injury attorney, had simply gotten a big payoff, then run away rather than share it with his clients.

Once it dawned on people—in particular, those fifty or so clients who were owed 50 percent of that settlement—they would look high and low for Imperiale and never find him.

Because he was already dead.

Meanwhile, I was sure Barry had found a way to pump the escrow account dry. That money was probably already offshore somewhere. Perhaps in Switzerland. Perhaps on a little Caribbean island where Barry figured he and Lisa could live quite happily on eight million dollars for the rest of his life.

And I should have known. I should have known the moment I saw Elizabeth McAlister's tiny angel statue was missing the night before. It hadn't been knocked over by fire trucks or anything of the sort. It had been taken by a man who was still strangely sentimental over the wife who had run off. It may well have been among Barry's last acts: lovingly wrapping up that piece of marble and packing it away for a long trip to wherever.

Around the time I got this all worked out, Marcia had signed all five copies. Barry had dumped her onto the floor next to Tommy and was wrapping her in duct tape. I watched him working, looking like a Just For Men dropout with his bad dye job.

That's when I figured out the last piece. Why Barry had dyed his hair black. Why Lisa was suddenly brunette. Or at least I had a theory. One way to confirm it:

"Marcia," I said. "Do you keep your passport in your house somewhere?"

"Yeah, why?" she said.

"Shut up," Barry ordered. "Both of you."

I didn't need to say any more to her. It would just have discouraged her.

But I knew why her house had been broken into this morning: Barry needed her passport.

These weren't just random disguises. Barry was trying to pass as Will Imperiale. And it would work, too. They both had big noses and ridiculous hair-dye jobs. No one looking at their passport photos would be able to see beyond those things.

Lisa was a less-convincing Marcia Fenstermacher. But she was still probably good enough. While their bodies were different, you couldn't see that on a head shot. They were roughly the same age and their faces were close enough that a random customs worker or Transportation Security Administration employee—bored and tired and with a long line behind him—wouldn't bother to stop her. After all, she was just a nice woman from the suburbs going on vacation to the British Virgin Islands. Or wherever.

If investigators ever really started working on it—which was doubtful—it would appear that Willard R. Imperiale, Esq., had taken an eight-million-dollar payday and run off with Marcia Fenstermacher, the woman whose signature was on the settlement papers.

I thought about how Barry had likely snookered Imperiale into playing his part. Barry had probably waltzed into Imperiale's office and told him he was about to get the easiest payday of his life. In exchange for some portion of the proceeds, Barry was going to agree to settle this lawsuit. That's why Imperiale had been promising his clients quick money. Barry had told him that's what he was going to get.

"How much of a kickback did Imperiale think he was giving you?" I asked Barry, who was almost finished with Marcia. "That was the deal, wasn't it? You told Imperiale that McAlister

Properties had eight million bucks that was ripe for the plucking and he only had to give you, what, a million? Two million?"

Barry was ignoring me. But I saw what looked like a little bit of a smile cross his face.

It all worked out. Barry was getting a comfortable retirement—and running off with a woman he'd always had a crush on. Lisa was getting her escape from all those creditors and piddling lawsuits and was being given the life of luxury that she had married Vaughn for in the first place. Plus, she was getting a pretty good slice of revenge on the woman who had wrecked her marriage.

And all they had to do to make it work was kill the man whom they both had once professed to love.

And a lawyer.

And a secretary.

And a pair of newspaper reporters.

Even though we weren't integral to the scheme, there was no way they could leave Tommy and me alive. I had known that already. Now I really understood why: the moment anyone knew Barry McAlister was not dead, the whole jig was up. The banks would never let him get away with what was obviously a scheme to pump money out of a failing business before it went belly-up. The courts would seize whatever money he had.

So Tommy and I were just the poor sots who got in the wrong place at the wrong time. I was assuming Barry was going to arrange for all three of us not to be found. Hired killers tended to be good at that sort of thing. And there was enough money on the line that Barry could afford the best.

I glanced over at Tommy, both of us looking ridiculous in our duct-tape bondage, and shook my head. "Remember what I said about outliving Brittany Murphy?"

"Yeah?"

"I take it back."

He was never allowed to say it. He wasn't allowed even to think it. He felt like some kind of deviant for admitting it to himself.

We live in a society that constantly reinforces the belief—through books, through movies, through Hallmark cards and commercials and Father's Day nostalgia—that the birth of a child ought to be a joyous, precious event, one of the great days in any human's existence.

But the way Barry McAlister viewed things, Vaughn's birth had ruined his life.

He was married to a gorgeous woman before that baby came. They lived in a nice house in the suburbs. They enjoyed themselves. He worked hard to provide for them. She had been sort of self-centered, sure. But there was enough attention and affection left over for him. And he felt the pride of having a beautiful woman on his arm. He could remember thinking how fortunate he was, how happy he was. He couldn't wait to get home and see her every night. He had the perfect life.

Then, wham. Baby. And it was like a dark cloud had passed over everything. She had a difficult delivery. She couldn't nurse the child. She suffered through a horrible case of what he now realized was postpartum depression—back then they called it "baby blues"—and, in some ways, never really recovered. She was miserable all the time. She stopped paying any attention to him, stopped having any energy for him. It was like she stopped loving him. She was constantly angry. Before long, so was he. Coming home at night became like walking into a dungeon. Even her looks faded.

Then she just took off, leaving behind the kid and her feeble excuses. When he heard about her death a few years later, it was like completing the circle of agony. He had always held out hope that she might come back to him. No. More than that: he knew she would come back to him. Then the cancer got her. He told himself that if he had been around, she would have gone to the doctor more regularly. Or he might have noticed the lump. Instead, she was gone forever.

And maybe Barry should have resented only his wife, not his child. But it wasn't that easy to separate the two of them. All he knew was that he had been fine, and then he was miserable. And the clear dividing line between the two was the birth of his son.

Things certainly didn't get any easier when his wife left. He was a single dad at a time when there was really no such thing. He struggled constantly to find child care. He had no social life because of Vaughn—there was no going out on nights or weekends when you had a kid to watch. He had no sex life because of Vaughn—no woman seemed to want Barry when it meant also taking on his little anchor. He had nothing beyond work and parenting. Because of Vaughn.

So, yeah, Vaughn had ruined Barry's personal life. And he could sort of accept that. He could tell himself it wasn't the kid's fault.

But when Vaughn ruined his business as well, that was too much.

Barry could never understand why Vaughn hadn't been satisfied to stick just with residential. They had a good thing going with their apartment buildings. Yeah, it was hard work. And it wasn't *particularly glamorous. But what was wrong with hard work? Who needed glamour? It gave them a good, steady income. They could prudently expand their holdings without too much risk.*

But Vaughn was like his mother. Always concerned with appearances. Always wanting flashy things. Always having this dream of the Really Big Deal.

And somehow he persuaded Barry—against Barry's better judgment—to sell off everything and let him chase it. So that's what Barry did, putting the proceeds from his life's work into Vaughn's hands and letting him go into the high-stakes world of commercial real estate.

It worked for a while. Then Vaughn just flat screwed it up. He got so wrapped up dreaming of deals that would run into the hundreds of millions that he forgot the basic principle of property management: you need to keep the tenants happy. If you don't have tenants, you don't have anything.

His cash flow went negative right about the same time he came up with this other scheme—to take millions of dollars of cleanup money for a brownfields site, pocket it, then use it as seed money for this new project that would supposedly get him back in the black.

When Barry learned about the brownfields thing, he wanted to kill Vaughn right there. It went against everything Barry stood for in business, every principle upon which he had built McAlister Properties, everything he thought he had taught his son. They were going to get caught. He knew they were going to get caught.

Then those construction workers started getting sick. And Barry started thinking about his options. He couldn't just let Vaughn ruin everything and bankrupt them. He started coming up with a plan to save them.

It was when Vaughn lost Best Buy that Barry realized he needed to put his plan into action. The thing was hopeless. McAlister Place and McAlister Center were money sieves. Now

McAlister Arms was destined be a loser before Vaughn would even be able to get a foundation poured.

They owed millions. What little equity there was in those buildings was going to go to the banks. Barry was going to lose everything.

So Barry put a plan into place to get it all back. Then he convinced the former Lisa McAlister there were eight million reasons to join him.

CHAPTER 9

As his final step in turning us into duct-tape mummies, Barry McAlister used what remained of the roll to gag us.

So there we were. Totally immobilized. Huddled in the corner next to one another. And mute.

Lisa was mostly just pacing around the room, looking at various pictures and renderings of McAlister Arms, McAlister Place, and McAlister Center—like she was just a random visitor to the office, waiting for a meeting.

Barry had taken a seat at Marcia's desk. He had put both guns down next to the keyboard and was typing on her computer. What he was doing, I couldn't see. Was there a Web site called FugitivesFromJustice.org where he could get tips for a well-funded life on the lam? But, no; he kept swearing occasionally, like he didn't like what the machine was showing him. He kept glancing at his watch.

Every time I felt like neither of them was looking in my direction, I would test my bonds to see if I could get them to budge, even a little. If I could get a little wiggle room going, I thought maybe I could get some leverage and . . .

And, well, nothing. Even if I did manage to, say, get my hands free, my legs were still wrapped up tight. And my captors were still armed.

The only thing we had going for us—and it wasn't much—was that if Barry had planned to blow our heads off here at the office, we would have long ago been dead. He planned to kill us somewhere else. And maybe in the process of moving us, we'd have a chance to do . . . something.

This, mind you, is the equivalent of the football team down three scores thinking it still has a chance with under two minutes left. But I had to cling to something.

Barry continued looking at his watch, continued his swearing and muttering. Finally, he said, "Okay, where the hell are those guys?"

"I don't know," Lisa said. "Why don't you call them?"

"I told you, that's not how it works with guys like that," he said. "I don't even have their number."

"Well, I don't know what to tell you, sugar."

Barry looked at the computer screen a little more, then decided, "We'll be fine. This is why I had us fly tomorrow morning. We're okay."

They eventually switched places, with Barry pacing and Lisa seated at the desk. I had no idea how much time was passing. I couldn't see a clock, and my cell phone, which is how I usually checked the time, was currently in about eight hundred tiny pieces inside a cloth bag. The tinting of the windows made it tough to tell how close to sunset it was getting, but the shadows cast by the buildings were definitely getting longer.

Meanwhile—and not that this was my biggest problem at the moment, but still—I was starting to get incredibly uncomfortable. I could shift positions only so much. I wanted to lie down—if only to take some pressure off my seriously numb ass—but I worried that if I went on my side, I'd never be able to get up again. So I stayed where I was, trying to battle through the various parts of my body that kept getting pins and needles. I swore my butt was never going to regain circulation.

Still, the gag was the worst. Not only did it make it impossible to talk—one of my favorite things to do—it made it hard to breathe, perhaps the only thing I liked to do more. He had left our noses exposed, but have you ever tried breathing with only your nose for an extended period of time? It's hard to fight the feeling that you're just not getting enough oxygen.

Occasionally I'd make eye contact with Tommy or Marcia. They didn't seem to be having any more fun than I was. Tommy was mostly staring at the carpet. Marcia kept intermittently closing her eyes.

"Why don't you call the guy who calls them?" Lisa said after a while.

"No," Barry insisted. "They'll be here. They must have gotten caught in traffic or something."

Maybe, if we were lucky, they—whoever "they" were—had gotten caught in the mess on I-280. Even if it was just delaying the inevitable, it was something.

I tried to distract myself by thinking about what was going on at my parents' house. I was, by now, at least an hour late. My poor mother had probably been in a full panic by 4:35 and turned into an absolute wreck when I hadn't shown up by 4:45. My brother and sister and their respective mates would have given up trying to calm her down by 4:50. At 5:00, my father would have insisted they just leave without me. Either that, or he would have found a tranquilizer gun. Tina was probably plotting a variety of creative ways to kill me—as if that weren't already being taken care of.

Thinking about Tina naturally turned my thoughts to the baby that would soon be stirring in her womb. My baby. Suddenly, I was convinced she was a girl—I don't know why—and I found myself thinking of all the things I wanted to say to her;

how I would hold her when she was scared and laugh with her when she was happy; how I planned to play princesses with her or climb trees with her or braid her hair or teach her how to shoot a layup; how I was going to scare the hell out of her first boyfriend and dance with her at her wedding if she ever found a guy perfect enough to deserve her.

I imagined what she was going to look like. She would have dark hair, no doubt about that, perhaps curly like Tina's. Maybe she would get my blue eyes. She would probably end up being tall and slender—again, like her parents. I hoped she'd be smart and passionate, like her mother. And maybe my greatest gift to her would be my sense of curiosity about the world and my joy for all the things in it. Could that be hereditary?

I wasn't ever going to get the chance find out. I felt my throat constrict and my eyes begin to water and I immediately tried to think of something else. Anything else. Turning into a teary heap wasn't going to help me get out of this.

Finally, there was a knock at the door.

"About time," Barry grumbled. He grabbed one of the guns off the desk and went over to the door. "Who is it?" he asked.

"It's the cleaning service," came a voice from the other side.

"Where have you been?" Barry said as he opened the door.

Three men walked in: two thick guys and a thin guy. They were dressed in janitor's uniforms. One of the thick guys had a radio, a bucket, and a mop. The other guy was pushing a large garbage trolley, brimming with bags full of what appeared to be shredded paper. But they were most certainly not the cleaning service.

They were here to kill us.

I'm not sure if the thin guy arrived in a bad mood, but he seemed to get into one the moment he got an eyeful of Tommy and me.

"What the . . . You said one woman," he said, then gestured toward us. "You didn't say nothing about two guys. What's with them?"

"Unexpected visitors," Barry said. "I'll triple what I was going to pay you."

"Damn straight you will. But that's not the only issue. There are logistics to consider. We weren't planning on three," he said. He rubbed his jaw for a moment, then said, "Okay. Think you can get us two more carts?"

"Yeah, sure," Barry said.

"All right," the thin guy said, then turned to one of the thick guys. "We're also going to need some more garbage. Why don't you go down to the Dumpster and grab some nice, full bags."

Barry instructed Lisa how to reach the janitor's supply closet and told the thick guy where to find the Dumpster. He gave them each keys to open the doors they would encounter. As they disappeared to run their respective errands, everyone fell silent.

Then the thin guy walked over to Tommy and me and toed me with the black loafer he was wearing, like I was a dog and he wanted to see if I would snap at him. "So who are these guys?" he asked.

"Just a couple of newspaper reporters," Barry said.

"Newspaper reporters!" the thin guy said. "Don't you think someone is going miss them?"

"I'm sure someone will," Barry said. "But it doesn't matter, because no one is going to find them, right?"

"Yeah," the thin guy said. "That's what we do."

He stopped talking and went to work, pulling a hood out of the bucket and placing it over Marcia's head. She had been fully immobilized, so there wasn't much she could do about it as he secured the hood with duct tape. He wrapped several extra layers around where her mouth was—as if the muzzle she already had weren't enough—then started removing the garbage bags from the trolley, emptying it out. When he was done, he lifted her torso.

"Get her feet," he said to the thick guy, who complied. They dumped her roughly into the trolley and covered her with garbage bags.

So that was how they planned to get us out of the office unseen: wheeled out like so much trash.

"Give me your shirt," the thin guy said to Barry.

"Why?" Barry asked.

"Just give me your shirt," the thin guy said, lacing the instruction with an impolite word.

Barry complied, stripping down to his T-shirt and handing over his plaid, button-down oxford. The thin guy tore it into two roughly equal strips, then wrapped one of the halves around my head. It was a makeshift hood, one he secured with duct tape.

With my world now dark—and my chances for a heroic escape dimmed that much further—I could only listen to what came next. There was more duct tape being unpeeled as Tommy's head got its wrap job. Then there was a knock at the door and Lisa saying, "It's me." The door opened and I made out the jouncing of plastic wheels as two more trolleys were brought into the room.

Then there was another knock, more affirmations of identity, and I heard the rustling of trash bags. "This good?" one of the thick guys said.

"Yeah," the thin guy replied. "Help me load these guys."

I felt myself being lifted—they had no problem with my 185 pounds—then being dropped into the bottom of one of the trolleys. I was soon covered in a cascade of garbage bags. None of them was terribly heavy, but they still added to the feeling that I was being smothered. As if being bound, gagged, and hooded weren't enough. I had never known myself to be claustrophobic, but I'm not sure I had ever been wedged into such a narrow space without the ability to move.

Merely breathing had now become a difficult task. There was but the smallest pocket of air surrounding me, and I could only draw at it with my nose, through a layer of what had once been Barry McAlister's shirt. It was all I could do to keep myself calm enough and to quiet the thought that I was slowly suffocating. I knew the moment I started panicking, it would only make it worse.

I heard Tommy being placed in a trolley, followed by his own blanket of trash bags.

"We good to go?" the thin guy asked.

Someone must have nodded, because the radio was turned up. It was blaring out some Journey, but with all due respect to that classic American rock band's most-revered anthem, I had definitely stopped believing.

The next thing I knew, we were rolling. And that's when I felt a deep fear settling in. Yes, it was terrifying that I could no longer see, that I couldn't hear anything over the radio, that I was enclosed in this suffocating prison, that I had no control over what would happen to me next. But it wasn't so much that my senses had been dulled or my liberties disabled.

It was that I felt suddenly and irrevocably alone. I no longer knew if Tommy or Marcia was being wheeled alongside me or if we had been separated. I was totally isolated, and my biggest fear—strange as it may sound—was that I was going to die that way. Without Tommy. Without Tina. Without my parents or my unborn child or my siblings. Without anyone who cared to take pity on me in my final moments.

It was the most terrifying way I could think of to leave this world.

.   .   .

All I could really feel anymore was motion. Or, sporadically, the lack of it. And all I could do was imagine where that motion was taking me. So it was—I think—we went out of the office. Then down the hall. Then into the elevator. Then down to the parking garage.

Or maybe, for all I knew, we were going up to the roof. I was quickly becoming disoriented, and for as hard as I worked to keep my brain engaged in my surroundings, it was a struggle. I wanted to scream—just in the hope someone would hear me— but the radio kept up its full-throated blaring. Plus, I couldn't really get a lungful of air. I was fearful that even trying to yell would waste what little oxygen I had.

It was just darkness. And despair. And I couldn't very well get myself free or spare myself whatever fate I had coming if I couldn't move, see, or speak. I wondered if I should start to pray. Nothing in my power was going to change my situation. Maybe I needed a higher one.

Then the soundtrack changed. Maybe I was just imagining it, but I swore I heard a sharp, percussive banging. Followed by a lot of shouting. The words were mostly blurred. But the ones that came through the loudest, clearest, and sweetest were "state police" and "get down."

My next sensation was of garbage bags being removed from on top of me.

"Hey, someone help me with this guy," a voice said.

I was being lifted. Again. But this time in a much better direction. I was being placed gently down on a hard surface. Concrete.

"Get me some scissors," the voice said again. Someone shouted something—I couldn't make it out—and the voice said, "Yeah, from the med kit."

Moments later, the tape that encircled my head was being gently cut away. "Just bear with me, sir," the voice said.

Since I was quite sure I could bear with anything that didn't involve a bullet in the head, I held still. Finally, Barry's shirt was lifted from my head.

"Oh, thank God," I heard myself say, and then I sucked in a few large gasps of air until my lungs started realizing they were going to be okay.

With that taken care of, I started looking around. The first thing I saw was a New Jersey state trooper in riot gear. The next thing I saw was a whole bunch of state troopers in riot gear.

I was underground, in the parking garage. Perhaps twenty feet away was Barry McAlister, facedown, with handcuffs securing his wrists behind his back.

The three thugs were getting the same treatment. I didn't know if they had resisted or even tried. Based on the noises I had heard, I wasn't sure if they'd had time. The troopers had been on them too quickly. The whole thing had been over in less than thirty seconds.

The trooper who removed my hood moved on to my arms and legs next, cutting the tape off me in methodical, efficient fashion. It was around then that I saw my future brother-in-law—still dressed for a rehearsal dinner, but with his badge attached to his belt—idly strolling around, looking like he was doing nothing more taxing than considering the parked cars.

"Gary!" I said. It came out choked. And surprised. And, I hoped, grateful.

"You really ought to know better than to be late on your mother," he said, walking toward me.

"I figured she'd send the National Guard," I said. "I didn't realize she'd start with you guys first."

"The National Guard was probably next on her list. But I convinced her we could handle this."

"Yeah, I can see that," I said, as Barry and the three thugs were being led to a waiting van.

"Don't say nothing," the thin guy was warning his charges. "Don't say nothing but 'lawyer, lawyer, lawyer.' And remember, whatever they tell you is a lie."

Then he was gone. So were the two thick guys. I wasn't going to miss them.

"You were very lucky," Gary was saying. "We had a TEAMS Unit doing a training mission in Kearney this afternoon. So when we figured out you weren't just late, that you were probably in some kind of trouble, they were already decked out and ready to rumble. From there, it was just a question of getting them here."

Gary helped me to my feet. I was a little stiff but otherwise no worse off. I had never known how glorious it could feel to have blood circulating in all parts of my body again.

He continued: "That editor of yours, Tina, told us that your last known location was the McAlister Properties offices, so that was the first place we looked for you. We had our guys in the second floor of the building across the street, looking in on you with the infrared—those guys *love* having an excuse to use their infrared. They could see you had been tied up and weren't moving. It wasn't hard to figure out that something very wrong was happening, so they went on full alert."

"How long were you guys over there?" I said, still flexing various muscles that were overcoming having been seriously cramped.

"Only about twenty minutes or so," he said. "We were still assessing the situation, trying to come up with an action plan. We knew you were still alive, because of the infrared. We were fairly certain you were okay for the time being. Then we saw you were on the move. We knew we couldn't let you out of the building, so we decided to take them out down here."

"You seem to have done a pretty good job of it."

"It was a fairly straightforward operation," Gary said.

"TEAMS stands for Technical Emergency and Missions Specialists. These guys train for this sort of thing."

"They're good at it," I said, still swiveling my head, taking in the scene. Then I realized someone was missing. "Where's Lisa Denbigh?" I asked. "There was a woman with them, too."

"She's over there," he said, pointing behind me. I turned to see Lisa, with her hands behind her back, talking earnestly to a state trooper with a pad in his hand. "She was begging us for a deal before we even got the cuffs on her. The first thing she said was, 'I want to testify against Barry.'"

"Yeah, that sounds like Lisa," I said. "Self-preservation runs strong in her."

"Anyhow, let's get out of here," he said.

In the coming days, I would spend no small amount of time with prosecutors from the attorney general's office, helping them assemble evidence that would send Barry McAlister to jail for the rest of his life. I would also write a series of articles that, among other things, had legislators in Trenton taking a serious look at the LSRP program and questioning the wisdom of allowing government to outsource its responsibility to protect the health of its citizens. It helped that when my Open Public Records Act request came through, the signature belonging to "Scott Colston" was an easy match for Vaughn McAlister's handwriting. He had been forging all the documents and using the pizza place as a safe mail drop.

The law firm of Imperiale & Trautwig announced it would disburse the settlement money—recovered from an account in Grand Cayman—to Newark's cadmium-poisoning sufferers and continue to pursue the lawsuit filed by Will Imperiale. Quint Jorgensen even kicked a million bucks into the fund. Not because he had to. Just because.

It would make for a busy series of days.

But first I had a rehearsal dinner to attend.

· · ·

The event was being held in a large, private banquet facility. By the time I made it there, word of my imprisonment and pending death—and of the daring rescue—had spread among the guests, a portion of whom were state troopers who were, naturally, pretty charged up about it.

The first person I saw as I entered the double doors to the room was my dad.

"You're late," he said, grinning, then wrapped me in an extra-tight bear hug.

Then Mom came running up. She wept on me for a minute or two, begged me to consider a career in public relations, then dried her tears before they smudged her makeup and reminded me that I had a speech to give. And it had better be nice. And thoughtful. And she could look up some Auden on her phone if I wanted.

A guy from the banquet facility was next. He didn't cry on me, thankfully. He wanted to affix a small wireless microphone to me. I guess they took their speechifying seriously at this facility and wanted my every precious word to be heard—Gary's father had been outfitted with one, too.

As the sound guy fiddled with my blazer, I looked out at the dance floor, where Tommy and my cousin Glenn had already discovered each other. The deejay was playing a peppy pop song. Strangely, Tommy and Glenn were slow-dancing to it. They looked positively enthralled.

As soon as the mic was secure, my sister glided across the room in a very bride-to-be manner. She gave me a kiss on the cheek, then a punch on the shoulder.

"I'm putting you under house arrest tomorrow," she said playfully. "You're allowed to outshine me during the rehearsal dinner but I'll be damned if everyone is going to be talking about *you* during my wedding."

"So does that mean I can't wear white?" I asked.

"You are such a dork," she said. "You always have been."

"Thanks, Amanda. Love you, too."

My brother and his wife came next, and I took another heaping portion of good-natured ribbing—because, unsurprisingly, my family is incapable of being serious about anything for too long. Even near-death experiences.

Tina approached as soon as my family was done. My city editor/baby mama was wearing a black cocktail dress that I had seen before but that made me grateful to be male every time.

"Nice entrance, Carter," she said.

"Gotta find a way to keep it fresh."

"You're terrible," she said, but at least she was smiling.

"So from what Gary tells me, I owe you a pretty big thank-you," I said.

"Actually, you should be thankful that Pigeon is deathly afraid of dogs."

"Oh?"

"Well, I guess you told her to hit Barry McAlister's neighborhood and ask around about him?"

"Oh, right," I said, forgetting I had even done that.

"Well, apparently, she was in the midst of fleeing a particularly vicious-looking cocker spaniel when she ran into a guy who saved her from the terror. They got to talking, and he swore to her he had seen Barry at a Rite Aid in Maplewood earlier that day. The guy said he had called out to Barry but that Barry just ran away. I don't think the guy was even aware Barry had been declared a homicide victim at that point. He just wanted to ask his neighbor if everything was okay after the big fire."

"Obviously, this is someone who needs to read our Web site a little more carefully," I noted.

"Pigeon told the neighbor what was going on and the guy said he was absolutely certain it was Barry—but that he had dyed his hair."

"Worst dye job ever."

"Yeah, well, Pigeon was smart enough to realize this was a heck of a development but she didn't know what to do with it," Tina said. "I mean, a single source saying a dead guy is not dead. How do you handle that, right?"

"Right."

"Anyhow, like a good little intern, she asked her editor what to do. And then her editor called me. At that point, I was already at your parents' house and we were all wondering where you were. We had been trying to call your cell and it was going straight to voice mail. Your mother kept saying, 'He's never late, he's never late, he's never late.' And I had a hunch that if Barry McAlister was on the loose—with some kind of bad disguise, no less—he was probably up to no good and that you might be in trouble."

"Good hunch," I said.

"But I still didn't know what to do about it. It was actually that little offhand comment you made about Gary being a state trooper that saved you," she said. "I called him up, told him what was going on. He was able to locate the TEAMS Unit and send them over to Newark to check out the building. And, of course, they found you there and . . ."

She glanced over her shoulder to make sure no one was paying too careful attention, then planted a kiss directly on my lips, followed by a full-body hug that made my toes curl.

"Wow," I said when she released me.

"I really shouldn't reward behavior like this on your part," she said. "But I think a lot of stuff hit me afterward, when I thought about how close you came to not making it. I mean, if

Pigeon hadn't bumped into that guy, if she hadn't made that phone call, if your sister weren't marrying a state trooper . . . I thought about how easily I could have lost you and I—" She stopped herself. "I'm sorry," she said in a raspy voice. "Would you just come out in the lobby with me for a second?"

"Yeah, just let me check to make sure I don't have to give this speech right now," I said.

I confirmed with my mother that I had at least five minutes until people would be seated for the toasts. I paused at the double doors to give the microphone guy the thumbs-up, so he would know I was heading out for a minute or two. He responded with his own thumbs-up and I slipped through the doors.

Tina and I found a private corner just outside the room, out of earshot, where she half collapsed on me, leaning in and resting her head on my shoulder.

"I just kept thinking about you and the baby," she said. "I know I said I would raise this baby without you and that I didn't want you to have anything to do with it. But then I started thinking about my child *really* growing up without a father and . . . Carter, this is your baby too. I get that. And I want you to be a part of this baby's life, if that's okay with you."

"Okay with me?" I said, feeling my throat constrict. "It's the best thing you could say to me. Tina, I want to raise this baby with you more than anything."

And then, because I think we were both crying a little—and maybe both feeling a little silly about it all—we just held each other for a moment.

Not that the moment lasted long. I was suddenly hearing all kinds of noise coming from the banquet hall. The doors had been opened and a small crowd was pouring out, led by my mother—looking as wide-eyed and wild as I had ever seen her.

"Baby!" she screamed. "There's going to be a baby!?"

She rushed up to Tina and hugged her, more or less knocking me out of the way in the process.

I was just watching the whole thing, bewildered by how my mother knew. I mean, sure, mothers have special powers and all, but I didn't realize mine had suddenly been blessed with supersonic hearing.

Then my brother walked up and clapped me on the shoulder. "Congratulations, Dad," he said.

"But how did you guys . . ."

"We heard it over the speaker system, genius," he said.

"Speaker? But—"

My brother mocked my voice: "I want to raise this baby with you more than anything!"

And that's when it occurred to me that when I had given the sound guy the thumbs-up, he had taken it as the signal to switch on my microphone. Every private word Tina and I had just shared had been broadcast to the entire room.

Well. At least no one could complain they hadn't been first to get the news.

My father and sister had joined Tina. No one was paying much attention to me—something I supposed I was going to have to get used to—so Kira came up to me and gave me a quick hug and a peck on the cheek.

"Congratulations. I'll see you later," she said, and started peeling away.

"Wait, are you leaving?"

"You have enough on your hands," she said, in a way that felt friendly. "Don't worry about me. I've still got time to make it to the Zombie Ball."

"Are you sure you're okay?"

"Oh, Carter. You're sweet. But at this stage of my life, if it comes down to babies or zombies, I'll go with the undead every time."

She waved and skipped out. I turned my attention back to Tina, who was still being mobbed by my family. There was all kinds of excited yelping and chirping—mostly from my mother—and it was making it difficult to hear. I remembered what Tina had said about needing me as a buffer, so I started trying to shuck Rosses off her.

"Okay, break it up, break it up," I said.

No one was budging. So I just leaned in and kissed Tina on the cheek.

"Love you," I whispered in her ear. "Welcome to the family."

ACKNOWLEDGMENTS

There's a shelf in my living room where I display the merry band of books I've published.

The hardcovers are the front men, propped up on their own little stands. The paperback, large print, and audio versions of those same books are arranged behind, like background singers.

I was wandering past the shelf the other day when I noticed it was starting to get a little crowded in there. And somehow, for the very first time—five books and counting into this whole mad adventure—it struck me: Wow, I *really* am an author.

Call me a slow study. But sometimes I still have to pinch myself that I get to do this for a living. And I'm endlessly grateful to all the people who make it possible.

That starts with you, o gentle reader. I consider it an incredible privilege that you let me into your life and allow me—if all goes well, I hope—to entertain you for a few hours. Each day when I sit down to write, my goal is to be the equal of the amazing opportunity you've given me.

Kelley Ragland, my editor at Minotaur Books, also deserves a heaping helping of thanks. She and her assistant, Elizabeth Lacks, do a marvelous job of keeping me out of trouble, both on the page and elsewhere. (I still get in trouble, of course, but only when I don't listen to them.)

I'd also like to acknowledge the untiring efforts of the rest of the Minotaur mafia, including publicist Hector DeJean, library goddess Talia Sherer, the marketing team headed by Matt Baldacci, the Criminal Element crew (including Claire Toohey, who I'm pretty sure meant it as a compliment not long ago when she called me a whore), publisher Andy Martin, and the big boss, Sally Richardson.

Also, I know I'm not the only St. Martin's Press author who will miss the huge presence of Matthew Shear, taken from us much too soon after a battle with cancer he kept far too quiet. He was a gem of a man whose enthusiasm for books was surpassed only by the size of his smile.

Taking my praise outside the Flatiron Building, just down the street to Writers House, I count myself fortunate to have the counsel of Dan Conaway, the best agent in the business. It's no accident that his clientele represented 40 percent of the Anthony Award nominees this past year.

Elsewhere, Becky Kraemer of Cursive Communications is a joy to work with. But I warn my fellow authors: Hire her only if you want to get more attention and sell more books.

Speaking of selling books, I remain indebted to book peddlers across the nation, who push my work on people. In particular, I'd like to thank Kelly Justice of Fountain Bookstore in Richmond. She is a friend to me and authors everywhere.

Libraries are also close to my heart and I am constantly asking people to support their local branch. In that spirit, here's to the library scientists in my backyard: Alice Cooper at the Northumberland Public Library, Bette Dillehay at the Mathews Public Library, Bess Haile at the Essex Public Library, and Ralph Oppenheim at the Middlesex Public Library.

And, no, Lancaster County, I haven't forgotten Lindsy

Gardner. I just felt like she deserved her own paragraph. Roll Tide, Miss Lindsy.

Moving on, I am nourished by friendships in the crime fiction community, truly the best bunch of readers and writers you could ever want to be around. I will borrow the words of my friend, Erica Ruth Neubauer, who recently attended her first Bouchercon and came home gushing, "I have met my tribe." I know exactly how she feels.

On the road—a place an author finds himself in a lot—I appreciate the continuing hospitality of Tony Cicatiello, James Lum, Jorge Motoshige, and all the folks who have joined me for a meal or beverage during my travels.

Closer to home, I keep doing the bulk of my writing at a Hardees (yes, really) where Teresa Owens and the gang treat me like family and where Avis Webster provides excellent protective services. Thanks for letting me clutter up the corner all day.

And now, finally, to my actual family: a million thank-yous and a million more to my in-laws, Joan and Allan Blakely; my brother, Greg, and sister-in-law, Shevon; to my parents, Marilyn and Bob Parks, who are my anchors; and to Mary Lou Olson, to whom this book is dedicated. Sometimes we don't realize the lessons we learn from our grandparents until we have gotten along a bit in life. My grandmother is a model of elegance, grace and humility—and a thousand other traits I'm still trying to acquire. I feel blessed by the time we've spent together through the years.

Finally, I need to thank my children, both of whom, I'm proud to say, are now readers themselves (but, I hope, will not pick up this particular book for several more years yet); and my wife, Melissa, the lough of my life (private joke, don't ask). Living with a man who spends his days having conversations with imaginary people—and then killing them—is not always easy. Thanks for putting up with me, guys. I love you more than air.